PRAISE FOR

# BRUCE STERLING

AND

# SCHISMATRIX PLUS

"A tsunami of imagination!"

—PHILIP JOSE FARMER

"If you want to know what the future might really be like, read Sterling."

—GARDNER DOZOIS

"A powerful feat of sustained imagination, presenting a panoramic chunk of future history as broad and diverse as it is fast and furious . . . This is science fiction as it should be."

—BARRINGTON J. BAYLEY,
AUTHOR OF *THE GARMENTS OF CAEAN*

"An author of dazzling range and insight. With *Schismatrix,* Bruce Sterling joins the ranks of those daring SF creators who invent futures of startling complexity."

—*LOCUS*

"Crisp, colorful and superbly stimulating . . . Sterling is one of the best in the business!"

—*BEST SELLERS*

# Schismatrix Plus

*INCLUDES SCHISMATRIX AND SELECTED STORIES FROM CRYSTAL EXPRESS*

*BRUCE STERLING*

ACE BOOKS, NEW YORK

This Ace Book includes *Schismatrix* and selected stories
from *Crystal Express*. It has been completely reset in a
typeface designed for easy reading, and was
printed from new film.

SCHISMATRIX PLUS

An Ace Book / published by arrangement with the author

PRINTING HISTORY
Ace trade edition / December 1996

The Putnam Berkley World Wide Web site address is:
http://www.berkley.com/berkley

Make sure to check out *PB Plug*, the science fiction/fantasy newsletter, at
http://www.pbplug.com

ISBN: 0-441-00370-2

ACE®
Ace Books are published by The Berkley Publishing Group,
200 Madison Avenue, New York, NY 10016.
ACE and the "A" design are trademarks
belonging to Charter Communications, Inc.

PRINTED IN THE UNITED STATES OF AMERICA

10   9   8   7   6   5

# ACKNOWLEDGMENTS

# Introduction:
# The Circumsolar Frolics

**I wrote this** book, and these stories, eleven years ago. I finished the manuscript of SCHISMATRIX just before I turned thirty. Then I quit my day-job.

When I completed the Shaper/Mechanist series, I knew that I finally had a
hot and sticky ten-fingered grip on the genre. I'd learned how to make science
fiction address my own concerns, express my own ideas, and speak in my own
voice. It was a hugely exciting feeling. I've never gotten over it. Also, I've never
had a real job since.

This is the first book that I wrote on a word processor. My first two novels
were written on manual typewriters. They were the best books I could do at the
time, and they had quite a lot of rebellious kicking and thrashing in them, but
they couldn't be classed with SCHISMATRIX.

It was a revelation when I first saw my text become electric vapor on the
screen of a computer. I realized that I'd become part of a new generation in science fiction, a generation that had profound, genuine, "technical" advantages
over all our predecessors. This freed me almost overnight from any sense that I
still dwelt in the long shadows of Verne, Wells, or Stapledon. Those writers were
titans of the imagination, but they were one and all confined to analog technologies of ink and woodpulp. Now I could do what I liked with words—bend them,
break them, jam them together, pick them apart again. It was like patiently
studying blues guitar and suddenly finding a fire-engine-red Fender Stratocaster.

When I began work on the Shaper/Mechanist pieces, I had learned how to
stop reading quite so much science fiction. By that time, I was already brimful.
Instead, I learned to absorb the kind of material that science fiction professionals
themselves like to read. Three books in particular had a huge influence on my
thinking, and on the composition of the Shaper/Mechanist world.

First among them was THE WORLD, THE FLESH, AND THE DEVIL by J. D. Bernal. This book was written in the 1920s, and would be universally acknowledged as a stellar masterpiece of cosmic speculation, except for the uncomfortable fact that J. D. Bernal was a lifelong fervent Communist. His work simply couldn't be metabolized during most of the twentieth century, because the author himself was politically unacceptable. I never had much use for Communism, but I had plenty of use for J. D. Bernal.

The second book was Freeman Dyson's DISTURBING THE UNIVERSE. Freeman Dyson could have been a mighty figure in the genre if he'd become a science fiction writer instead of a mere world-class physicist at Princeton. I was lucky enough to have lunch with Freeman Dyson a couple of years ago. I was able to thank him for the fact that I had filed the serial numbers off his prose, hot-wired it and employed it in my work. Professor Dyson had never read SCHISMATRIX, but he was astonishingly good-humored about the fact that I had boldly hijacked thirty or forty of his ideas. What a gentleman and scholar!

The third book was Ilya Prigogine's FROM BEING TO BECOMING. This book boasted some of the most awesomely beautiful scientific jargon that I had ever witnessed in print. The writing was of such dense, otherworldly majesty that it resembled Scripture. It was very like the "crammed Prose" and "eyeball kicks" that we cyberpunks were so enamored of, with the exception of course that Prigogine's work was actual science and bore some coherent relation to consensus reality. So naturally I used his terminology as the basis for the Shaper/Mechanist mysticism. It worked like a charm. Eventually a fan of mine who happened to be one of Professor Prigogine's students gave him a copy of CRYSTAL EXPRESS, which contained the Shaper/Mechanist short stories. Professor Prigogine remarked perceptively that these stories had nothing whatever to do with his Nobel Prizewinning breakthroughs in physical chemistry. Well, that was very true, but charms are verbal structures. They work regardless of chemistry or physics.

I wrote the stories before the novel. I used the Shaper/Mechanist short stories as a method of exploration, a way to creep methodically into the burgeoning world of the book. First came "Swarm," which involves two characters only, and is set light-years away from the eventual center of the action. Next I wrote "Spider Rose," set on the fringes of the solar system, and the fringes of Schismatric society. After that came "Cicada Queen," which thundered headlong into a major Shaper/Mechanist city and examined their society as it boiled like a techno-crazed anthill. "Sunken Gardens" was set late in my future-history, a framing work. The experimental "Twenty Evocations" was my final word on the subject. It was a dry-run for the forthcoming novel, and with that effort, I was carrying my "crammed-prose" technique as far as it would go.

These were my first published short stories. I had one other story, "Man-Made Self," published when I was a teenager; but alas, the manuscript pages were scrambled at the printer's, and the published story was rendered unintelligible. I had to disown it. That made "Swarm" my official story premiere. "Swarm" was also my first magazine sale (to THE MAGAZINE OF FANTASY

AND SCIENCE FICTION, in April 1982). "Swarm" is still the story of mine most often reprinted. I'm still fond of it: I can write a better prose now, but with that story, I finally gnawed my way through the insulation and got my teeth set into the buzzing copper wire.

SCHISMATRIX was my third novel, but the first to go into an immediate second-printing—in Japan. I've valued the Japanese SF milieu very highly ever since. Recently SCHISMATRIX became my first novel to come out in Finland. Perhaps there's a quality in a good translation that can't be captured with the original. One might not think that a book this weird and idiosyncratic could survive translation into non-Indo-European languages; but on the contrary, it's that very weirdness that seems to push it through the verbal and cultural barriers. SCHISMATRIX is a creeping sea-urchin of a book—spikey and odd. It isn't very elegant, and it lacks bilateral symmetry, but pieces of it break off inside people and stick with them for years.

These stories, and this novel, are the most "cyberpunk" works I will ever write. I wrote them in a fine fury of inspiration, in those halcyon days when me and my ratty little cyberpunk co-conspirators first saw our way clear into literary daylight. I think I could write another book as surprising as this one, or even as weird as this one; but it would no longer surprise people that I can be surprising. My audience would no longer find it weird to discover that I can be weird. When I wrote this book, I was surprising myself every day.

In those days of yore, cyberpunk wasn't hype or genre history; it had no name at all. It hadn't yet begun to be metabolized by anyone outside a small literary circle. But it was very real to me, as real as anything in my life, and when I was hip-deep into SCHISMATRIX chopping my way through circumsolar superpower conflicts and grimy, micro-nation terrorist space pirates, it felt like holy fire.

Now all the Shaper/Mechanist stuff is finally here in one set of covers. At last I can formally tell a skeptical public that the title of SCHISMATRIX is pronounced "Skiz-mat´-rix." With a short a. Like "Schismatics," but with an R. Also, SCHISMATRIX is spelled without a "Z." I do hope this helps in future.

People are always asking me about—demanding from me even—more Shaper/Mechanist work. Sequels. A trilogy maybe. The Schismatrix sharecropping shared-universe "as created by" Bruce Sterling. But I don't do that sort of thing. I never will. This is all there was, and all there is.

Bruce Sterling—bruces@well.com
Austin, Texas: 29-11-'95

# Schismatrix

**P**ainted aircraft flew through the core of the world. Lindsay stood in knee-high grass, staring upward to follow their flight.

Flimsy as kites, the pedal-driven ultralights dipped and soared through the free-fall zone, far overhead. Beyond them, across the diameter of the cylindrical world, the curving landscape glowed with the yellow of wheat and the speckled green of cotton fields.

Lindsay shaded his eyes against the sunlit glare from one of the world's long windows. An aircraft, its wings elegantly stenciled in blue feathers on white fabric, crossed the bar of light and swooped silently above him. He saw the pilot's long hair trailing as she pedaled back into a climb. Lindsay knew she had seen him. He wanted to shout, to wave frantically, but he was watched.

His jailers caught up with him: his wife and his uncle. The two old aristocrats walked with painful slowness. His uncle's face was flushed; he had turned up his heart's pacemaker. "You ran," he said. "You ran!"

"I stretched my legs," Lindsay said with bland defiance. "House arrest cramps me."

His uncle peered upward to follow Lindsay's gaze, shading his eyes with an age-spotted hand. The bird-painted aircraft now hovered over the Sours, a marshy spot in the agricultural panel where rot had set into the soil. "You're watching the Sours, eh? Where your friend Constantine's at work. They say he signals you from there."

"Philip works with insects, Uncle. Not cryptography."

Lindsay was lying. He depended on Constantine's covert signals for news during his house arrest.

He and Constantine were political allies. When the crackdown came, Lindsay had been quarantined within the grounds of his family's mansion. But Philip

Constantine had irreplaceable ecological skills. He was still free, working in the Sours.

The long internment had pushed Lindsay to desperation. He was at his best among people, where his adroit diplomatic skills could shine. In isolation, he had lost weight: his high cheekbones stood out in sharp relief and his gray eyes had a sullen, vindictive glow. His sudden run had tousled his modishly curled black hair. He was tall and rangy, with the long chin and arched, expressive eyebrows of the Lindsay clan.

Lindsay's wife, Alexandrina, took his arm. She was dressed fashionably, in a long pleated skirt and white medical tunic. Her pale, clear complexion showed health without vitality, as if her skin were a perfectly printed paper replica. Mummified kiss-curls adorned her forehead.

"You said you wouldn't talk politics, James," she told the older man. She looked up at Lindsay. "You're pale, Abelard. He's upset you."

"Am I pale?" Lindsay said. He drew on his Shaper diplomatic training. Color seeped into his cheeks. He widened the dilation of his pupils and smiled with a gleam of teeth. His uncle stepped back, scowling.

Alexandrina leaned on Lindsay's arm. "I wish you wouldn't do that," she told him. "It frightens me." She was fifty years older than Lindsay and her knees had just been replaced. Her Mechanist teflon kneecaps still bothered her.

Lindsay shifted his bound volume of printout to his left hand. During his house arrest, he had translated the works of Shakespeare into modern circumsolar English. The elders of the Lindsay clan had encouraged him in this. His antiquarian hobbies, they thought, would distract him from plotting against the state.

To reward him, they were allowing him to present the work to the Museum. He had seized on the chance to briefly escape his house arrest.

The Museum was a hotbed of subversion. It was full of his friends. Preservationists, they called themselves. A reactionary youth movement, with a romantic attachment to the art and culture of the past. They had made the Museum their political stronghold.

Their world was the Mare Serenitatis Circumlunar Corporate Republic, a two-hundred-year-old artificial habitat orbiting the Earth's Moon. As one of the oldest of humankind's nation-states in space, it was a place of tradition, with the long habits of a settled culture.

But change had burst in, spreading from newer, stronger worlds in the Asteroid Belt and the Rings of Saturn. The Mechanist and Shaper superpowers had exported their war into this quiet city-state. The strain had split the population into factions: Lindsay's Preservationists against the power of the Radical Old, rebellious plebes against the wealthy aristocracy.

Mechanist sympathizers held the edge in the Republic.

The Radical Old held power from within their governing hospitals. These ancient aristocrats, each well over a century old, were patched together with advanced Mechanist hardware, their lives extended with imported prosthetic technology. But the medical expenses were bankrupting the Republic. Their world was already deep in debt to the medical Mech cartels. The Republic would soon be a Mechanist client state.

But the Shapers used their own arsenals of temptation. Years earlier, they had trained and indoctrinated Lindsay and Constantine. Through these two friends, the leaders of their generation, the Shapers exploited the fury of the young, who saw their birthrights stolen for the profit of the Mechanists.

Tension had mounted within the Republic until a single gesture could set it off.

Life was the issue. And death would be the proof.

Lindsay's uncle was winded. He touched his wrist monitor and turned down the beating of his heart. "No more stunts," he said. "They're waiting in the Museum." He frowned. "Remember, no speeches. Use the prepared statement."

Lindsay stared upward. The bird-painted ultralight went into a power dive.

"No!" Lindsay shouted. He threw his book aside and ran.

The ultralight smashed down in the grass outside the ringed stone seats of an open-air amphitheatre.

The aircraft lay crushed, its wings warped in a dainty convulsion of impact. "Vera!" Lindsay shouted.

He tugged her body from the flimsy wreckage. She was still breathing; blood gushed from her mouth and nostrils. Her ribs were broken. She was choking. He tore at the ring-shaped collar of her Preservationist suit. The wire of the collar cut his hands. The suit imitated space-suit design; its accordioned elbows were crushed and stained.

Little white moths were flying up from the long grass. They milled about as if drawn by the blood.

Lindsay brushed a moth from her face and pressed his lips to hers. The pulse stopped in her throat. She was dead.

"Vera," he groaned. "Sweetheart, you're burned. . . ."

A wave of grief and exultation hit him. He fell into the sun-warmed grass, holding his sides. More moths sprang up.

She had done it. It seemed easy now. It was something the two of them had talked about a hundred times, deep into the night at the Museum or in bed after their adultery. Suicide, the last protest. An enormous vista of black freedom opened up in Lindsay's head. He felt a paradoxical sense of vitality. "Darling, it won't be long. . . ."

His uncle found him kneeling. The older man's face was gray.

"Oh," he said. "This is vile. What have you done?"

Lindsay got dizzily to his feet. "Get away from her."

His uncle stared at the dead woman. "She's dead! You damned fool, she was only twenty-six!"

Lindsay yanked a long dagger of crudely hammered metal from his accordioned sleeve. He swept it up and aimed it at his own chest. "In the name of humanity! And the preservation of human values! I freely choose to—"

His uncle seized his wrist. They struggled briefly, glaring into one another's eyes, and Lindsay dropped the knife. His uncle snatched it out of the grass and slipped it into his lab coat. "This is illegal," he said. "You'll face weapons charges."

Lindsay laughed shakily. "I'm your prisoner, but you can't stop me if I choose to die. Now or later, what does it matter?"

"You're a fanatic." His uncle watched him with bitter contempt. "The Shaper schooling holds to the end, doesn't it? Your training cost the Republic a fortune, and you use it to seduce and murder."

"She died clean! Better to burn in a rush than live two hundred years as a Mechanist wirehead."

The elder Lindsay stared at the horde of white moths that swarmed on the dead woman's clothing. "We'll nail you for this somehow. You and that upstart plebe Constantine."

Lindsay was incredulous. "You stupid Mech bastard! Look at her! Can't you see that you've killed us already? She was the best of us! She was our muse."

His uncle frowned. "Where did all these insects come from?" He bent and brushed the moths aside with wrinkled hands.

Lindsay reached forward suddenly and snatched a filigreed gold locket from the woman's neck. His uncle grabbed his sleeve.

"It's mine!" Lindsay shouted. They began to fight in earnest. His uncle broke Lindsay's clumsy stranglehold and kicked Lindsay twice in the stomach. Lindsay fell to his knees.

His uncle picked up the locket, wheezing. "You assaulted me," he said, scandalized. "You used violence against a fellow citizen." He opened the locket. A thick oil ran out onto his fingers.

"No message?" he said in surprise. He sniffed at his fingers. "Perfume?"

Lindsay knelt, panting in nausea. His uncle screamed.

White moths were darting at the man, clinging to the oily skin of his hands. There were dozens of them.

They were attacking him. He screamed again and batted at his face.

Lindsay rolled over twice, away from his uncle. He knelt in the grass, shaking. His uncle was down, convulsing like an epileptic. Lindsay scrambled backward on his hands and knees.

The old man's wrist monitor glared red. He stopped moving. The white moths crawled over his body for a few moments, then flew off one by one, vanishing into the grass.

Lindsay lurched to his feet. He looked behind him, across the meadow. His wife was walking toward them, slowly, through the grass.

# Part 1

## Sundog Zones

# Chapter 1

## THE MARE TRANQUILLITATIS PEOPLE'S CIRCUMLUNAR ZAIBATSU: 27-12-'15

They shipped Lindsay into exile in the cheapest kind of Mechanist drogue. For two days he was blind and deaf, stunned with drugs, his body packed in a thick matrix of deceleration paste.

Launched from the Republic's cargo arm, the drogue had drifted with cybernetic precision into the polar orbit of another circumlunar. There were ten of these worlds, named for the lunar mares and craters that had provided their raw materials. They'd been the first nation-states to break off all relations with the exhausted Earth. For a century their lunar alliance had been the nexus of civilization, and commercial traffic among these "Concatenate worlds" had been heavy.

But since those glory days, progress in deeper space had eclipsed the Concatenation, and the lunar neighborhood had become a backwater. Their alliance had collapsed, giving way to peevish seclusion and technical decline. The circumlunars had fallen from grace, and none had fallen further than the place of Lindsay's exile.

Cameras watched his arrival. Ejected from the drogue's docking port, he floated naked in the free-fall customs chamber of the Mare Tranquillitatis People's Circumlunar Zaibatsu. The chamber was of dull lunar steel, with strips of ragged epoxy where paneling had been ripped free. The room had once been a honeymoon suite, where newlyweds could frolic in free-fall. Now it was bleakly transformed into a bureaucratic clearing area.

Lindsay was still drugged from the trip. A drip-feed cable was plugged into the crook of his right arm, reviving him. Black adhesive disks, biomonitors, dotted his naked skin. He shared the room with a camera drone. The free-fall videosystem had two pairs of piston-driven cybernetic arms.

Lindsay's gray eyes opened blearily. His handsome face, with its clear pale skin and arched, elegant brows, had the slack look of stupor. His dark, crimped hair fell to high cheekbones with traces of three-day-old rouge.

His arms trembled as the stimulants took hold. Then, abruptly, he was back to himself. His training swept over him in a physical wave, flooding him so suddenly that his teeth clacked together in the spasm. His eyes swept the room, glittering with unnatural alertness. The muscles of his face moved in a way that no human face should move, and suddenly he was smiling. He examined himself and smiled into the camera with an easy, tolerant urbanity.

The air itself seemed to warm with the sudden radiance of his good-fellowship.

The cable in his arm disengaged itself and snaked back into the wall. The camera spoke.

"You are Abelard Malcolm Tyler Lindsay? From the Mare Serenitatis Circumlunar Corporate Republic? You are seeking political asylum? You have no biologically active materials in your baggage or implanted on your person? You are not carrying explosives or software attack systems? Your intestinal flora has been sterilized and replaced with Zaibatsu standard microbes?"

"Yes, that's correct," Lindsay said, in the camera's own Japanese. "I have no baggage." He was comfortable with the modern form of the language: a streamlined trade patois, stripped of its honorific tenses. Facility with languages had been part of his training.

"You will soon be released into an area that has been ideologically decriminalized," the camera said. "Before you leave customs, there are certain limits to your activities that must be understood. Are you familiar with the concept of civil rights?"

Lindsay was cautious. "In what context?"

"The Zaibatsu recognizes one civil right: the right to death. You may claim your right at any time, under any circumstances. All you need do is request it. Our audio monitors are spread throughout the Zaibatsu. If you claim your right, you will be immediately and painlessly terminated. Do you understand?"

"I understand," Lindsay said.

"Termination is also enforced for certain other behaviors," the camera said. "If you physically threaten the habitat, you will be killed. If you interfere with our monitoring devices, you will be killed. If you cross the sterilized zone, you will be killed. You will also be killed for crimes against humanity."

"Crimes against humanity?" Lindsay said. "How are those defined?"

"These are biological and prosthetic efforts that we declare to be aberrant. The technical information concerning the limits of our tolerance must remain classified."

"I see," Lindsay said. This was, he realized, carte blanche to kill him at any time, for almost any reason. He had expected as much. This world was a haven for sundogs: defectors, traitors, exiles, outlaws. Lindsay doubted that a world full of sundogs could be run any other way. There were simply too many strange technologies at large in circumsolar space. Hundreds of apparently innocent actions, even the breeding of butterflies, could be potentially lethal.

We are all criminals, he thought.

"Do you wish to claim your civil right?"

"No, thank you," Lindsay said politely. "But it's a great solace to know that the Zaibatsu government grants me this courtesy. I will remember your kindness."

"You need only call out," the camera said, with satisfaction.

The interview was over. Wobbling in free-fall, Lindsay stripped away the biomonitors. The camera handed him a credit card and a pair of standard-issue Zaibatsu coveralls.

Lindsay climbed into the baggy clothing. He'd come into exile alone. Constantine, too, had been indicted, but Constantine, as usual, had been too clever.

Constantine had been his closest friend for fifteen years. Lindsay's family had disapproved of his friendship with a plebe, but Lindsay had defied them.

In those days the elders had hoped to walk the fence between the competing superpowers. They'd been inclined to trust the Shapers and had sent Lindsay to the Ring Council for diplomatic training. Two years later, they'd sent Constantine as well, for training in biotechnology.

But the Mechanists had overwhelmed the Republic, and Lindsay and Constantine were disgraced, embarrassing reminders of a failure in foreign policy. But this only united them, and their dual influence had spread contagiously among the plebes and the younger aristos. In combination they'd been formidable: Constantine, with his subtle long-term plans and iron determination; Lindsay as the front man, with his persuasive glibness and theatrical elegance.

But then Vera Kelland had come between them. Vera: artist, actress, and aristocrat, the first Preservationist martyr. Vera believed in their cause; she was their muse, holding to the conviction with an earnestness they couldn't match. She too was married, to a man sixty years her senior, but adultery only added spice to the long seduction. At last Lindsay had won her. But with the possession of Vera came her deadly resolve.

The three of them knew that an act of suicide would change the Republic when all else was hopeless. They came to terms. Philip would survive to carry on the work; that was his consolation for losing Vera and for the loneliness that was to come. And the three of them had worked toward death in feverish intimacy, until her death had truly come, and made their sleek ideals into a sticky nastiness.

The camera opened the customs hatch with a creak of badly greased hydraulics. Lindsay shook himself free of the past. He floated down a stripped hallway toward the feeble glow of daylight.

He emerged onto a landing pad for aircraft, cluttered with dirty machines.

The landing pad was centered at the free-fall zone of the colony's central axis. From this position, Lindsay could stare along the length of the Zaibatsu, through five long kilometers of gloomy, stinking air.

The sight and shape of the clouds struck him first. They were malformed and bloated, with an ugly yellowish tinge. They rippled and distorted in fetid updrafts from the Zaibatsu's land panels.

The smell was vile. Each of the ten circumlunar worlds of the Concatenation had its own native smell. Lindsay remembered that his own Republic had seemed to reek when he first returned to it from the Shaper academy. But here the air seemed foul enough to kill. His nose began to run.

Every Concatenate world faced biological problems as the habitat aged.

Fertile soil required a minimum of ten million bacterial cells per cubic centimeter. This invisible swarm formed the basis of everything fruitful. Humanity had carried it into space.

But humanity and its symbionts had thrown aside the blanket of atmosphere. Radiation levels soared. The circumlunar worlds had shields of imported lunar rubble whole meters deep, but they could not escape the bursts of solar flares and the random shots of cosmic radiation.

Without bacteria, the soil was a lifeless heap of imported lunar dust. With them, it was a constant mutational hazard.

The Republic struggled to control its Sours. In the Zaibatsu, the souring had become epidemic. Mutant fungi had spread like oil slicks, forming a mycelial crust beneath the surface of the soil. This gummy crust repelled water, choking trees and grass. Dead vegetation was attacked by rot. The soil grew dry, the air grew damp, and mildew blossomed on dying fields and orchards, gray pinheads swarming into blotches of corruption, furred like lichen. . . .

When matters reached this stage, only desperate efforts could restore the world. It would have to be evacuated, all its air decompressed into space, and the entire inner surface charred clean in vacuum, then reseeded from scratch. The expense was crippling. Colonies faced with this had suffered breakaways and mass defections, in which thousands fled to frontiers of deeper space. With the passage of time, these refugees had formed their own societies. They joined the Mechanist cartels of the Asteroid Belt, or the Shaper Ring Council, orbiting Saturn.

In the case of the People's Zaibatsu, most of the population had gone, but a stubborn minority refused defeat.

Lindsay understood. There was a grandeur in this morose and rotting desolation.

Slow whirlwinds tore at the gummy soil, spilling long tendrils of rotten grit into the twilit air. The glass sunlight panels were coated with filth, a gluey amalgam of dust and mildew. The long panels had blown out in places; they were shored up with strut-braced makeshift plugs.

It was cold. With the glass so filthy, so cracked, with daylight reduced to a smeared twilight, they would have to run the place around the clock simply to keep it from freezing. Night was too dangerous; it couldn't be risked. Night was not allowed.

Lindsay scrabbled weightlessly along the landing deck. The aircraft were moored to the scratched metal with suction cups. There were a dozen man-powered models, in bad repair, and a few battered electrics.

He checked the struts of an ancient electric whose fabric wings were stenciled with a Japanese carp design. Mud-smeared skids equipped it for gravity landings. Lindsay floated into the skeletal saddle, fitting his cloth-and-plastic shoes into the stirrups.

He pulled his credit card from one of the coverall's chest pockets. The gold-trimmed black plastic had a red LED readout displaying credit hours. He fed it into a slot and the tiny engine hummed into life.

He cast off and caught a downdraft until he felt the tug of gravity. He oriented himself with the ground below.

To his left, the sunlight panel had been cleaned in patches. A cadre of lumpy robots were scraping and mopping the fretted glass. Lindsay nosed the ultralight down for a closer look. The robots were bipedal; they were crudely designed. Lindsay realized suddenly that they were human beings in suits and gas masks.

Columns of sunlight from the clean glass pierced the murk like searchlights. He flew into one, twisted, and rode its updraft.

The light fell upon the opposite land panel. Near its center a cluster of storage tanks dotted the land. The tanks brimmed with oozing green brew: algae. The last agriculture left in the Zaibatsu was an oxygen farm.

He swooped lower over the tanks. Gratefully, he breathed the enriched air. His aircraft's shadow flitted over a jungle of refinery pipes.

As he looked down, he saw a second shadow behind him. Lindsay wheeled abruptly to his right.

The shadow followed his movement with cybernetic precision. Lindsay pulled his craft into a steep climb and twisted in the seat to look behind him.

When he finally spotted his pursuer, he was shocked to see it so close. Its splattered camouflage of dun and gray hid it perfectly against the interior sky of ruined land panels. It was a surveillance craft, a remotely controlled flying drone. It had flat, square wings and a noiseless rear propeller in a camouflaged exhaust cowling.

A knobbed array of cylinders jutted from the robot aircraft's torso. The two tubes that pointed at him might be telephoto cameras. Or they might be x-ray lasers. Set to the right frequency, an x-ray laser could char the interior of a human body without leaving a mark on the skin. And x-ray beams were invisible.

The thought filled him with fear and profound disgust. Worlds were frail places, holding precious air and warmth against the hostile nothingness of space. The safety of worlds was the universal basis of morality. Weapons were dangerous, and that made them vile. In this sundog world, only weapons could keep order, but he still felt a deep, instinctive outrage.

Lindsay flew into a yellowish fog that roiled and bubbled near the Zaibatsu's axis. When he emerged, the aircraft had vanished.

He would never know when they were watching. At any moment, unseen fingers might close a switch, and he would fall.

The violence of his feelings surprised him. His training had seeped away. There flashed behind his eyes the uncontrollable image of Vera Kelland, plunging downward, smashing to earth, her craft's bright wings crumpling on impact. . . .

He turned south. Beyond the ruined panels he saw a broad ring of pure white, girdling the world. It abutted the Zaibatsu's southern wall.

He glanced behind him. The northern wall was concave, crowded with abandoned factories and warehouses. The bare southern wall was sheer and vertical. It seemed to be made of bricks.

The ground below it was a wide ring of blazingly clean, raked white rocks. Here and there among the sea of pebbles, enigmatically shaped boulders rose like dark islands.

Lindsay swooped down for a closer look. A squat guardline of black weapons bunkers swiveled visibly, tracking him with delicate bluish muzzles. He was over the Sterilized Zone.

He climbed upward rapidly.

A hole loomed in the center of the southern wall. Surveillance craft swarmed like hornets in and around it. Microwave antennae bristled around its edges, trailing armored cables.

He could not see through the hole. There was half a world beyond that wall, but sundogs were not allowed to glimpse it.

Lindsay glided downward. The ultralight's wire struts sang with tension.

To the north, on the second of the Zaibatsu's three land panels, he saw the work of sundogs. Refugees had stripped and demolished wide swaths of the industrial sector and erected crude airtight domes from the scrap.

The domes ranged from small bubbles of inflated plastic, through multicolored caulked geodesics, to one enormous isolated hemisphere.

Lindsay circled the largest dome closely. Black insulation foam covered its surface. Mottled lunar stone armored its lower rim. Unlike most of the other domes, it had no antennae or aerials.

He recognized it. He'd known it would be here.

Lindsay was afraid. He closed his eyes and called on his Shaper training, the ingrained strength of ten years of psychotechnic discipline.

He felt his mind slide subtly into its second mode of consciousness. His posture altered, his movements were smoother, his heart beat faster. Confidence seeped into him, and he smiled. His mind felt sharper, cleaner, cleansed of inhibitions, ready to twist and manipulate. His fear and his guilt faltered and warped away, a tangle of irrelevance.

As always, in this second state, he felt contempt for his former weakness. *This* was his true self: pragmatic, fast-moving, free of emotional freight.

This was no time for half measures. He had his plans. If he was to survive here, he would have to take the situation by the throat.

Lindsay spotted the building's airlock. He brought the ultralight in for a skidding landing. He unplugged his credit card and stepped off. The aircraft sprang into the muddy sky.

Lindsay followed a set of stepping-stones into a recessed alcove in the dome's wall. Inside the recess, an overhead panel flicked into brilliant light. To his left, in the alcove's wall, a camera lens flanked an armored videoscreen. Below the screen, light gleamed from a credit-card slot and the steel rectangle of a sliding vault.

A much larger sliding door, in the interior wall, guarded the airlock. A thick layer of undisturbed grit filled the airlock's groove. The Nephrine Black Medicals were not partial to visitors.

Lindsay waited patiently, rehearsing lies.

Ten minutes passed. Lindsay tried to keep his nose from running. Suddenly the videoscreen flashed into life. A woman's face appeared.

"Put your credit card in the slot," she said in Japanese.

Lindsay watched her, weighing her kinesics. She was a lean, dark-eyed woman of indeterminate age, with close-cropped brown hair. Her eyes looked dilated. She wore a white medical tunic with a metal insignia in its collar: a golden staff with two entwined snakes. The snakes were black enamel with jeweled red eyes. Their open jaws showed hypodermic fangs.

Lindsay smiled. "I haven't come to buy anything," he said.

"You're buying my attention, aren't you? Put in the card."

"I didn't ask you to appear on this screen," Lindsay said in English. "You're free to sign off at any time."

The woman stared at him in annoyance. "Of course I'm free," she said in English. "I'm free to have you hauled in here and chopped to pieces. Do you know where you are? This isn't some cheap sundog operation. We're the Nephrine Black Medicals."

In the Republic, they were unknown. But Lindsay knew of them from his days in the Ring Council: criminal biochemists on the fringes of the Shaper underworld. Reclusive, tough, and vicious. He'd known that they had strongholds: black laboratories scattered through the System. And this was one of them.

He smiled coaxingly. "I would like to come in, you know. Only not in pieces."

"You must be joking," the woman said. "You're not worth the credit it would cost us to disinfect you."

Lindsay raised his brows. "I have the standard microbes."

"This is a sterile environment. The Nephrines live clean."

"So you can't come in and out freely?" said Lindsay, pretending surprise at the news. "You're trapped in there?"

"This is where we *live*," the woman said. "You're trapped *outside*."

"That's a shame," Lindsay said. "I wanted to do some recruiting here. I was trying to be fair." He shrugged. "I've enjoyed our talk, but time presses. I'll be on my way."

"Stop," the woman said. "You don't go until I say you can go."

Lindsay feigned alarm. "Listen," he said. "No one doubts your reputation. But you're trapped in there. You're of no use to me." He ran his long fingers through his hair. "There's no point in this."

"What are you implying? Who are you, anyway?"

"Lindsay."

"Lin Dze? You're not of oriental stock."

Lindsay looked into the lens of the camera and locked eyes with her. The impression was hard to simulate through video, but its unexpectedness made it very effective on a subconscious level. "And what's *your* name?"

"Cory Prager," she blurted. *"Doctor* Prager."

"Cory, I represent Kabuki Intrasolar. We're a commercial theatrical venture." Lindsay lied enthusiastically. "I'm arranging a production and I'm recruiting a cast. We pay generously. But, as you say, since you can't come out, frankly, you're wasting my time. You can't even attend the performance." He sighed. "Obviously this isn't my fault. I'm not responsible."

The woman laughed unpleasantly. Lindsay had grasped her kinesics, though, and her uneasiness was obvious to him. "You think we care what they do on the outside? We have a seller's market cornered here. All we care about is their credit. The rest is of no consequence."

"I'm glad to hear you say that. I wish other groups shared your attitude. I'm an artist, not a politician. I wish I could avoid the complications as easily as you do." He spread his hands. "Since we understand each other now, I'll be on my way."

"Wait. What complications?"

"It's not my doing," Lindsay hedged. "It's the other factions. I haven't even finished assembling the cast, and already they're plotting together. The play gives them a chance to negotiate."

"We can send out our monitors. We can watch your production."

"Oh, I'm sorry," Lindsay said stiffly. "We don't allow our plays to be taped or broadcast. It would spoil our attendance." He was rueful. "I can't risk disappointing my cast. Anyone can be an actor these days. Memory drugs make it easy."

"We sell memory drugs," she said. "Vasopressins, carbolines, endorphins. Stimulants, tranquilizers. Laughers, screamers, shouters, you name it. If there's a market for it, the Nephrine black chemists can make it. If we can't synthesize it, we'll filter it from tissue. Anything you want. Anything you can think of." She lowered her voice. "We're friends with Them, you know. The ones beyond the Wall. They think the world of us."

Lindsay rolled his eyes. "Of course."

She looked offscreen; he heard the rapid tapping of a keyboard. She looked up. "You've been talking to the whores, haven't you? The Geisha Bank."

Lindsay looked cautious. The Geisha Bank was new to him. "It might be best if I kept my dealings confidential."

"You're a fool to believe their promises."

Lindsay smiled uneasily. "What choice do I have? There's a natural alliance between actors and whores."

"They must have warned you against us." The woman put a pair of headphones against her left ear and listened distractedly.

"I told you I was trying to be fair," Lindsay said. The screen went silent suddenly and the woman spoke rapidly into a pinhead microphone. Her face flashed offscreen and was replaced by the wrinkle-etched face of an older man. Lindsay had a brief glimpse of the man's true appearance—white hair in spiky disarray, red-rimmed eyes—before a video-manicuring program came on line. The program raced up the screen one scan line at a time, subtly smoothing, deleting, and coloring.

"Look, this is useless," Lindsay blustered. "Don't try to talk me into something I'll regret. I have a show to put on. I don't have time for this—"

"Shut up, you," the man said. The steel vault door slid open, revealing a folded packet of transparent vinyl. "Put it on," the man said. "You're coming inside."

Lindsay unfolded the bundle and shook it out. It was a full-length decontamination suit. "Go on, hurry it up," the Black Medical insisted. "You may be under surveillance."

"I hadn't realized," Lindsay said. He struggled into the booted trousers. "This is quite an honor." He tunneled into the gloved and helmeted top half of the suit and sealed the waist.

The airlock door shunted open with a scrape of grit. "Get in," the man said. Lindsay stepped inside, and the door slid shut behind him.

Wind stirred the dust. A light, filthy rain began to fall. A skeletal camera robot minced up on four tubular legs and trained its lens on the door.

An hour passed. The rain stopped and a pair of surveillance craft kited silently overhead. A violent dust storm blew up in the abandoned industrial zone, to the north. The camera continued to watch.

Lindsay emerged from the airlock, weaving a little. He set a black diplomatic bag on the stone floor beside him and struggled out of the decontamination suit. He stuffed the suit back into the vault, then picked his way with exaggerated grace along the stepping-stones.

The air stank. Lindsay stopped and sneezed. "Hey," the camera said. "Mr. Dze. I'd like a word with you, Mr. Dze."

"If you want a part in the play you'll have to appear in person," Lindsay said.

"You astonish me," the camera remarked. It spoke in trade Japanese. "I have to admire your daring, Mr. Dze. The Black Medicals have the foulest kind of reputation. They could have rendered you for your body chemicals."

Lindsay walked north, his flimsy shoes scuffing the mud. The camera tagged after him, its left rear leg squeaking.

Lindsay descended a low hill into an orchard where fallen trees, thick with black smut, formed a loose, skeletal thicket. Below the orchard was a scum-covered pond with a decayed teahouse at its shore. The once-elegant wooden and ceramic building had collapsed into a heap of dry rot. Lindsay kicked one of the timbers and broke into a coughing fit at the explosion of spores. "Someone ought to clean this up," he said.

"Where would they put it?" the camera said.

Lindsay looked around quickly. The trees screened him from observation. He stared at the machine. "Your camera needs an overhaul," he said.

"It was the best I could afford," the camera said.

Lindsay swung his black bag back and forth, narrowing his eyes. "It looks rather slow and frail."

The robot prudently stepped backward. "Do you have a place to stay, Mr. Dze?"

Lindsay rubbed his chin. "Are you offering one?"

"You shouldn't stay in the open. You're not even wearing a mask."

Lindsay smiled. "I told the Medicals that I was protected by advanced anti- septics. They were very impressed."

"They must have been. You don't breathe raw air here. Not unless you want your lungs to end up looking like this thicket." The camera hesitated. "My name is Fyodor Ryumin."

"I am pleased to make your acquaintance," Lindsay said in Russian. They had injected him with vasopressin through the suit, and his brain felt impossibly keen. He felt so intolerably bright that he was beginning to crisp a little around the edges. Changing from Japanese to his little-used Russian felt as easy as switching a tape.

"Again you astonish me," the camera said in Russian. "You pique my cu- riosity. You understand that term, 'pique'? It's not common to trade Russian. Please follow the robot. My place isn't far. Try to breathe shallowly."

Ryumin's place was a small inflated dome of gray-green plastic near the smeared and broken glass of one window panel. Lindsay unzipped the fabric air- lock and stepped inside.

The pure air within provoked a fit of coughing. The tent was small, ten strides across. A tangle of cables littered the floor, connecting stacks of battered video equipment to a frayed storage battery propped on ceramic roof tiles. A central support pole, wreathed in wire, supported an air filter, a lightbulb, and the roots of an antenna complex.

Ryumin was sitting cross-legged on a tatami mat with his hands on a portable joystick. "Let me take care of the robot first," he said. "I'll be with you in a moment."

Ryumin's broad face had a vaguely Asiatic cast, but his thinning hair was blond. Age spots marked his cheeks. His knuckles had the heavy wrinkles com- mon to the very old. Something was wrong with his bones. His wrists were too thin for his stocky body, and his skull looked strangely delicate. Two black adhe- sive disks clung to his temples, trailing thin cords down his back and into the jungle of wires.

Ryumin's eyes were closed. He reached out blindly and tapped a switch beside his knee. He peeled the disks from his temples and opened his eyes. They were bright blue.

"Is it bright enough in here?" he said.

Lindsay glanced at the bulb overhead. "I think so."

Ryumin tapped his temple. "Chip grafts along the optic nerves," he said. "I suffer a little from video burn. I have trouble seeing anything not on scan lines."

"You're a Mechanist."

"Does it show?" Ryumin asked, ironically.

"How old are you?"

"A hundred and forty. No, a hundred and forty-two." He smiled. "Don't be alarmed."

"I'm not prejudiced," Lindsay said falsely. He felt confusion, and, with that, his training seeped away. He remembered the Ring Council and the long, hated sessions of anti-Mech indoctrination. The sense of rebellion recalled him to himself.

He stepped over a tangle of wires and set his diplomatic bag on a low table beside a plastic-wrapped block of synthetic tofu. "Please understand me, Mr. Ryumin. If this is blackmail, you've misjudged me. I won't cooperate. If you mean me harm, then do it. Kill me now."

"I wouldn't say that too loudly," Ryumin cautioned. "The spyplanes can burn you down where you stand, right through that tent wall."

Lindsay flinched.

Ryumin grinned bleakly. "I've seen it happen before. Besides, if we're to murder each other, then you should be killing me. I run the risks here, since I have something to lose. You're only a fast-talking sundog." He wrapped up the cord of his joystick. "We could babble reassurances till the sun expands and never convince each other. Either we trust each other or we don't."

"I'll trust you," Lindsay decided. He kicked off his mud-smeared shoes.

Ryumin rose slowly to his feet. He bent to pick up Lindsay's shoes, and his spine popped loudly. "I'll put these in the microwave," he said. "When you live here, you must never trust the mud."

"I'll remember," Lindsay said. His brain was swimming in mnemonic chemicals. The drugs had plunged him into a kind of epiphany in which every tangled wire and pack of tape seemed of vital importance. "Burn them if you want," he said. He opened his new bag and pulled out an elegant cream-colored medical jacket.

"These are good shoes," Ryumin said. "They're worth three or four minutes, at least."

Lindsay stripped off his coveralls. A pair of injection bruises mottled his right buttock.

Ryumin squinted. "I see you didn't escape unscathed."

Lindsay pulled out a pair of creased white trousers. "Vasopressin," he said.

"Vasopressin," Ryumin mused. "I thought you had a Shaper look about you. Where are you from, Mr. Dze? And how old are you?"

"Three hours old," Lindsay said. "Mr. Dze has no past."

Ryumin looked away. "I can't blame a Shaper for trying to hide his past. The System swarms with your enemies." He peered at Lindsay. "I can guess you were a diplomat."

"What makes you think so?"

"Your success with the Black Medicals. Your skill is impressive. Besides, diplomats often turn sundog." Ryumin studied him. "The Ring Council had a secret training program for diplomats of a special type. The failure rate was high. Half the alumni were rebels and defectors."

Lindsay zipped up his shirt.

"Is that what happened to you?"

"Something of the sort."

"How fascinating. I've met many borderline posthumans in my day, but never one of you. Is it true that they enforced an entire second state of consciousness? Is it true that when you're fully operational, you yourself don't know if you're speaking the truth? That they used psychodrugs to destroy your capacity for sincerity?"

"Sincerity," Lindsay said. "That's a slippery concept."

Ryumin hesitated. "Are you aware that your class is being stalked by Shaper assassins?"

"No," Lindsay said sourly. So it had come to this, he thought. All those years, while the spinal crabs burned knowledge into every nerve. The indoctrinations, under drugs and brain taps. He'd gone to the Republic when he was sixteen, and for ten years the psychotechs had poured training into him. He'd returned to the Republic like a primed bomb, ready to serve any purpose. But his skills provoked panic fear there and utter distrust from those in power. And now the Shapers themselves were hunting him. "Thank you for telling me," he said.

"I wouldn't worry," Ryumin said. "The Shapers are under siege. They have bigger concerns than the fate of a few sundogs." He smiled. "If you really took that treatment, then you must be less than forty years old."

"I'm thirty. You're a cagey old bastard, Ryumin."

Ryumin took Lindsay's well-cooked shoes out of the microwave, studied them, and slipped them on his own bare feet. "How many languages do you speak?"

"Four, normally. With memory enhancement I can manage seven. And I know the standard Shaper programming language."

"I speak four myself," Ryumin said. "But then, I don't clutter my mind with their written forms."

"You don't read at all?"

"My machines can do that for me."

"Then you're blind to mankind's whole cultural heritage."

Ryumin looked surprised. "Strange talk for a Shaper. You're an antiquarian, eh? Want to break the Interdict with Earth, study the so-called humanities, that sort of thing? That explains why you used the theatrical gambit. I had to use my lexicon to find out what a 'play' was. An astonishing custom. Are you really going through with it?"

"Yes. And the Black Medicals will finance it for me."

"I see. The Geisha Bank won't care for that. Loans and finance are their turf."

Lindsay sat on the floor beside a nest of wires. He plucked the Black Medicals pin from his collar and twirled it in his fingers. "Tell me about them."

"The Geishas are whores and financiers. You must have noticed that your credit card is registered in hours."

"Yes."

"Those are hours of sexual service. The Mechanists and Shapers use kilowatts as currency. But the System's criminal element must have a black market to survive. A great many different black currencies have seen use. I did an article on it once."

"Did you?"

"Yes. I'm a journalist by profession. I entertain the jaded among the System's bourgeoisie with my startling exposés of criminality. Low-life antics of the sundog canaille." He nodded at Lindsay's bag. "Narcotics were the standard for a while, but that gave the Shaper black chemists an edge. Selling computer time had some success, but the Mechanists had the best cybernetics. Now sex has come into vogue."

"You mean people come to this godforsaken place just for sex?"

"It's not necessary to visit a bank to use it, Mr. Dze. The Geisha Bank has contacts throughout the cartels. Pirates dock here to exchange loot for portable black credit. We get political exiles from the other circumlunars, too. If they're unlucky."

Lindsay showed no reaction. He was one of those exiles.

His problem was simple now: survival. It was wonderful how this cleared his mind. He could forget his former life: the Preservationist rebellion, the political dramas he'd staged at the Museum. It was all history.

Let it fade, he thought. All gone now, all another world. He felt dizzy, suddenly, thinking about it. He'd lived. Not like Vera.

Constantine had tried to kill him with those altered insects. The quiet, subtle moths were a perfect modern weapon: they threatened only human flesh, not the world as a whole. But Lindsay's uncle had taken Vera's locket, boobytrapped with the pheromones that drove the deadly moths to frenzy. And his uncle had died in his place. Lindsay felt a slow, rising flush of nausea.

"And the exhausted come here from the Mechanist cartels," Ryumin went on. "For death by ecstasy. For a price the Geisha Bank offers *shinju:* double suicide with a companion from the staff. Many customers, you see, take a deep comfort in not dying alone."

For a long moment, Lindsay struggled with himself. Double suicide—the words pierced him. Vera's face swam queasily before his eyes in the perfect focus of expanded memory. He pitched onto his side, retching, and vomited across the floor.

The drugs overwhelmed him. He hadn't eaten since leaving the Republic. Acid scraped his throat and suddenly he was choking, fighting for air.

Ryumin was at his side in a moment. He dropped his bony kneecaps into Lindsay's ribs, and air huffed explosively through his clogged windpipe. Lindsay rolled onto his back. He breathed in convulsively. A tingling warmth invaded his hands and feet. He breathed again and lost consciousness.

Ryumin took Lindsay's wrist and stood for a moment, counting his pulse. Now that the younger man had collapsed, an odd, somnolent calm descended over the old Mechanist. He moved at his own tempo. Ryumin had been very old for a long time. The feeling changed things.

Ryumin's bones were frail. Cautiously, he dragged Lindsay onto the tatami mat and covered him with a blanket. Then he stepped slowly to a barrel-sized ceramic water cistern, picked up a wad of coarse filter paper, and mopped up Lindsay's vomit. His deliberate movements disguised the fact that, without video input, he was almost blind.

Ryumin donned his eyephones. He meditated on the tape he had made of Lindsay. Ideas and images came to him more easily through the wires.

He analyzed the young sundog's movements frame by frame. The man had long, bony arms and shins, large hands and feet, but he lacked any awkwardness. Studied closely, his movements showed ominous fluidity, the sure sign of a nervous system subjected to subtle and prolonged alteration. Someone had devoted great care and expense to that counterfeit of footloose ease and grace.

Ryumin edited the tape with the reflexive ease of a century of practice. The System was wide, Ryumin thought. There was room in it for a thousand modes of life, a thousand hopeful monsters. He felt sadness at what had been done to the man, but no alarm or fear. Only time could tell the difference between aberration and advance. Ryumin no longer made judgments. When he could, he held out his hand.

Friendly gestures were risky, of course, but Ryumin could never resist the urge to make them and watch the result. Curiosity had made him a sundog. He was bright; there'd been a place for him in his colony's soviet. But he had been driven to ask uncomfortable questions, to think uncomfortable thoughts.

Once, a sense of moral righteousness had lent him strength. That youthful smugness was long gone now, but he still had pity and the willingness to help. For Ryumin, decency had become an old man's habit.

The young sundog twisted in his sleep. His face seemed to ripple, twisting bizarrely. Ryumin squinted in surprise. This man was a strange one. That was nothing remarkable; the System was full of the strange. It was when they *escaped control* that things became interesting.

Lindsay woke, groaning. "How long have I been out?" he said.

"Three hours, twelve minutes," Ryumin said. "But there's no day or night here, Mr. Dze. Time doesn't matter."

Lindsay propped himself up on one elbow.

"Hungry?" Ryumin passed Lindsay a bowl of soup.

Lindsay looked uneasily at the warm broth. Circles of oil dotted its surface and white lumps floated within it. He had a spoonful. It was better than it looked.

"Thank you," he said. He ate quickly. "Sorry to be troublesome."

"No matter," Ryumin said. "Nausea is common when Zaibatsu microbes hit the stomach of a newcomer."

"Why'd you follow me with that camera?" Lindsay said.

Ryumin poured himself a bowl of soup. "Curiosity," he said. "I have the Zaibatsu's entrance monitored by radar. Most sundogs travel in factions. Single passengers are rare. I wanted to learn your story. That's how I earn my living, after all." He drank his soup. "Tell me about your future, Mr. Dze. What are you planning?"

"If I tell you, will you help me?"

"I might. Things have been dull here lately."

"There's money in it."

"Better and better," Ryumin said. "Could you be more specific?"

Lindsay stood up. "We'll do some acting," he said, straightening his cuffs. " 'To catch birds with a mirror is the ideal snare,' as my Shaper teachers used to say. I knew of the Black Medicals in the Ring Council. They're not genetically altered. The Shapers despised them, so they isolated themselves. That's their habit, even here. But they hunger for admiration, so I made myself into a mirror and showed them their own desires. I promised them prestige and influence, as patrons of the theatre." He reached for his jacket. "But what does the Geisha Bank want?"

"Money. Power," Ryumin said. "And the ruin of their rivals, who happen to be the Black Medicals."

"Three lines of attack." Lindsay smiled. "This is what they trained me for." His smile wavered, and he put his hand to his midriff. "That soup," he said. "Synthetic protein, wasn't it? I don't think it's going to agree with me."

Ryumin nodded in resignation. "It's your new microbes. You'd better clear your appointment book for a few days, Mr. Dze. You have dysentery."

# Chapter 2

## THE MARE TRANQUILLITATIS PEOPLE'S CIRCUMLUNAR ZAIBATSU: 28-12-'15

Night never fell in the Zaibatsu. It gave Lindsay's sufferings a timeless air: a feverish idyll of nausea.

Antibiotics would have cured him, but sooner or later his body would have to come to terms with its new flora. To pass the time between spasms, Ryumin entertained him with local anecdotes and gossip. It was a complex and depressing history, littered with betrayals, small-scale rivalries, and pointless power games.

The algae farmers were the Zaibatsu's most numerous faction, glum fanatics, clannish and ignorant, who were rumored to practice cannibalism. Next came the mathematicians, a proto-Shaper breakaway group that spent most of its time wrapped in speculation about the nature of infinite sets. The Zaibatsu's smallest domes were held by a profusion of pirates and privateers: the Hermes Breakaways, the Gray Torus Radicals, the Grand Megalics, the Soyuz Eclectics, and others, who changed names and personnel as easily as they cut a throat. They feuded constantly, but none dared challenge the Nephrine Black Medicals or the Geisha Bank. Attempts had been made in the past. There were appalling legends about them.

The people beyond the Wall had their own wildly varying mythos. They were said to live in a jungle of overgrown pines and mimosas. They were hideously inbred and afflicted with double thumbs and congenital deafness.

Others claimed there was nothing remotely human beyond the Wall: just a proliferating cluster of software, which had acquired a sinister autonomy.

It was, of course, possible that the land beyond the Wall had been secretly invaded and conquered by—*aliens*. An entire postindustrial folklore had sprung up around this enthralling concept, buttressed with ingenious arguments. Everyone expected aliens sooner or later. It was the modern version of the Millennium.

Ryumin was patient with him; while Lindsay slept feverishly, he patrolled the Zaibatsu with his camera robot, looking for news. Lindsay turned the corner on his illness. He kept down some soup and a few fried bricks of spiced protein.

One of Ryumin's stacks of equipment began to chime with a piercingly clear electronic bleeping. Ryumin looked up from where he sat sorting cassettes. "That's the radar," he said. "Hand me that headset, will you?"

Lindsay crawled to the radar stack and untangled a set of Ryumin's adhesive eyephones. Ryumin clamped them to his temples. "Not much resolution on radar," he said, closing his eyes. "A crowd has just arrived. Pirates, most likely. They're milling about on the landing pad."

He squinted, though his eyes were already shut. "Something very large is moving about with them. They've brought something huge. I'd better switch to telephoto." He yanked the headset's cord and its plug snapped free.

"I'm going outside for a look," Lindsay said. "I'm well enough."

"Wire yourself up first," Ryumin said. "Take that earset and one of the cameras."

Lindsay attached the auxiliary system and stepped outside the zippered airlock into the curdled air.

He backed away from Ryumin's dome toward the rim of the land panel. He turned and trotted to a nearby stile, which led over the low metal wall, and trained his camera upward.

"That's good," came Ryumin's voice in his ear. "Cut in the brightness amps, will you? That little button on the right. Yes, that's better. What do you make of it, Mr. Dze?"

Lindsay squinted through the lens. Far above, at the northern end of the Zaibatsu's axis, a dozen sundogs were wrestling in free-fall with a huge silver bag.

"It looks like a tent," Lindsay said. "They're inflating it." The silver bag wrinkled and tumesced suddenly, revealing itself as a blunt cylinder. On its side was a large red stencil as wide as a man was tall. It was a red skull with two crossed lightning bolts.

"Pirates!" Lindsay said.

Ryumin chuckled. "I thought as much."

A sharp gust of wind struck Lindsay. He lost his balance on the stile and looked behind him suddenly. The glass window strip formed a long white alley of decay. The hexagonal metaglass frets were speckled with dark plugs, jackstrawed here and there with heavy reinforcement struts. Leaks had been sprayed with airtight coats of thick plastic. Sunlight oozed sullenly through the gaps.

"Are you all right?" Ryumin said.

"Sorry," Lindsay said. He tilted the camera upward again.

The pirates had gotten their foil balloon airborne and had turned on its pair of small pusher-propellers. As it drifted away from the landing pad, it jerked once, then surged forward. It was towing something—an oddly shaped dark lump larger than a man.

"It's a meteorite," Ryumin told him. "A gift for the people beyond the Wall. Did you see the dark rocks that stand in the Sterilized Zone? They're all gifts from pirates. It's become a tradition."

"Wouldn't it be easier to carry it along the ground?"

"Are you joking? It's death to set foot in the Sterilized Zone."

"I see. So they're forced to drop it from the air. Do you recognize these pirates?"

"No," Ryumin said. "They're new here. That's why they need the rock."

"Someone seems to know them," Lindsay said. "Look at that."

He focused the camera to look past the airborne pirates to the sloping gray-brown surface of the Zaibatsu's third land panel. Most of this third panel was a bleak expanse of fuzz-choked mud, with surging coils of yellowish ground fog.

Near the third panel's blasted northern suburbs was a squat, varicolored dome, built of jigsawed chunks of salvaged ceramic and plastic. A foreshortened, antlike crowd of sundogs had emerged from the dome's airlock. They stared upward, their faces hidden by filter masks. They had dragged out a large crude machine of metal and plastic, fitted with pinions, levers, and cables. They jacked the machine upward until one end of it pointed into the sky.

"What are they doing?" Lindsay said.

"Who knows?" Ryumin said. "That's the Eighth Orbital Army, or so they call themselves. They've been hermits up till now."

The airship passed overhead, casting blurred shadows onto all three land panels. One of the sundogs triggered the machine.

A long metal harpoon flicked upward and struck home. Lindsay saw metal foil rupture in the airship's tail section. The javelin gleamed crazily as it whirled end over end, its flight disrupted by the collision and the curve of Coriolis force. The metal bolt vanished into the filthy trees of a ruined orchard.

The airship was in trouble. Its crew kicked and thrashed in midair, struggling to force their collapsing balloon away from the ground attackers.

The massive stone they were towing continued its course with weightless, serene inertia. As its towline grew tight, it slowly tore off the airship's tail.

With a *whoosh* of gas, the airship crumpled into a twisted metal rag. The engines fell, tugging the metal foil behind them in a rippling streamer.

The pirates thrashed as if drowning, struggling to stay within the zone of weightlessness. Their plight was desperate, since the zone was riddled with slow, sucking downdrafts that could send fliers tumbling to their deaths.

The rock blundered into the rippling edge of a swollen cloudbank. The dark mass veered majestically downward, wobbling a bit, and vanished into the mist. Moments later it reappeared below the cloud, plummeting downward in a vicious Coriolis arc.

It slammed into the glass and patchwork of the window strip. Lindsay, following it with his camera, heard the sullen crunch of impact. Glass and metal grated and burst free in a sucking roar.

The belly of the cloud overhead bulged downward and began to twist. A white plume spread above the blowout with the grace of creeping frost. It was steam, condensing from the air in the suddenly lowered pressure.

Lindsay held the camera above his head and leaped down onto the grimy floor of the window. He ran toward the blowout, ignoring Ryumin's surprised protests.

A minute's broken-field running brought him as close as he dared go. He crouched behind the rusted steel strut of a plug, ten meters from the impact site. Looking down past his feet through the dirty glass, Lindsay saw a long tail of freezing spray fanning out in rainbowed crystals against the shine of the sunlight mirrors.

A roaring vortex of sucking wind sprang up, slinging gusts of rain. Lindsay cupped one hand around the camera's lens.

Motion caught his eye. A group of oxygen farmers in masks and coveralls were struggling across the glass from the bordering panel. They cradled a long hose in their arms. They lurched forward doggedly, staggering in the wind, weaving among the plugs and struts.

Caught by the wind, a camouflaged surveillance plane crashed violently beside the hole. Its wreckage was sucked through at once.

The hose jerked and bucked with a gush of fluid. A thick spray of gray-green plastic geysered from its nozzle, hardening in midair. It hit the glass and clung there.

Under the whirlwind's pressure the plastic warped and bulged, but held. As more gushed forth, the wind was choked and became a shrill whistle.

Even after the blowout was sealed, the farmers continued to pump plastic sludge across the impact zone. Rain fell steadily from the agitated clouds. Another knot of farmers stood along the window wall, leaning their masked heads together and pointing into the sky.

Lindsay turned and looked upward with the rest.

The sudden vortex had spawned a concentric surf of clouds. Through a crescent-shaped gap, Lindsay saw the dome of the Eighth Orbital Army, across the width of the Zaibatsu. Tiny forms in white suits ringed the dome, lying on the ground. They did not move.

Lindsay focused the telephoto across the interior sky. The fanatics of the Eighth Orbital Army lay sprawled on the fouled earth. A knot of them had been caught trying to escape into the airlock; they lay in a tangle, their arms outstretched.

He saw no sign of the airship pirates. He thought for a moment that they had all escaped back to the landing port. Then he spotted one of them, mashed flat against another window panel.

"That was excellent footage," Ryumin said in his ear. "It was also very stupid."

"I owed you a favor," Lindsay said. He studied the dead. "I'm going over there," he decided.

"Let me send the robot. There'll be looters there soon."

"Then I want them to know me," Lindsay said. "They might be useful."

He crossed another stile onto the land panel. His lungs felt raw, but he had decided never to wear a breathing mask. His reputation was more important than the risk.

He skirted the Black Medicals' stronghold and crossed a second window strip. He walked north to the ragtag junk dome of the Orbital Army. It was the only outpost in the entire third panel, which had been abandoned to a particularly virulent form of the blight. This had once been an agricultural zone, and the heightened fertility of the soil brought forth a patchy crop of ankle-high mold. Farm buildings, all pastel ceramic and plastic, had been looted but not demolished, and their stiff inorganic walls and gaping windows seemed to long to lapse into an unattainable state of rot.

The recluses' dome was built of plastic door panels, chopped to shape and caulked.

The corpses lay frozen, their limbs oddly bent, for they had been dead before they hit the ground, and their arms and legs had bounced a little, loosely, with the impact. There was a curious lack of horror about the scene. The faceless masks and watertight body suits of the dead fanatics conveyed a sense of bloodless, prim efficiency. Nothing marked the dead as human beings except the military insignia on their shoulders. He counted eighteen of them.

The lenses on the faces of the dead were fogged over with internal steam.

He heard the quiet whir of aircraft. A pair of ultralights circled once and skidded in for a landing. Two of the airship pirates had arrived.

Lindsay trained his camera on them. They dismounted, unplugging their credit cards, and the aircraft taxied off.

They walked toward him in the half-crouching shuffle of people unused to gravity. Lindsay saw that their uniforms were full-length silver skeletons etched over a blood-red background.

The taller pirate prodded a nearby corpse with his foot. "You saw this?" he said in English.

"The spyplanes killed them," Lindsay said. "They endangered the habitat."

"The Eighth Orbital Army," the taller pirate mused, examining a shoulder patch. The second pirate muttered through her mask's filters, "Fascists. Antinationalist scum."

"You knew them?" Lindsay said.

"We dealt with them," said the first pirate. "We didn't know they were here, though." He sighed. "What a burn. Do you suppose there are others inside?"

"Only dead ones," Lindsay said. "The planes use x-ray lasers."

"Really?" the first pirate said. "Wish I could get my hands on one of those."

Lindsay twirled his left hand, a gesture in surveillance argot stating that they were watched. The taller pirate looked upward quickly. Sunlight glinted on the silver skull inlaid over his face.

He looked at Lindsay, his eyes hidden behind gleaming silver-plated eye sockets. "Where's your mask, citizen?"

"Here," Lindsay said, touching his face.

"A negotiator, huh? Looking for work, citizen? Our last diplomat just took the plunge. How are you in free-fall?"

"Be careful, Mr. President," the second pirate warned. "Remember the confirmation hearings."

"Let me handle the legal implications," the President said impatiently. "I'll introduce us. I'm the President of the Fortuna Miners' Democracy, and this is my wife, the Speaker of the House."

"Lin Dze, with Kabuki Intrasolar," Lindsay said. "I'm a theatrical impresario."

"That some kind of diplomat?"

"Sometimes, your excellency."

The President nodded. The Speaker of the House warned, "Don't trust him, Mr. President."

"The executive branch handles foreign relations, so shut the fuck up," the President snarled. "Listen, citizen, it's been a hard day. Right now, we oughta be in the Bank, having a scrub, maybe getting juiced, but instead these fascists cut in on us with their surface-to-air stuff, a preemptive strike, you follow me? So now our airship's burned and we've lost our fuckin' rock."

"That's a shame," Lindsay said.

The President scratched his neck. "You just can't make plans in this business. You learn to take it as it comes." He hesitated. "Let's get out of this stink, anyway. Maybe there's loot inside."

The Speaker of the House took a hand-held power saw out of a holster on her red webbing belt and began to saw through the wall of the sundog dome. The caulk between the plastic panels powdered easily. "You got to go in unexpected if you want to live," the President explained. "Don't ever, never go in an enemy airlock. You never know what's in 'em." Then he spoke into a wrist attachment. He used a covert operational jargon; Lindsay couldn't follow the words.

Together the two pirates kicked out the wall and stepped inside. Lindsay followed them, holding his camera. They replaced the burst-out panel, and the woman sprayed it with sealant from a tiny propellant can.

The President pulled off his skull mask and sniffed the air. He had a blunt, pug-nosed, freckled face; his short ginger-colored hair was sparse, and the skin of his scalp gleamed oddly. They had emerged into the communal kitchen of the Eighth Orbital Army: there were cushions and low tables, a microwave, a crate of plastic-wrapped protein, and half a dozen tall fermenting units, bubbling loudly. A dead woman whose face looked sunburned sprawled on the floor by the doorway.

"Good," the President said. "We eat." The Speaker of the House unmasked herself; her face was bony, with slitted, suspicious eyes. A painful-looking skin rash dotted her jaw and neck.

The two pirates stalked into the next room. It was a combination bunkroom and command center, with a bank of harsh, flickering videos in a central cluster. One of the screens was tracking by telephoto: it showed a group of nine red-clad pirates approaching on foot down the Zaibatsu's northern slope, picking their way through the ruins.

"Here come the rest of us," the Speaker said.

The President glanced about him. "Not so bad. We stay here, then. At least we'll have a place to keep the air in."

Something rustled under one of the bunks. The Speaker of the House flung herself headlong under the bed. Lindsay swung his camera around. There was a high-pitched scream and a brief struggle; then she emerged, dragging out a small child. The Speaker had pinned the child in a complicated one-handed armlock. She got it to its feet.

It was a dark-haired, glowering, filthy little creature of indeterminate sex. It wore an Eighth Orbital Army uniform, cut to size. It was missing some teeth. It looked about five years old.

"So they're not all dead!" the President said. He crouched and looked the child in the eye. "Where are the rest of you?"

He showed it a knife. The blade flickered into his hand from nowhere. "Talk, citizen! Otherwise I show you your guts!"

"Come on!" said Lindsay. "That's no way to talk to a child."

"Who are you kidding, citizen? Listen, this little squealer might be eighty years old. There are endocrine treatments—"

Lindsay knelt by the child and tried to approach it gently. "How old are you? Four, five? What language do you speak?"

"Forget it," the Speaker of the House said. "There's only one small-sized bunk, see it? I guess the spyplanes just missed this one."

"Or spared it," Lindsay said.

The President laughed skeptically. "Sure, citizen. Listen, we can sell this thing to the whore bankers. It ought to be worth a few hours' attention for us, at least."

"That's slavery," Lindsay protested.

"Slavery? What are you talking about? Don't get theological, citizen. I'm talking about a national entity freeing a prisoner of war to a third party. It's a perfectly legal commercial transaction."

"I don't want to go to the whores," the child piped up suddenly. "I want to go to the farmers."

"The farmers?" said the President. "You don't want to be a farmer, micro-citizen. Ever had any weapons training? We could use a small assassin to sneak through the air ducts—"

"Don't underestimate those farmers," Lindsay said. He gestured at one of the video screens. A group of two dozen farmers had walked across the interior slope of the Zaibatsu. They were loading the dead Eighth Orbitals onto four flat sledges, drawn by shoulder harnesses.

"Blast!" the President said. "I wanted to roll them myself." He smirked. "Can't blame 'em, I guess. Lots of good protein in a corpse."

"I want to go with the farmers," the child insisted.

"Let it go," Lindsay spoke up. "I have business with the Geisha Bank. I can treat your nation to a stay."

The Speaker of the House released the child's arm. "You can?"

Lindsay nodded. "Give me a couple of days to negotiate it."

She caught her husband's eye. "This one's all right. Let's make him Secretary of State."

## THE MARE TRANQUILLITATIS PEOPLE'S CIRCUMLUNAR ZAIBATSU: 2-1-'16

The Geisha Bank was a complex of older buildings, shellacked airtight and connected by a maze of polished wooden halls and sliding paper airlocks. The area had been a red-light district even before the Zaibatsu's collapse. The Bank was proud of its heritage and continued the refined and eccentric traditions of a gentler age.

Lindsay left the eleven nationals of the Fortuna Miners' Democracy in an antiseptic sauna vault, being scrubbed by impassive bathboys. It was the first real bath the pirates had had in months. Their scrawny bodies were knobbed with muscle from constant practice in free-fall jujutsu. Their sweating skins were bright with fearsome tattoos and septic rashes.

Lindsay did not join them. He stepped into a paneled dressing room and handed over his Nephrine Medicals uniform to be cleaned and pressed. He slipped into a soft brown kimono. A low-ranking male geisha in kimono and obi approached him. "Your pleasure, sir?"

"I'd like a word with the *yarite,* please."

The geisha looked at him with well-bred skepticism. "One moment. I will ask if our chief executive officer is prepared to accept guests."

He vanished. After half an hour a blonde female geisha in business suit and obi appeared. "Mr. Dze? This way, please."

He followed her to an elevator guarded by two men armed with electrode-studded clubs. The guards were giants; his head barely came to their elbows. Their long, stony faces were acromegalic: swollen jaws, clifflike jutting cheekbones. They had been treated with hormonal growth factors.

The elevator surged up three floors and opened.

Lindsay faced a thick network of brightly colored beads. Thousands of dangling, beaded wires hung from floor to ceiling. Any movement would disturb them.

"Take my hand," the banker said. Lindsay shuffled behind her, thrashing and clattering. "Step carefully," she said. "There are traps."

Lindsay closed his eyes and followed. His guide stopped; a hidden door opened in a mirrored wall. Lindsay stepped through it, into the *yarite*'s private chamber.

The floor was of ancient wood, waxed to a dark gleam. There were flat square cushions underfoot, in patterns of printed bamboo. In the long wall to Lindsay's left, glass double-doors showed a sunlit wooden balcony and a splendid garden, where crooked pines and tall japonicas arched over curving paths of raked white pebbles. The air in the room smelled of evergreen. He was gazing on this world before its rot, an image of the past, projected on false doors that could never open.

The *yarite* was sitting cross-legged on a cushion. She was a wizened old Mech with a tight-drawn mouth and hooded, reptilian eyes. Her wrinkled head was encased in a helmetlike lacquered wig, skewered with pins. She wore an angular flowered kimono supported by starch and struts. There was room in it for three of her.

A second woman knelt silently with her back to the right-hand wall, facing the garden's image. Lindsay knew at once that she was a Shaper. Her startling beauty alone was proof, but she had that strange, intangible air of charisma that spread from the Reshaped like a magnetic field. She was of mixed Asiatic-African gene stock: her eyes were tilted, but her skin was dark. Her hair was long and faintly kinked. She knelt before a rack of white keyboards with an air of meek devotion.

The *yarite* spoke without moving her head. "Your duties, Kitsune." The girl's hands darted over the keyboards and the air was filled with the tones of that most ancient of Japanese instruments: the synthesizer.

Lindsay knelt on a cushion, facing the old woman. A tea tray rolled to his side and poured hot water into a cup with a chaste tinkling sound. It dipped a rotary tea whisk into the cup.

"Your pirate friends," the old woman said, "are about to bankrupt you."

"It's only money," Lindsay said.

"It is our sweat and sexuality. Did you think it would please us to squander it?"

"I needed your attention," Lindsay said. His training had seized him at once, but he was still afraid of the girl. He hadn't known he would be facing a Shaper. And there was something drastically wrong with the old woman's kinesics. It looked like drugs or Mechanist nerve alteration.

"You came here dressed as a Nephrine Black Medical," the old woman said. "Our attention was guaranteed. You have it. We are listening."

With Ryumin's help, Lindsay had expanded his plans. The Geisha Bank had the power to destroy his scheme; therefore, they had to be co-opted into it. He knew what they wanted. He was ready to show them a mirror. If they recognized their own ambitions and desires, he would win.

Lindsay launched into his spiel. He paused midway to make a point. "You can see what the Black Medicals hope to gain from the performance. Behind their walls they feel isolated, paranoid. They plan to gain prestige by sponsoring our play.

"But I must have a cast. The Geisha Bank is my natural reservoir of talent. I can succeed without the Black Medicals. I can't succeed without you."

"I see," the *yarite* said. "Now explain to me why you think we can profit from your ambitions."

Lindsay looked pained. "I came here to arrange a cultural event. Can't that be enough?"

He glanced at the girl. Her hands flickered over the keyboards. Suddenly she looked up at him and smiled, slyly, secretly. He saw the tip of her tongue behind her perfect teeth. It was a bright, predatory smile, full of lust and mischief. In an instant it burned itself into his bloodstream. Hair rose on the back of his neck. He was losing control.

He looked at the floor, his skin prickling. "All right," he said heavily. "It isn't enough, and that shouldn't surprise me. . . . Listen, madame. You and the Medicals have been rivals for years. This is your chance to lure them into the open and ambush them on your own ground. They're naive about finance. Naive, but greedy. They hate dealing in a financial system that you control. If they thought they could succeed, they'd leap at the chance to form their own economy.

"So, let them do it. Let them commit themselves. Let them pile success on success until they lose all sense of proportion and greed overwhelms them. Then burst their bubble."

"Nonsense," the old woman said. "How can an actor tell a banker her business?"

"You're not dealing with a Mech cartel," Lindsay said intensely, leaning forward. He knew the girl was staring at him. He could feel it. "These are three hundred technicians, bored, frightened, and completely isolated. They are perfect prey for mass hysteria. Gambling fever will hit them like an epidemic." He leaned back. "Support me, madame. I'll be your point man, your broker, your go-between. They'll never know you were behind their ruin. In fact, they'll come to you for help." He sipped his tea. It tasted synthetic.

The old woman paused as if she were thinking. Her expression was very wrong. There were none of the tiny subliminal flickers of mouth and eyelid, the movements of the throat, that accompanied human thought processes. Her face was more than calm. It was inert.

"It has possibilities," she said at last. "But the Bank must have control. Covert, but complete. How can you guarantee this?"

"It will be in your hands," Lindsay promised. "We will use my company, Kabuki Intrasolar, as a front. You will use your contacts outside the Zaibatsu to issue fictitious stock. I will offer it for sale here, and your Bank will be ambivalent. This will allow the Nephrines to score a financial coup and seize control of the company. Fictitious stockholders, your agents, will react in alarm and send in pleas and inflated offers to the new owners. This will flatter their self-esteem and overwhelm any doubts.

"At the same time, you will cooperate with me openly. You will supply me with actors and actresses; in fact, you will jealously fight for the privilege. Your geishas will talk of nothing else to every customer. You will spread rumors about me: my charm, my brilliance, my hidden resources. You will underwrite all my extravagances, and establish a free-wheeling, free-spending atmosphere of carefree hedonism. It will be a huge confidence trick that will bamboozle the entire world."

The old woman sat silently, her eyes glazed.

The low, pure tones of the synthesizer stopped suddenly. A tense hush fell over the room. The girl spoke softly from behind her keyboards. "It will work, won't it?"

He looked into her face. Her meekness had peeled off like a layer of cosmetics. Her dark eyes shocked him. They were full of frank, carnivorous desire. He knew at once that she was feigning nothing, because her look was beyond pretense. It was not human.

Without knowing it, he rose to one knee, his eyes still locked with hers. "Yes," he said. His voice was hoarse. "It will work, I swear it to you." The floor was cold under his hand. He realized that, without any decision on his part, he had begun to move toward her, half crawling.

She looked at him in lust and wonder. "Tell me what you are, darling. Tell me really."

"I'm what you are," Lindsay said. "Shaper's work." He forced himself to stop moving. His arms began to tremble.

"I want to tell you what they did to me," the girl said. "Let me tell you what I am."

Lindsay nodded once. His mouth was dry with sick excitement.

"All right," he said. "Tell me, Kitsune."

"They gave me to the surgeons," she said. "They took my womb out, and they put in brain tissue. Grafts from the pleasure center, darling. I'm wired to the ass and the spine and the throat, and it's better than being God. When I'm hot, I sweat perfume. I'm cleaner than a fresh needle, and nothing leaves my body that you can't drink like wine or eat like candy. And they left me bright, so that I would know what submission was. Do you know what submission is, darling?"

"No," Lindsay said harshly. "But I know what it means not to care about dying."

"We're not like the others," she said. "They put us past the limits. And now we can do anything we like to them, can't we?"

Her laugh sent a shuddering thrill through him. She leaped with balletic grace over her deck of keyboards.

She kicked the old woman's shoulder with one bare foot, and the *yarite* fell over with a crunch. Her wig ripped free with a shredding of tape. Beneath it, Lindsay glimpsed her threadbare skull, riddled with cranial plugs. He stared. "Your keyboards," he said.

"She's my front," Kitsune said. "That's what my life is. Fronts and fronts and fronts. Only the pleasure is real. The pleasure of control."

Lindsay licked his dry lips.

"Give me what's real," she said.

She undid her obi sash. Her kimono was printed in a design of irises and violets. The skin beneath it was like a dying man's dream of skin.

"Come here," she said. "Put your mouth on my mouth."

Lindsay scrambled forward and threw his arms around her. She slipped her warm tongue deep into his mouth. It tasted of spice.

It was narcotic. The glands of her mouth oozed drugs.

They sprawled on the floor in front of the old woman's half-lidded eyes.

She slipped her arms inside his loose kimono. "Shaper," she said, "I want your genetics. All over me."

Her warm hand caressed his groin. He did what she said.


## THE MARE TRANQUILLITATIS PEOPLE'S CIRCUMLUNAR ZAIBATSU: 16-1-'16

Lindsay lay on his back on the floor of Ryumin's dome, his long fingers pressed to the sides of his head. His left hand had two glittering impact rubies set in gold bands. He wore a shimmering black kimono with a faint pattern of irises set in the weave. His hakama trousers were of the modern cut.

The right sleeve of his kimono held the fictitious corporate emblem of Kabuki Intrasolar: a stylized white mask striped across the eyes and cheeks with flaring bands of black and red. His sleeves had fallen back as he clutched his head and revealed an injection bruise on his forearm. He was on vasopressin.

He dictated into a microphone. "All right," he said. "Scene Three: Amijima. Jihei says: No matter how far we walk, there'll never be a place marked for suicides. Let us kill ourselves here.

"Then Koharu: Yes, that's true. One place is as good as another to die. But I've been thinking. If they find our dead bodies together, people will say that Koharu and Jihei committed a lovers' suicide. I can imagine how your wife will resent and envy me. So you should kill me here, then choose another spot, far away, for yourself.

"Then Jihei says—" Lindsay fell silent. As he had been dictating, Ryumin had occupied himself with an unusual handicraft. He was sifting what appeared to be tiny bits of brown cardboard onto a small slip of white paper. He carefully rolled the paper into a tube. Then he pinched the tube's ends shut and sealed it with his tongue.

He put one end of the paper cylinder between his lips, then held up a small metal gadget and pressed a switch on its top. Lindsay stared, then screamed. "Fire! Oh my God! Fire, fire!"

Ryumin blew out smoke. "What the hell's wrong with you? This tiny flame can't hurt anything."

"But it's fire! Good God, I've never seen a naked flame in my life." Lindsay lowered his voice. "You're sure you won't catch fire?" He watched Ryumin anxiously. "Your lungs are smoking."

"No, no. It's just a novelty, a small new vice." The old Mechanist shrugged. "A little dangerous maybe, but aren't they all."

"What is it?"

"Bits of cardboard soaked in nicotine. They've got some kind of flavoring, too. It's not so bad." He drew on the cigarette; Lindsay stared at the glowing tip and shuddered. "Don't worry," Ryumin said. "This place isn't like other colonies. Fire's no danger here. Mud doesn't burn."

Lindsay sagged back to the floor and groaned. His brain was swimming in memory enhancements. His head hurt and he had an indescribable tickling sensation, like the first fraction of a second during an onset of déjà vu. It was like being unable to sneeze.

"You made me lose my place," he said peevishly. "What's the use? When I think of what this used to mean to me! These plays that hold everything worth preserving in human life. . . . Our heritage, before the Mechs, before the Shapers. Humanity, morality, a life not tampered with."

Ryumin tapped ashes into an upended back lens cap. "You're talking like a circumlunar native, Mr. Dze. Like a Concatenate. What's your home world? Crisium S.S.R.? Copernican Commonwealth?"

Lindsay sucked air through his teeth.

Ryumin said, "Forgive an old man's prying." He blew more smoke and rubbed a red mark on his temple, where the eyephones fit. "Let me tell you what I think your problem is, Mr. Dze. So far, you've recited three of these compositions: *Romeo and Juliet, The Tragical History of Doctor Faustus,* and now *The Love Suicide at Amijima.* Frankly, I have some problems with these pieces."

"Oh?" said Lindsay on a rising note.

"Yes. First, they're incomprehensible. Second, they're impossibly morbid. And third and worst of all, they're preindustrial.

"Now let me tell you what I think. You've launched this audacious fraud, you're creating a huge stir, and you've set the whole Zaibatsu on its ear. For this much trouble, you should at least repay the people with a little fun."

"Fun?" Lindsay said.

"Yes. I know these sundogs. They want to be entertained, not clubbed by some ancient relic. They want to hear about real people, not savages."

"But that's not human culture."

"So what?" Ryumin puffed his cigarette. "I've been thinking. I've heard three 'plays' now, so I know the medium. There's not much to it. I can whip one up for us in two or three days, I think."

"You think so?"

Ryumin nodded. "We'll have to scrap some things."

"Such as?"

"Well, gravity, first of all. I don't see how you can get any good dancing or fighting done except in free-fall."

Lindsay sat up. "Dancing and fighting, is it?"

"That's right. Your audience are whores, oxygen farmers, two dozen pirate bands, and fifty runaway mathematicians. They would all love to see dancing and fighting. We'll get rid of the stage; it's too flat. The curtains are a nuisance; we can do that with lighting. You may be used to these old circumlunars with their damned centrifugal spin, but modern people love free-fall. These poor sundogs have suffered enough. It'll be like a holiday for them."

"You mean, get up to the free-fall zone somehow."

"Yes indeed. We'll build an aerostat: a big geodesic bubble, airtight. We'll launch it off the landing zone and keep it fixed up there with guy wires, or some such thing. You have to build a theatre anyway, don't you? You might as well put it in midair where everyone can see it."

"Of course," Lindsay said. He smiled as the idea sank in. "We can put our corporate logo on it."

"Hang pennants from it."

"Sell tickets inside. Tickets and stock." He laughed aloud. "I know just the ones to build it for me, too."

"It needs a name," Ryumin said. "We'll call it . . . the Kabuki Bubble!"

"The Bubble!" Lindsay said, slapping the floor. "What else?"

Ryumin smiled and rolled another cigarette.

"Say," Lindsay said. "Let me try some of that."

WHEREAS, Throughout this Nation's history, its citizens have always confronted new challenges; and

WHEREAS, The Nation's Secretary of State, Lin Dze, finds himself in need of aeronautic engineering expertise that our citizens are uniquely fitted to supply; and

WHEREAS, Secretary Dze, representing Kabuki Intrasolar, an autonomous corporate entity, has agreed to pay the Nation for its labors with a generous allocation of Kabuki Intrasolar corporate stock;

NOW, THEREFORE, BE IT RESOLVED by the House of Representatives of the Fortuna Miners' Democracy, the Senate concurring, that the Nation will construct the Kabuki Bubble auditorium, provide promotional services for Kabuki stock, and extend political and physical protection to Kabuki staff, employees, and property.

"Excellent," Lindsay said. He authenticated the document and replaced the Fortuna State Seal in his diplomatic bag. "It truly eases my mind to know that the FMD will handle security."

"Hey, it's a pleasure," said the President. "Any dip of ours who needs it can depend on an escort twenty-four hours a day. Especially when you're going to the Geisha Bank, if you get my meaning."

"Have this resolution copied and spread through the Zaibatsu," Lindsay said. "It ought to be good for a ten-point stock advance." He looked at the President seriously. "But don't get greedy. When it reaches a hundred and fifty, start selling out, slowly. And have your ship ready for a quick getaway."

The President winked. "Don't worry. We haven't been sitting on our hands. We're lining up a class assignment from a Mech cartel. A bodyguard gig ain't bad, but a nation gets restless. When the *Red Consensus* is shipshape again, then our time has come to kill and eat."

# THE MARE TRANQUILLITATIS PEOPLE'S CIRCUMLUNAR ZAIBATSU: 13-3-'16

Lindsay slept, exhausted, with his head propped against the diplomatic bag. An artificial morning shone through the false glass doors. Kitsune sat in thought, toying quietly with the keys of her synthesizer.

Her proficiency had long since passed the limits of merely technical skill. It had become a communion, an art sprung from dark intuition. Her synthesizer could mimic any instrument and surpass it: rip its sonic profile into naked wave forms and rebuild it on a higher plane of sterilized, abstract purity. Its music had the painful, brittle clarity of faultlessness.

Other instruments struggled for that ideal clarity but failed. Their failure gave their sound humanity. The world of humanity was a world of losses, broken hopes, and original sin, a flawed world, yearning always for mercy, empathy, compassion. . . . It was not her world.

Kitsune's world was the fantastic, seamless realm of high pornography. Lust was ever present, amplified and tireless, broken only by spasms of superhuman intensity. It smothered every other aspect of life as a shriek of feedback might overwhelm an orchestra.

Kitsune was an artificial creature, and accepted her feverish world with a predator's thoughtlessness. Hers was a pure and abstract life, a hot, distorted parody of sainthood.

The surgical assault on her body would have turned a human woman into a blank-eyed erotic animal. But Kitsune was a Shaper, with a Shaper's unnatural resilience and genius. Her narrow world had turned her into something as sharp and slippery as an oiled stiletto.

She had spent eight of her twenty years within the Bank, where she dealt with customers and rivals on terms she thoroughly understood. Still, she knew there was a realm of mental experience, taken for granted by humanity, that was closed to her.

Shame. Pride. Guilt. Love. She felt these emotions as dim shadows, dark reptilian trash burnt to ashes in an instant by searing ecstasy. She was not incapable of human feeling; it was simply too mild for her to notice. It had become a second subconscious, a buried, intuitive layer below her posthuman mode of thought. Her consciousness was an amalgam of coldly pragmatic logic and convulsive pleasure.

Kitsume knew that Lindsay was handicapped by his primitive mode of thought. She felt a kind of pity for him, a compassionate sorrow that she could not recognize or admit to herself. She believed he must be very old, from one of the first generations of Shapers. Their genetic engineering had been limited and they could scarcely be told from original human stock.

He must be almost a hundred years old. To be so old, yet look so young, meant that he had chosen sound techniques of life extension. He dated back to an era before Shaperism had reached its full expression. Bacteria still swarmed through his body. Kitsune never told him about the antibiotic pills and supposi-

tories she took, or the painful antiseptic showers. She didn't want him to know
he was contaminating her. She wanted everything between them to be clean.

She had a cool regard for Lindsay. He was a source of lofty and platonic
satisfaction to her. She had the craftsmanlike respect for him that a butcher
might have for a sharp steel saw. She took a positive pleasure in using him. She
wanted him to last a long time, so she took good care of him and enjoyed giving
him what she thought he needed to go on functioning.

For Lindsay, her affections were ruinous. He opened his eyes on the tatami
mat and reached out at once for the diplomatic bag behind his head. When his
fingers closed over the smooth plastic handle, an anxiety circuit shut off in his
head, but that first relief only triggered other systems and he came fully awake
into a queasy combat alertness.

He saw that he was in Kitsune's chamber. Morning was breaking over the
image of the long-dead garden. False daylight slanted into the room, gleaming
from inlaid clothes chests and the perspex dome of a fossilized bonsai. Some repressed part of him cried out within him, in meek despair. He ignored it. His
new diet of drugs had brought the Shaper schooling back in full force and he
was in no mood to tolerate his own weaknesses. He was full of that mix of steel-
trap irritability and slow gloating patience that placed him at the keenest edges
of perception and reaction.

He sat up and saw Kitsune at the keyboards. "Good morning," he said.

"Hello, darling. Did you sleep well?"

Lindsay considered. Some antiseptic she used had scorched his tongue. His
back was bruised where her Shaper-strengthened fingers had dug in carelessly.
His throat had an ominous rawness—he had spent too much time without a
mask in the open air. "I feel fine," he said, smiling. He opened the complex lock
of his diplomatic bag.

He slipped on his finger rings and stepped into his hakama trousers.

"Do you want something to eat?" she said.

"Not before my shot."

"Then help me plug in the front," she said.

Lindsay repressed a shudder. He hated the *yarite*'s withered, waxlike, cy-
borged body, and Kitsune knew it. She forced him to help her with it because it
was a measure of her control.

Lindsay understood this and wanted to help her; he wanted to repay her, in
a way she understood, for the pleasure she had given him.

But something in him revolted at it. When his training faltered, as it did between shots, repressed emotions rose and he was aware of the terrible sadness of
their affair. He felt a kind of pity for her, a compassionate sorrow that he would
never insult her by admitting. There were things he had wanted to give her: simple companionship, simple trust and regard.

Simple irrelevance. Kitsune hauled the *yarite* out of its biomonitored cradle
beneath the floorboards. In some ways the thing had passed the limits of the
clinically dead; sometimes they had to slam it into operation like push-starting a
balky engine.

Its maintenance technology was the same type that supported the Mechanist cyborgs of the Radical Old and the Mech cartels. Filters and monitors clogged the thing's bloodstream; the internal glands and organs were under computer control. Implants sat on its heart and liver, prodding them with electrodes and hormones. The old woman's autonomous nervous system had long since collapsed and shut down.

Kitsune examined a readout and shook her head. "The acid levels are rising as fast as our stocks, darling. The plugs are degrading its brain. It's very old. Held together with wires and patchwork."

She sat it up on a floor mat and spooned vitaminized pap into its mouth.

"You should seize control on your own," he said. He inserted a dripping plug into a duct on the *yarite*'s veiny forearm.

"I'd like that," she said. "But I have a problem getting rid of this one. The sockets on its head will be hard to explain away. I could cover them with skin grafts, but that won't fool an autopsy. . . . The staff expect this thing to live forever. They've spent enough on it. They'll want to know why it died."

The *yarite* moved its tongue convulsively and dribbled out its paste. Kitsune hissed in annoyance. "Slap its face," she said.

Lindsay ran a hand through his sleep-matted hair. "Not this early," he said, half pleading.

Kitsune said nothing, merely straightened her back and shoulders and set her face in a prim mask. Lindsay was defeated at once. He jerked his hand back and swung it across the thing's face in a vicious open-handed slap. A spot of color showed in its leathery cheek.

"Show me its eyes," she said. Lindsay grabbed the thing's gaunt cheeks between his thumb and fingers and twisted its head so that it met Kitsune's eyes. With revulsion, he recognized a dim flicker of debased awareness in its face.

Kitsune took his hand away and lightly kissed his palm. "That's my good darling," she said. She slipped the spoon between the thing's slack lips.

## THE MARE TRANQUILLITATIS PEOPLE'S CIRCUMLUNAR ZAIBATSU: 21-4-'16

The Fortuna pirates floated like red-and-silver paper cutouts against the interior walls of the Kabuki Bubble. The air was loud with the angry spitting of welders, the whine of rotary sanders, the wheeze of the air filters.

Lindsay's loose kimono and trousers ruffled in free-fall. He reviewed the script with Ryumin. "You've been rehearsing this?" he said.

"Sure," said Ryumin. "They love it. It's great. Don't worry."

Lindsay scratched his floating, puffy hair. "I don't quite know what to make of this."

A camouflaged surveillance plane had forced itself into the Bubble just before the structure was sealed shut. Against the bright triangular pastels, its dreary camouflage made it as obvious as a severed thumb. The machine yawed and dipped within the fifty-meter chamber, its lenses and shotgun microphones swiveling relentlessly. Lindsay was glad it was there, but it bothered him.

"I have the feeling I've heard this story before," he said. He flipped through the printout's pages. The margins were thick with cartoon stick figures scribbled there for the illiterate. "Let me see if I have it right. A group of pirates in the Trojan asteroids have kidnapped a Shaper woman. She's some kind of weapons specialist, am I right?"

Ryumin nodded. He had taken his new prosperity in stride. He wore ribbed silk coveralls in a tasteful shade of navy and a loose beret, high fashion in the Mech cartels. A silver microphone bead dotted his upper lip.

Lindsay said, "The Shapers are terrified by what the pirates might do with her expertise. So they form an alliance and put the pirates under seige. Finally they trick their way in and burn the place out." Lindsay looked up. "Did it really happen, or didn't it?"

"It's an old story," Ryumin said. "Something like that actually happened once; I feel sure of it. But I filed off the serial numbers and made it my own."

Lindsay smoothed his kimono. "I could swear that . . . hell. They say if you forget something while you're on vasopressin, you'll never remember it. It causes mnemonic burnout." He shook the script in resignation.

"Can you direct it?" Ryumin said.

Lindsay shook his head. "I wanted to, but it might be best if I left it to you. You do know what you're doing, don't you?"

"No," Ryumin said cheerfully. "Do you?"

"No. . . . The situation's getting out of hand. Outside investors keep trying to buy Kabuki stock. Word got out through the Geisha Bank's contacts. I'm afraid that the Nephrine Black Medicals will sell their Kabuki holdings to some Mech cartel. And then . . . I don't know . . . it'll mean—"

"It'll mean that Kabuki Intrasolar has become a legitimate business."

"Yes." Lindsay grimaced. "It looks like the Black Medicals will escape unscathed. They'll even profit. The Geisha Bank won't like it."

"What of it?" said Ryumin. "We have to keep moving forward or the whole thing falls apart. The Bank's already made a killing selling Kabuki stock to the Black Medicals. The old crone who runs the Bank is crazy about you. The whores talk about you constantly."

He gestured at the center stage. It was a spherical area crisscrossed with padded wires, where a dozen actors were going through their paces. They flung themselves through free-fall aerobatics, catching the wires, spinning, looping, and rebounding.

Two of them collided bruisingly and clawed the air for a handhold. Ryumin said, "Those acrobats are pirates, you understand? Four months ago they would have slit each other's throats for a kilowatt. But not now, Mr. Dze. Now they have too much at stake. They're stage-struck."

Ryumin laughed conspiratorially.

"For once they're more than pocket terrorists. Even the whores are more than sex toys. They're real actors, with a real script and a real audience. It doesn't

matter that you and I know it's a fraud, Mr. Dze. A symbol has meaning if someone gives it meaning. And they're giving it everything they have."

Lindsay watched the actors begin their routine again. They flew from wire
to wire with feverish determination. "It's pathetic," he said.

"A tragedy to those who feel. A comedy to those who think," Ryumin said.

Lindsay stared at him suspiciously. "What's gotten into you, anyway? What
are you up to?"

Ryumin pursed his lips and looked elaborately nonchalant. "My needs are
simple. Every decade or so I like to return to the cartels and see if they've made
any progress with these bones of mine. Progressive calcium loss is not a laughing matter. Frankly, I'm getting brittle." He looked at Lindsay. "And what about
you, Mr. Dze?"

He patted Lindsay's shoulder.

"Why not tag along with me? It would do you good to see more of the System. There are two hundred million people in space. Hundreds of habitats, an
explosion of cultures. They're not all scraping out a living on the edge of survival, like these poor *bezprizorniki*. Most of them are the bourgeoisie. Their
lives are snug and rich! Maybe technology eventually turns them into something
you wouldn't call human. But that's a choice they make—a rational choice."
Ryumin waved his hands expansively. "This Zaibatsu is only a criminal enclave.
Come with me and let me show you the fat of the System. You need to see the
cartels."

"The cartels . . ." Lindsay said. To join the Mechanists would mean surren-
dering to the ideals of the Radical Old. He looked around him, and his pride
flared. "Let them come to me!"

## THE MARE TRANQUILLITATIS PEOPLE'S CIRCUMLUNAR ZAIBATSU: 1-6-'16

For the first performance, Lindsay gave up his finery for a general-issue jumpsuit. He covered his diplomatic bag with burlap to hide the Kabuki decals.

It seemed that every sundog in the world had filtered into the Bubble. They
numbered over a thousand. The Bubble could not have held them, except in free-
fall. There were light opera-box frameworks for the Bank elite, and a jackstraw
complex of padded bracing wires where the audience clung like roosting sparrows.

Most floated freely. The crowd formed a percolating mass of loose concentric spheres. Broad tunnels had opened spontaneously in the mass of bodies, following the complex kinesics of crowd flow. There was a constant excited
murmur in a flurry of differing argots.

The play began. Lindsay watched the crowd. Brief shoving matches broke
out during the first fanfare, but by the time the dialogue started the crowd had
settled. Lindsay was thankful for that. He missed his usual bodyguard of Fortuna
pirates.

The pirates had finished their obligations to him and were busy preparing
their ship for departure. Lindsay, though, felt safe in his anonymity. If the play

failed disastrously, he would simply be one sundog among others. If it went well, he could change in time to accept the applause.

In the first abduction scene, pirates kidnapped the young and beautiful weapons genius, played by one of Kitsune's best. The audience screamed in delight at the puffs of artificial smoke and bright free-fall gushes of fake blood.

Lexicon computers throughout the Bubble translated the script into a dozen tongues and dialects. It seemed unlikely that this polyglot crowd could grasp the dialogue. To Lindsay it sounded like naive mush, mangled by mistranslation. But they listened raptly.

After an hour, the first three acts were over. A long intermission followed, in which the central stage was darkened. Rude claques had formed spontaneously for the cast members, as pirate groups shouted for their own.

Lindsay's nose stung. The air inside the Bubble had been supercharged with oxygen, to give the crowd a hyperventilated élan. Despite himself, Lindsay too felt elation. The hoarse shouts of enthusiasm were contagious. The situation was moving with its own dynamics. It was out of his hands.

Lindsay drifted toward the Bubble's walls, where some enterprising oxygen farmers had set up a concessions stand.

The farmers, clinging awkwardly to footloops on the Bubble's frame, were doing a brisk business. They sold their own native delicacies: anonymous green patties fried up crisp, and white blobby cubes on a stick, piping hot from the microwave. Kabuki Intrasolar took a cut, since the food stands were Lindsay's idea. The farmers paid happily in Kabuki stock.

Lindsay had been careful with the stock. He had meant at first to inflate it past all measure and thereby ruin the Black Medicals. But the miraculous power of paper money had seduced him. He had waited too long, and the Black Medicals had sold their stock to outside investors, at an irresistible profit.

Now the Black Medicals were safe from him—and grateful. They sincerely respected him and nagged him constantly for further tips on the market.

Everyone was happy. He foresaw a long run for the play. After that, Lindsay thought, there would be other schemes, bigger and better ones. This aimless sundog world was perfect for him. It only asked that he never stop, never look back, never look farther forward than the next swindle.

Kitsune would see to that. He glanced at her opera box and saw her floating with carnivorous meekness behind the Bank's senior officers, her dupes. She would not allow him any doubts or regrets. He felt obscurely glad for it. With her limitless ambition to drive him, he could avoid his own conflicts.

They had the world in their pocket. But below his giddy sense of triumph a faint persistent pain roiled through him. He knew that Kitsune was simply and purely relentless. But Lindsay had a fault line through him, an aching seam where his training met his other self. Now, at his finest moment, when he wanted to relax and feel an honest joy, it came up tainted.

All around him the crowd was exulting. Yet something within him made him shrink from joining them. He felt cheated, twisted, robbed of something that he couldn't grip.

He reached for his inhaler. A good chemical whiff would boost his discipline.

Something tugged the fabric of his jumpsuit, from behind him, to his left. He glanced quickly over his shoulder.

A black-haired, rangy young man with flinty gray eyes had seized his jumpsuit with the muscular bare toes of his right foot. "Hey, target," the man said. He smiled pleasantly. Lindsay watched the man's face for kinesics and realized with a dull shock that the face was his own.

"Take it easy, target," the assassin said. Lindsay heard his own voice from the assassin's mouth.

The face was subtly wrong. The skin looked too clean, too new. It looked synthetic.

Lindsay twisted around. The assassin held a bracing wire with both hands, but he reached out with his left foot and caught Lindsay's wrist between his two largest toes. His foot bulged with abnormal musculature and the joints looked altered. His grip was paralyzing. Lindsay felt his hand go numb.

The man jabbed Lindsay's chest with the toe of his other foot. "Relax," he said. "Let's talk a moment."

Lindsay's training took hold. His adrenaline surge of terror transmuted into icy self-possession. "How do you like the performance?" he said.

The man laughed. Lindsay knew that he was hearing the assassin's true voice; his laugh was chilling. "These moondock worlds are full of surprises," he said.

"You should have joined the cast," Lindsay said. "You have a talent for impersonation."

"It comes and goes," the assassin said. He bent his altered ankle slightly, and the bones of Lindsay's wrist grated together with a sudden lancing pain that made blackness surge behind his eyes. "What's in the bag, targ? Something they'd like to know about back home?"

"In the Ring Council?"

"That's right. They say they have us under siege, all those Mech wireheads, but not every cartel is as straight as the last. And we're well trained. We can hide under the spots on a dip's conscience."

"That's clever," Lindsay said. "I admire a good technique. Maybe we could arrange something."

"That would be interesting," the assassin said politely. Lindsay realized then that no bribe could save him from this man.

The assassin released Lindsay's wrist. He reached into the breast pocket of his jumpsuit with his left foot. His knee and hip swiveled eerily. "This is for you," he said. He released a black videotape cartridge. It spun in free-fall before Lindsay's eyes.

Lindsay took the cartridge and pocketed it. He snapped the pocket shut and looked up again. The assassin had vanished. In his place was a portly male sundog in the same kind of general-issue dun-brown jumpsuit. He was heavier than the assassin and his hair was blond. The man looked at him indifferently.

Lindsay reached out as if to touch him, then snatched his hand back before the man could notice.

The lights went up. Dancers came onstage. The Bubble rang with howls of enthusiasm. Lindsay fled along the Bubble's walls through a nest of legs tucked through footloops and arms clutching handholds. He reached the anterior airlock.

He hired one of the aircraft moored outside the lock and flew at once to the Geisha Bank.

The place was almost deserted, but his credit card got him in. The enormous guards recognized him and bowed. Lindsay hesitated, then realized he had nothing to say. What could he tell them? "Kill me, next time you see me?"

To catch birds with a mirror was the ideal snare.

The *yarite*'s network of beads would protect him. Kitsune had taught him how to work the beads from within. Even if the assassin avoided the traps, he could be struck down from within by high voltage or sharp fléchettes.

Lindsay walked the pattern flawlessly and burst into the *yarite*'s quarters. He opened a videoscreen, flicked it on, and loaded the tape.

It was a face from his past: the face of his best friend, the man who had tried to kill him, Philip Khouri Constantine.

"Hello, cousin," Constantine said.

The term was aristocratic slang in the Republic. But Constantine was a plebe. And Lindsay had never heard him put such hatred into the word.

"I take the liberty of contacting you in exile." Constantine looked drunk. He was speaking a little too precisely. The ring-shaped collar of his antique suit showed sweat on the olive skin of his throat. "Some of my Shaper friends share my interest in your career. They don't call these agents assassins. The Shapers call them 'antibiotics.'

"They've been operating here. The opposition is much less troublesome with so many dead from 'natural causes.' My old trick with the moths looks juvenile now. Very brash and risky.

"Still, the insects worked well enough, out here in the moondocks. . . . Time flies, cousin. Five months have changed things.

"The Mechanist siege is failing. When the Shapers are trapped and squeezed, they ooze out under pressure. They can't be beaten. We used to tell each other that, when we were boys, remember, Abelard? When our future seemed so bright we almost blinded each other, sometimes. Back before we knew what a bloodstain was. . . .

"This Republic needs the Shapers. The colony's rotting. They can't survive without the biosciences. Everyone knows it, even the Radical Old.

"We never really talked to those old wireheads, cousin. You wouldn't let me; you hated them too much. And now I know why you were afraid to face them. They're tainted, Abelard, like you are. In a way, they're your mirror image. By now you know what a shock it is to see one." Constantine grinned and smoothed his wavy hair with a small, deft hand.

"But I talked to them, I came to terms. . . . There's been a coup here, Abelard. The Advisory Council is dissolved. Power belongs to the Executive

Board for National Survival. That's me, and a few of our Preservationist friends. Vera's death changed everything, as we knew it would. Now we have our martyr. Now we're full of steel and fury.

"The Radical Old are leaving. Emigrating to the Mech cartels, where they belong. The aristocrats will have to pay the costs for it.

"There are others coming your way, cousin. The whole mob of broken-down aristos: Lindsays, Tylers, Kellands, Morrisseys. Political exiles. Your wife is with them. They're squeezed dry between their Shaper children and their Mechanist grandparents, and thrown out like garbage. They're all yours.

"I want you to mop up after me, tie up my loose ends. If you won't accept that, then go back to my messenger. He'll settle you." Constantine grinned, showing small, even teeth. "Except for death, you can't escape the game. You and Vera both knew that. And now I'm king, you're pawn."

Lindsay shut off the tape.

He was ruined. The Kabuki Bubble had assumed a grotesque solidity; it was his own ambitions that had burst.

He was trapped. He would be unmasked by the Republic's refugees. His glittering deceptions would fly apart to leave him naked and exposed. Kitsune would know him for what he was: a human upstart, not her Shaper lover.

His mind raced within the cage. To live here under Constantine's terms, in his control, in his contempt—the thought scalded him.

He had to escape. He had to leave this world at once. He had no time left for scheming.

Outside, the assassin was waiting, with Lindsay's own stolen face. To meet him again was death. But he might escape the man if he disappeared at once. And that meant the pirates.

Lindsay rubbed his bruised wrist. Slow fury built in him: fury at the Shapers and the destructive cleverness they had used to survive. Their struggle left a legacy of monsters. The assassin. Constantine. Himself.

Constantine was younger than Lindsay. He had trusted Lindsay, looked up to him. But when Lindsay had come back on furlough from the Ring Council, he'd painfully felt how deeply the Shapers had changed him. And he had deliberately sent Constantine into their hands. As always, he had made it sound plausible, and Constantine's new skills were truly crucial. But Lindsay knew that he had done it selfishly, so that he'd have company, outside the pale.

Constantine had always been ambitious. But where there had been trust, Lindsay had brought a new sophistication and deceit. Where he and Constantine had shared ideals, they now shared murder.

Lindsay felt an ugly kinship with the assassin. The assassin's training must have been much like his own. His own self-hatred added sudden venom to his fear of the man.

The assassin had Lindsay's face. But Lindsay realized with a sudden flash of insight that he could turn the man's own strength against him.

He could pose as the assassin, turn the situation around. He could commit some awful crime, and the assassin would be blamed.

Kitsune needed a crime. It would be his farewell gift to her, a message only she would understand. He could free her, and his enemy would pay the price.

He opened the diplomatic bag and tossed aside his paper heap of stocks. He opened the floorboards and stared at the body of the old woman, floating naked on the wrinkled surface of the waterbed. Then he searched the room for something that would cut.

# Chapter 3

When the last slave rocket from the Zaibatsu had peeled away, and the engines of the *Red Consensus* had cut in, Lindsay began to think he might be safe.

"So how about it, citizen?" the President said. "You sundogged off with the loot, right? What's in the bag, State? Ice-cold drugs? Hot software?"

"No," Lindsay said. "It can wait. First we have to check everyone's face. Make sure it's their own."

"You're twisted, State," said one of the Senators. "That 'antibiotic' stuff is just agitprop crap. They don't exist."

"You're safe," the President said. "We know every angstrom on this ship, believe me." He brushed an enormous crawling roach from the burlapped surface of Lindsay's diplomatic bag. "You've scored, right? You want to buy into one of the cartels? We're on assignment, but we can detour to one of the Belt settlements—Bettina or Themis, your choice." The President grinned evilly. "It'll cost you, though."

"I'm staying with you," Lindsay said.

"Yeah?" said the President. "Then this belongs to us!" He snatched up Lindsay's diplomatic bag and threw it to the Speaker of the House.

"I'll open it for you," Lindsay said quickly. "Just let me explain first."

"Sure," the Speaker said. "You can explain how much it's worth." She pressed her portable power saw against the bag. Sparks flew and the reek of melted plastic filled the spacecraft. Lindsay averted his face.

The Speaker groped within the bag, bracing her knee against it in free-fall.

With a wrenching motion she dragged out Lindsay's booty. It was the *yarite*'s severed head.

She let go of the head with the sudden hiss of a scorched cat. "Get 'im!" the President yelled.

Two of the Senators bounced off the spacecraft's walls and seized Lindsay's arms and legs in painful jujutsu holds.

*"You're* the assassin!" the President shouted. "You were hired to hit this old Mechanist! There's no loot at all!" He looked at the input-studded head with a grimace of disgust. "Get it into the recycler," he told one of the representatives. "I won't have a thing like that aboard this ship. Wait a second," he said as the representative took tentative hold of a lock of sparse hair. "Take it up to the machine shop first and dig out all the circuitry."

He turned to Lindsay. "So that's your game, eh, citizen? An assassin?"

Lindsay clung to their expectations. "Sure," he said reflexively. "Whatever you say."

There was an ominous silence, overlaid by distant thermal pops from the engines of the *Red Consensus*. "Let's throw his ass out the airlock," suggested the Speaker of the House.

"We can't do that," said the Chief Justice of the Supreme Court. He was a feeble old Mechanist who was subject to nosebleeds. "He is still Secretary of State and can't be sentenced without impeachment by the Senate."

The three Senators, two men and a woman, looked interested. The Senate didn't see much action in the government of the tiny Democracy. They were the least trusted members of the crew and were outnumbered by the House.

Lindsay shrugged. It was an excellent shrug; he had captured the feel of the President's own kinesics, and the subliminal mimicry defused the situation for the crucial instant it took him to start talking. "It was a political job." It was a boring voice, the leaden sound of moral exhaustion. It defused their bloodlust, made the situation into something predictable and tiresome. "I was working for the Mare Serenitatis Corporate Republic. They had a coup there. They're shipping a lot of their population to the Zaibatsu soon and wanted me to pave the way."

They were believing him. He put some color into his voice. "But they're fascists. I prefer to serve a democratic government. Besides, they set an 'antibiotic' on my track—at least, I think it was them." He smiled and spread his hands innocently, twisting his arms in the loosened grips of his captors. "I haven't lied to you, have I? I never claimed that I wasn't a killer. Besides, think of the money I made for you."

"Yeah, there's that," the President said grudgingly. "But did you have to saw its head off?"

"I was following orders," Lindsay said. "I'm good at that, Mr. President. Try me."

## ABOARD THE RED CONSENSUS: 13-6-'16

Lindsay had stolen the cyborg's head to free Kitsune, to guarantee that her power games would not come to light. He had deceived her, but he had freed her as a message of apology. The Shaper assassin would bear the blame for it. He hoped the Geisha Bank would tear the man apart.

He put aside the horror. His Shaper teachers had warned him about such feelings. When a diplomat was thrown into a new environment, he should re-press all thoughts of the past and immediately soak up as much protective col-oration as possible.

Lindsay surrendered to his training. Crammed into the tiny spacecraft with the eleven-member Fortuna nation, Lindsay felt the environment's semiotics as an almost physical pressure. It would be hard to keep a sense of perspective, trapped in a can with eleven lunatics.

Lindsay had not been in a real spacecraft since his schooldays in the Shaper Ring Council. The Mech cargo drogue that had shipped him into exile didn't count; its passengers were drugged meat. The *Red Consensus* was lived in; it had been in service for two hundred and fifteen years.

Within a few days, following bits of evidence present within the spacecraft, Lindsay learned more about its history than the Fortuna Miners knew them-selves.

The living decks of the *Consensus* had once belonged to a Terran national entity, an extinct group calling themselves the Soviet Union, or CCCP. The decks had been launched from Earth to form one of a series of orbiting "defense stations."

The ship was cylindrical, and its living quarters were four interlocked round decks. Each deck was four meters tall and ten meters across. They had once been equipped with crude airlock safety doors between levels, but those had been wrenched out and replaced with modern self-sealing pressure fila-ments.

The stern deck had been ripped clean to the padded walls. The pirates used it for exercise and free-fall combat practice. They also slept there, although, hav-ing no day or night, they were likely to doze off anywhere at any time.

The next deck, closer to the bow, held their cramped surgery and sick bay, as well as the "sweatbox," where they hid from solar flares behind lead shield-ing. In the "broom closet," a dozen antiquated spacesuits hung flabbily beside a racked-up clutter of shellac sprayers, strap-on gas guns, ratchets, clamps, and other "outside" tools. This deck had an airlock, an old armored one to the out-side, which still had a series of peeling operations stickers in green Cyrillic capi-tals.

The next deck was a life-support section, full of gurgling racks of algae. It had a toilet and a food synthesizer. The two units were both hooked directly to the algae racks. It was an object lesson in recycling, but not one that Lindsay relished much. This deck also had a small machine shop; it was tiny, but the lack of gravity allowed the use of every working surface.

The bow deck had the control room and the power hookups to the solar panels. Lindsay grew to like this deck best, mostly because of the music. The control room was an old one, but nowhere near as old as the *Consensus* itself. It had been designed by some forgotten industrial theorist who believed that instruments should use acoustic signals. The cluster of systems, spread out along a semicircular control panel, had few optical readouts. They signaled their functions by rumbles, squeaks, and steady modular beeping.

Bizarre at first, the sounds were designed to sink unobtrusively into the backbrain. Any change in the chorus, though, was immediately obvious. Lindsay found the music soothing, a combination of heartbeat and brain.

The rest of the deck was not so pleasant: the armory, with its nasty racks of tools, and the ship's center of corruption: the particle beam gun. Lindsay avoided that compartment when he could, and never spoke of it.

He could not escape the knowledge that the *Red Consensus* was a ship of war.

"Look," the President told him, "taking out some feeble old Mech whose brain's shut down is one thing. But taking out an armed Shaper camp full of hot genetics types is a different proposition. There's no room for feebs or thumbsitters in the Fortuna National Army."

"Yes sir," said Lindsay. The Fortuna National Army was the military arm of the national government. Its personnel were identical to the personnel of the civilian government, but this was of no consequence. It had an entirely different organization and set of operating procedures. Luckily the President was commander in chief of the armed forces as well as head of state.

They did military drills in the fourth deck, which had been stripped down to the ancient and moldy padding. It held three exercycles and some spring-loaded weights, with a rack of storage lockers beside the entrance port.

"Forget up and down," the President advised. "When we're talking free-fall combat, the central rule is *haragei*. That's this." He punched Lindsay suddenly in the stomach. Lindsay doubled over with a wheeze and his velcro slippers ripped free from the wall, shredding loudly.

The President grabbed Lindsay's wrist, and with a sinuous transfer of torque he stuck Lindsay's feet to the ceiling. "Okay, you're upside down now, right?" Lindsay stood on the upward or bow side of the deck; the President crouched on the sternward side, so that their feet pointed in opposite directions. He glared upside down into Lindsay's eyes. His breath smelled of raw algae.

"That's what they call the local vertical," he said. "The body was built for gravity and the eyes look for gravity in any situation; that's the way the brain's wired. You're gonna look for straight lines that go up and down and you're going to orient yourself to those lines. And you're gonna get killed, soldier, understand?"

"Yes sir!" Lindsay said. In the Republic, he'd been taught from childhood to despise violence. Its only legitimate use was against one's self. But his brush with the antibiotic had changed his thinking.

"That's what haragei's for." The President slapped his own belly. "This is your center of gravity, your center of torque. You meet some enemy in free-fall, and you grapple with him, well, your head is just a *stalk,* see? What happens depends on your center of mass. Your haragei. Your actions, the places where you can punch out with hands and feet, form a sphere. And that sphere is centered on your belly. You think of that bubble around you all the time."

"Yes sir," Lindsay said. His attention was total.

"That's number one," the President said. "Now we're gonna talk about number two. Bulkheads. Control of the bulkhead is control of the fight. If I pull my feet up, off this bulkhead, how hard do you think I can hit you?"

Lindsay was prudent. "Hard enough to break my nose, sir."

"Okay. But if I have my feet planted, so my own body holds me fast against the recoil, what then?"

"You break my neck. Sir."

"Good thinking, soldier. A man without bracing is a helpless man. If you got nothing else, you use the enemy's own body as bracing. Recoil is the enemy of impact. Impact is damage. Damage is victory. Understand?"

"Recoil is impact's enemy. Impact is damage, damage is victory," Lindsay said immediately. "Sir."

"Very good," the President said. He then reached out, and, with a quick pivoting movement, he broke Lindsay's forearm over his knee with a wet snap. "That's number three," he said over Lindsay's sudden scream. "Pain."

"Well," said the Second Justice, "I see he showed you the old number three."

"Yes, ma'am," Lindsay said.

The Second Justice slid a needle into his arm. "Forget that," she said kindly. "This isn't the army, this is sick bay. You can just call me Judge Two."

A rubbery numbness spread over the fractured arm. "Thanks, Judge." The Second Justice was an older woman, maybe close to a century. It was hard to tell; her constant abuse of hormone treatments had made her metabolism a patchwork of anomalies. Her jawline was freckled with acne, but her wrists and shins were flaky and varicose-veined.

"You're okay, State, you'll do," she said. She stuck Lindsay's anesthetized arm into the wide rubber orifice of an old-fashioned CAT scanner. Multiple x-rays whirred from its ring, and a pivoting three-D image of Lindsay's arm appeared on the scanner's screen.

"Good clean break, nothin' to it," she said analytically. "We've all had it. You're almost one of us now. Want me to scroll you up while the arm's still numb?"

"What?"

"Tattoos, citizen."

The thought appalled him. "Fine," he said at once. "Go right ahead."

"I knew you were okay from the beginning," she said, nudging him in the ribs. "I'll do you a favor: vein-pop you with some of those anabolic steroids. You'll muscle up in no time; the Prez'll think you're a natural." She pulled gently on his forearm; the sullen grating of jagged bone ends was like something happening at the other end of a telescope.

She pulled a needled tattoo rig from the wall, where it clung by a patch of velcro. "Any preferences?"

"I want some moths," Lindsay said.

The history of the Fortuna Miners' Democracy was a simple one. Fortuna was a major asteroid, over two hundred kilometers across. In the first flush of success, the original miners had declared their independence.

As long as the ore held out, they did well. They could buy their way out of political trouble and could pay for life-extension treatments from other more advanced worlds.

But when the ore was gone and Fortuna was a mined-out heap of rubble, they found they had crucially blundered. Their wealth had vanished, and they had failed to pursue technology with the cutthroat desperation of rival cartels. They could not survive on their outmoded expertise or sustain an information economy. Their attempts to do so only hastened their bankruptcy.

The defections began. The nation's best and most ambitious personnel were brain-drained away to richer worlds. Fortuna lost its spacecraft, as defectors decamped with anything not nailed down.

The collapse was exponential, and the government devolved upon smaller and smaller numbers of diehards. They got into debt and had to sell their infrastructure to the Mech cartels; they even had to auction off their air. The population dwindled to a handful of knockabout dregs, mostly sundogs who'd meandered to Fortuna out of lack of alternatives.

They were, however, in full legal control of a national government, with its entire apparat of foreign relations and diplomatic protocol. They could grant citizenship, coin money, issue letters of marque, sign treaties, negotiate arms control agreements. There might be only a dozen of them, but that was irrelevant. They still had their House, their Senate, their legal precedents, and their ideology.

They therefore redefined Fortuna, their national territory, as the boundaries of their last surviving spacecraft, the *Red Consensus.* Thus equipped with a mobile nation, they were able to legally annex other people's property into their national boundaries. This was not theft. Nations are not capable of theft, a legal fact of great convenience to the ideologues of the FMD. Protests were forwarded to the Fortuna legal system, which was computerized and of formidable intricacy.

Lawsuits were the chief source of income for the pirate nation. Most cases were settled out of court. In practice, this was a simple process of bribing the pirates to make them go away. But the pirates were very punctilious about form and took great pride in preserving the niceties.

## ABOARD THE RED CONSENSUS: 29-9-'16

"What are you doing in the sweatbox, State?"

Lindsay smiled uneasily. "The State of the Nation address," he said. "I'd prefer to escape it." The President's rhetoric filled the spacecraft, filtering past the slight figure of the First Representative. The girl slipped into the radiation shelter and wheeled the heavy hatch shut behind her.

"That ain't very patriotic, State. You're the new hand here; you ought to listen."

"I wrote it for him," Lindsay said. He knew he had to treat this woman carefully. She made him nervous. Her sinuous movements, the ominous perfection of her features, and the sharp, somehow overattentive intensity of her gaze all told him that she was Reshaped.

"You Shaper types," she said. "You're slick as glass."

"Are we?" he said.

"I'm no Shaper," she said. "Look at these teeth." She opened her mouth and showed a crooked overlapping incisor and canine. "See? Bad teeth, bad genetics."

Lindsay was skeptical. "You had that done yourself."

"I was born," she insisted. "Not decanted."

Lindsay rubbed a fading combat-training bruise on his high cheekbone. It was hot and close in the box. He could smell her.

"I was a ransom," the girl admitted. "A fertilized ovum, but a Fortuna citizen brought me to term." She shrugged. "I did do the teeth, it's true."

"You're a rogue Shaper, then," Lindsay said. "They're rare. Ever had your quotient done?"

"My IQ? No. I can't read," she said proudly. "But I'm Rep One, the majority whip in the House. And I'm married to Senator One."

"Really? He never mentioned it."

The young Shaper adjusted her black headband. Beneath it, her red-blonde hair was long and done up with bright pink alligator clips. "We did it for tax reasons. I'd throw you a juice otherwise, maybe. You're looking good, State." She drifted closer. "Better now that the arm's healed up." She ran one fingertip along the tattooed skin of his wrist.

"There's always Carnaval," Lindsay said.

"Carnaval don't count," she said. "You can't tell it's me, tripped out on aphrodisiacs."

"There's three months left till rendezvous," Lindsay said. "That gives me three more chances to guess."

"You been in Carnaval," she said. "You know what it's like, shot up on 'disiacs. After that, you ain't you, citizen. You're just wall-to-wall meat."

"I might surprise you," Lindsay said. They locked eyes.

"If you do I'll kill you, State. Adultery's a crime."

## ABOARD THE RED CONSENSUS: 13-10-'16

One of the shipboard roaches woke Lindsay by nibbling his eyelashes. With a start of disgust, Lindsay punched it and it scuttled away.

Lindsay slept naked except for his groin cup. All the men wore them; they prevented the testicles from floating and chafing in free-fall. He shook another roach out of his red-and-silver jumpsuit, where it feasted on flakes of dead skin.

He got into his clothes and looked about the gym room. Two of the Senators were still asleep, their velcro-soled shoes stuck to the walls, their tattooed bodies curled fetally. A roach was sipping sweat from the female senator's neck.

If it weren't for the roaches, the *Red Consensus* would eventually smother in a moldy detritus of cast-off skin and built-up layers of sweated and exhaled effluvia. Lysine, alanine, methionine, carbamino compounds, lactic acid, sex pheromones: a constant stream of organic vapors poured invisibly, day and night, from the human body. Roaches were a vital part of the spacecraft ecosystem, cleaning up crumbs of food, licking up grease.

Roaches had haunted spacecraft almost from the beginning, too tough and adaptable to kill. At least now they were well-trained. They were even housebroken, obedient to the chemical lures and controls of the Second Representative. Lindsay still hated them, though, and couldn't watch their grisly swarming and free-fall leaps and clattering flights without a deep conviction that he ought to be somewhere else. Anywhere else.

Dressed, Lindsay meandered in free-fall through the filamented doors between decks. The plasticized doors unraveled into strands as he approached and knitted themselves shut behind him. They were thin but airtight and as tough as steel when pressed. They were Shaper work. Stolen, probably, Lindsay thought.

He wandered into the control room, drawn by the instrumental music. Most of the crew was there. The President, two Reps, and Justice 3 were watching a Shaper agit-broadcast with strap-on videogoggles.

The Chief Justice was strapped in beside the waist-high console, monitoring deep-space broadcasts with the ship's drone. The Chief Justice was by far the oldest member of the crew. He never took part in Carnaval. This, his age, and his office made him the crew's impartial arbiter.

Lindsay spoke loudly beside the man's earphones. "Any news?"

"The siege is still on," the Mech said, without any marked satisfaction. "The Shapers are holding." He stared emptily at the control boards. "They keep boasting about their victory in the Concatenation."

Justice 2 came into the control room. "Who wants some ketamine?"

Rep 1 took off her videogoggles. "Is it good?"

"Fresh out of the chromatograph. I just made it myself."

"The Concatenation was a real power in my day," the Chief Justice said. With his earphones on, he hadn't seen or heard the two women. Something about the broadcast he had monitored had stirred some deep layer of ancient indignation. "In my day the Concatenation was the whole civilized world."

Through long habit, the women ignored him, raising their voices. "Well, how much?" Rep 1 said.

"Forty thousand a gram?" the Judge bargained.

"Forty thousand? I'll give you twenty."

"Come on, girl, you charged me twenty thousand just to do my nails."

Lindsay listened with half an ear, wondering if he could cut himself in. The FMD still had its own banks, and though its currency was enormously inflated, it was still in circulation as the exclusive legal tender of eleven billionaires. Lindsay, unfortunately, as junior crew member, was already deeply in debt.

"Mare Serenitatis," the old man said. "The Corporate Republic." He fixed Lindsay suddenly with his ash-gray eyes. "I hear you worked for them."

Lindsay was startled. The unwritten taboos of the *Red Consensus* suppressed discussion of the past. The old Mech's face had brightened with a reckless upwash of memory. Decades of the same expressions had dug deep furrows into his ancient muscle and skin. His face was an idiosyncratic mask.

"I was only there briefly," Lindsay lied. "I don't know the moondocks well."

"I was born there."

Rep 1 cast an alarmed glance in the old man's direction. "All right, forty thousand," she said. The two women left for the lab. The President lifted his videogoggles. He looked sardonically at Lindsay, then deliberately turned up the volume on his headset. The other two, Rep 2 and the grizzled Justice 3, ignored the whole situation.

"The Republic had a system in my day," the Mech said. "Political families. The Tylers, the Kellands, the Lindsays. Then there was an underclass of refugees we'd taken in, just before the Interdict with Earth. The plebes, we called them. They were the last ones to get off the planet, just before things fell apart. So they had nothing. We had the kilowatts in our pockets, and the big mansions. And they had the little plastic slums."

"You were an aristocrat?" Lindsay said. He couldn't restrain his fatalistic interest.

"Apples," the Mech said sadly. The word was heavy with nostalgia. "Ever had an apple? They're a kind of vegetable growth."

"I think so."

"Birds. Parks. Grass. Clouds. Trees." The Mech's right arm, a prosthetic job, whirred softly as he whacked a roach from the console with one wire-tendoned finger. "I knew it would come to trouble, this business with the plebes. . . . I even wrote a play about it once."

"A play? For the theatre? What was it called?"

Vague surprise showed in the old man's eyes. *"The Conflagration."*

"You're Evan James Tyler Kelland," Lindsay blurted. "I—ah . . . I saw your play. In the archives." Evan Kelland was Lindsay's own great-granduncle. An obscure radical, his play of social protest had been lost for years until Lindsay, hunting for weapons, had found it in the Museum. Lindsay had staged the play's revival to annoy the Radical Old. The men who had exiled Kelland were still in power, sustained by Mech technologies after a hundred years. When the time was right they had exiled Lindsay too.

Now they were in the cartels, he remembered suddenly. Constantine, the descendant of plebes, had cut a deal with the wireheads. And the aristocracy had paid at last, as Kelland had prophesied. Lindsay, and Evan Kelland, had only paid early.

"You happened to see my play," Kelland said. Suspicion turned the lines in his face to deep crevasses. He looked away, his ash-gray eyes full of pain and obscure humiliation. "You shouldn't have presumed."

"I'm sorry," Lindsay said. He looked with new dread at his old kinsman's mechanical arm. "We won't speak of this again."

"That would be best." Kelland turned up his earphones and seemed to lose the grip on his fury. His eyes grew mild and colorless. Lindsay looked at the others, deliberately blind behind their videogoggles. None of this had happened.

## ABOARD THE RED CONSENSUS: 27-10-'16

"Sleep troubles, citizen?" said the Second Judge. "Those steroids getting under your skin, stepping on your dream time? I can fix it." She smiled, showing three ancient, discolored teeth amid a rack of gleaming porcelain.

"I'd appreciate it," Lindsay said, struggling for politeness. The steroids had covered his long arms with ropes of muscle, healed the constellation of bruises from constant jujutsu drills, and filled him with hot flashes of aggressive fury. But they robbed him of sleep, leaving only feverish catnaps.

As he watched the Fortuna medic through red-rimmed eyes, he was reminded of his ex-wife. Alexandrina Lindsay had had just that same china-doll precision of movement, the same parchmentlike skin, the same telltale age wrinkles on the knuckles. His wife had been eighty years old. And, watching the Judge, Lindsay felt stifled by secondhand sexual attraction.

"This'll do it," Judge Two said, drawing up a hypo of muddy fluid from a plastic-topped vial. "Some REM promoter, serotonin agonists, muscle relaxant, and just a taste of mnemonics to pry loose troublesome memories. Use it all the time myself; it's fabulous. While you're out, I'll scroll up the other arm."

"Not just yet," Lindsay said through gritted teeth. "I haven't decided what I want on it yet."

The Second Judge put away her tattoo rig with a moue of disappointment. She seemed to live, eat, and breathe needles, Lindsay thought. "Don't you like my work?" she said.

Lindsay examined his right arm. The bone had knitted well, but he'd put on so much muscle that the designs were distorted: coax-cable snakes with television eyes, white death's-heads with flat solar-panel wings, knives wreathed in lightning, and everywhere, fluttering along and between them, a horde of white moths. The skin of his arm from wrist to bicep was so laden with ink that it felt cold to the touch and no longer sweated.

"It was well done," he said as the hypo sank into his arm through the hollow eye of a skull. "But wait till I've finished muscling for the rest, all right, citizen?"

"Sweet dreams," she said.

At night, the Republic was truest to itself. The Preservationists preferred the night, when watchful older eyes were closed in sleep.

Truths hidden in daylight revealed themselves in blazing nightlights. The solar energy of the power panels was the Republic's currency. Only the wealthiest could squander financial power.

To his right, at the world cylinder's north end, light poured from the hospitals. In their clinics around the cylinder's axis, the frail bones of the Radical Old rested easily, almost in free-fall. Gouts of light spilled from distant windows and landing pads, a smeared and bogus Milky Way of wealth.

Suddenly Lindsay, looking up, was behind those windows. It was his Great-Grandfather's suite. The old Mechanist floated in a matrix of life-support tubes, his eye sockets wired to a video input, in a sterile suite flooded with oxygen.

"Grandfather, I'm leaving," Lindsay said. The old man raised one hand, so crippled with arthritis that its swollen knuckles bulged, and rippled, and suddenly burst into a hissing net of needle-tipped tubes. They whipped into Lindsay, clinging, piercing, sucking. Lindsay opened his mouth to scream—

The lights were far away. He was walking across the fretted glass windowpane. He emerged onto the Agricultural panel.

A faint smell of curdling rot came with the wind. He was near the Sours.

Lindsay's shoes hissed through genetically altered wiregrass at the swamp's margins. Grasshoppers creaked in the undergrowth, and a chitinous thing the size of a rat scurried away from him. Philip Constantine had the rot under siege.

The wind gusted. Constantine's tent flapped loudly in the darkness. By the tent's doorflaps, two globes on stakes shone with yellow bioluminescence.

Constantine's sprawling tent dominated the wiregrass borderlands, with the Sours to its north and the fertile grainfields shielded behind it. The no-man's land, where he battled the contagion, clicked and rustled with newly minted vermin from his labs.

From within, he heard Constantine's voice, choked with sobs.

"Philip!" he said. He went inside.

Constantine sat at a wooden bench before a long metal lab bureau, cluttered with Shaper glassware. Racks of specimen cases stood like bookshelves, loaded with insects under study. Globes on slender, flexible supports cast a murky yellow light.

Constantine seemed smaller than ever, his boyish shoulders hunched beneath his lab jacket. His round eyes were bloodshot and his hair was disheveled.

"Vera's burned," Constantine said. He trembled silently and put his face into his gloved hands. Lindsay sat on the bench beside him and threw his long, bony arm over Constantine's back.

They were sitting together as they had sat so often, so long ago. Side by side as usual, joking together in their half-secret argot of Ring Council slang, passing a spiked inhaler back and forth. They laughed together, the quiet laughter of shared conspiracy. They were young, and breaking all the rules, and after a few long whiffs from the inhaler they were brighter than anyone human had a right to be.

Constantine laughed happily, and his mouth was full of blood. Lindsay came awake with a start, opened his eyes, and saw the sick bay of the *Red Consensus*. He closed his eyes and slept again at once.

Lindsay's cheeks were wet with tears. He was not sure how long they had been sitting together, sobbing. It seemed a long time. "Can we talk freely here, Philip?"

"They don't need police spies here," Constantine said bitterly. "That's why we have wives."

"I'm sorry for what's come between us, Philip."

"Vera's dead," Constantine said. He closed his eyes. "You and I did this. We engineered her death. We share that guilt. We know our power now. And we've discovered our differences." He wiped his eyes with a round disk of filter paper.

"I lied to them," Lindsay said. "I said my uncle died of heart failure. The inquest said as much. I let them think so, so that I could shield you. You killed him, Philip. But it was me you meant to kill. Only my uncle stumbled into the trap."

"Vera and I discussed it," Constantine said. "She thought you would fail, that you wouldn't carry out the pact. She knew your weaknesses. I knew them. I bred those moths for stings and poison. The Revolution needs its weapons. I gave her the pheromones to drive them into frenzy. She took them gladly."

"You didn't trust me," Lindsay said.

"And you're not dead."

Lindsay said nothing.

"Look at this!" Constantine peeled off one of his lab gloves. Beneath it his olive skin was shedding like a reptile's. "It's a virus," he said. "It's immortality. A Shaper kind, from the cells themselves, not those Mech prosthetics. I'm committed, cousin."

He picked at an elastic shred of skin. "Vera chose you, not me. I'm going to live forever, and to hell with you and your cant about humanities. Mankind's a dead issue now, cousin. There are no more souls. Only states of mind. If you think you can deny that, then here." He handed Lindsay a dissection scalpel. "Prove yourself. Prove your words weren't empty. Prove you're better dead and human."

The knife was in Lindsay's hand. He stared at the flesh of his wrist. He stared at Constantine's throat. He raised the knife over his head, poised it, and screamed aloud.

The sound woke him, and he found himself in sick bay, drenched in sweat, while the Second Judge, her eyes heavy with intoxicants, ran one veiny hand along the inside of his thigh.

## ABOARD THE <u>RED CONSENSUS</u>: 20-11-'16

The Third Representative, or Rep 3 as he was commonly called, was a stocky, perpetually grinning young man with a scarred nose and short, brush-cut sandy hair.

Like many EVA experts, he was a space fanatic and spent most of his time outside the ship, towed on long kilometers of line. Stars talked to him, and the Sun was his friend. He always wore his spacesuit, even inside the craft, and the whiff of long-fermented body odor came through its open helmet collar with eye-watering pungency.

"I'm gonna send out the drone," he said to Lindsay as they ate together in the control room. "You can hook up to it from in here. It's almost like being Outside."

Lindsay put aside his empty canister of green paste. The drone was an ancient planetary probe, found in long-forgotten orbit by some long-forgotten crew, but its telescopes and microwave antennae were still useful, and it could broadcast as well. Hundreds of klicks out on its fiber-optic cable, the unmanned drone could pick up deep-space broadcasts and mislead enemy radar with electronic countermeasures. "Sure, citizen," Lindsay said. "What the hell."

Rep 3 nodded eagerly. "It'll be beautiful, State. Your brain'll spread out so-fast-so-thin be like a second skin for you."

"I won't take any drugs," Lindsay said guardedly.

"You can't take drugs," Rep 3 said. "If you take drugs the Sun won't talk to you." He picked a pair of strap-on videogoggles from the console and adjusted them over Lindsay's head. Within the goggles, a tiny video system projected images directly onto the eyeballs. The drone was shut down at the moment; Lindsay saw only an array of cryptic blue alphanumeric readouts across the bottom of his vision. There was no sense of a screen. "So far so good," he said.

He heard a series of keyboard clicks as Rep 3 activated the drone. Then the whole ship shook gently as the robot probe cast off. Lindsay heard his guide strap on another pair of showphones, and then, through the drone's cameras, he saw the outside of the *Consensus* for the first time.

It was pitiful how shabby and makeshift it looked. The old engines had been ripped off the stern and replaced with a jury-rigged attack tunnel, a long, flexible, accordioned tube with the jagged teeth of a converted mining drill at its end. A new engine, one of the old-fashioned Shaper electromagnetic SEPS types, had been welded on at the end of four long stanchions. The globular engine was a microwave hazard and was kept as far as possible from the crew's quarters. Foil-wrapped control cables snaked up the stanchions, which had been clumsily bolted to the stern deck.

Beside the stanchions crouched the inert hulk of a mining robot. Seeing it waiting there, powered down, Lindsay realized what a powerful weapon it was; its gaping, razor-sharp claws could rip a ship like tinfoil.

Another mechanism clung to the hull: a parasite rocket. The old corrugated

hull, painted an ugly shade of off-green, bore scrapes and scratches from the little rocket's magnetic feet. Being mobile, the parasite handled all the retrorocket
work.

The third deck, with its life-support system, was an untidy mashed tangle of
fat ventilation and hydraulics tubes, some so old that their insulation had burst
and hung in puffy free-fall streamers. "Don't worry, we don't use those," Rep 3
said conversationally.

The four jointed solar panels spread laterally from the fourth deck, a gleaming cross of black silicon cut by copper gridwork. The nasty muzzle of the particle beam gun was just visible around the curve of the hull.

"Little star nation under the Sun's eye," the Rep said. He swung the drone
around so that, briefly, Lindsay saw the drone's own tether line. Then its cameras focused on the rigging of the spacecraft's solar sail. In the bow was a storage chamber of accordioned fabric, but it was empty now; the nineteen tons of
metallic film were spread for light pressure in a silver arc two kilometers across.
The camera zoomed in and Lindsay saw as the sail expanded that it too was old:
creased a bit here and there, and peppered with micrometeor holes.

"Prez says, next time, if we can afford it, we get a monolayer sprayer, stencil a big mother-burner skull and crossed lightnings on the outside of that," the
Rep offered.

"Good idea," Lindsay said. He was off steroids now, and feeling a lot more
tolerant.

"I'll take it out," the Rep said. Lindsay heard more clicks, and suddenly the
drone unreeled its way into deep space at frightening speed. In seconds, the *Red
Consensus* shrank to thimble-size beside the tabletop smear of its sail. Lindsay
was seized with a gut-wrenching vertigo and clutched blindly at the console. He
closed his eyes tightly within the goggles, then opened them onto the cosmic
panorama of deep space.

"Milky Way," the Rep said. An enormous arc of white spread itself across
half of reality. Lindsay lost control of perspective: he felt for a moment that the
billion white pinpoints of the galactic ridge were pressing pitilessly down onto
his eyeballs. He closed his eyes again, deeply thankful that he was not actually
out there.

"That's where the aliens will come from," the Rep informed him.

Lindsay opened his eyes. It was just a bubble, he told himself, with white
specks spattered on it: a bubble with himself at its center—there, now he had it
stabilized. "What aliens?"

"*The* aliens, State." The Rep was genuinely puzzled. "You know they're
out there."

"Sure," Lindsay said.

"Wanna watch the Sun a while? Maybe it'll tell us something."

"How about Mars?" Lindsay suggested.

"No good, it's in opposition. We can try asteroids, though. Check out the
ecliptic." There was a moment's silence, filled by the low-key music of the control room, as the stars wheeled. Lindsay used haragei and felt the drone's turning

as a smooth movement around his own center of gravity. The constant training paid off; he felt solid, secure, confident. He breathed from the pit of his stomach.

"There's one," the Rep said. A distant pinpoint of light centered itself in his field of vision and swelled into a smudge. When it seemed about finger-sized, its edges fuzzed out and lost definition. The Rep kicked in the computer resolution and the image grew into a sausage-shaped cylinder, glowing in false data-bit colors.

"It's a decoy," the Rep said.

"You think so?"

"Yeah, I've seen 'em. Shaper work. Just a polymer skin, a balloon. Airtight, though. There might be someone in it."

"I've never seen one," Lindsay said.

"There's thousands." It was true. Shaper claim-jumpers in the Belt had been manufacturing the decoys for years. The polymer skins were large enough to house a small outpost of data spies, drone hijackers, or defectors. Would-be Mech sundogs could hide from police agencies there, or Shaper cypher experts could lurk within them, tapping inter-cartel broadcasts.

The strategy was to overload Mech tracking systems with a swarm of potential hideouts. The Shapers had made a strong early showing in the struggle for the Belt, and there were still isolated groups of Shaper agents moving from cell to cell behind Mech lines while the Ring Council was under siege. Many decoys were outfitted with propaganda broadcasting systems or with solar wind-tracking devices that could distort their orbits; some could shrink and expand repeatedly, disappearing from Mech radar. It was cheaper to manufacture them than it was to track down and destroy them, giving the Shapers a financial edge.

The outpost the *Red Consensus* had been hired to hit was one of those manufacturing centers.

"When there's peace," the Rep told him, "you get a dozen of these, link 'em up with tubeways, and you got a good cheap nation-station."

"Will there ever be peace?" Lindsay said.

The walls hummed as the *Red Consensus* reeled in line. "When the aliens come," the Rep said.

## ABOARD THE RED CONSENSUS: 30-11-'16

They were training in the gym. "That's enough for today," the President said. "You're all looking good. Even State has the fundamentals down."

The three Reps laughed, lifting off their helmets. Lindsay popped the seal and pulled the suit helmet over his head. The combat session had lasted longer than he'd expected. He had hidden the wad from an inhaler inside the suit; he'd soaked it in vasopressin. He knew what was coming next, and he knew he would need his training at its finest pitch. But the fumes had been stronger than he'd realized; he felt dizzy, and his bladder ached.

"You're flushed, State," the President said. "Feel winded?"

"It's the air inside the suit, sir," Lindsay lied, the words ringing loudly in his own ears. "The oxygen, sir." The vasopressin had dilated the blood vessels beneath his skin.

Rep 1 laughed and made a face. "State's a feeb."

"At ease, the rest of you citizens. State and I have business."

The suits were entered through a long horseshoe-shaped inseam along the crotch and thighs. The others, except for Rep 3, were out of their suits in seconds. Lindsay unzipped his seam and kicked his legs out of the heavy magnetic boots.

The others left, leaving Lindsay and the President. Lindsay shrugged the suit over his head, and as he did so he squeezed his right hand shut within the suit's bulky arm, driving a hypo needle deep into the base of his palm. He plucked the needle loose and let it float down into the glove fingers.

He left the suit open to air it out and tucked it under one arm. No one would bother it; it was Lindsay's now, with the diplomatic seal of the FMD on both shoulders. He followed the President up a deck and stowed the suit on its rack.

The two of them were alone in the "broom closet." The President's face was anxious. "You're ready, soldier? You feel okay? Ideologically, I mean?"

"Yes, sir," Lindsay said. "My mind's made up, sir."

"Then follow me." They went up two more decks to the control room. The President hauled himself head first through the narrow armory room and into the gun compartment.

Lindsay followed. His head throbbed, dilated blood vessels pounding rhythmically. He felt sharper than broken glass. He took a deep breath and pulled himself feet first into the gunroom. He plunged at once into an underworld of paranoia.

"You're ready?"

"Yes, sir," Lindsay said. Slowly, he strapped himself into the skeletal control chair. The ancient gun was grisly and impressive. He felt a flash of intuition suddenly, a cold steel certainty that the muzzle of the gun was pointed at his own gut. To pull the trigger would be to blow himself apart.

Lindsay remembered the procedures. In his state they might as well have been stenciled on his brain. He ran his hand over the matte-black surface of the control panel and kicked in power with a tap of the rocker switch. Behind him, the muffled music of the control room dropped an octave as the power drain set in. A rack of evil red blips and readouts sprang into life below the eerie blue of the target screen.

Lindsay looked past the screen, his eyes blurring. There was a light sheen of oil on the ribbed struts along the gun barrel. Thick black hard-edged ribs: superconducting magnets, oozing gutlike coils of foil-covered power cables.

It was a pornography of death. A degradation of the human genius in abject whoredom to racial suicide.

Lindsay tripped an arming switch and flipped up the first safety seal. He stuck his right hand within the hollow behind the seal. His fingers settled around a ribbed plastic grip. He flicked aside another catch with his thumb. The machine began to whine.

"We all have to do it," the President said. "It can't rest on any one of us."

"I understand, sir," Lindsay said. He had rehearsed the words. The gun was not aimed at anything; it pointed off the ecliptic into empty galactic space. No one would be harmed. All he had to do was pull the trigger. He was not going to be able to do it.

"We all hate it," the President said. "The gun's under seal at all times, I swear it. But we gotta have it. You never know what you'll find in the next action. Maybe the big score. The score that'll buy us into a cartel, make us a nation again. Then we can junk this monster."

"Yes, sir." It was not something he could confront directly, not something he could coldly think through. It was too deep for that. It was the basis of the universe.

*Worlds could burst.* The walls held life itself, and outside those locks and bulkheads loomed utterly pitiless darkness, the lethal nothingness of naked space. In the old circumlunars, in the modern Mech cartels, in the Shaper Ring Council, even in the far-flung outposts of the cometary miners and the blazing smelters of intra-Mercurian orbit, every single thinking being carried this knowledge. Too many generations had lived and died under the shadow of catastrophe. It had soaked itself into everyone from childhood.

Habitats were sacred; sacred because they were frail. The frailty was universal. Once the world was deliberately destroyed, there could be no more safety anywhere, for anyone. Every world would burst in a thousand infernos of total war.

There was no true safety. There had never been any. There were a hundred ways to kill a world: fire, explosion, poison, sabotage. The constant vigilance exercised by all societies could only reduce the risk. The power of destruction was in the hands of anyone and everyone. Anyone and everyone shared the burden of responsibility. The specter of destruction had shaped the moral paradigm of every world and every ideology.

The destinies of man in space had not been easy, and Lindsay's universe was not a simple one. There were epidemics of suicide, bitter power struggles, vicious techno-racial prejudices, the crippling suppression of entire societies.

And yet the ultimate madness had been avoided. There was war, yes: small-scale ambushes, spacecraft destroyed, tiny mining camps claim-jumped with the murder of their inhabitants: all the grim and obscure conflicts that burst like sparks from the grinding impact of the Mech and Shaper superpowers. But humankind had survived and flourished.

It was a deep and fundamental triumph. On the same deep level of the mind that held the constant fear, there was a stronger hope and confidence. It was a victory that belonged to everyone, a victory so thorough and so deep that it had vanished from sight, and belonged to that secret realm of the mind on which everything else is predicated.

And yet these pirates, as pirates must, controlled a weapon of mass destruction. It was an ancient machine: a relic of a lunatic era when men first pried open the Pandora crypts of physics. An age when cosmic explosives had spread across the surface of Earth like bleeding scabs across the brain of a paretic.

"I fired it myself last week," the President said, "so I know the Zaibatsu security didn't booby-trap the bastard. Some of the Mech cartels will do that. Pick you up with frontier craft four thousand klicks out, shut down your weaponry, then put a delay chip in the wiring—you pull the trigger, chip vaporizes, nerve gas. . . . It makes no difference. You pull that trigger in combat you're dead anyway, ninety-nine percent. The Shapers we're attacking have Armageddon stuff too. We gotta have anything they have. We gotta do anything they can do. That's nuclear war, soldier; otherwise, we can't talk together. . . . Now, fire."

"Fire!" cried Lindsay. There was nothing. The gun was silent.

"Something's wrong," Lindsay said.

"Gun down?"

"No, it's my arm. My arm." He pulled backward. "I can't get it off the pistol grip. The muscles have knotted."

"They what?" the President said. He gripped Lindsay's forearm. The muscles stood out like cables, cramped in paralytic rigor.

"Oh, God," Lindsay said, a well-practiced edge of hysteria in his voice. "I can't feel your hand. Squeeze my arm."

The President crushed his forearm with bruising force. "Nothing," Lindsay said. He had filled his arm with anesthetic in the spacesuit. The cramping was a diplomatic trick. It was not an easy one. He hadn't meant to get his fingers caught around the grip.

The President dug his calloused fingertips into the outside groove of Lindsay's elbow. Even past the anesthetic, pain knifed through the crushed nerves. His hand jumped slightly, releasing the grip. "I felt that, just a little," he said calmly. There was something he could do with pain, if the vasopressin would help him remember. . . . There. The pain transformed itself, lost its color, became something nastily close to pleasure.

"I could try it left-handed," Lindsay said gamely. "Of course, if that arm goes too, then—"

"What the hell's wrong with you, State?" The President dug his thumb cruelly into the complex of nerves in Lindsay's wrist. Lindsay felt the agony as a cool black sheet draped across his brain. He almost lost consciousness; his eyes fluttered and he smiled faintly.

"It must be some Shaper thing," he said. "Neural programming. They fixed it so that I could never do this." He swallowed hard. "It's like it's not my arm." Sweat beaded on his forehead. He was so wired on vasopressin that he could feel each muscle in his face as a separate entity, just like they taught at the Academy.

"I can't accept this," the President told him. "If you can't pull the trigger then you can't be one of us."

"It might be possible to rig up some kind of mechanical thing," Lindsay said adroitly. "Some kind of piston-powered glove I could fit over it. I'm willing, sir. It's this that's not." He lifted the arm, stiffly, from the shoulder, then slammed it down on the hard-edged ridge of the gun. He hit it again. "I can't feel it." Skin peeled from the muscle. Bright microglobes of blood leaped up to float in midair. The arm stayed rigid. A flat amoebalike ripple of blood oozed from the long scrape.

"We can't try an arm for treason," the President said.

Lindsay shrugged one-sidedly. "I'm doing my best, sir." He knew that he would never pull that trigger. He thought they might kill him for it, though he hoped to escape that. Life was important, but not so crucial as the trigger.

"We'll see what Judge Two says," the President said.

Lindsay was willing. This much had gone according to plan.

Judge Two was asleep in sick bay. She came awake with a start, her eyes wild. She saw the blood, then stared at the President. "Burn it, you've hurt him again."

"Not me," said the President, with a flicker of confusion and guilt. The President explained while Judge 2 examined the arm and bandaged it. "Might be psychosomatic."

"I want that arm moving," the President said. "Do it, soldier."

"Yes sir," said the Judge, startled. She hadn't realized they were under military rule. She scratched her head. "I'm outa my depth. I'm just a mechanic, not some Shaper psychotech." She looked sidelong at the President; he was adamant. "Lemme think. . . . This should do it." She produced another vial, labeled in an impenetrable scrawl. "Convulsant. Five times as powerful as the nerves' own firing signals." She drew up three cc's. "We'd better tourniquet that arm. If this hits his bloodstream it'll really rack him up." She looked guiltily at Lindsay. "This'll hurt some. A lot."

Lindsay saw his chance. His arm was full of anesthetic, but he could fake the pain. If he seemed to suffer badly enough, they might forget about the test. They would feel he'd been punished enough, for something that wasn't his fault. The Judge was sympathetic; he could play her against the President. Their guilt would do the rest.

He spoke sternly. "The President knows best. You should follow his orders. Never mind my arm, it's numb anyway."

"You'll feel this, State. If you ain't dead." The needle went in. She twisted the hose tight around his bicep. The tattoos rippled as his veins began to bulge.

When agony hit he knew the anesthetic was useless. The convulsant scorched him like acid. "It's burning!" he screamed. "It's burning!" His arm rippled, its muscles writhing eerily. It began to flop in spasms, yanking one end of the hose loose from the Judge's grip.

Congested blood seeped past the tourniquet into Lindsay's chest. He choked on a scream and bent double, his face gray. The drug crept like hot wires around his heart. He swallowed his tongue and went into convulsions.

He was near death for two days. By the time he'd recovered, the others had reached a decision. No one ever spoke of the test again. It had never happened.

## ABOARD THE RED CONSENSUS: 19-12-'16

"It's just a rock," said Rep 2. She brushed a roach from the videoscreen.

"It's the target," said the Speaker of the House. The control room was powered down, and the familiar chorus of pops, squeaks, and rumbles had dwindled to a faint, tense scratching. The Speaker's face was greenish with screen light. "It's camouflage. They're in there. I can feel it."

"It's a rock," said Senator 3. Her tool belt rattled as she drifted overhead, watching the screen. "They've scrammed, they've scarpered. There's no infrareds."

Lindsay drifted quietly in a corner of the control room, not watching the screen. He was rubbing the tattooed skin of his right arm, slowly, absently, staring at nothing. The skin had healed, but the combination of drugs had burned the crushed nerves. His skin felt rubbery below the cold ink of his tattoos. His right-hand fingertips were numb.

He had no faith in the Shapers' restraint. The billowing sunsail of the *Red Consensus* was supposed to hide the ship itself from radar, preventing a preemptive strike from the asteroid. But he expected at any moment to feel the last half second of impact as Shaper weapons tore the ship apart. From within the gun room, he heard the whine of the gunner's seat as Justice 3 shifted nervously.

"They're waiting for us to drift past," the President said. "They're waiting for a shot past the sail."

"They can't just blow us away," Senator 2 said plaintively. "We might be sundogs. Mech defectors."

"Stay on that drone, Rep Three!" the President ordered.

Smiling sunnily, Rep 3 removed his earphones and turned his goggled face toward the others. "What's that, Mr. President?"

"I said stay on those frequencies, God damn it!" the President shouted.

"Oh, that," said Rep 3. He scratched within his spacesuit collar, holding the doubled phones to one ear. "I was doing that already. And—oh, yeah." He paused, while the crew held their breath. The goggles blocked his eyesight, but he reached out unerringly and touched switches on the board before him. The control room was filled with a high-pitched staccato whine.

"Cut it in on visuals," Rep 3 explained, tapping the keyboard. The asteroid vanished, replaced on the screen by column after column of alphanumeric gibberish:

TCGAGGCTATCGTAGCTAAAGCTCTCCCGATCGATATCGTCTCGAGATCGATCGATGC-
TTAGCTAGCTAGTTGTCGATCGTAGGGCTCGAGCTA . . .

"Shaper genetics code," the Speaker said. "I told you so."

"Their last signal before we take them out," the President said boldly. "I'm declaring martial law as of this moment. I want everyone in battle gear—except you, State. Hop to it."

The crew scrambled, their nerves unkinking in a burst of action. Lindsay watched them go, thinking of the stream of data to the Ring Council that had betrayed the outpost.

The Shapers might have thrown their lives away with that last cry. But the enemy, at least, had someone who would know their deaths, and mourn.

# Chapter 4

## ESAIRS XII: 21-12-'16

They called the asteroid ESAIRS 89-XII, the only name it had ever had, drawn from an ancient catalog. ESAIRS XII was a potato-shaped lump of slag, half a kilometer long.

The *Red Consensus* hovered over its bulging equator, anchored by a guy line.

Lindsay pulled himself one-handed down the line. Glimpsed through his faceplate, the asteroid was dark, with long coal-powder streaks of carbonaceous ore. Cold gray and white blurs marked the charred impact points of primeval collisions. The biggest craters were eighty meters across, huge lava sumps of cracked slag and splattered glass.

Lindsay landed. The expanse beneath his boots was like pumice, a static off-white surf of petrified bubbles. He could see up and down the asteroid's length, but its width curved out of sight behind a horizon a dozen steps away.

He bent and pulled himself along, gripping knobs and cavities with the rough fingers of his gauntlets. The right hand was bad. The tough interior fabric of the glove felt soft as cotton to his nerve-burned fingers.

He crawled, legs bobbing aimlessly, over the rim of an oblong crater, the scarred gouge of some glancing collision. It was five times as deep as he was tall, and its floor was a long gas-smoothed blister of greenish basalt. A long bloated ridge of molten rock had almost lifted free into space but then frozen, preserving every last ripple and warp. . . .

It slid aside. The rock ridge shriveled, crumpling like silk, its warps and bumps revealed as shaded camouflage on a plastic film.

A cavern yawned below. It was a tunnel, curving just below the surface.

Lindsay picked his way cautiously down the slope and flung himself into the tunnel. He braced himself against its walls. Stretching overhead, he pushed against the tunnel's ceiling to plant his feet.

Sunlight dawned over the tiny horizon and fell into the tunnel.

It was precisely circular and inhumanly smooth. Six tracks of thin metallic ribbon had been epoxied into place, running lengthwise along the corridor. In raw sunlight the tracks had the gleam of copper.

The tunnel apparently girdled the asteroid. It curved rapidly, like the horizon. Before him, almost hidden by the tunnel's curvature, he glimpsed the dim sheen of brown plastic. Jumping and shoving along the walls, he bounced toward it in free-fall.

It was a plastic film with an inert fabric airlock. Lindsay pulled the zippered airlock tag and stepped in. He zipped it up behind him, undid a second zipper in the lock's inner wall, and climbed through.

He was in a cavernous black and ocher balloon. It had been blown up within the tunnel, filling it tightly.

A figure in a plastic decontamination suit floated upside down below the ceiling, a bright green silhouette against hand-sprayed black arabesques on an ocher background.

Lindsay's suit had gone flat, indicating air pressure. He took his helmet off and inhaled cautiously. It was an oxy-nitrogen mix, standard air.

Lindsay held his right arm across his chest with deliberate awkwardness. "I, uh, have a prepared statement to read. If you have no objection."

"Please proceed." The woman's voice was thin, half muffled. He glimpsed her face behind the plate: cold eyes, tawny skin, dark hair held in a green net.

Lindsay read the words slowly, without inflection. "Greetings from the Fortuna Miners' Democracy. We are an independent nation, operating under the rule of law, firmly predicated on a basis of individual civil rights. As emigrants into our national territory, new members of the body politic are subject to a brief naturalization process before assuming full citizenship. We regret any inconvenience caused by the imposition of a new political order.

"It is our policy that ideological differences be settled by a process of negotiation. To that end, we have deputized our Secretary of State to establish preliminary terms, subject to ratification by the Senate. It is the wish of the Fortuna Miners' Democracy, as expressed in House Joint Resolution Sixteen, Sixty-Seventh Session, that you begin negotiation without delay under the Secretary's aegis, so that the interim period may be as brief and as secure as possible.

"We extend to our future citizens the hand of friendship and warm congratulations.

"Signed, President."

Lindsay looked up.

"You'll want a copy of this," he said, extending it.

The Shaper woman floated closer. Lindsay saw that she was beautiful. It meant very little. Beauty was cheap among Shapers.

She took the document. Lindsay pulled more from a hip valise, with his left hand. "These are my credentials." He handed them over: a wad of recycled printout gaudy with Fortuna foil seals.

The woman said, "My name is Nora Mavrides. The rest of the Family has asked me to convey to you our impression of the situation. We feel that we can convince you that the actions you've taken are rash, and that you can profit by turning your attention elsewhere. We ask for nothing but the time to convince you. We have even shut down our main gun."

Lindsay nodded. "That's nice. Very good. Should impress the government very much. I'd like to see this gun."

"We are inside it," said Nora Mavrides.

## ABOARD THE RED CONSENSUS: 22-12-'16

Lindsay said, "I played dumb. But I don't think she bought it." He was addressing a joint session of the House and Senate, with the Speaker of the House presiding. The President was in the audience. The Supreme Court Justices were manning the gun and control room, listening in on an intercom.

The President shook his head. "She believed it. Shapers always think we're stupid. Hell, to Shapers we *are* stupid."

Lindsay said, "We're tethered just past the outlet of their launch ring. It's a long circular tunnel, a ring around the rock's center of gravity, cored just under the surface. It has magnetic strips for acceleration and some kind of magnetic launch bucket."

"I heard of those," said Justice 3, over the intercom. He was their regular gunner, a former miner, close to a century old. "It starts with just a little boost, get that bucket up, magnetized. Rides on a magnetic cushion, then you accelerate it, let it zip around a while, then brake it just behind the outlet. The bucket slows but the cargo shoots out at klicks per second."

"Klicks per second?" said the Speaker of the House. "That could blow us away."

"No," said the President. "They'd have to use a lot of power for a launch. This close, we'd pick up the magnetics."

"They won't let us in," Lindsay said. "Their Family lives clean. No microbes, or only tailored ones. And we have Zaibatsu stuff in every pore. They're going to offer us loot to go away."

"That's not our assignment," the Speaker said.

"We can't judge their loot unless we see their quarters," Rep 1 said. The young Shaper renegade brushed at her hair with enameled fingertips. She had been dressing well lately.

"We can dig our way in with the excavator," the President said. "We'll use the sonar readings we made. We got a good idea of the closest tunnels to the surface. We could core in in five-ten minutes, while State negotiates." He hesitated. "They might kill us for it."

The Speaker's voice held cold certainty. "We're dead anyway, if they keep holding us off at arm's length. Our gun is short-range. That launch ring can plaster us hours after we leave."

"They didn't do it before," said Rep 1.

"Now they know who we are."

"There's only one thing for it," the President said. "Put it to a vote."

## ESAIRS XII: 23-12-'16

"We're a miners' democracy after all," Lindsay told Nora Mavrides. "According to Fortuna ideology, we had a perfect right to drill. If you'd mapped your tunnel network for us, this wouldn't have happened."

"You risked everything," Nora Mavrides said.

"You have to admit there were benefits," Lindsay said. "Now that your network has been, as you say, 'contaminated,' we can at least meet face to face, without spacesuits."

"It was reckless, Secretary."

Lindsay touched his chest left-handed. "Look at it from our perspective, Dr. Mavrides. The FMD will not wait indefinitely to take possession of its own property. I think we've been quite reasonable.

"You keep assuming that we mean to leave. We are settlers, not brigands. We won't be turned aside by nebulous promises and anti-Mechanist propaganda. We are miners."

"Pirates. Mech hirelings."

Lindsay shrugged one-sidedly.

"Your arm," she said. "Is it really hurt? Or do you pretend it, to make me think you're harmless?"

Lindsay said nothing.

"I take your point," she said. "There's no true negotiation without trust. Somewhere we have common ground. Let's find it."

Lindsay straightened his arm. "All right, Nora. If this is between just the two of us, role-playing aside, let's hear you. I can bear any level of frankness you're willing to advance."

"Tell me your name, then."

"It won't mean anything to you." She was silent. "It's Abelard," he said. "Call me Abelard."

"What's your gene-line, Abelard?"

"I'm no Shaper."

"You're lying, Abelard. You move like one of us. The arm business camouflaged it, but your clumsiness is too deliberate. How old are you? A hundred? Less? How long have you been sundogging it?"

"Does that matter?" Lindsay said.

"You can go back. Believe me, it's different now. The Council needs you.

I'll sponsor you. Join us, Abelard. We're your people. Not these germy renegades."

Lindsay reached out. Nora drew back, the long laces of her sleeve ties jerking in free-fall.

"You see," Lindsay said. "I'm as filthy as they are." He watched her closely.

She was beautiful. The Mavrides clan was a gene-line he hadn't seen before. Wide, hazel eyes, with a trace of epicanthic fold, more Amerindian than oriental. High cheekbones, straight aquiline nose. Feathery black eyebrows, and a wealth of shimmering black hair, which in free-fall formed a bushy mass of curled tendrils. Nora's hair was confined in a loose free-fall headdress, a jade-green plastic turban with a crimson drawstring at the back and a serrated fringe of forest green above her bangs. Her coppery skin was clear and inhumanly smooth, with a dusting of rouge.

There were six of them. They had a close family resemblance, but they were not identical clones. The six were that tiny percentage of the Mavrides gene-line which had been drafted: Kleo, Paolo, Fazil, Ian, Agnes, and Nora Mavrides. Kleo was their leader. She was forty. Nora was twenty-eight. The rest were all seventeen years old.

Lindsay had seen them. He'd pitied them. The Ring Council did not waste investment. A seventeen-year-old genius was more than sufficient for the assignment, and they were cheap. They had looked him over with cold hazel eyes, with the alert and revolted stare that a man reserves for vermin. They longed to kill him, with a hunger tempered only by disgust.

It was too late for that now. They should have killed him far away, when they could have stayed clean. Now he was too close. His skin, his breath, his teeth, even his blood seethed with corruption.

"We have no antiseptics," Nora said. "We never thought we'd need them. It won't be pleasant for us, Abelard. Boils, weals, rashes. Dysentery. There's no help for it. Even if you left tomorrow, the air from your ship . . . it was crawling." She spread her hands. Her blouse had scarlet drawstrings at the wrists, with puffed slashed sleeves showing the smooth skin of her forearms. The blouse was a wraparound garment, tied with short strings at each hip and belted at the waist. She'd sewn it herself, embroidering the lapels in pink-and-white gridwork. Below it she wore shorts cinched at the knee and lace-up crimson sandals.

"I'm sorry," Lindsay said. "But it's better than dying. The Shapers are burned, Nora. They're finished. I have no love for the Mechs, believe me." For the first time, he gestured with his right arm. "Let me tell you something I'll deny if you repeat. The Mechs wouldn't exist if it weren't for you. Their Union of Cartels is a sham. It's only united by fear and hatred of the Reshaped. When they've destroyed the Ring Council, as they must, the Mechs themselves will fly to pieces.

"Please, Nora. See it my way for a moment, for the sake of argument. I know you're committed, I know you're loyal to your gene-line, your people back home. But your death won't save them. They're burned, doomed. It's just you and us now. Eighteen people. I've lived with these Fortunans. We know what they are. They're scum, pirates, marauders. Failures. Victims, Nora. They live in the gap between what's right and what's possible.

"But if you go along, they won't kill you. It's your chance, a chance for the six here. . . . After they've shut you down, they'll go back to the cartels. If you surrender, they'll take you along. You're all young. Disguise your pasts, and in a century you could be running those cartels. Mech, Shaper, those are only labels. The point is that we *live.*"

"You're tools," the woman said. "Victims, yes, I'll accept that. We're victims ourselves. But victims in a better cause than yours. We came here naked, Abelard. We were shipped here in a one-way drogue, and the only reason we weren't blown away in flight is because the Council launches fifty decoys for every real mission. It costs the cartels more to kill us than we're worth.

"That's why they hired you. The rich Mechs, the ones in power, have turned you on us. And we were surviving. We made this base from nothing with our hands, brains, and wetware. It was you who came to kill us."

"But we're here now," Lindsay said. "What's past can't be helped. I'm begging you to let me live, and you give me ideology. Please, Nora, bend a little. Don't kill us all."

"I want to live," she said. "It's you who should join us here. Your lot won't be of much use, but we could tolerate you. You'll never be true Shapers, but there's room for the unplanned under our aegis. In one way or another, we outflank every move the cartels make against us."

"You're under siege," Lindsay said.

"We break out. Haven't you heard? The Concatenation will declare for us. We have one circumlunar already: the Mare Serenitatis Circumlunar Corporate Republic."

Even here Constantine's shadow had touched him. "You call that a triumph?" he said. "Those decadent little worlds? Those broken-down relics?"

"We will rebuild them," she said with chilling confidence. "We own their youth."

## ABOARD THE RED CONSENSUS: 1-1-'17

"Welcome aboard, Dr. Mavrides," the President said. He extended his hand. Nora shook it without hesitation; her skin was protected under the thin plastic of her spacesuit.

"A fine beginning for the new year," Lindsay said. They were on the control deck of the *Red Consensus*. Lindsay realized how much he'd missed the familiar pop-blip-and-squeak of the instruments. The sound settled into him, releasing tension he hadn't known he had.

The negotiations were twelve days old. He'd forgotten how bad the pirates looked, how consummately grubby. They had clogged pores, hair rank with grease, teeth rimmed with plaque. To a Shaper's eyes they looked like wild animals.

"This is our third agreement," the President said formally. "First the Open Channels Act, then the Technological Assessment and Trade Consensus, and now a real breakthrough in social justice policy, the Integration Act. Welcome to the *Red Consensus,* doctor. We hope you'll regard every angstrom of the craft as part of your national heritage."

The President pinned the printout treaty to a bulkhead and signed it with a flourish. Lindsay printed the state seal with his left hand. The flimsy paper ripped a little.

"We're all nationals here," the President said. "Let's relax a little. Get to, uh, know each other." He pulled a gunmetal inhaler and sniffed at it ostentatiously.

"You sew that spacesuit yourself?" the Speaker of the House said.

"Yes, Madam Speaker. The seams are threadwire and epoxy from our wetware tanks."

"Clever."

"I like your roaches," said Rep 2. "Pink and gold and green. Hardly look like roaches at all. I'd like to have some of those."

"That can be arranged, I'm sure," Nora said.

"Trade you some relaxant for it. I have lots."

"Thank you," Nora said. She was doing well. Lindsay felt obscurely proud of her.

She unzipped her spacesuit and stepped out of it. Below it she wore a triangular over-the-shoulders poncho, geometrically embroidered in white and ice blue. The poncho's tapering ends were laced across her hips, leaving her legs bare except for lace-up velcro sandals.

The pirates had tactfully given up their red-and-silver skeleton jumpsuits. Instead they wore dun-brown Zaibatsu coveralls. They looked like savages.

"I could do with one of these," said Rep 3. He held the accordioned arm of his ancient spacesuit next to the thin plastic of hers. "How you breathe in that sucker?"

"It's not for deep space. We just fill it with pure oxygen and breathe as long as we can. Ten minutes."

"I could hook tanks to one. More spacey, citizen-to-be. The Sun would like it."

"We could teach you to sew one. It's an art worth knowing." She smiled at Rep 3, and Lindsay shuddered inwardly. He knew how the sweaty reek of the Rep's suit must turn her stomach.

He drifted between the two of them, unobtrusively nudging Rep 3 to one side. And, for the first time, he touched Nora Mavrides. He put his hand gently on the soft blue and white shoulder of her poncho. The muscle beneath his hand was as stiff as wire.

She smiled again, quickly. "I'm sure the others will find this ship fascinating. We came here in a drogue. Our cargo was nine-tenths ice, for the wetware tanks. We were in paste, close to dead. We had our robot and our pocket toka-mak. The rest was bits and pieces. Wire, a handful of microchips, some salt and trace minerals. The rest's genetics. Eggs, seeds, bacteria. We came here naked, to save launch weight. Everything else we've done with our hands, friends. Flesh against rock. Flesh wins, if it's smart enough."

Lindsay nodded. She had not mentioned their electromagnetic pulse weapon. No one talked about the guns.

She struggled to charm the pirates, but her pride stung them. The pride of the Family was justified. They'd bootstrapped themselves into prosperity with bacterial wetware from gelatin capsules no bigger than pinheads. They had mastered plastics; they conjured them out of the rock. Their artifacts were as cheap as life itself.

They had *grown* themselves into the rock; wormed their way in with soft-bodied relentless persistence. ESAIRS was riddled with tunnels; their sharp-toothed tunneling hoops ran around the clock. They had air blowers rigged from vinyl sacks and ribs of memory plastic. The ribs *breathed.* They were wired to the tokamak fusion plant, and a small change in voltage made them bend and flex, bend and flex, sucking in air with a pop of plastic lung and an animal wheeze of exhalation. It was the sound of life inside the rock, the rasp of the hoops, the blowers breathing, the sullen gurgling of the fermenters.

They had plants. Not just algae and protein goo but flowers: roses, phlox, daisies—or plants that had known those names before their DNA had felt the scalpel. Celery, lettuce, dwarf corn, spinach, alfalfa. Bamboo: with fine wire and merciless patience they could warp bamboo into complex pipes and bottles. Eggs: they even had chickens, or things that had once been chickens before Shaper gene-splicers turned them into free-fall protein tools.

They were powerful, subtle, and filled with desperate hatred. Lindsay knew that they were waiting for their chance, weighing odds, calculating. They would attack to kill if they could, but only when they could maximize the chance of their own survival.

But he also knew that with each day that passed, with each minor concession and agreement, another frail layer of shellac was laid over the open break between them. Day by day a new status quo struggled to form, a frail détente supported by nothing but habit. It was not much, but it was all he had: the hope that, with time, the facade of peace would take on substance.

## ESAIRS XII: 3-2-'17

"Hey, Secretary of State."

Lindsay woke. In the ghostlike gravity of the asteroid he had settled imperceptibly to the bottom of his cavern. They called his dugout "the Embassy." With the passage of the Integration Act, Lindsay had moved into the rock, with the rest of the FMD.

Paolo had spoken. Fazil was with him. The two young men wore embroidered ponchos and stiff plastic crowns holding floating manes of shoulder-length hair.

The skin bacteria had hit them badly. Every day they looked worse. Paolo's neck was so badly inflamed that his throat looked cut. Fazil's left ear was infected; he carried his head tilted to one side.

"We want to show you something," Paolo said. "Can you come with us, Mr. Secretary? Quietly?" His voice was gentle, his hazel eyes so clear and guileless that Lindsay knew at once that he was up to something. Would they kill him? Not yet. Lindsay laced on a poncho and struggled with the complex knots of his sandals. "I'm at your disposal," he said.

They floated into the corridor. The corridors between dugouts were no more than long wormholes, a meter across. The Mavrides clansmen propelled themselves along with a quick side-to-side lizardlike skittering. Lindsay was slower. His injured arm was bad today, and his hand felt like a club.

They glided silently through the soft yellow light of one of the fermenting rooms. The blunt, nippled ends of three wetware bags jutted into the room. They were stuffed like a string of sausages into stone tunnels. Each tunnel held a series of bags, united by filters, each bag passing its output to the next. The last bag had a spinneret running, a memory-plastic engine, clacking slowly. A hollow tube of flawless clear acrylic coiled in free-fall, reeking as it dried.

They entered another black tunnel. The tunnels were all identical, all perfectly smooth. There was no need for lighting. Any genius could easily memorize the nexus.

To his left Lindsay heard the slow *clack-rasp, clask-rasp* of a tunneling hoop. The hoops were handmade, their teeth hand-set in plastic, and they each sounded slightly different. They helped him navigate. They could gnaw two meters a day through the softer rock. In two years they had gnawed over twenty thousand tons of ore.

When the ore was processed, the tailings were shot into space. Everything launched away left a hole behind it. A hole ten kilometers long, pitch black, and as knotted as snarled fishline, beaded with living caverns, greenhouses, wetware rooms, and private hideyholes.

They took a turn Lindsay had never used before. Lindsay heard the grating sound of a stone plug hauled away.

They went a short distance, squirming past the flaccid bulk of a deactivated air blower. As Lindsay crawled past it in the darkness, the blower came to life with a gasp.

"This is our secret place," Paolo said. "Mine and Fazil's." His voice echoed in the darkness.

Something fizzed loudly with a leaping of white-hot sparks. Startled, Lindsay braced to fight. Paolo was holding a short white stick with flame gnawing at one end. "A candle," he said.

"Kindle?" said Lindsay. "Yes, I see."

"We play with fire," Paolo said. "Fazil and I."

They were in a workshop cavern, dug into one of the large stony veins within ESAIRS XII. The walls looked like granite to Lindsay's untrained eye: a grayish-pink rock studded with little gleams of rock crystal.

"There was quartz here," Paolo said. "Silicon dioxide. We mined it for oxygen, then Kleo forgot about it. So we drilled this room ourselves. Right, Fazil?"

Fazil spoke eagerly. "That's right, Mr. Secretary. We used hand drills and expansion plastic. See where the rock shattered and came loose? We hid the chunks in the debris for launch, so that no one knew. We worked for days and saved the biggest chunk."

"Look," Paolo said. He touched the wall, and the stone wrinkled in his hand and came away. In a broken-out rough cavity the size of a closet, an oblong boulder floated, kept from falling by a thread. Paolo snapped the thread and pulled the boulder out. It moved sluggishly; Fazil helped him stop its inertia.

It was a two-ton sculpture of Paolo's head.

"Very fine work," Lindsay said. "May I?" He ran his fingertips across the slickly polished cheekbone. The eyes, wide and alert, cored out for pupils, were as big as his outstretched hands. There was a faint smile on the enormous lips.

"When they sent us out here, we knew we weren't coming back," Paolo said. "We'll die here, and why? Not because our genetics are bad. We're a good line. Mavrides *rule*." He was talking faster now, falling into the cadences of Ring Council slang.

Fazil nodded silently.

"It's just bad percentages. Chance. We were burned by chance before we were twenty years old. You can't edit out chance. Some of the gene-line are bound to fall so the rest can live. If it weren't me and Fazil, it would be our crèchemates."

"I understand," Lindsay said.

"We're young and cheap. They throw us into the enemy's teeth so the ink is black not red. But we're alive, me and Fazil. There's something inside us. We'll never see ten percent of the life the others back home will see. But we were here. We're real."

"Living is better," Lindsay said.

"You're a traitor," Paolo said without resentment. "Without a gene-line you're bloodless, you're just a system."

"There are more important things than living," Fazil said.

"If you had enough time you'd outlive this war," Lindsay said.

Paolo smiled. "This is no war. This is evolution in action. You think you'll outlive that?"

Lindsay shrugged. "Maybe. What if aliens come?"

Paolo looked at him wide-eyed. "You believe in that? The aliens?"

"Maybe."

"You're all right," Paolo said.

"How can I help you?" Lindsay said.

"It's the launch ring. We plan to launch this head. An oblique launch, top velocity, full power, off the plane of the ecliptic. Maybe somebody sees it someday. Maybe some thing, five hundred million years, no trace of human life, picks it up, my face. There's no debris off the plane, no collisions, just dead-space vacuum, perfect. And it's good hard rock. Out this far the sun could go red giant and barely warm it. It could orbit till white dwarf stage, maybe till black cinder, till the galaxy bursts or the Kosmos eats its own tail. My image forever."

"Only first we have to launch it," said Fazil.

"The President won't like it," Lindsay said. "The first treaty we signed said no more launches for the duration. Maybe later, when our trust is stronger."

Paolo and Fazil traded glances. Lindsay knew at once that things were out of hand.

"Look," he said. "You two are talented. You have a lot of time on your hands since the launch ring's down. You could do heads of all of us."

"No!" Paolo shouted. "It's between us two, that's it."

"What about you, Fazil? Don't you want one?"

"We're dead," Fazil said. "This took us two years. There was only time for one. Chance burned us both. One of us had to give everything for nothing. So we decided. Show him, Paolo."

"He shouldn't look," Paolo said sullenly. "He doesn't understand."

"I want him to know, Paolo." Fazil was stern. "Why I have to follow, and you get to lead. Show him, Paolo."

Paolo reached under his poncho and pulled out a hinged box of clear acrylic. There were two stone cubes in it, black cubes with white dots on their faces. Dice.

Lindsay licked his lips. He had seen this in the Ring Council: endemic gambling. Not just for money, but for the core of personality. Secret agreements. Dominance games. Sex. The struggles within gene-lines, between people who knew with flat certainty that they were equally matched. The dice were quick and final.

"I can help you," Lindsay said. "Let's negotiate."

"We're supposed to be on duty," Paolo said. "Monitoring radio. We're leaving, Mr. Secretary."

"I'll come along," Lindsay said.

The two Shapers resealed the stone lid of their secret workshop and scuttled off in the darkness. Lindsay followed as best he could.

The Shapers had listening dishes dug in all over the asteroid. The bowl-shaped impact craters were ready-made for their camouflaged gridworks of copper mesh. All antennae fed into a central processor, whose delicate semiconductors were sheltered in a tough acrylic console. Slots in the console held cassettes of homemade recording tape, constantly spooling on a dozen different heads. Another cutout on the acrylic deck held a flat liquid crystal display for video copy and a hand-lettered keyboard.

The two genetics combed the waveband, flickering through a spectrum of general-issue cartel broadcasts. Most bands were cypher-static, anonymous blips of cybernetic datapulse. "Here's something," Paolo said. "Triangulate it, Fazil."

"It's close," Fazil said. "Oh, it's just the madman."

"What?" Lindsay said. A huge green roach speckled in lustrous violet flew past with a clatter of wings.

"The one who always wears the spacesuit." The two glanced at one another. Lindsay read their eyes. They were thinking about the man's stench.

"Is he talking?" Lindsay said. "Put him on, please."

"He always talks," Paolo said. "Sings, mostly. He raves into an open channel."

"He's in his new spacesuit," Lindsay said urgently. "Put him on."

He heard Rep 3. "—granulated like my mother's face. And sorry not to say goodbye to my friend Mars. Sorry for Carnaval, too. I'm out kilometers, and that hiss. I thought it was a new friend, trying to talk. But it's not. It's a little hole in my back, where I glued the tanks in. Tanks work fine, hole works better. It's me and my two skins, soon both cold."

"Try and raise him!" Lindsay said.

"I told you he keeps the channel open. The unit's two hundred years old if it's a day. He can't hear us when he talks."

"I'm not reeling back in, I'm staying out here." His voice was fainter. "No air to talk with, and no air to listen. So I'll try and climb out. Just a zipper. With any luck I can skin out completely." There was a light crackling of static. "Goodbye, Sun. Goodbye, Stars. Thanks for—"

The words were lost in a rush of decompression. Then the crackling of static was back. It went on and on.

Lindsay thought it through. He spoke quietly. "Was I your alibi, Paolo?"

"What?" Paolo was shocked.

"You sabotaged his suit. And then you carefully weren't here when we could have helped him."

Paolo was pale. "We were never near his suit, I swear!"

"Then why weren't you here at your post?"

"Kleo set me up!" Paolo shouted. "Ian walks point, the dice said so! I'm supposed to be clean!"

"Shut up, Paolo." Fazil grabbed his arm.

Paolo tried to stare him down, then turned to Lindsay. "It's Kleo and Ian. They hate my luck—" Fazil shook him.

Paolo slapped him hard across the face. Fazil cried out and threw his arms around Paolo, holding him close.

Paolo looked stricken. "I was upset," he said. "I lied about Kleo; she loves all of us. It was an accident. An accident."

Lindsay left. He scrambled headlong down the tunnels, passing more wetware and a greenhouse where a blower gusted the smell of fresh-cut hay.

He entered a cavern where grow-lights shone dusky red through a gas-permeable membrane. Nora's room branched off from the cavern, blocked by the wheezing bulk of her private air blower. Lindsay squeezed past it on the exhale and slapped the lights.

Violet arabesques covered the room's round walls. Nora was sleeping.

Her arms, her legs, were gripped in wire. Braces circled her wrists and elbows, ankles and knees. Black myoelectrodes studded the muscle groups beneath her naked skin. The arms, the legs, moved quietly, in unison, side, side, forward, back. A long carapace knobbed her back, above the branching nerve clumps of her spine.

It was a diplomatic training device. A spinal crab. Memory flashed behind Lindsay's eyes and he went berserk. He jumped off the wall and rocketed toward her. Her eyes snapped open blearily as he shouted in fury.

He seized her neck and jerked it forward, digging his nails into the rubbery rim where the spinal crab met her skin. He tore at it savagely. Part of it ripped free. The skin shone red beneath it, slick with sweat. Lindsay grabbed the left-arm cable and snapped it loose. He pulled harder; she wheezed as a strap dug in under her ribs.

The crab was peeling away. Its underside was ghastly, a hundred-footed mass of damp translucent tubes, pored with hair-thin wires. Lindsay ripped again. A cable nexus stretched and snapped, extruding colored wires.

He braced his feet against her back and pulled. She gagged and clawed at the strap's buckle; the belt whipped loose, and Lindsay had the whole thing. With its programming disrupted, it flopped and curled like a live thing. Lindsay whirled it by the straps and slammed it into the wall with all his strength. The interlapping segments of its back split open, their brittle plastic crackling. He whiplashed it into the stone. Brown lubricant oozed, then spattered into free-fall drops as he smashed it again. He crushed it underfoot, tore at the strap until it gave way. Its guts showed beneath the plates: lozenge-shaped biochips nested in multicolored fiberoptics.

He slammed it again, more slowly. The fury was leaving him. He felt cold. His right arm trembled uncontrollably.

Nora was against the wall, gripping a clothes rack. The sudden loss of nerve programming left her shaking with palsy.

"Where's the other one?" Lindsay demanded. "The one for your *face?*"

Her teeth chattered. "I didn't bring it," she said.

Lindsay kicked the crab away. "How long, Nora? How long have you been under that thing?"

"I wear it every night."

"Every night! My God!"

"I have to be the best," she said, shaking. She fumbled a poncho from the rack and ducked her head through the collar.

"But the pain," Lindsay said. "The way it burns!"

Nora smoothed the bright fabric from her shoulders to hips. "You're one of them," she said. "The early classmates. The failures. The defectors."

"What was your class?" Lindsay said.

"Fifth. The last one."

"I was first," Lindsay said. "The foreign section."

"Then you're not even a Shaper."

"I'm a Concatenate."

"You're all supposed to be dead." She peeled the crab's broken braces from her knees and ankles. "I should kill you. You attacked me. You're a traitor."

"When I smashed that thing I felt real freedom." He rubbed his arm absently, marveling. He'd truly lost control. Rebellion had overwhelmed him. For a moment, sincere human fury had burned through the training, touched a hot core of genuine rage. He felt shaken, but more whole, more truly himself, than he'd been for years.

"Your kind ruined it for the rest of us," Nora said. "We diplomats should be on top, coordinating things, making peace. But they shut down the whole program. We're undependable, they said. A bad ideology."

"They want us dead," Lindsay said. "That's why you were drafted."

"I wasn't drafted. I volunteered." She tied the poncho's last hip-lace. "I'll have a hero's welcome if I make it back. That's the only chance I'll ever have at power in the Rings."

"There are other powerful places."

"None that count."

"Rep Three is dead," Lindsay told her. "Why did you kill him?"

"Three reasons," she said. They were past pretense. "It was easy. It helps our odds against you. And third, he was crazy. Worse even than the rest of your crew. Too unpredictable. And too dangerous to let live."

"He was harmless," Lindsay said. "Not like the two of us." His eyes filled with tears.

"If you had my control you wouldn't weep. Not if they tore your heart out."

"They already have," Lindsay said. "And yours as well."

"Abelard," she said, "he was a pirate."

"And the rest?"

"You think they'd weep over us?"

"No," Lindsay said. "And not much, even over their own. It's vengeance they'll want. How would you feel if Ian disappears tomorrow? And two months from now you find his bones in the sludge drain of some fermenter? Or, better yet, if your nerves are so well steeled, what about yourself? How would *power* taste to you if you were retching bloody foam outside some airlock?"

"It's in your hands," she said. "I've told you the truth, as we agreed between us. It's up to you to control your faction."

"I won't be put in this position," Lindsay said. "I thought we had an understanding."

She pointed at the oozing wreckage of her spinal crab. "You didn't ask my permission to attack me. You saw something you couldn't bear, and you destroyed it. We did the same."

"I want to talk to Kleo," he said.

She looked hurt. "That's against our understanding. You talk through me."

"This is murder, Nora. I have to see her."

Nora sighed. "She's in her garden. You'll have to put on a suit."

"Mine's in the *Consensus*."

"We'll use one of Ian's, then. Come on." She led him back into the glowing cavern, then down a long fissured-out mining vein to Ian Mavrides's room.

The spacesuit maker and graphic artist was awake and working. He had refused to put his decontamination suit aside and wore it constantly, a one-man sterile environment.

Ian was point man for the Mavrides Family, a focus for threats and resentment. Paolo had blurted as much, but Lindsay knew it already.

The round walls of Ian's dugout were neatly stenciled in gridwork. For weeks he'd been decorating it with an elaborate geometric mosaic of interlocking L-shapes. With the passage of time the shapes were smaller, more tightly packed, crammed together in obsessive, crawling rigor. Its intricacy was claustrophobic, smothering; the tiny squares seemed to writhe and flicker.

When they entered, Ian whirled, putting his hand to one bulky sleeve-pocket. "It's us," Nora said.

Behind the faceplate, Ian's eyes were wild. "Oh," he said. "Get burned."

"Save it for the others," Lindsay said. "I'd be more impressed if you got some sleep, Ian."

"Sure," said Ian. "So you could come in here and pull my suit off. And contaminate me."

Nora said, "We need a suit, Ian. State is going to the garden."

"Fuck him! He's not stinking up one of my suits! He can sew his own, like Rep Three did."

"You're clever with suits, Ian." Lindsay wondered if Ian had been the one to murder Rep Three. They had probably rolled dice for the privilege. He pulled a suit from the rack. "If you take your suit off, I might not put this on. What do you say? I'll roll you."

Ian pressed an oxygen balloon against the intake nozzle of his suit. "Don't test your luck. Cripple."

Kleo lived in the largest greenhouse. It was ornamental; it grew more slowly than the wormholed industrial gardens, where vegetation rioted under grow-lights in pure carbon dioxide. The room was oblong, and its long walls had the ribbed look of a seashell. Brilliant light poured from fluorescent tubes along each ridge.

The soil was mine tailings, held by dampness and a fine plastic mesh. Like the Shapers themselves, the plants were altered to live without bacteria. They were flowers, mostly: roses, daisies, buttercups the size of fists.

Kleo's bed was of roofed-in wickerwork, grown from curved bamboo. She was awake, working on an embroidery hoop. Her skin was darker than the others'—the grow-lights had tanned her. She wore a sleeveless white blouse cinched at the waist, hanging in multiple thin folds. Her legs and feet were bare. There was an embroidered logo of rank above her heart.

"Hello, dear," she said.

"Kleo." Nora floated into the wickerwork structure and lightly kissed Kleo's cheek. "At his insistence, I—"

Kleo nodded once. "I hope you'll make this brief," she told Lindsay. "My garden is not for the unplanned."

"I want to discuss the murder of the Third Representative."

Kleo tucked a lock of curled hair into her braided hairnet. The proportions of her wrist, palm, and forearm showed that she was older than the rest, from an earlier production run. "Nonsense," she said. "An absurd allegation."

"I know you had him killed, Kleo. Maybe you did it yourself. Be frank with me."

"That man's death was an accident. There's no proof otherwise. Therefore, we bear no blame."

"I'm trying to save our lives, Kleo. Please, spare me the party line. If Nora admits the truth, why can't you?"

"What you discuss with our negotiator in secret session is not our business, Mr. Secretary. The Mavrides Family cannot acknowledge anything unproven."

"That's it, then?" Lindsay said from behind his faceplate. "Crimes don't exist outside your ideology? You expect me to join that fiction, lie for you, protect you?"

"We're your people," Kleo said, fixing him with her clear hazel eyes.

"But you've killed my friend."

"That is not a valid allegation, Mr. Secretary."

"This is useless," Lindsay said. He bent, grabbed a thornless rosebush, and ripped it up by the roots. He shook it; blobs of wet dirt flew. Kleo winced. "Look!" Lindsay said. "Don't you understand?"

"I understand that you're a barbarian," Kleo said. "You destroyed a thing of beauty to make a point in an argument you know I can't accept."

"Bend a little," Lindsay pleaded. "Have mercy."

"That's not our assignment," Kleo told him.

Lindsay turned and left, stripping off the clammy spacesuit just beyond the airlock.

"I told you not to try it," Nora said.

"She's suicidal," Lindsay said. "Why? Why do you follow her?"

"Because she loves us."

## ESAIRS XII: 23-2-'17

"Let me tell you about sex," Nora said. "Give me your hand."

Lindsay gave her his left hand. Nora gripped his wrist, pulled him forward, and put his thumb deep into her mouth. She held it there, then released him. "Tell me what you felt."

"It was warm," Lindsay said. "Wet. And uncomfortably intimate."

"That's what sex is like on suppressants," she said. "We have love in the Family, but not erotics. We're soldiers."

"You're chemically castrated, then?"

"You're prejudiced," she said. "You haven't lived it. That's why the orgy you propose is out of the question."

"Carnaval isn't an orgy," Lindsay said. "It's a ceremony. It's trust, it's communion. It holds the group together. Like animals huddling."

"It's too much to ask," she said.

"You don't realize what's at stake. It's not your body they want. They want to kill you. They hate your sterile guts. You don't know how I talked, persuaded, coaxed them. . . . Listen, they use hallucinogens. Your brain turns to pudding in Carnaval. You don't know what your own *hands* are, much less someone else's genitals. . . . You're helpless. Everyone is helpless, that's the point. No more games, no politics, no ranks and grudges. No *self.* When you come out of Carnaval it's like the first day of Creation. Everyone smiles." Lindsay looked aside, blinking. "It's real, Nora. It's not their government that sustains them, that's just the brain. Carnaval is the blood, the spine, the groin."

"It's not our way, Abelard."

"But if you could join us, even once, for a few hours! We'd dissolve these tensions, truly trust each other. Listen, Nora, sex is not some handicraft. It's real, it's human, it's one of the last things we have left. Burn it! What do you have to lose?"

"It could be an ambush," she said. "You could bend our minds with drugs and kill us. It's a risk."

"Of course it is, but there are ways around that." He locked eyes with her. "I'm telling you this on the basis of all the trust we have between us. At least we can give it a trial."

"I don't like this," Nora said. "I don't like sex. Especially with the unplanned."

"It's that or juice your own gene-line," Lindsay said. He pulled a loaded hypodermic from inside his lapel and attached its needle. "I have mine ready."

She looked at it sidelong, then produced her own. "You may not take well to this, Abelard."

"What is it?"

"Suppressant. With phenylxanthine to kick your IQ up. So you'll see how we feel."

"This isn't the full Carnaval mixture," Lindsay said. "Just the aphrodisiacs, half strength, and muscle relaxant. I think you need it since I smashed the spinal crab. You seem jumpy."

"You seem to know all too well what I need."

"That makes two of us." Lindsay pulled aside the loose sleeve of his wraparound blouse. "This is it, Nora. You could kill me now and call it allergic reaction, stress, anything." He looked at the gaudy tattoos on the skin of his arm. "Don't do it."

She shared his suspicion. "Are you taping this?"

"I don't allow tapes in my room." He pulled a pair of elastic cords from a styrene cabinet and passed her one.

He tied off his bicep. She did the same. With their sleeves rolled up, they waited quietly for the veins to swell. It was the most intimate moment they had ever had together. The thought aroused him.

She slipped her hypodermic into the crook of his elbow, and found the vein by the sudden rosette of blood at the needle's root. He did the same. They stared into each other's eyes and pressed the plungers home.

The moment passed. Lindsay withdrew the needle and pressed a sterile plastic dot against her puncture. Then he did his own. They loosened the cords.

"Neither of us seems to be dying," she said.

"It's a good sign," Lindsay said. He tossed the cords aside. "So far so good."

"Oh." She half closed her eyes. "It's hitting me. Oh, Abelard."

"How do you feel?" He took her shoulder. The nexus of bone and muscle seemed to soften under his hand. She was breathing shallowly, lips parted, her eyes dark.

"Like I'm melting," she said.

The phenylxanthine hit him first. He felt like a king. "You wouldn't hurt me," he said. "We're two of a kind, you and I."

He undid the ties and pulled her blouse off, then peeled the trousers inside out over her feet. He left the sandals on. His clothes flapped as he threw them off. They spun slowly in midair.

He pulled her close, his eyes blazing.

"Help me breathe," she whispered. The relaxant had hit her lungs. Lindsay took her chin in his hands, opened her mouth, and sealed his lips around it. He puffed gently and felt her ribs expand against his chest. Her head lolled back; the muscles of her neck were like wax. He hooked his legs around hers, from the inside, and breathed for her.

She let her arms drift, sluggishly, around his neck. She pulled her mouth back a fraction of an inch. "Try now."

He tried to enter her. Despite his own excitement, it was useless; the aphrodisiacs hadn't hit her yet, and she was dry.

"Don't hurt me," she said.

"I want you," Lindsay said. "You belong to me. Not to those others."

"Don't say that," she said, her voice slurring. "This is an experiment."

"For them, maybe. Not for us." The phenylxanthine had made him certain, and reckless in his certainty. "The rest don't matter. I'd kill any one of them at a word from you. I love you, Nora. Tell me you love me."

"I can't say that." She winced. "You're hurting me."

"Say you trust me, then."

"I trust you. There, it's done. Hold still a moment." She wrapped her legs around him, then rocked her hips from side to side, settling around him. "This is it, then. Sex."

"Haven't you had it before?"

"In the Academy once, on a bet. It wasn't like this."

"You feel all right?"

"I'm comfortable. Go ahead, Abelard."

But now his curiosity was aroused. "Did they give you the pleasure tap too? I had it once. An interrogation drill."

"Of course they did. But that was nothing human, just white ecstasy." She was sweating. "Come on, darling."

"No, wait a minute." He blinked as she clutched his waist. "I see what you mean. This is stupid, isn't it? We're friends already."

"I want you, Abelard! Come on, finish me!"

"We've proven our point. Besides, I'm filthy!"

"I don't care how fucking filthy you are! For God's sake, hurry!"

He tried to oblige her, then, and worked away mechanically for almost a minute. She bit her lip and groaned in anticipation, rolling her head back. But all the meaning had leached out of it for him. "I can't go on," he said. "I just don't see why we should bother."

"Just let me use you. Come on!"

He tried to think of something arousing. The usual damp whirl of his mind's erotic imagery seemed abstract and distant to him, like something done by another species. He thought of his ex-wife. Sex with Alexandrina had been something like this, an act of politeness, an obligation.

He held still, letting her slam herself against him. At last a cry of desperate pleasure escaped her.

She pulled away, patting sweat from her face and neck with the sleeve of her blouse. She smiled shyly.

Lindsay shrugged. "I see your point. It's a waste of time. I may have some trouble talking the others into it, but if I can reason with them. . . ."

She looked at him hungrily. "I made a mistake. It shouldn't have been this awful for us. I feel selfish now, since you had nothing."

"I feel fine," Lindsay insisted.

"You said you loved me."

"That was just hormones talking. Of course I have deep respect for you, a sense of comradeship. . . . I'm sorry I told you that. Forgive me, I didn't mean it, of course."

"Of course," she said, putting on her blouse.

"Don't be bitter," Lindsay said. "You should take some of this. I'm grateful for it. I see it now in a way I never did before. Love . . . it has no substance. It might be right for other people, other places, another time."

"Not us."

"No. I feel bad about it, now. Reducing our negotiations to a sexual stereotype. You must have found it insulting. And inconvenient."

"I feel sick," she said.

## ESAIRS XII: 24-2-'17

"You're okay now, huh?" the President said, wrinkling his pug nose. "No more of that crap about dryin' up our juice?"

"No, sir, no." Lindsay shook his head, shivering. "I'm better now."

"Good enough. Untie him, Rep Two."

The woman undid Lindsay's ropes, uncoupling him from the cavern wall.

"I lost it," Lindsay said. "I can see that now, but when those suppressants hit me, everything just went crystal clear. Seamless."

"That's okay for you, but we have marriages," Senator 1 said sternly. He clutched the hand of Rep 1.

"I'm sorry," Lindsay said, rubbing his arms. "They're all under that stuff, here. Except Nora, now. I never realized how deep it went. These people are *relentless,* they don't have the decent muddiness and confusion that comes with sex. They all fit together as clean as cogwheels. We'll have to seduce them." He looked them over: Senator 3 with her close-cropped, pumpkinlike head, Justice 3 calmly picking his teeth with a shred of thumbnail. "It won't be easy."

"Relax, State." The President smoothed one of the red plastic ribbons of his openwork sleeve. "You've held this mess together long enough. The fuckers blew away Rep Three."

"There's no proof of that."

"You know they killed him, and we know it. You covered up for them, State, and maybe that was right, but it means you're in too deep. It's not our job to kill all these people. If we wanted to kill 'em, we wouldn't have moved our gun out of the *Consensus* and into this rock."

"But that was our triumph. Everyone's. We got the Armageddon guns shut down, didn't we? After that, anything's possible!"

"We have to kill the threat. That's our assignment. That's what the Mechs will pay us for. We've been exploring all the time you talked your head off. The tunnels are mapped. We know the machinery well enough to wreck it. We'll vandalize the place. Then off to the cartels and the high life."

"You'll leave them here in the wreckage?"

The Speaker of the House grinned tightly. "They can have our gun. We won't need it where we're going."

Justice 2 touched Lindsay's sandaled foot. "It's easy, State. We'll be in Themis Cartel before you know it, juicing in some dogtown. We'll stun the Mechs in this getup." She tugged at the shoulder of her plastic gown with one veiny hand. Two of the Senators snickered.

"When?" Lindsay said.

"You'll know. In the meantime, you just keep a lid on things."

"What if one of them wants to defect with us?" Lindsay said.

"Bring her along," the President said.

## ESAIRS XII: 1-3-'17

Lindsay pulled himself through the darkness, tugging the loading crate behind him. He tapped at the rock as he went. "Paolo! Fazil!"

A stone plug grated aside and Paolo appeared in an eerie glow of candlelight. He pulled himself out to the elbows and leaned toward Lindsay. "Yes? What can we do for you?"

"Let's talk terms, Paolo."

"Is it that orgy business again?"

"We're doing a launch," Lindsay said. He jerked his thumb at the loaded crate behind him. "We could do two launches if we can come to an agreement." Lindsay smiled. "Favor for favor, all right? I'll get you your launch. In return you back me up on the Carnaval proposal."

Paolo's face wrinkled. He rubbed gently at the oozing sores beneath his chin. "Trade our bodies for our art. Forget it, State. The rest would never go along with it. Can you imagine Kleo"—his voice fell—"her legs open to that thug captain?"

"I didn't say it would actually happen," Lindsay said. "I only want you to agree to back me up. Do you want the head launched or don't you?"

Paolo glanced back into the tunnel. "I say yes," came Fazil's voice.

"Then I want one of you to go to the launch room and help set parameters," Lindsay said. "And the other to come with me and help me load the launch ring. And not a word to anyone about our agreement, understood?"

"You get us our launch. Then we'll make you look good with the others. Like you talked us into it with sheer charisma, right?"

"Those are my terms," Lindsay said. "You keep my secrets, I'll keep yours. Now, which of you is going to set the launch?"

"I will," said Paolo. He squirmed past Lindsay in the tunnel and vanished in the darkness, headed for the launch control room.

Fazil peered out. "What's in the crate?" he said.

"Evidence," Lindsay said. "Souvenirs from past raids and the like. Things that might embarrass us, now that we've settled here for good." It was half the truth, as Lindsay understood it. The embarrassment would not come within ESAIRS but at the Mech cartel, when the pirates would have to be on their best behavior. Major cartels like Themis were particular; even in their dogtowns, open piracy was not condoned.

The pirates had loaded the crate without his knowledge and told him to launch it. By this token he knew that their coup was close.

Fazil moved into the tunnel with his candle. "May I look?" He reached past Lindsay and put one hand on the packing crate. A pitch-black roach squeezed head first out between the plastic slats, waving whip-thin antennae as long as a forearm. Fazil snatched his hand back with a hiss of disgust. Lindsay made a quick grab at the roach but missed.

"Filthy," Fazil muttered. "Help me with the head."

Lindsay followed him into the workshop. Together, they heaved and wrestled the massive head out into the corridor. It was a tight fit in the narrow tunnel. "Maybe we should grease it," Lindsay said.

"Paolo's face isn't going into eternity with a snotty nose," said Fazil. He blew out the candle and resealed the workshop. He pushed the sculpture ahead of him, toward the launch ring. Lindsay followed, towing the crate.

The route was devious, traversing gnawed-out rock veins where the air was stale. The ring's loading dock was near the surface of the asteroid, set in one wall of ESAIRS' major industrial center. Here, next to the launch ring, they manufactured the decoys.

The decoy complex was a grapelike cluster of fermentation bags, connected by flaccid hydraulic tubes, anchored with guy ropes and ringed by harsh banks of bluish grow-lights. The cluster hung in midair, its translucent chambers churning sluggishly.

The complex had not been shut down completely; that would have killed the wetware. But its production was cut almost to nothing. The blowpipes had been unplugged from their output duct into the launch ring. Instead of thin decoy film, they were producing a thick, colorless froth. The air reeked with the sharp fever stench of hot plastic.

The Family's robot was on duty. It stopped in mid-program as Fazil floated past it, clutching the head. As Lindsay drifted by, the robot crouched quietly, a powder bellows gripped in its forward manipulators. Its huge single eye tilted to follow him in movement, with a ratchetlike clicking.

The robot was all wires and joints, its six skeletal limbs made of lightweight foamed metal. It was bigger than Lindsay. Its brain and motor were shielded in its torso, behind barrel-like ribs. The forward end held the sensors and two long, jointed pincer arms. A cross-shaped junction of four swiveling limbs sprouted from its aft end, set that way for work in free-fall. It had a rotary spindle tail for drilling.

The robot lacked the smoothness of a Mech unit, but there was an alarming liveliness about it. It was like an animated skeleton, a vivisected animal stripped down to jumpy knee-jerk reflex.

When Lindsay drifted out of range, the robot clicked back into motion, kicked off a wall, and plugged its bellows into the wet duct of a fermentation bag.

Fazil crawled over the head and caught it against the wall.

The launching ring had an airlock of translucent plastic. Fazil plucked a tightly wrapped green spacesuit from the wall and shook it out. He zipped himself into it and unzipped the airlock wall. He stepped inside.

Lindsay passed him the crate.

Fazil zipped the airlock shut and opened the loading chamber. A curved rectangular section of wall slid up on spring-loaded exterior hinges. Air gusted out into the vacuum of the launch ring. The airlock's flimsy walls sucked in, clinging like soap film to an interior support trellis.

Five huge roaches and a cloud of smaller ones burst from the crate's interior, kicking in the vacuum. Fazil shrieked silently behind his transparent faceplate. He batted around his head as the roaches convulsed, their paper-thin wings beating in crippled angles. Decompression bloated their abdomens. Froth oozed from their joints and rumps.

A roach clung vomiting to the plastic, near Lindsay's face. It had been eating something within the crate. Something viscous and red.

Faint wisps of steam were coming from the crate. Fazil didn't notice; he was swatting the roaches out into the launch ring.

Fazil stepped through the hatchway into the ring and pulled the crate after him. He wrestled it into the launch cage.

He emerged, then knocked the last of the dead insects through the chamber hatch and locked it shut. A green ready-light came on as the hatch door sealed the circuit. An LED raced through numbers as launch power hit the magnets.

Fazil pulled the entrance zipper and air rushed in. The plastic airlock flapped like a sail. Fazil climbed out, shaking. His shouts were muffled by the suit. "Did you see that?" He pulled his own zip down to mid-chest. "What was in there? What were they eating?"

"I didn't see them pack the crate," Lindsay said. "Could have been anything."

Fazil examined the smeared sleeve of his suit. "Looks like blood."

Lindsay leaned closer. "Doesn't smell like blood."

"This is evidence," Fazil said, tapping the suit.

Lindsay was thoughtful. The pirates had lied to him. They had tried to be clever, as clever as the Shapers. They had tried to make someone disappear. "It might be best, Fazil, if we launched that suit."

"Have you seen Ian today?" Fazil said.

"I wasn't looking for him."

They eyed one another. Lindsay said nothing. Fazil glanced quickly, warily, over one shoulder at the LED. "It's launched away," he said.

"If you'll launch the suit," Lindsay said, "I'll scrub the inside of the airlock."

"I'm not launching this suit with the head," Fazil said.

"You could feed it into one of the chambers," Lindsay said, pointing. "The fermentation vats." He thought fast. "If you'll do that, I'll help you set this complex to full capacity. You can make decoys again." Lindsay pulled another suit from the wall and shook it out. "We'll launch the head. We'll dump the suit. We'll do those two things first, and then we'll talk. All right?"

The moment to attack was when Lindsay had his legs half trapped in the suit. That moment passed, and once again Lindsay knew he had bought time.

He and Fazil manhandled the head into the airlock. Fazil zipped the lock shut behind the two of them. Lindsay opened the rectangular hatch.

Light spilled into the launch ring's glassy interior, gleaming off its inset copper tracks. The iron bars of the launch cage shone with a faint rime of condensed steam from the body that had been within the crate.

Lindsay stepped into the launch ring. He shoved the head within the cage and set the clamps.

Fazil's shadow passed across the light. He was slamming the hatch. Lindsay wheeled and jumped.

He got his right arm through. The hatch door bounded off flesh and bone and Lindsay's suit began at once to fill with blood.

Lindsay snarled as he jammed his head and shoulders past the hatch. He snagged Fazil's leg with his left hand. His fingertips dug deep into the socket of the Shaper's ankle and he smashed the man's shin against the sharp edge of the hatch. Bone grated and Fazil, levered backward, lost his grip.

Lindsay slithered out into the airlock, still grappling, and jacked his foot into Fazil's crotch. As Fazil convulsed, Lindsay seized the man's leg and bent it double, jamming one arm behind Fazil's knee. He braced himself against the Shaper's body and yanked upward, wrenching the man's thighbone from its socket.

In agony, Fazil scrabbled for a hold. His hand struck the edge of the hatch and slammed it shut. The launch ring's circuit sealed and the ready-light came on.

Lindsay held the leg and twisted. Two globes of his own blood floated up within his faceplate. He sneezed, blinded, and Fazil kicked him in the neck. He lost his grip, and the Shaper attacked.

He threw his arms around Lindsay's chest with the panic strength of desperation. Lindsay wheezed, and black unconsciousness loomed close for four loud heartbeats. Then he kicked wildly, and his foot caught the edge of the airlock's support trellis.

They spun, grappling. Lindsay slammed his elbow into the side of the Shaper's head. The grip loosened. Lindsay swung his free arm over Fazil's head and seized his neck in a hammerlock. Fazil squeezed again and Lindsay's ribs bent in the power of his Shaper-strengthened arms.

Lindsay locked eyes with him through his blood-spattered faceplate. Lindsay's face rippled hideously. Fazil went wall-eyed in terror and tried to claw his way free. Lindsay broke his neck.

Lindsay was panting. The suits had no air tanks; they were for brief exposures only. He had to get out into air.

He turned for the airlock's exit. Kleo was there. Her eyes were dark with fascination and terror. She held the zipper's outside tag.

Lindsay stared at her, blinking as a microglobe of blood clung to his lashes. Kleo pulled her favorite weapon: a needle and thread.

Lindsay kicked off from Fazil's body. He fumbled for the tag. With a few deft moves, Kleo sewed the zipper shut.

Lindsay pulled at it frantically. The slender pink thread was like steel wire. He shook his head: "No!" Vacuum surrounded him. He was cut off; the words that had always saved him could not leap the gap.

She waited to watch him die. Overhead, the LED raced through its readout. The lights were dimming. A launch off the ecliptic required full power.

Lindsay pulled left-handed at the hatch. There was a faint vibration through his fingers. He kicked the hatch, savagely, three times, and something gave. He pulled with all his strength. The hatch opened, just a finger's width.

Safety fuses tripped. And all the lights went out.

The hatch opened easily, then. The darkness was total.

He didn't know how long it would take the circling launch cage to grate to a stop within the ring. If it were still whirring by at klicks per second, it would shear his arm or leg off as neatly as a laser.

He couldn't wait long. The air inside the suit was thick with his own breath and the reek of blood. He made up his mind and thrust his head into the ring.

He lived.

Now he faced another problem. The cage was resting within the ring, somewhere, blocking it. If he reached it on his way to the Outside, he would have to turn around, wasting air. Left or right?

Left. Breathing shallowly, favoring his arm, he leaped along the inside of the ring. He cradled his arms against his chest, using his legs, bounding, somersaulting, skidding.

Three hundred meters—that was half the length of the ring. All he would have to go. But what if the camouflage plastic was sealing the ring's launch exit? What if he had already passed the exit in the blackness, noticing nothing?

Starlight. Lindsay leaped upward frantically, remembering only at the last moment to catch himself on the rim. ESAIRS' gravity was so weak that his leap would have put him into circumsolar orbit.

Once again he was outside the asteroid, amid streaks of charred black and off-white blast sumps.

He leaped across a buckled crater, almost missing the far rim. When he grappled along a stretch of pumice, rock powdered under his fingers and went into slow orbit just above the surface.

He was gasping when he found the second airlock: plastic film dappled with camouflage, inset into the surface of ESAIRS where the Family's first drill had bitten in. He brushed the film aside and twisted the hatch wheel. His right arm was bleeding steadily. It felt broken again.

The hatch popped free. He slipped into the airlock and slammed the outside hatch behind him. Then there was another. He was panting steadily; each lungful offered less, and he tasted inhaled blood.

The second hatch opened. He pulled himself through, and there was a sudden flurry of movement in darkness. He heard his suit rip. Cold steel nicked his throat, his legs were seized, and he screamed as hands in the blackness grabbed his wounded arm and twisted.

"Talk!"

"Mr. President!" Lindsay gasped at once. "Mr. President!"

The knife against his throat drew back. He heard a deafening buzz-saw grinding, and sparks flew. In the sudden gory light Lindsay saw the President, the Speaker of the House, the Chief Justice, and Senator 3.

The sparks went out. The Speaker had held the blade of her small power saw against a length of pipe.

The President ripped the head from Lindsay's suit. "The arm, the arm," Lindsay yelped. The Chief Justice released it; Senator 3 released his legs. Lindsay breathed deeply, filling his lungs with air.

"Fucking preemptive strike," the President muttered. "Hate 'em."

"They tried to kill me," Lindsay said. "The equipment—you destroyed it? We can leave now?"

"Something tipped 'em off," the President growled. "We were in the launch center with Paolo. Learning how to smash the launch controls. Then Agnes and Nora show up. Supposed to be sleeping. And all of a sudden, black as fire—"

"Power blackout," said the Speaker.

"I yell ambush," said the President. "Only it's black. They have the advantage: fewer of them, less chance of hitting their own. So, I go for machinery. Sleeve knife into the circuitry. We hear Second Senator howl, meat breaks open."

"Something wet touched my face," the Chief Justice said. His ancient voice was heavy with doomed satisfaction. "The air was full of blood."

"They were armed," the President said. "I caught this in the scuffle. Feel it, State."

In the darkness, the President pressed something into Lindsay's left hand. It was the size of his palm—a flattened disk of dense stone, wrapped in braided thread. Part of it was sticky.

"Had 'em taped to their ribs, I think. Swinging weapons. Bludgeons. Stranglers. Those threads are thin enough to cut. Opened my thumb to the bone when I caught it."

"Where are the rest of us?" Lindsay said.

"We got a contingency plan. The two Reps were cleaning up after Ian— they're aboard the *Consensus* now, getting ready to lift."

"Why'd you kill Ian?"

"Kill him?" the Speaker said. "There's no proof. He evaporated."

"The FMD don't take a wound without returning it," the President said. "We thought we'd be gone by morning, and we thought, Hah, let 'em think he defected with us! Cute, huh?" He snorted. "The Senate were with us but two got lost. They'll show up here, 'cause this is rendezvous. Justices Two and Three are looting, lifting some of that hot Shaper wetware. Good loot for us. We figured— we seize the exit. If we have to, we jump to the *Consensus,* naked. We could make it with just nosebleeds and gut ache, hard vacuum thirty seconds."

Tapping echoed down the corridor. It had crept up imperceptibly under the sound of their voices. It continued with faint, rhythmic precision, the flat click of plastic against stone.

"Aw, shit," said the President.

"I'll go," said the Chief Justice.

"It's nothing," Senator 3 said. "A blower settling." Lindsay heard the rattle of her tool belt.

"I'm gone," the Chief Justice said. Lindsay felt a light movement of air as the old Mechanist floated past him.

Fifteen seconds passed in darkness. "We need light," the Speaker hissed. "I'll use the saw and—"

The tapping stopped. The Chief Justice called out. "I have it! It's a piece of—"

A sudden nasty crunch cut him off.

"Justice!" the President cried. They rushed down the corridor, bumping and colliding blindly.

When they reached the spot, the Speaker pulled her saw, and sparks flew. The noisemaker was a simple flap of stiff plastic, glued to the mouth of a branching tunnel and tugged by a long thread. The assassin—Paolo—had waited deep within the tunnel. When he'd heard the old Mechanist's voice he had fired his weapon, a slingshot. A heavy stone cube—Paolo's six-sided die—was half buried in the dead pirate's fractured skull.

In the brief blazing light of sparks, Lindsay saw the dead man's head covered by a flattened mass of blood, held by surface tension to the skin around the wound.

"We could leave," Lindsay said.

"Not without our own," the President said. "And not leaving the one who did this. They got only five left."

"Four," Lindsay said. "I killed Fazil. Three, if I can talk to Nora."

"No time for talk," the President said. "You're wounded, State. Stay here and guard the airlock. When you see the others, tell 'em we've gone to kill the four."

Lindsay forced himself to speak. "If Nora surrenders, Mr. President, I hope that you'll—"

"Mercy was *his* job," said the President. Lindsay heard him tug at the dead judge's body. "You got a weapon, State?"

"No."

"Take this, then." He handed Lindsay the dead man's mechanical arm. "If one of 'em strays by here, kill them with the old man's fist."

Lindsay clutched the cabled ridges of the stiff prosthetic wrist. The others went quickly, with a click, a rustle, and the whisper of calloused skin against stone. Lindsay floated back up the tunnel to the airlock, bouncing along the smooth stone with knees and shoulders, thinking of Nora.

The old woman wouldn't die, that was the horror of it. If it had only been as quick and clean as Kleo had said it would, Nora could have borne it, endured it as she endured all things. But in the darkness, when she whipped the weighted sash around the pirate's neck and pulled, it had not been quiet, it had not been clean.

The old woman—Judge 2, the pirates called her—her throat was a mass of cartilage and gristle, tough as wire beneath her skin's false smoothness. Twice, when Nora thought she was dead at last, the pirate woman had lurched shudderingly into life again with a tortured rasp in the darkness. Nora's wrists bled freely from the old woman's splintered nails. The body stank.

Nora smelled her own sweat. Her armpits were a tormenting mass of rashes. She floated quietly in the pitch-black launch control room, her bare feet perched on the dead woman's shoulders, one end of the sash in each hand.

She had not fought well when the pirates had launched their strike in the sudden blackout. She had hit someone, swinging her stone bola, but then lost it in the struggle. Agnes had fought hard and been wounded by the Speaker's handsaw. Paolo had fought like a champion.

Kleo murmured a password from the door, and in a few moments there was light in the room. "I told you they worked," Paolo said.

Kleo held the plastic candle away; the sodium at the tip of the wick was still sputtering where it had ignited. The waxy plastic reeked as the wick burned down. "I brought all you made," Kleo told Paolo. "You're a bright boy, dear."

Paolo nodded proudly. "My luck beat this contingency. And I've killed *two*."

"You made the candles," Agnes said. "*I* said they wouldn't work." She looked at him adoringly. "You're the one, Paolo. Give me orders."

Nora saw the dead pirate's face in candlelight. She unwrapped the strangling sash and tied it around her waist.

She felt another siege of weakness. Her eyes filled with tears and she felt a sudden horror and regret for the woman she had killed.

It was the drugs Abelard had given her. She had been a fool to take that first injection. Firing up with aphrodisiacs had been a surrender, not just to the enemy but to those bits and pieces of temptation and doubt that lurked within her. Throughout her life, the brighter her convictions had burned, the darker these shadows had been, flitting, creeping.

On her own, she might have held her ground. But there was the fatal example of the other diplomats. The traitors. The Academy had never officially spoken of them, leaving that to the covert world of gossip and rumor that boiled unceasingly in every Shaper colony. The rumors festered in darkness, taking on all the distorted forms of the forbidden.

In her own mind, Nora had become a criminal: sexual, ideological, professional. Things had happened to her that she dared not speak of, even to Kleo. Her Family knew nothing of the diplomatic training, the burning glare in every muscle, the attack on face and brain that had made her own body into an alien object before she turned sixteen.

If it had been anyone but another diplomat, she could have fought and died with the conviction and serenity that Kleo showed. But she had faced him now and understood. Abelard was not as bright as she was, but he was resilient and quick. She could become what he was. It was the first real alternative she had ever known.

"I gave us light," Paolo bragged. He whirled his bola in a twisting figure-eight, catching the string on his padded forearms. "I played odds, even the farthest. I beat Ian, I beat Fazil, and I killed two." Sleeve ties flailed at his elbows as he slapped his chest. "I say ambush, ambush, ambush!" The bola whirled to a stop, wrapping his arm, and he pulled his slingshot from his belt.

"They mustn't escape," Kleo said. Her face was warm and calm in the candlelight, framed by the fringed gold crown of her hairnet. "If survivors leave, they'll bring others. We can live, darlings. They're *stupid*. And they're split. We've lost two, they seven." A flicker of pain crossed her face. "The diplomat was quick, but odds say he died in the launch ring. The others we can outflank, like the Judges."

"Where are the two Representatives?" said Agnes. The Speaker's handsaw had slashed her above the left knee; she was pale but still full of fight. "We have to get the rogue genetic. She's trouble."

"What about the wetware?" Nora said. "It'll stale if we stay powered down. We have to get power back."

"They'd know we were in the power plant!" Paolo said. "One could start it, the others wait in ambush! Strike and fall back, strike and fall back!"

"First we hide the bodies," Kleo said. She turned, bracing her feet near the doorway, and tugged hand over hand on a line. The third Judge appeared, his wrinkled neck almost slashed through by Kleo's wire-thin garotte. The syringes on his belt were filled with stolen wetware. Like Judge 2, he had been caught at his theft.

Paolo peeled camo plastic from the launch room's secret alcove. The bodies of Senators 1 and 2 already floated within it, killed by Agnes and Paolo. They shoved the other dead inside, reluctant to touch them. "They'll know they're here," Agnes said. "They'll smell them." She sneezed violently.

"They'll think it's themselves," Paolo said, smoothing the filmy false wall back into place.

"To the tokamak," Kleo said. "I'll take the candles; Agnes, you take point."

"All right." Agnes stripped off her blouse and heavy hairnet. She attached them together with a few loose stitches. Puffing out in free-fall, they looked like a human form in the dimness. She slipped into the narrow corridor, pushing the decoy ahead of her with her extended arm.

The others followed, Nora as rear guard.

At each intersection they halted, listening, smelling. Agnes would push her clothes ahead, then peer quickly around the lip of the opening. Kleo would pass her the candle and she would check for ambushers.

As they neared the tokamak power plant, Agnes sneezed loudly again. After a moment Nora smelled it as well: an appalling alien stench. "What is it?" she whispered to Kleo, ahead of her.

"Fire, I think. Smoke." Kleo was grim. "The Reshaped one is smart, I think she has gone to the tokamak."

"Look!" Agnes whispered loudly. From the corridor branching to their left, a thin gray stream undulated in the candle's light. Agnes ran her fingers through it, and the smoke broke into dissipating wisps. Agnes coughed rawly and caught herself against the wall, her naked ribs heaving silently.

Kleo blew out the candle. In the darkness they saw a feeble gleam reflected along the bends and curves of the tunnel's smooth stone.

"Fire," Kleo said. For the first time, Nora heard fear in her leader's voice. "I'll go first."

"No!" Agnes brushed her lips against Kleo's ear and whispered to her rapidly. The two women embraced, and Agnes sneaked forward, leaving her clothes and pressing herself against the tunnel wall. When Nora followed the others she felt Agnes's smeared sweat cold against the stone.

Nora peered behind her, guarding their back. Where was Abelard? He wasn't dead, she thought. If only he were here now, with his incessant glibness, and his gray eyes glowing with an animal's determination to survive. . . .

A sudden sharp *clack* echoed up the tunnel. A second passed, Agnes screamed, and the air filled with the sharp metallic stench of acid. There were howls of pain and hatred, the snap of Paolo's slingshot. Nora's back and shoulders tightened so suddenly that they cramped in agony and she scrambled head first down the tunnel, deafened by her own screams.

The rogue genetic whirled in the red gleam of firelight, slashing Agnes across the face with the spout of her weapon, a bellows. The air was full of flying globes of corrosive acid, drawn from a wetware tank. Steam curled from Agnes's naked chest. To the side, Kleo grappled, slashing and kicking, with the stocky Rep 2, whose arm was broken by Paolo's shot. Paolo was pulling another heavy stone from his belt pouch.

Nora yanked the sash from her waist with a silken hiss and launched herself at the enemy Shaper. The woman saw her coming. She wrapped a leg around Agnes's throat, crushing it, and swung forward, arms spread to grapple.

Nora swung her weighted sash at the woman's face. She caught it, grinned with her crooked teeth, and darted a hand at Nora's face, two fingers spread to spear her eyes. Nora twisted and the nails drew blood from her cheeks. She kicked, missed, kicked with the other leg, felt a sudden searing pain as the combat-trained pirate sank her fingers into the joint of her knee. She was strong, with a genetic's smooth, deceptive strength. Nora fumbled at the other end of the sash and smashed the weight against the pirate's cheek. Rep 1 grinned and Nora felt something snap as her kneecap soggily gave way. Suddenly blood sprayed across her as Paolo's slung shot broke the woman's jaw.

Her mouth hung open, bloody, in the firelight, as the pirate woman fought with the sudden wild strength of desperation. The back of her heel slammed bruisingly into Nora's solar plexus as she launched herself at Paolo. Paolo was ready; his bola whipped overhand from nowhere with the force of a hatchet, taking the woman's ear off and slashing deep into her collarbone. She faltered and Paolo stamped her body into the wall.

The pirate's head cracked against the stone and Paolo was on her at once, slashing into her throat with the bola's cord. Behind him Kleo and the other woman struggled in midair, the pirate flailing with legs and a broken arm as Kleo's braced thumbs pressed relentlessly into the woman's throat.

Nora, winded by the kick, struggled for breath. Her whole rib cage locked in a sudden radiating cramp. Somehow she forced a thin gasp of smoky air into her lungs, wheezed, then breathed again, feeling as if her chest were full of molten lead. Agnes died before her eyes, skin steaming from the acid spray.

Paolo finished the Shaper woman. Kleo was still strangling the second woman, who had died; Paolo slammed his bola into the back of the dead woman's head and Kleo released her, yanking her stiffened hands away. She rubbed them together as if spreading on lotion, breathing hard. "Put out that fire," she said.

Paolo approached the flaming, gluey mass of hay and plastics carefully. He shrugged out of his heavy blouse, which was speckled with pinholes of acid, and threw it over the fire as if trapping an animal. He stamped it vindictively, and there was darkness. Kleo spat on the sodium tip of another candle, which sputtered into life.

"Not good," she said. "I'm hurt. Nora?"

Nora looked down at her leg, felt it. The kneecap was loose beneath the skin. There was no pain yet, only a shocked numbness. "My knee," she said, and coughed. "She killed Agnes."

"There's just three left," Kleo said. "The Speaker, her man, and Senator Three. We have them. My poor precious darlings." She threw her arms around Paolo, who stiffened at the sudden gesture but then relaxed, cradling his head in the hollow at Kleo's neck and shoulder.

"I'll start the power plant," Nora said. She drifted to the wall panel and tapped switches for the preliminary sequence.

"Paolo and I will cover the entrances and wait for them," Kleo said. "Nora, you go to the radio room. Raise the Council, report in. We'll regroup there." She gave Nora the candle and left.

Nora stuck the candle above the tokamak's control board and got it up into stage one. A bluish glow seeped through the polarized blast shield as magnetic fields uncurled within the chamber. The tokamak flickered uneasily as it bootstrapped its way up to fusion velocities. False sunlight flared yellow as the ion streams collided and burned. The field stabilized, and suddenly all the lights were on.

Holding it warily, Nora snuffed the candle against the wall.

Paolo brushed petulantly at the acid blisters on his unprotected hands. "I'm the one, Nora," he said. "The one percent destined for survival."

"I know that, Paolo."

"I'll remember you, though. All of you. I loved you, Nora. I wanted to tell you one more time."

"It's a privilege to live in your memory, Paolo."

"Goodbye, Nora."

"If I ever had luck," Nora said, "it's yours."

He smiled, hefting his slingshot.

Nora left. She skidded quickly through the tunnels, holding one leg stiff. Waves of pain dug into her, knotting her body. Without the spinal crab, she could no longer stop the cramps.

The pirates had been through the radio room. They had smashed about them wildly in the darkness. The transmitters were saw-torn wreckage; the table-top console had been wrenched off and flung aside.

Fluid leaked from the liquid crystal display. Nora pulled needle and thread from her hairnet and sewed up the gash in the screen. The CPU was still working; there were signals incoming from the dishes outside. But the deciphering programs were down. Ring Council transmissions were gibberish.

She picked up a general frequency propaganda broadcast. The slashed television still worked, though it blurred around the stitches.

And there it was: the outside world. There was not much to it: words and pictures, lines on a screen. She ran her fingertips gently over the scalding pain in her knee.

She could not believe what the faces on the screen were telling her, what the images showed. It was as if the little screen in its days of darkness had fermented somehow, and the world behind it was frothing over, all its poisons wetwared into wine. The faces of the Shaper politicos were alight with astounded triumph.

She watched the screen, transfixed. The shocked public statements of Mechanist leaders: broken men, frightened women, their routines and systems stripped away. The Mech armor of plans and contingencies had been picked off like a scab, showing the raw flesh of their humanity. They gabbled, they scrambled for control, each contradicting the last. Some with tight smiles that looked wired on by surgery, others misty-eyed with secondhand religious awe, gesturing vaguely, their faces bright as children's.

And the doyens of the Shaper academic-military complex: the smooth-faced Security types, facile, triumphant, still too pleased at the amazing coup to show their ingrained suspicion. And the intelligentsia, dazzled by potential, speculating wildly, their objectivity in rags.

Then she saw one. There were more, a dozen of them. They were *huge.* Their legs alone were as tall as men, enormous corded masses of muscle, bone, and tendon under slickly polished corrugated hide. Scales. Brown scaled hide showed under their clothing: they wore skirts, glittering beads on wire. Their mighty chests were bare, with great keelbone ridges of sternum. Compared to the treelike legs and the massive jutting tails, their arms were long and slender, with quick, swollen-tipped fingers and oddly socketed thumbs. Their heads were huge, the size of a man's torso, split with great cavernous grins full of thumb-sized flat peg teeth. They seemed to have no ears, and their black eyeballs, the size of fists, were shielded under pebbly lids and grayish nictitating membranes. Ribbed, iridescent frills draped the backs of their heads.

There were people talking to them, holding cameras. Shaper people. They seemed to be hunched in fear before the aliens; their backs were bent, they shuffled subserviently from one to another. It was gravity, Nora realized. The aliens used a heavy gravity.

They were real! They moved with relaxed, ponderous grace. Some were holding clipboards. Others were talking, with fluted, birdlike tongues as long as a forearm.

By size alone they dominated the proceedings. There was nothing formalized or stagy about it; even the solemn narration could not hide the essential nature of the meeting. The aliens were not frightened or even much impressed. They had no bluster, no mystique. They were *businesslike.* Like tax collectors.

Paolo burst in suddenly, his eyes wild, his long hair matted with blood. "Quickly! They're right behind me!" He glanced around. "Give me that panel cover!"

"It's over, Paolo!"

"Not yet!" Paolo snatched the broad console top from midair. Wiring trailed behind it. He catapulted across the room and slammed the console across the tunnel entrance. Placed flat against it, it formed a crude barricade; Paolo whipped a tube of epoxy from his belt and glued the console top against the stone.

There was a gap to one side; Paolo pulled his slingshot and fired down the corridor. They heard a distant howl. Paolo jammed his face against the gap and screamed with laughter.

"The television, Paolo! News from the Council! The siege is over!"

"The *siege?*" Paolo said, glancing back at her. "What the fuck does that have to do with us?"

"The siege, the war," she said. "There never *was* any war, it's the new party line. There were just . . . misunderstandings. Bottlenecks." Paolo ignored her, staring down the tunnel, readying another shot. "We were never soldiers. Nobody was ever trying to kill anyone. The human race is peaceful, Paolo, just— *good trading partners.* . . . Aliens are here, Paolo. The aliens."

"Oh, God," Paolo moaned. "I just have to kill two more, that's all, and I already winged the woman. Just help me kill them first, then you can tell me anything you want." He pressed his shoulder against the barricade, waiting for the epoxy to set.

Nora drifted over him and shouted through one of the console's instrument holes into the darkness. "Mr. President! This is the diplomat! I want a parley!"

There was silence for a moment. Then: "You crazy bitch! Come out and die!"

"It's over, Mr. President! The siege is lifted! The System is at peace, do you understand? Aliens, Mr. President! Aliens have arrived, they've been here for days already!"

The President laughed. "Sure. Come on out, baby. Send that little fucker with the slingshot out first." She heard the sudden whine of the power saw.

Paolo pushed her aside with a snarl and fired down the hall. They heard half a dozen sharp clicks as the shot ricocheted far down the tunnel. The President cawed triumphantly. "We're gonna eat you," he said, very seriously. "We're gonna eat your fuckin' livers." He lowered his voice. "Take 'em out, State."

Nora clawed past Paolo and screamed aloud. "Abelard! Abelard, it's true, I swear it by everything between us! Abelard, you're not stupid, let us live! I want to live—"

Paolo clamped his hand over her mouth and pulled her back. She clung to the barricade, now glued firm, staring down the hall. A white form was drifting there. A spacesuit. Not a Mavrides one, but one of the bloated armored ones from the *Red Consensus.*

Paolo's slingshot was useless against the suit. "This is it," he muttered.

"The cusp." He released Nora and pulled a candle and a flat bladder of liquid from within his blouse. He wrapped the bladder around the candle, cinching it with a sleeve-tie. He hefted the bomb. "Now they burn."

Nora threw her sash around his neck. She put her good knee into his back and pulled savagely. Paolo made a sound like broken pipes and kicked away from the entrance. He clawed at the sash. He was strong. He was the one with luck.

Nora pulled harder. Abelard was alive. The idea gave her strength. She pulled harder. Paolo was pulling just as hard. His fists were locked around the belt's gray fabric so hard that blood oozed from his nail-cut palms in little crescent blisters.

There were screams down the hall. Screams and the sound of the power saw.

And now the knot that had never left her shoulders had spread into her arms and Paolo was pulling against muscle that had set like iron. He was not breathing in the sudden silence that followed. The wrinkled ridge of the sash had vanished into his neck. He was dead, still pulling.

She let the ends of the sash slide through her cramped fingers. Paolo twisted slowly in free-fall, his face blackened, his arms locked in place. He seemed to be strangling himself.

A gauntleted hand, drenched in blood, came through the crescent hole at the side of the barricade. There was a muffled buzzing from within the spacesuit. He was trying to talk.

She rushed to his side. He leaned his head against the outside of the barricade, shouting within the helmet. "Dead!" he said. "They're dead!"

"Take off the helmet," she said.

He shrugged his right shoulder within the suit. "My arm!" he said.

She stuck one hand through the crevice and helped him twist the helmet off. It popped free with a suck of air and the familiar reek of his body. There were half-dried scabs of blood under his nostrils and one in his left ear. He had been decompressed.

Carefully, she ran her hand across his sweating cheek. "We're alive, aren't we?"

"They were going to kill you," he said. "I couldn't let them."

"The same for me." She looked backward at Paolo. "It was like suicide to kill him. I think I'm dead."

"No. We belong to each other. Say so, Nora."

"Yes, we do," she said, and pressed her face blindly against the gap between them. He kissed her with the bright salt taste of blood.

The demolition had been thorough. Kleo had finished the job. She had crept out in a spacesuit and soaked the inside of the *Red Consensus* with sticky contact venom.

But Lindsay had gone there before her. He had leaped the gap of naked space, decompressing himself, to get one of the armored spacesuits. He'd caught

Kleo in the control room. In her thin suit she was no match for him; he'd ripped her suit open and she'd died of the poison.

Even the Family's robot had suffered. The two Reps had lobotomized it while passing through the decoy room. Operations by the launch ring ran at manic speed, the brain-stripped robot loading ton after ton of carbon ore into the overstuffed and belching wetware. A frothing mass of plastic output gushed into the launch ring, which was itself ruined by the skidding launch cage. But that was the least of their problems.

The worst was sepsis. The organisms brought from the Zaibatsu wreaked havoc on the delicate biosystems of ESAIRS XII. Kleo's garden was a leprous parody five weeks after the slaughter.

The attenuated blossoms of the Shaper garden mildewed and crumbled at the touch of raw humanity. The vegetation took strange forms as it suffered and contorted, its stems corkscrewing in rot-dusted perversions of growth. Lindsay visited it daily, and his very presence hastened the corruption. The place smelled of the Zaibatsu, and his lungs ached with its nostalgic stench.

He had brought it with him. No matter how fast he moved, he dragged behind him a fatal slipstream of the past.

He and Nora would never be free of it. It was not just the contagion, or his useless arm. Nor the galaxy of rashes that disfigured Nora for days, crusting her perfect skin and filling her eyes with flinty stoicism. It dated back to the training they had shared, the damage done to them. It made them partners, and Lindsay realized that this was the finest thing that life had ever offered him.

He thought about death as he watched the Shaper robot at its task. Ceaselessly, tirelessly, it loaded ore into the distended guts of the decoy wetware. After the two of them had smothered, this machine would continue indefinitely in its hyperactive parody of life. He could have shut it down, but he felt a kinship with it. Its headlong, blind persistence cheered him somehow. And the fact that it was pumping tons of frothing plastic into the launch ring, ruining it, meant that the pirates had won. He could not bear to rob them of that useless victory.

As the air grew fouler they were forced to retreat, sealing the tunnels behind them. They stayed near the last operative industrial gardens, shallowly breathing the hay-scented air, making love and trying to heal each other.

With Nora, he reentered Shaper life, with its subtleties, its allusions, its painful brilliance. And slowly, with him, her sharpest edges were smoothed. She lost the worst kinks, the hardest knots, the most insupportable levels of stress.

They turned down the power so that the tunnels grew colder, retarding the spread of the contagion. At night they clung together for warmth, swaddled in a carpet-sized shroud that Nora compulsively embroidered.

She would not give up. She had a core of unnatural energy that Lindsay could not match. For days she had worked on repairs in the radio room, though she knew it was useless.

Shaper Ring Security had stopped broadcasting. Their military outposts had become embarrassments. Mechanists were evacuating them and repatriating their Shaper crews to the Ring Council with exquisite diplomatic courtesy. There had never been any war. No one was fighting. The cartels were buying out their pirate clients and hastily pacifying them.

All this was waiting for them if they could only raise their voices. But their broadcast equipment was ruined; the circuits were irreplaceable, and the two of them were not technicians.

Lindsay had accepted death. No one would come for them; they would assume that the outpost was wiped out. Eventually, he thought, someone would check, but not for years.

One night, after making love, Lindsay stayed up, toying with the dead pirate's mechanical arm. It fascinated him, and it was a solace; by dying young, he thought, he had at least escaped this. His own right arm had lost almost all feeling. The nerves had deteriorated steadily since the incident with the gun, and his battle wounds had only hastened it.

"Those damned guns," he said aloud. "Someone will find this place someday. We ought to tear those fucking guns apart, to show the world that we had decency. I'd do it but I can't bear to touch them."

Nora was drowsy. "So what? They don't work."

"Sure, they're disarmed." That had been one of his triumphs. "But they could be armed again. They're evil, darling. We should smash them."

"If you care that much . . ." Nora's eyes opened. "Abelard. What if we fired one?"

"No," he said at once.

"What if we blew up the *Consensus* with the particle beam? Someone would see."

"See what? That we were criminals?"

"In the past it would just be dead pirates. Business as usual. But now it would be a scandal. Someone would have to come after us. To see that it never happened again."

"You'd risk this facade of peace that they're showing the aliens? Just on the chance that someone would rescue us? Fire, imagine what they'd do to us when they came."

"What? Kill us? We're dead already. I want us to live."

"As criminals? Despised by everyone?"

Nora smiled bitterly. "That's nothing new for me."

"No, Nora. There are limits."

She caressed him. "I understand."

Two nights later he woke in terror as the asteroid shook. Nora was gone. At first he thought it was a meteor strike, a rare but terrifying event. He listened for the hiss of blowout, but the tunnels were still sound.

When he saw Nora's face he realized the truth. "You fired the gun."

She was shaken. "I cast the *Consensus* loose before I shot it. I went out on the surface. There's something weird there, Abelard. Plastic has been leaking out of the launch ring into space."

"I don't want to hear about it."

"I had to do it. For us. Forgive me, darling. I swear I'll never deceive you again."

He brooded. "You think they'll come?"

"It's a chance. I wanted a chance for us." She was distracted. "Tons of plastic. Squeezing out like paste. Like a huge worm."

"An accident," Lindsay said. "We'll have to tell them that it was an accident."

"I'll destroy the gun now." She looked at him guiltily.

"What's done is done." He smiled sadly and reached toward her. "Let it wait."

## ESAIRS XII: 17-7-'17

Somewhere in his dreams Lindsay heard a repeated pounding. As always, Nora woke first and was instantly alert. "Noise, Abelard."

Lindsay woke painfully, his eyelids gummy. "What is it? A blowout?"

She slipped out of the sheets, launching herself off his hip with one bare foot. She hit the lights. "Get up, darling. Whatever it is, we're meeting it head on."

It was not the way Lindsay would have preferred to meet death but he was willing to go along with her. He pulled on drawstring pants and a poncho.

"There's no breeze," she said as he struggled with a complex Shaper knot. "It's not decompression."

"Then it's a rescue! The Mechs!"

They hurried through darkened tunnels to the airlock.

One of their rescuers—he must have been a courageous one—had managed to force his vast bulk through the airlock and into the loading room. He was picking fussily at the huge birdlike toes of his spacesuit as Lindsay peered out of the access tunnel, squinting and shielding his eyes.

The alien had a powerful searchlight mounted on the nasal bridge of his cavernous spacesuit helmet. The light gushing from it was as vivid as a welding torch: harsh and electric blue, heavily tinged with ultraviolet. The spacesuit was brown and gray, dotted with input sockets and accordion-ribbed around the alien's joints.

The light swept across them and Lindsay squinted, averting his face. "You may call me the Ensign," the alien said in trade English. He politely aligned himself with their vertical axis, stretching overhead to finger-walk along the wall.

Lindsay put his hand on Nora's forearm. "I'm Abelard," he said. "This is Nora."

"How do you do? We want to discuss this property." The alien reached into a side pocket and pulled out a wad of tissue. He shook it out with a quick birdlike motion, and it became a television. He put the screen against the wall. Lindsay, watching carefully, saw that the television had no scan lines. The image was formed in millions of tiny colored hexagons.

The image was ESAIRS XII. Bursting from the launch ring's exit hole was an extruded tube of foamed plastic almost half a kilometer long. There was a rough knob at the tip of the wormlike coil. Lindsay realized with instantly smothered shock that it was Paolo's stone head, neatly framed in the flowerlike wreckage of the launch cage. The entire mass had been smoothly embedded in the decoy complex's leakage of plastic, then squeezed out under pressure into a coiling helical arc.

"I see," Lindsay said.

"Are you the artist?"

"Yes," Lindsay said. He pointed at the screen. "Notice the subtle shading effect where our recent blast darkened the sculpture."

"We noticed the explosion," the alien said. "An unusual artistic technique."

"We are unusual," Lindsay said. "We are unique."

"I agree," the Ensign said politely. "We seldom see work on this scale. Do you accept negotiations for purchase?"

Lindsay smiled. "Let's talk."

# Part 2

## Community and Anarchy

# Chapter 5

By fits and starts the world entered a new age. The aliens benignly accepted a semidivine mystique. Millennial fervor swept the System. Détente came into vogue. People began to speak, for the first time, of the Schismatrix—of a posthuman solar system, diverse yet unified, where tolerance would rule and every faction would have a share.

The aliens—they called themselves the Investors—seemed unlimited in power. They were ancient, so old that they remembered no tradition earlier than starflight. Their mighty starships ranged a vast economic realm, buying and selling among nineteen other intelligent races. Obviously they possessed technologies so potent that, if they chose, they could shatter the narrow world a hundred times over. Humanity rejoiced that the aliens seemed so serenely affable. The goods they offered were almost always harmless, often artworks of vast academic interest and surprisingly small practicality.

Human wealth poured into the alien coffers. Tiny embassies traveled to the stars in Investor ships. They failed to accomplish much, and they remained tiny, because the Investors charged fares that were astronomical.

The Investors recycled the riches they tapped from the human economy. They bought into human enterprises. With a single technological novelty from one of their packed holds, the aliens could transform a flagging industry into a rocketing growth stock. Factions competed wildly for their favor. And uncooperative worlds soon learned how easily they could be outflanked and rendered obsolete.

Trade flourished in the new Investor Peace. Open warfare became vulgar, replaced by the polite covertness of rampant industrial espionage. With each new year, a golden age seemed just out of reach. And the years passed, and passed.

## GOLDREICH-TREMAINE COUNCIL STATE: 3-4-'37

The crowd pleased Lindsay. People filled the air around him: colored jackets with a froth of lace, legs in patterned stockings with sleek five-toed foot-gloves. The air in the theatre lobby reeked of Shaper perfumes.

Lindsay lounged against one patterned velvet wall, his jacketed elbow hooked through a mooring-loop. He dressed in the cutting edge of fashion: sea-green brocade jacket, green satin kneelongs, stockings pinstriped in yellow. His feet were elegantly gloved for free-fall. A gold-chained video monocle gleamed in his waistcoat.

Braids interlaced with yellow cord bound his long, graying hair.

Lindsay was fifty-one. Among the Shapers he passed for one much older—some genetic from the dawn of Shaper history. There were many such in Goldreich-Tremaine, one of the oldest Shaper city-states in the Rings of Saturn.

A Mechanist emerged into the lobby from the theatre. He wore a ribbed one-piece suit in tasteful mahogany brown. He noticed Lindsay and kicked off from the doorway, floating toward him.

Lindsay reached out in friendly fashion and stopped the man's momentum. Beneath his sleeve, Lindsay's prosthetic right arm whined slightly with the movement. "Good evening, Mr. Beyer."

The handsome Mechanist nodded and took a mooring-loop. "Good evening, Dr. Mavrides. Always a pleasure."

Beyer was with the Ceres Legation. He was Undersecretary for Cultural Affairs, a colorless title meant to camouflage his affiliation with Mech intelligence.

"I don't often see you during this day-shift, Mr. Beyer."

"I'm slumming," Beyer said comfortably. Life in Goldreich-Tremaine ran around the clock; the graveyard shift, from midnight to eight, was the loosest and least policed. A Mechanist could mingle during the graveyard shift without attracting stares.

"Are you enjoying the play, sir?"

"A triumph. As good as Ryumin, I'd say. This author—Fernand Vetterling—his work is new to me."

"He's a local youngster. One of our best."

"Ah. One of your protégés. I appreciate his Détentiste sentiments. We're having a little soiree at the Embassy later this week. I'd like to meet Mr. Vetterling. To express my admiration."

Lindsay smiled evasively. "You're always welcome at my home, Mr. Beyer. Nora speaks of you often."

"How flattering. Colonel-Doctor Mavrides is a charming hostess." Beyer hid his disappointment, but his kinesics showed signs of impatience.

Beyer wanted to leave, to touch base with some other social doyen. Lindsay bore him no resentment for it; it was the man's job.

Lindsay himself held a rank in Security. He was Captain-Doctor Abelard Mavrides, an instructor in Investor sociology at Goldreich-Tremaine Kosmosity.

Even in these days of the Investor Peace, a rank in Security was mandatory for those in the Shaper academic-military complex. Lindsay played the game, as they all did.

In his role as theatrical manager, Lindsay never alluded to his rank. But Beyer was well aware of it, and only the grease of diplomatic politesse allowed them to be friends.

Beyer's light-blue eyes scanned the crowded lobby, and his face stiffened. Lindsay followed the man's gaze.

Beyer had spotted someone. Lindsay sized the man up at once: microphone lip bead, ear-clasp audiophones, clothing that lacked finesse. A bodyguard. And not a Shaper: the man's hair was sleeked back with antiseptic oils, and his face lacked Shaper symmetry.

Lindsay reached for his video monocle, fitted it to his right eye, and began filming.

Beyer noticed the gesture and smiled with a hint of sourness. "There are four of them," he said. "Your production has attracted a man of distinction."

"They look like Concatenates," Lindsay said.

"A state visit," Beyer said. "He is here incognito. It's the head of state from the Mare Serenitatis Republic. Chairman Philip Khouri Constantine."

Lindsay turned aside. "I don't know the gentleman."

"He is not a friend of Détente," Beyer said. "I know him only by reputation. I can't introduce you."

Lindsay moved along the wall, keeping his back to the crowd. "I must visit my office. Will you join me for a smoke?"

"Lung-smoking?" Beyer said. "I never acquired the habit."

"Then you must excuse me." Lindsay fled.

"After twenty years," said Nora Mavrides. She sat before her console, her Security jacket thrown carelessly over her shoulders, a black cape over her amber-colored blouse.

"What's possessed him?" Lindsay demanded. "Isn't the Republic enough for him?"

Nora thought aloud. "The militants must have brought him here. They need him to back their cause here in the capital. He has prestige. And he's no Détentiste."

"That's plausible," Lindsay said, "but only if you turn it around. The militants think Constantine is their pet unplanned, their loyal general, but they don't know his ambitions. Or his potential. He's manipulated them."

"Did he see you?"

"I don't think so. I don't think he would have recognized me if he had." Lindsay stuck his spoon moodily into a carton of medicinal yogurt. "My age disguises me."

"My heart sank when I saw the film from your monocle. Abelard, these years, they've been so good to us. If he knew who you were, he could ruin us."

"Not completely." Lindsay forced himself to eat, grimacing. The yogurt was a special preparation for non-Shapers whose intestines had been rendered antiseptic. It was bitter with digestive enzymes. "Constantine could denounce me. But what if he does? We'd still have the aliens. The Investors don't give a damn about my genetics, my training. . . . The aliens could be our refuge."

"We should attack Constantine. He's a killer."

"We're not the ones to talk on that score, darling." Lindsay gripped the carton with his mechanical hand; its thin walls buckled precisely. "I always meant to avoid him if I could. It was something I fell into, a roll of the dice. . . ."

"Don't talk that way. As if it were something we can't help."

Lindsay drummed his iron fingers. Even the arm was part of his disguise. The antique prosthetic had once belonged to the Chief Justice, and Lindsay's affectation of it hinted at great age.

On the wall of Nora's office, a huge satellite telephoto of the Saturnian surface crawled slowly, red winds interlacing streams of muddy gold. "We could leave," Lindsay said. "There are other Council States. Kirkwood Gap's all right. Cassini-Kluster."

"And give up everything we've built here?"

Lindsay watched the screen abstractly. "You're all I want."

"I want that tenure, Abelard. That Colonel-Professorship. If we go, what about the children? What about our Clique? They depend on us."

"You're right. This is our home."

"You're making too much of this," Nora said. "He'll return to the Republic soon. If Goldreich-Tremaine weren't the capital now, he wouldn't be here."

Children laughed in the next room; from her console, Nora turned down the audio. Lindsay said, "There's a horror between Philip and myself. We know too much about each other."

"Don't be a fatalist, darling. I'm not going to sit with folded hands while some unplanned upstart attacks my husband."

Nora left her console and walked across to him. A centrifugal half-gravity tugged at her skirt and sleeve laces. Lindsay pulled her into his lap and ran his human hand across the serpentine curls of her hair. "Let him be, Nora. Otherwise it will come to killing again."

She kissed him. "You were alone in the past. Now you're a match for him. We have our Midnight Clique. We have the Mavrides line, the Investors, my rank in Security. We have our good trust. This life belongs to us."

## GOLDREICH-TREMAINE COUNCIL STATE: 13-4-'37

Philip Constantine watched his ship's departure through his video monocle. The monocle pleased him. He liked its stylishness. Constantine took pains to stay abreast of such developments. Fashions were powerful manipulations.

Especially among the Reshaped. Behind his ship, the *Friendship Serene,* the Goldreich-Tremaine complex spun in gyroscopic counterclockwork. Constantine studied the city's image, broadcast to his monocle from a camera mounted on the ship's hull.

The orbiting city taught an object lesson in Shaper history.

Its core was the dark, heavily shielded cylinder that had sheltered the earliest settlers: desperate pioneers, driven to mine the Rings of Saturn despite their sleets of radiation and complex electrical storms. The central core of Goldreich-Tremaine was as dark as a nut, a stubborn acorn that had endured and broken forth at last into fantastic growth. Hubbed spheres wheeled about it, radar installations slid with sleek precision on external tracks, two huge tubed suburbs turned in counterbalanced array on white ceramic stems. And all about the inner complex was a lacy network of habitats in free-fall. Outside the bubbled suburbs—the "subbles"—loomed the immaterial walls of the Bottle.

The *Friendship Serene* hit the flaw in the Bottle. Colored static raced across Constantine's monocle, and Goldreich-Tremaine disappeared. It was visible now only by its absence: a lozenge of dark fog in the white ice-rubble of the Ring. The dark fog was the Bottle itself: a magnetic tokamak field eight kilometers long, shielding the Shaper city-state within a fusion-powered web.

This far from the sun, solar kilowatts were useless. The Reshaped had their own suns, bright fusion cores in every Council State: Goldreich-Tremaine, Dermott-Gold-Murray, Tauri Phase, Kirkwood Gap, Synchronis, Cassini-Kluster, Encke-Kluster, Skimmers Union, Arsenal. . . . Constantine knew them all.

Ghost acceleration wafted across him as the engines cut in. The Goldreich-Tremaine weather station had cleared them for launch; there was no chance of a crippling ring-lightning strike. Background radiation was light. With the new Shaper drives he faced mere weeks of travel.

The playwright, Zeuner, entered the cabin and seated himself beside Constantine. "It's gone," he said.

"Homesick already, Carl?" Constantine looked up at the larger man.

"For Goldreich-Tremaine? Yes. For the people? That's another matter."

"Someday you'll return in triumph."

"Very kind of you to say so, your excellency." Zeuner ran one fawn-colored glove over his chin. Constantine noted that the Republic's standard bacteria were already spotting the man's neck.

"Forget titles of state," Constantine said. "In the Ring Council it's politesse. In the Republic, it smacks of aristocracy. Our local form of bad ideology."

"I see, Dr. Constantine. I'll be more careful in the future." Zeuner's clean-shaven face had the anonymous beauty of the Reshaped. He dressed with fussy precision in understated browns and beiges.

Constantine tucked the monocle into his copper-threaded velvet waistcoat. Beneath his embroidered linen jacket, his back had begun to sweat. The skin of his back was peeling where the rejuvenation virus ate at aging cells. For twenty years the infestation had wandered over his body, the first reward for his loyalty to the Shaper cause. Where the virus had worked, his olive skin had a child's smoothness.

Zeuner examined the cabin walls. The heavy insulation was stitched with pointillistic tapestries depicting the Republic. Orchards spread under bright clouds, sunlight fell with cathedral-like solemnity across golden wheatfields, ultralight aircraft dipped over stone-walled mansions with red-tiled roofs. The vistas were as clean as a travel brochure's. Zeuner said, "What's it really like, your Republic?"

"A backwater," Constantine said. "An antique. Before our Revolution, the Republic was rotting. Not just socially. Physically. An ecosystem that large needs total genetic control. But the builders didn't care about the long run. In the long run they were all dead."

Constantine steepled his fingers. "Now we inherit their mess. The Concatenation exiled its visionaries. Their genetics theorists, for instance, who formed the Ring Council. The Concatenates were squeamish. Now they have lost all power. They are client states."

"You think we'll win, doctor? The Shapers?"

"Yes." Constantine gave the man one of his rare smiles. "Because we understand what this struggle is about. Life. I don't mean that the Mechs will be annihilated. They may totter on for whole centuries. But they will be cut off. They'll be cybernetic, not living flesh. That's a dead end, because there's no will behind it. No imperatives. Only programming. No imagination."

The playwright nodded. "Sound ideology. Not like what you hear in Goldreich-Tremaine these days. Détentiste slogans. Unity in diversity, where all the factions form one vast Schismatrix. Humankind reuniting when faced by aliens."

Constantine shifted in his chair, surreptitiously rubbing his back against the cushion. "I've heard that rhetoric. On the stage. This producer you were mentioning—"

"Mavrides?" Zeuner was eager. "They're a powerful clan. Goldreich-Tremaine, Jastrow Station, Kirkwood Gap. They've never had a genetic on the Council itself, but they share genes with the Garzas and the Drapers and the Vetterlings. The Vetterlings have authority."

"This man is a Mavrides by marriage, you said. A nongenetic."

"A eunique, you mean? Yes. He's not allowed to contribute his genes to the line." Zeuner was pleased to tell this bit of scandal. "He's also an Investor pet. And a cepheid."

"Cepheid? You mean he has a rank in Security?"

"He's Captain-Doctor Abelard Mavrides, C.-Ph.D. It's a low rank for one so old. He was a sundog once, a cometary miner, they say. He met the aliens on the rim of the System, wormed his way into their good graces somehow. . . . They'd been here only a few months when they brought Mavrides and his wife into Goldreich-Tremaine in one of their starships. Since then he's moved from success to success. Corporations hire him as a go-between with the aliens. He teaches Investor studies and speaks their language fluently. He's wealthy enough to keep his past obscure."

"Old-line Shapers guard their privacy closely."

Zeuner brooded. "He's my enemy. He blighted my career."

Constantine thought it through. He knew more about Mavrides than Zeuner did. He had recruited Zeuner deliberately, knowing that Mavrides must have enemies, and that finding them was easier than creating them.

Zeuner was frustrated. His first play had failed; the second was never produced. He was not privy to the behind-the-scenes machinations of Mavrides and his Midnight Clique. Zeuner was harshly anti-Mechanist; his gene-line had suffered cruelly in the War. The Détentistes rejected him.

So Constantine had charmed him. He had lured Zeuner to the Republic with promises of the theatrical archives, a living tradition of drama that Zeuner could study and exploit. The Shaper was grateful, and because of that gratitude he was Constantine's pawn.

Constantine was silent. Mavrides troubled him. Tentacles of the man's influence had spread throughout Goldreich-Tremaine.

And the coincidences went beyond chance. They hinted at deliberate plot.

A man who chose to call himself Abelard. An impresario of the theatre. Staging political plays. And his wife was a diplomat.

At least Constantine knew that Abelard Lindsay was dead. His agents in the Zaibatsu had taped Lindsay's death at the hands of the Geisha Bank. Constantine had even spoken to the woman who had had Lindsay killed, a Shaper renegade called Kitsune. He had the whole sorry story: Lindsay's involvement with pirates, his desperate murder of the Geisha Bank's former leader. Lindsay had died horribly.

But why had Constantine's first assassin never reported back from the Zaibatsu? He had not thought the man would turn sundog. Assassins had failsafes implanted; few traitors survived.

For years Constantine had lived in fear of this lost assassin. The elite of Ring Council Security assured him that the assassin was dead. Constantine did not believe them, and had never trusted them again.

For years he had worked his way into the mirrored underworld of Shaper covert action. Assassins and bodyguards—the two were often one and the same, since they specialized in one another's tradecraft—these had become his closest allies.

He knew their subterfuges, their fanatic loyalties. He struggled constantly to win their trust. He sheltered them in his Republic, hiding from pacifist persecution. He used his prestige freely to further their militarist ends.

Some Shapers still despised him for his unplanned genes; from many others he had won respect. Personal hatreds did not bother him. But it bothered him that he might be cut short before he had measured himself against the world. Before he had satisfied the soaring ambition that had driven him since childhood.

Who knew about Lindsay, the only man who had ever been his friend? When he was young, and weaker, before the armor of distrust had sealed around him, Lindsay had been his intimate. Who let this phantom loose, and to what end?

## GOLDREICH-TREMAINE COUNCIL STATE: 26-12-'46

Wedding guests surrounded the garden. From his hiding place behind the boughs of a dwarf magnolia, Lindsay saw his wife lightly bounding toward him, in half a gravity. Green fronds brushed at the spreading wings of her headdress. Nora's formal gown was a dense ocher weave beaded in silver, with openwork amber sleeves. "You're all right, darling?"

Lindsay said, "My sleeve hems, burn it. I was dancing and popped a whole weave loose."

"I saw you leave. Do you need help?"

"I can get it." Lindsay struggled with the complex interweave. "I'm slow, but I can do it."

"Let me help." She stepped to his side, pulled inlaid knitting needles from her headdress, and tatted his sleeves with a smooth dexterity he could not hope to match. He sighed and tucked his own needles carefully back into his braids. "The Regent is asking about you," she said. "The senior genetics are here."

"Where'd you put them?"

"In the veranda discreet. I had to clear out a raft of kids." She finished the sleeve. "There. Good enough?"

"You're a wonder."

"No kissing, Abelard. You'll smear your makeup. After the party." She smiled. "You look grand."

Lindsay ran his mechanical hand over his coils of gray hair. The steel knuckles glittered with inlaid seed-gems; the wire tendons sparkled with interwoven strands of fiberoptics. He wore a formal Goldreich-Tremaine Kosmosity academic's ruffled overvest, its lapels studded with pins of rank. His kneelongs were a rich coffee-brown. Brown stockings relieved the dignity of his outfit with a hint of iridescence. "I danced with the bride," he said. "I think I surprised them a bit."

"I heard the shouts, dear." She smiled and took his arm, placing her hand on his sleeve above the steel of his artificial ulna. They left the garden.

On the patio outside, the bride and groom were dancing on the ceiling, heads downward. Their feet darted nimbly in and out of the dance rig, a broad complex of padded footloops for use in light gravity. Lindsay watched the bride, feeling a rush of happiness close to pain.

Kleo Mavrides. The young bride was the dead woman's clone, sharing her name and her genes. There were times when Lindsay felt that behind the merry eyes of the younger Kleo there lurked an older spirit, as a sound might still vibrate in the glass of a crystal just after it had ceased to ring. He had done what he could. Since her production, the younger Kleo had been his special care. He and Nora found satisfaction in these amends. It was more than penance. They had taken too many pains to call it simply recompense. It was love.

The groom danced powerfully; he had the bearlike build of all the Vetterling genetics. Fernand Vetterling was a gifted man, a standout even in a society of genius. Lindsay had known the man for twenty years, as playwright, architect, and Clique member. Vetterling's creative energy still filled Lindsay with a kind of awe, even subdued fear. How long would the marriage last, he wondered, between Kleo and her fleet graces and the sober Vetterling, with his mind like a sharp steel ax? It was a marriage of state as well as a love match. Much capital had been invested in it, economic and genetic.

Nora led him on through a crowd of children, who were lashing speed into whirring gyroscopes with dainty braided whips. As usual, Paolo Mavrides was winning, his nine-year-old face alight with preternatural concentration. "Don't hit my wheel, Nora," he said.

"Paolo's been gambling," said Randa Vetterling, a muscular six-year-old. She grinned mischievously, showing missing front teeth.

"Nyaah," Paolo said, not looking up. "Randa's an informer."

"Play nicely," Nora said. "Don't bother the seniors."

The senior genetics were sitting around the buhl table in Lindsay's veranda, with its Investor centerpiece. They were conversing strictly in Looks, a language which to the untrained eye seemed to consist entirely of sidelong glances. Lindsay, nodding, glanced under the table. Two children were squatting beneath it, playing in tandem with a long loop of string. Using all four hands and their largest toes they had formed a complex rack of angles. "Very nice," Lindsay said. "But go play your spiders' games elsewhere."

"All right," the older child said grudgingly. Careful not to disturb their structure, they wormed their way toward the open doorway on their heels and toes, their string-wrapped hands outspread.

"I gave them some candy," said Dietrich Ross when they had left. "They said they'd save it for later. Ever hear of kids that age saving candy for later? What the hell's becoming of the world?"

Lindsay sat down, opening a pocket mirror. He pulled a powder puff from the pocket of his vest.

"Sweating like a pig," Ross observed. "You're not the man you once were, Mavrides."

"You can talk when you've danced four measures, Ross, you old fraud," Lindsay said.

"Margaret has a new opinion on your centerpiece," said Charles Vetterling. The former Regent had gone frankly to seed since his loss of office; he looked tubby and choleric, his old-fashioned trimmed hair speckled with white.

Lindsay was interested. "What's that, Madam Chancellor?"

"It's erotica." Chancellor-General Margaret Juliano leaned over the inlaid table and pointed into the perspex pressure-dome. Beneath the dome was a complex sculpture. Speculation had been rife ever since the Investors had first given it to Lindsay.

The gift was carved out of water ice and plated in glimmering frozen ammonia. Machinery beneath the dome maintained it at 40 degrees Kelvin. The sculpture consisted of two oblate lumps covered in filigree spires of delicate crystalline frost. The tableau was set on a rippled surface, possibly meant to represent some unimaginably cold sludge-ocean. Off to one side, poking through the surface, was a smaller hinged lump that might have been an elbow.

"You'll notice there are two of them," the Shaper academic said. "I believe that the physical goings-on are tastefully concealed beneath the water. The fluid, rather."

"They don't look much alike," Lindsay said. "It seems more likely that one is eating the other. If they're alive at all."

"That's what I said," rasped Sigmund Fetzko. The Mechanist renegade, by far the oldest of the six of them, lay back in his chair in exhaustion. Words came to him with difficulty, propelled by flexing rib-braces beneath his heavy coat. "The second one has dimples. Shell collapsing. Juice sucked out of it."

A Vetterling child came into the room, chasing a runaway gyroscope. Vetterling Looked at Neville Pongpianskul, changing the subject. The child left. "It *is* a good marriage," Pongpianskul replied. "Mavrides grace with Vetterling determination: a formidable match. Mikhaila Vetterling shows promise, I think; what was her split?"

Vetterling was smug. "Sixty Vetterling, thirty Mavrides, and ten percent Garza on a general reciprocity deal. But I saw to it that the Garza genes were close to early-line Vetterling. None of that new-line Garza tampering. Not till there's proof behind it."

"Young Adelaide Garza is brilliant," said Margaret Juliano. "One of my advanced students. The Superbrights are astounding, Regent. A quantum leap." She smoothed the lapel of her medal-studded overvest with graceful, wrinkled hands.

"Really?" said Ross. "I was married to the older Adelaide once."

"What happened to Adelaide?" said Pongpianskul.

Ross shrugged. "Faded."

A faint chill crossed the room. Lindsay changed the subject. "We're planning a new veranda. Nora needs this one for her office."

"She needs a bigger place?" said Pongpianskul.

Lindsay nodded. "Tenure. And this is our best discreet. Wakefield Zaibatsu did the debugging. Otherwise we have to have the debuggers in again; it'll turn the place upside down."

"Building on credit?" Ross said.

"Of course." Lindsay smiled.

"Too flaming much loose credit in G-T these days," Ross said. "I don't hold with it."

"Ah, Ross," Vetterling said, "you haven't changed those digs of yours in eighty years. A man can't turn sideways in those core ratholes. Take us Vetterlings, now. The bridegroom just delivered us the specs for a new complex of inflatables."

"Jerry-built crap," Ross opined. "G-T's too crowded these days anyway. Too many young sharks. Things smell good now but there's crash in the air, I can feel it. When it comes, I'll pull up stakes and head for the cometaries. Been too long since I last tested my luck."

Pongpianskul Looked at Lindsay, communicating in the set of his wrinkled eyelids his amused contempt for Ross's incessant luck-bragging. Ross had made his big mining strike a century ago and had never let anyone forget it. Though he incessantly goaded others on, Ross's own risk-taking was confined almost entirely to his odd choice of waistcoats.

"I have a Clique candidate," Vetterling said. "Very polite, very well-spoken. Carl Zeuner."

"The playwright?" said Margaret Juliano. "I don't care for his work."

"You mean he's not a Détentiste," Vetterling said. "He doesn't fit your pacifism, Margaret. Mavrides, I believe you know the man."

"We've met," Lindsay said.

"Zeuner's a fascist," said Pongpianskul. The topic galvanized the elderly doctor; he leaned forward intently, knotting his hands. "He's Philip Constantine's man. He spent years in the Republic. A playground for Shaper imperialists."

Vetterling frowned. "Calm yourself, Neville. I know the Concatenation; I was born there. Constantine's work there should have been done a hundred years ago."

"You mean fill his garden world with broken-down assassins?"

"To bring a new world into the Shaper community—"

"Nothing but cultural genocide." Pongpianskul had just been rejuvenated; his lean body quivered with unnatural energy. Lindsay had never asked what technique he used; it left his skin smooth but leathery, and of a peculiar dusky color not found in nature. His knuckles were so heavily wrinkled that they looked like small rosettes. "The Circumlunar Republic should be left as a cultural museum. It's good policy. We need variety; not every society we form can hold together."

"Neville." Sigmund Fetzko spoke heavily. "You are talking as if you were a boy."

Pongpianskul leaned back. "I confess I've been reading my old speeches since my last rejuve."

"That's what got you purged," Vetterling said.

"My taste for antiquities? My own speeches are antiques by now. But the issues are still with us, friends. Community and anarchy. Politics pulls things together; technology blows them apart. Little enclaves like the Republic should be preserved intact. So that if our own tampering strikes us down, there'll be someone left to pick up the pieces."

"There's the Earth," said Fetzko.

"I draw the line at barbarians," Pongpianskul said. He sipped his drink, a tranquilizer frappé.

"If you had any guts, Pongpianskul," Ross said, "you'd go to the Republic and tackle things firsthand."

Pongpianskul sniffed. "I'll wager I could gather damning evidence there."

"Nonsense," said Vetterling.

"A wager?" Ross looked from one to the other. "Let me be arbiter, then.

Doctor, if you could find evidence that would offend my hardened sensibilities, we would all agree that right is on your side."

Pongpianskul hesitated. "It's been so long since I . . ."

Ross laughed. "Afraid? Better hang back and cultivate your mystique, then. You need a facade of mystery. Otherwise the young sharks will have you for breakfast."

"There were breakfasters after the purge," Pongpianskul said. "They couldn't digest me."

"That was two centuries back," Ross taunted. "I recall a certain episode—what was it—immortality from kelp?"

"What?" Pongpianskul blinked. Then the memory seemed to ooze up within him, buried under decades. "Kelp," he said. " 'The earth-ocean wonder plant.' " He was quoting himself. " 'You wonder, friends, why your catalytic balances vary. . . . The answer is kelp, the sea-born wonder plant, now genetically altered to grow and flourish in the primeval brine from which blood itself derives. . . .' My God, I'd forgotten entirely."

"He sold kelp pills," Ross confided. "Had a little dig in some inflatable slum, radiation so hard you could poach an egg against the bulkhead."

"Placebos," Pongpianskul said. "Goldreich-Tremaine was full of old unplanned types then. Miners, refugees cooked by radiation. It was before the Bottle shielded us. If they looked hopeless I used to slip a little painkiller into the mix."

"You don't get as old as we are without artifice," Lindsay said.

Vetterling snorted. "Don't start reminiscing, Mavrides. I want to know what my angle is, Ross. What are my winnings once Pongpianskul fails?"

"My domicile," Pongpianskul said. "In the Fitzgerald Wheel."

Vetterling's eyes widened. "Against?"

"Against your public denunciation of Constantine and Zeuner. And the expenses of the trip."

"Your beautiful place," Margaret Juliano told Pongpianskul. "How can you part with it, Neville?"

Pongpianskul shrugged. "If the future belongs to Constantine's friends then I don't care to live here."

"Don't forget you've just had a treatment," Vetterling said uncomfortably. "You're acting rashly. I hate to turn a man out of his digs. We can put the bet off until—"

"Off," Pongpianskul said. "That's our curse; there's always time for everything. While those younger than ourselves tear into every year as if there were no yesterday. . . . No, I'm settled, Regent." He entended his leathery hand to Vetterling.

"Fire!" Vetterling said. He took Pongpianskul's thin hand in his heavy one. "Sealed, then. The four of you are witnesses."

"I'll take the next ship out," said Pongpianskul. He stood up, his verdigris-colored eyes gleaming feverishly. "I must make arrangements. A delightful little fete, Mavrides."

Lindsay was startled. "Oh. Thank you, sir. The robot has your hat, I think."

"I must thank my hostess." Pongpianskul left.

"He's cracked," Vetterling said. "That new treatment's unhinged him. Poor Pongpianskul never was very stable."

"What treatment is he using?" Fetzko wheezed. "He seems so energetic."

Ross smiled. "An unproven one. He can't afford a registered treatment. I hear he's made an arrangement with a wealthier man to serve as test subject; they split the cost."

Lindsay Looked at Ross. Ross hid his expression by biting into a canapé.

"A risk," said Fetzko. "That's why the young ones bear us. So that we can take their risks. And weed out. Bad treatments. With our casualties."

"Could've been worse," Ross said. "He could have fallen for one of those skin-virus scams. He'd be peeling like a snake right now, hah!"

Young Paolo Mavrides stepped through the soundproof field in the doorway. "Nora says come see Kleo and Mr. Vetterling off."

"Thank you, Paolo." Juliano and the Regent Vetterling headed for the doorway, small-talking about construction costs. Fetzko tottered after them, his legs buzzing audibly. Ross took Lindsay by the arm.

"A moment, Abelard."

"Yes, Arts-Lieutenant?"

"It's not Security business, Abelard. You won't tell Juliano that I put Pongpianskul up to it?"

"The unproven treatment, you mean? No. It was cruel, though."

Ross smirked. "Look, I almost married Margaret a few decades back, and from what Neville tells me my marrying days may be back any day now. . . . Listen, Mavrides. It hasn't escaped me the way you've been looking these past few years. Frankly, you're in decay."

Lindsay touched his graying hair. "You're not the first to say so."

"It's not a money problem?"

"No." He sighed. "I don't want my genetics inspected. There are too many Security groups watching, and frankly I'm not all I seem. . . ."

"Who the hell is, at this age? Listen, Mavrides: I figured it was something like that, you being eunique. That's my point: I've gotten wind of something, very quiet, very confidential. It costs but there's no questions asked, no records: operations take place in a discreet. Out in one of the dogtowns."

"I see," Lindsay said. "Risky."

Ross shrugged. "You know I don't get along with the rest of my gene-line. They won't give me their records; I have to handle my own research. Can't we work out something?"

"Possibly. I have no secrets from my wife. May she know?"

"Surely, surely. . . . You'll do it?"

"I'll be in touch." Lindsay put his prosthetic arm on Ross's shoulder; Ross shuddered, just a little.

The wedding couple had made it as far as the alcove, where they had bogged down in a crowd of well-wishers and hat-fetching junior genetics. Lindsay embraced Kleo, and took Fernand Vetterling's arm left-handed. "You'll take good care of my sib, Fernand? You know she's very young."

Fernand met his eyes. "She's life and breath to me, friend."

"That's the spirit. We'll put the new play off awhile. Love is more important."

Nora kissed Fernand, smearing his makeup. Back within the domicile the younger set were hitting full stride. The dancing across the ceiling footloops had degenerated into a near brawl, where young Shapers, screaming with laughter, struggled to shove one another off the crowded dance rig. Several had fallen already and were clinging to others, dangling loosely in the half gravity.

High spirits, Lindsay thought. Soon many of these would be married as well; few would find the convenient meshing of love and politics that Fernand had. They were pawns in the dynastic games of their seniors, where money and genetics set the rules.

He looked over the crowd with the close judgment that thirty years of Shaper audiences had taught him. Some were hidden by the trees of the garden, a central rectangle of lush greenery surrounded by tessellated patio floors. Four Mavrides children were tormenting one of the serving robots, which wouldn't spill its drinks though they tugged it and tripped it up. Lindsay leaped upward in the mild gravity to look past the garden.

An argument was brewing on the other side: half a dozen Shapers surrounding a man in black coveralls. Trouble. Lindsay walked to the garden roofway and leaped up onto the ceiling. He pulled himself across the pathway with the ease of long habit, clinging deftly to knobs and foot-niches. He was forced to pause as a pack of three children raced past and over him, giggling excitedly. His sleeve lace came loose again.

Lindsay dropped to the floor on the other side. "Burn the sleeves," he muttered. By now everyone looked a little unraveled. He made his way toward the cluster of debaters.

A young Mechanist stood at the circle's center, wearing well-cut satin overalls with black frogging and a suggestion of Shaper lace at the throat. Lindsay recognized him: a disciple of Ryumin's, come in with the latest Kabuki Intrasolar tour. He called himself Wells.

Wells had a brash, sundoggish look: short matted hair, shifty eyes, a wide free-fall stance. He had the Kabuki mask logo on his coverall's shoulders. He looked drunk.

"It's an open-and-shut case," Wells insisted loudly. "When they used the Investors as a pretext to stop the war, that was one thing. But those of us who've known the aliens since we were children can recognize the truth. They're not saints. They have played on us for profit."

The group had not yet noticed Lindsay. He hung back, judging their kinesics. This was grim: the Shapers were Afriel, Besetzny, Warden, Parr, and Leng: his graduate class in alien linguistics. They listened to the Mechanist with polite contempt. Obviously they had not bothered to tell him who they were, though their predoctoral overvests marked their rank clearly.

"You don't feel they bear any credit for détente?" This was Simon Afriel, a cold and practiced young militant already making his mark in the Shaper academic-military complex. He had confessed once to Lindsay that he had his sights set on an alien diplomatic assignment. So did they all: surely, out of nineteen known alien races, there would be one with which the Shapers could establish strong rapport. And the diplomat who returned sane from that assignment would have the world at his feet.

"I'm an ardent Détentiste," said Wells. "I just want humanity to share the profit from it. For thirty years the Investors have bought and sold us. Do we have their secrets? Their stardrive? Their history? No. Instead they fob us off with toys and expensive joyrides to the stars. These scaly con artists have preyed on human weakness and division. I'm not alone in thinking this. There's a new generation in the Cartels these days—"

"What's the point?" This was Besetzny, a wealthy young woman who already spoke eight languages as well as Investor. She was the picture of young Shaper glamour in her slashed cordless sleeves and winged velvet headdress. "In the Cartels you're outnumbered by your old. They'll deal with us as they always have; that's their routine. Without the Investors to shield us—"

"That's just it, doctor-designate." Wells was not as drunk as he looked. "There are hundreds of us who long to see the Rings for what they are. You're not without your admirers, you know. We have third-hand Ring fashions, fourth-hand Ring art, passed around secretly. It's pathetic! We have so much to offer each other. . . . But the Investors have squeezed everything they can from the status quo. Already they've begun abetting warmongers: cut down Ring-Cartel interflights, encouraged bidding wars. . . . You know, the mere fact that I've come here is enough to brand me for life, possibly even as an agent for Ring Security: a bacillus, I think you call them? I'll never set foot in a Cartel again without eyes watching me—"

Afriel lifted his voice. "Good evening, Captain-Doctor." He had spotted Lindsay.

Making the best of it, Lindsay ambled forward. "Good evening, doctors-designate. Mr. Wells. I trust you're not embittering yourselves with youthful cynicism. This is a happy time. . . ."

But now Wells was nervous. All Mechanists were terrified of agents of Ring Security, not realizing that the academic-military complex permeated Shaper life so thoroughly that a quarter of the population was Security in one form or another. Besetzny, Afriel, and Parr, for instance, all ardent leaders in Goldreich-Tremaine paramilitary youth, were much more of a threat to Wells than Lindsay, with his reluctant captaincy. Wells, though, was galvanized with distrust. He mumbled pleasantries until Lindsay walked away.

The worst of it was that Wells was right. The Shaper students knew it. But they were not about to jeopardize their hard-won doctorates by publicly agreeing with a naive Mech. No one would have Ring Council clearance to visit other stars without an impeccable ideology.

Of course the Investors were profiteers. Their arrival had not brought the millennium humankind had expected. The Investors were not even particularly intelligent. They made up for that with a cast-iron gall and a magpie's lust for shiny loot. They were simply too greedy to become confused. They knew what they wanted, and that was their critical advantage.

They had been painted much larger than life. Lindsay had done as much himself, when he and Nora had parlayed their asteroid deathtrap into three months of language lessons and a free ride to the Ring Council. With his instant notoriety as a friend to aliens, Lindsay had done his best to inflate the Investor mystique. He was as guilty of the fraud as anyone.

He had even defrauded the Investors. The Investors' name for him was still a rasp and whistle meaning "Artist." Lindsay still had friends among the Investors: or, at least, beings whom he felt sure he could amuse.

Investors had a sense of something close to humor, a certain sadistic enjoyment in a sharp deal. That sculpture they had given him, which rested in a place of honor in his home, might well be two frost-eaten chunks of alien dung.

God only knew to what befuddled alien they had sold his own piece of found art. It was only to be expected that a young man like Wells would demand the truth and spread it. Not knowing the consequences of his action, or even caring; simply too young to live a lie. Well, the falsehoods would hold up awhile longer. Despite the new generation bred in the Investor Peace, who struggled to rip aside the veil, not knowing that it was the very canvas on which their world was painted.

Lindsay looked for his wife. She was in her office, closeted with her conspirator's crew of trained diplomats. Colonel-Professor Nora Mavrides cast a large shadow in Goldreich-Tremaine. Sooner or later every diplomat in the capital had drifted into it. She was the best known of her class's loyalists and served as their champion.

Lindsay hid within the comfort of his own mystique. As far as he knew, he was the last survivor of the foreign section. If other non-Shaper diplomats survived, it was not by advertising themselves.

He entered the room briefly for politeness' sake, but as usual their smooth kinesics made him nervous. He left for the smoking room, where two stagedoor hangers-on were being introduced to the modish vice by the cast of Vetterling's *Shepherd Moons*.

Here Lindsay sank at once into his role as impresario. They believed in what they saw of him: an older man, a bit slow, perhaps, without the fire of genius others had, but generous and with a tang of mystery. With that mystery came glamour; Doctor Abelard Mavrides had set his share of trends.

He drifted from one conversation to another: genetic marriage-politics, Ring Security intrigues, city rivalries, academic doctrines, day-shift clashes, artistic cliques—threads all of a single fabric. The sheen of it, the smooth brilliance of its social design, had lulled him into routine. He wondered sometimes about the placidity he felt. How much of it was age, the mellowness of decay? Lindsay was sixty-one.

The wedding party was ending. Actors left to rehearse, seniors crept to their antique warrens, the hordes of children scampered to the crèches of their gene-lines. Lindsay and Nora retired at last to their bedroom. Nora was bright-eyed, a little tipsy. She sat on the edge of their bed, unloosing the clasp at the back of her formal dress. She pulled it forward and the whole complex fretwork hissed loose across her back, in a web of strings.

Nora had had her first rejuvenation twenty years ago, at thirty-eight, and a second at fifty. The skin of her shoulders was glassily smooth in the bedside lamp's roseate light. Lindsay reached into his bedside table's upper drawer and took his old video monocle from its padded box. Nora pulled her slim arms from the gown's beaded sleeves and reached up to unwire her hat. Lindsay began filming.

"You're not undressing?" She turned. "Abelard, what are you doing?"

"I want to remember you like this," he said. "This perfect moment."

She laughed and threw the headdress aside. With a few deft movements she yanked the jeweled pins from her hair and tossed loose a surge of dark braids. Lindsay was aroused. He put the monocle aside and slid out of his clothes.

They made slow, comfortable love. Lindsay, though, had felt the sting of mortality that night, and it put the spur into him. Passion seized him; he made love with ardent urgency, and she responded. He climaxed hard, looking throughout the heartbeats of orgasm at his own iron hand on her sleek shoulder. He lay gasping, his heart beating loud in his ears. After a moment he moved aside. She sighed, stretched, and laughed. "Wonderful," she said. "I'm happy, Abelard."

"I love you, darling," he said. "You're my life."

She leaned up on one elbow. "You're all right, sweetheart?"

Lindsay's eyes were stinging. "I was talking with Dietrich Ross tonight," he said carefully. "He has a rejuving program he wants me to try."

"Oh," she said, delighted. "Good news."

"It's risky."

"Listen, darling, being *old* is risky. The rest of it is just a matter of tactics. All you need is some minor decatabolism; any lab can handle that. You don't need anything ambitious. That can wait another twenty years."

"It'll mean dropping my mask to someone. Ross says this lot is discreet, but I don't trust Ross. Vetterling and Pongpianskul had a peculiar scene tonight. Ross abetted them."

She unraveled one of her braids. "You're not old, darling, and you've been pretending it too long. Your history won't be a problem much longer. The diplomats are winning their rights back, and you're a Mavrides now. Regent Vetterling's unplanned, and no one thinks less of him."

"Of course they do."

"Maybe a little. That's not it, though. That's not why you've put this off. Your eyes look puffy, Abelard. Have you been taking your antioxidants?"

Lindsay was silent a moment. He sat up in bed, propping himself up with his untiring prosthetic arm. "It's my mortality," he said. "It meant so much to me once. It's all I have left of my old life, my old convictions. . . ."

"But you're not staying the same by letting yourself age. You should stay young if you want to preserve your old feelings."

"There's only one way to do that. Vera Kelland's way."

Her hands stopped with the braid half-twisted. "I'm sorry," Lindsay said. "But it's there somewhere: the shadow. . . . I'm afraid, Nora. If I'm young again it will change things. All these years that there's been such joy for us . . . I froze here, lying in the shadows, safe with you, and happy. To be young again, to take this risk—I'll be out in the open. Eyes will be watching."

She caressed his cheek. "Darling, I'll watch over you. I'll protect you. No one alive will hurt you without coming through me first."

"I know that, and I'm glad for it, but I can't shake off this feeling. Is it just guilt? Guilt, that life has been good to us, that we've had love while those others died like rats in a corner?" His voice trembled; he looked at the sienna weave of the bedspread in the lamp's mild glow. "How long can the Peace go on? The old despise us while the young see through us. Things must change, and how could they be better? It can only be worse for us. . . . Sweetheart. . . ." He met her eyes. "I remember the days when we had nothing, not even the air to breathe, and the rot crept in all around us. Everything we've gained since then has been sheer profit to us, but it's not been real . . . What's between us two is real, that's all. Tell me that if this all collapses, you'll still be with me. . . ."

She took his hands, curling the iron one over her own. "What's brought this on? Is it Constantine?"

"Vetterling wants to bring one of Constantine's men into the Clique."

"Burn him, I knew that despot came into this somehow. He's what frightens you, isn't he? Stirring up old tragedies. . . . I feel better now that I know who I'm facing!"

"It's not just him, darling. Listen: Goldreich-Tremaine can't stay on top forever. The Investor Peace is crumbling; it'll be open struggle again between Shaper and Mechanist. The military wing is bound to reassert itself. We'll lose the capitalship—"

"This is pure alarm, Abelard. We haven't lost anything yet. The Détentistes in G-T have never been stronger. My diplomats—"

"I know you're strong. You'll win, I think. But if you don't, if we have to sundog it—"

"Sundog? We're not refugees, darling, we're Mavrides genetics, with offices, property, tenure! This is our fortress! We can't just abandon this, when it's given us so much. . . . You'll feel different after the treatment. When your youth is back you'll see things differently."

"I know," Lindsay said. "And it scares me."

"I love you, Abelard. Tell me you'll call Ross tomorrow."

"Oh, no," Lindsay said. "It would be a bad mistake to seem too eager."

"When, then?"

"Oh, a few more years; that's nothing by Ross's standards. . . ."

"But Abelard . . . it hurts me, watching age cut into you. It's gone far enough. It's just not reasonable. . . ." Her eyes filled with tears.

Lindsay was startled and alarmed. "Don't cry, Nora. You'll hurt yourself." He put his arms around her.

She embraced him. "Can't we keep what we have? You've made me doubt myself."

"I'm a fool," Lindsay said. "I'm in good shape, there's no need to be rash. I'm sorry I've said all this."

Her eyes were dry again. "I'll win. We'll win. We'll be young and strong together. You'll see."

## GOLDREICH-TREMAINE COUNCIL STATE: 16-4-'53

Lindsay had put off this meeting as long as possible. Now antioxidants and his special diet were no longer enough. He was sixty-eight.

The demortalization clinic was in the outskirts of Goldreich-Tremaine, part of the growing cluster of inflatable subbles. The tube-linked bubbles could mushroom or vanish overnight, a perfect habitat for Black Medicals and other dubious enclaves.

Mechanists lurked here, hunting Shaper life-extension while evading Shaper law. Supply and demand had conjured up corruption, while Goldreich-Tremaine grew lax with success. The capital had overreached itself, and cracks in the economy were papered over with black money.

Fear had driven Lindsay to this point: fear that things might fall apart and find him weak.

Ross had promised him anonymity. He would be in and out in a hurry, two days at the most.

"I don't want anything major," Lindsay told the old woman. "Just a decatabolism."

"Did you bring your gene-line records?"

"No."

"That complicates matters." The black-market demortalist looked at him with an oddly girlish tilt of the head. "Genetics determine the nature of the side-effects. Is that natural aging or cumulative damage?"

"It's natural."

"Then we can try something less fine-tuned. Hormonals with a deoxidation flush for free radicals. Quick and dirty. But it'll bring your sparkle back."

Lindsay thought of Pongpianskul and his leathery skin. "What treatment do you use yourself?"

"That's confidential."

"How old are you?"

The woman smiled. "You shouldn't pry, friend. The less we know about each other, the better."

Lindsay gave her a Look. She failed to catch it. He Looked again. She didn't know the language.

He crawled with unease. "I can't go through with this," he said. "I find you too hard to trust." Lindsay floated toward the bubble's exit, away from its free-fall core of hospital scanners and samplers.

"Is our price too high, Dr. Abelard Mavrides?" the woman called out.

His mind raced as his worst fears were realized. He turned, determined to face her down. "Someone has misled you."

"We have our own intelligence."

He studied her kinesics warily. The wrinkles of her face were very slightly wrong, not matching the muscles beneath the skin. "You're young," he said. "You only look old."

"Then we share one fraud. For you, that's only one of many."

"Ross told me you were dependable," he said. "Why risk your situation by annoying me?"

"We want the truth."

He stared. "How ambitious. Try the scientific method. And in the meantime, let's talk sense."

The young woman smoothed her medical tunic with wrinkled hands. "Pretend I'm a theatre audience, Dr. Mavrides. Tell me about your ideology."

"I don't have one."

"What about the Investor Peace? All those Détentiste plays? Did you think you would heal the Schism with this Investor fraud?"

"You're younger than I thought," he said. "If you ask me that, you must have never seen the war."

She glared at him. "We were raised in the Peace! Children, told from the crèche that love and reason would sweep the war aside! But we read history. Not Juliano's version but the bitter truth. Do you know what happens to groups whose innovations fail? At best they're shuffled off to some wretched outpost. At worst they're hunted down, picked off, turned against each other—"

The truth of it stung him. "But some live!"

The girl laughed. "You're unplanned, so why should you care for us? Stupidity is life and breath to you."

"You're one of Margaret Juliano's people," he said. "The Superbrights." He stared at her. He had never met a Superbright before. They were supposed to be closely sheltered, constantly under study.

"Margaret Juliano," she said. "From your Midnight Clique. She helped design us. She's a Détentiste! When the Peace falls, we'll fall with her! They're always prying at us, spying, looking for flaws. . . ." Her eyes were wild in the wrinkled face. "Do you realize the potential we have? There are no rules, no souls, no limits! But dogmas hedge us in. False wars and stupid loyalties. The heaped-up garbage of the Schismatrix. Others wallow in it, hiding from total freedom! But we want all the truth, without conditions. We take our reality raw. We want all eyes open, always: and if it takes a cataclysm, then we have a thousand ready. . . ."

"No, wait," Lindsay said. The girl was a Superbright; she could be no more than thirty. It appalled him to see her so fanatic, so willing to repeat his errors: his, and Vera's. "You're too young for absolutes. For God's sake, no pure gestures. Give it fifty years first. Give it a hundred! You have all the time you want!"

"We don't think the way they want us to," the girl said. "And they'll kill us for it. But not until we've pried the worldskull open and put our needles in."

"Wait," Lindsay said. "Maybe the Peace is doomed. But you can save yourselves. You're clever. You can—"

"Life's a joke, friend. Death's the punch line." She raised her hand and vanished.

Lindsay gasped. "What have you—?" He stopped suddenly. His own voice sounded odd to him. The room's acoustics seemed different. The machines, however, were producing the same quiet hums and subdued beeps.

He approached the machines. "Hello? Young girl. Let's talk first. Believe me, I can understand." His voice had changed; it had lost the subtle raspiness of age. He touched his throat left-handed. His chin had a heavy growth of beard. Shocked, he tugged at it. It was his own hair.

He floated closer to the machines, touched one. It rustled beneath his hand. He seized it in a fury; it crumpled at once, showing a flimsy lathwork of cellulose and plastic. He tore into the next machine. Another mockup. In the center of the complex was a child's tape recorder, humming and beeping faithfully. He snatched it up left-handed and was suddenly aware of his left arm: a lingering soreness in the muscle.

He tore off his short and jacket. His stomach was taut, flat; the graying hair on his chest had been painstakingly depilated. Again he felt his face. He had never worn a beard, but it felt like two weeks' growth, at least.

The girl must have drugged him on the spot. Then someone had given him a cell-wash, reversed catabolism, reset the Hayflick limit on his skin and major organs, at the same time exercising his unconscious body to restore muscle tone. Then, when all was done, replaced him in the same position and somehow restored him to instant awareness.

Delayed shock struck him; the world seemed to shimmer. Compared to this, almost anything was easier to doubt: his name, his business here, his life. They left me the beard as a calendar, he thought dazedly. Unless that too was fraud.

He took a deep breath. His lungs felt tight, stretched. They had stripped them of the tar from smoking.

"Oh God," he said aloud. "Nora." By now she would be past panic: she would be full of reckless hatred for whoever had taken him. He hurried at once to the bubble's exit.

The grapelike cluster of cheap inflatables was hooked to an interurban tube-road. He floated at once down the lacquered corridor and emerged through a filament doorway into the swollen transparent nexus of crossroads. Below was Goldreich-Tremaine, with its Besetzny and Patterson Wheels spinning in slow majesty; with the moleculelike links and knobs of other suburbs shining purple, gold, and green, surrounding the city like beaded yarn. At least he was still in G-T. He headed at once for home.

# GOLDREICH-TREMAINE COUNCIL STATE: 18-9-'53

The chaos repulsed Constantine. Evacuations were untidy affairs. The docking port was littered with trash: clothing, ship schedules, inhaler wrappers, propaganda leaflets. Baggage limits were growing stricter by the hour. Not far away four Shapers were pulling items from their overweight luggage and spitefully smashing them against the walls and mooring-benches.

Long lines waited at the interaction terminals. The overloaded terminals were charging by the second. Some of the refugees were finding that it cost more money to sell their faltering stocks than the stocks themselves were worth.

A synthetic voice on the address system announced the next flight to Skimmers Union. Instant pandemonium swept the port. Constantine smiled. His own craft, the *Friendship Serene,* had that destination. Unlike the others, his berth was secure. Not simply in the ship but in the new capital as well.

Goldreich-Tremaine had overreached itself. It had leaned too heavily on the mystique of its capitalship. When that was gone, seized by militants in a rival city, G-T's web of credit had nothing to sustain it.

He liked Skimmers Union. It floated in circumtitanian orbit, above the bloody glimmer of the clouds of Titan. In Skimmers Union the source of the city's wealth was always reassuringly close: the inexhaustible mass of rich organics that choked the Titanian sky. Fusion-powered dredges punched through its atmosphere, sweeping up organics by the hundreds of tons. Methane, ethane, acetylene, cyanogen: a planetary feedstock for the Union's polymer factories.

Passengers were disembarking; a handful compared to those leaving, and not a savory handful. A group in baggy uniforms floated past customs. Sundogs, clearly, and not even Shaper sundogs: their skins shone with antiseptic oils.

Constantine's bodyguards murmured to one another in his earpiece, sizing up the latest arrivals. The four guards were unhappy with Constantine's reluctance to leave. Constantine's many local enemies were close to desperation as Goldreich-Tremaine's banks neared collapse. The guards were keyed to a fever pitch.

But Constantine lingered. He had defeated the Shapers on their own ground, and the pleasure of it was intense. He lived for moments like this one. He was perhaps the only calm man in a crowd of close to two thousand. Never had he felt so utterly in control.

His enemies had been crippled by their underestimation. They had taken his measure and erred completely. Constantine himself did not know that measure; that was the pang that drove him on.

He considered his enemies, one by one. The militants had chosen him to attack the Midnight Clique, and his success had been thorough and impressive. Regent Charles Vetterling had been the first to fall. Vetterling fancied himself a survivor. Encouraged by Carl Zeuner, he had thrown in his lot with the militants. The power of the Midnight Clique was broken from within. It splintered into warring camps. Those who held their ground were denounced by others more desperate.

The Mechanist defector, Sigmund Fetzko, had "faded." These days, those calling his residence received only ingenious delays and temporizing from his household's expert system. Fetzko's image lived; the man himself was dead, and too polite to admit it.

Neville Pongpianskul was dead, assassinated in the Republic at Constantine's order.

Chancellor-General Margaret Juliano had simply vanished. Some enemy of her own had finished her. This still puzzled Constantine; on the day of her disappearance he had received a large crate, anonymously. Cautiously opened by bodyguards, it had revealed a block of ice with her name elegantly chiseled on its surface: *Margaret Juliano,* on ice. She had not been seen since.

Colonel-Professor Nora Mavrides had drastically overplayed her hand. Her husband, the false Lindsay, had disappeared, and she had accused Constantine of kidnapping him. When her husband returned again, with a wild tale about Superbright renegades and black market clinics, she was disgraced.

Constantine was still not sure what had happened. The most likely explanation was that Nora Mavrides had been double-crossed by her burnt-out little cadre of diplomats. Probably they had seen what was coming and set up their one-time protectress, hoping that the new Skimmers Union regime would thank them for it. If so, they were grossly mistaken.

Constantine looked about the cavernous station, adjusting his videoshades for closeups. Amid the fretting Shapers in their overelaborate finery was a growing minority of others. An imported cargo of sundogs. Here and there shabbily clad ideological derelicts, their faces wreathed in smiles, were comparing lace-sleeved garments to their torsos or lurking with predatory nonchalance beside evacuees lightening their luggage.

"Vermin," Constantine said. The sight depressed him. "Gentlemen, it's time we moved on."

The guards led him across the chained-off entry to a private ramp padded in velcro. Constantine's clingtight boots crunched and shredded across the fabric.

He floated down the free-fall embarkation tube to the airlock of the *Friendship Serene.* Once inside he took his favorite acceleration chair and plugged in on video to enjoy the takeoff.

Within the port's skeletal gantryways, the smaller ships queued up for embarkation tubes, dwarfed by the stylized bulk of an Investor starship. Constantine craned his neck, causing the hull cameras of the *Friendship Serene* to swivel in slaved obedience. "Is that Investor ship still here?" he said aloud. He smiled. "Do you suppose they're hunting bargains?"

He lifted his videoshades. Within the ship's cabin his guards clustered around an overhead tank, huffing tranquilizer gas from breathing masks. One looked up, red-eyed. "May we go into suspension now, sir?"

Constantine nodded sourly. Since the war had started up again, his guards had lost all sense of humor.

# AN INVESTOR TRADE SHIP: 22-9-'53

Nora looked up at her husband, who sprawled above her in a towering chair. His face was hidden by a dark beard and opaque wraparound sunshades. His hair was close-cropped and he wore a Mech jumpsuit. His old, scarred diplomatic bag rested on the scratchy plush of the deck. He was taking it with him. He meant to defect.

The heavy gravity of the Investor ship weighed on both of them like iron. "Stop pacing, Nora," he said. "You'll only exhaust yourself."

"I'll rest later," she said. Tension knotted her neck and shoulders.

"Rest now. Take the other chair. If you'll close your eyes, sleep a little . . . in almost no time—"

"I'm not going with you." She pulled off her own sunshades and rubbed the bridge of her nose. The light in the cabin was the light Investors favored: a searing blaze of blue-white radiance, drenched in ultraviolet.

She hated that light. Somehow she had always resented the Investors for robbing her Family's deaths of meaning. And the three months she'd once spent in a ship like this one had been the eeriest time of her life. Lindsay had been quick, adaptable, the consummate sundog, as willing to deal with the aliens as he was with anyone. She'd wondered at it then. And now they had come full circle.

He said, "You came this far. You wouldn't have, if you didn't want to come with me. I know you, Nora. You're still the same, even if I've changed."

"I came because I wanted to be with you for every moment that I could." She fought down the tears, her face frozen. The sensation was horrifying, a black nausea. Too many tears, she thought, had been pushed away for too long. The day would come when she would choke on them.

Constantine used every weakness in Goldreich-Tremaine, she thought. And my special weakness was this man. When Abelard came back from the rejuvenation clinic, three weeks late and so changed that the household robots wouldn't let him in . . . But even that was not so bad as the days without him, hunting for him, finding that the black-market subble he'd gone to had been deflated and put away, wondering what furtive Star Chamber was picking him to shreds. . . .

"This is my fault," she said. "I accused Constantine with no proof, and he humiliated me. Next time I'll know better."

"Constantine had nothing to do with it," he said. "I know what I saw in that clinic. They were Superbrights."

"I can't believe in the Cataclysts," she said. "Those Superbrights are watched like jewels; they don't have room for wild conspiracies. What you saw was a fraud; the whole thing was staged to draw me out. And I fell for it."

"Don't be proud, Nora. It's blinded you. The Cataclysts abducted me, and you won't even admit they exist. You can't win, because you can't bring back the past. Let it go, and come with me."

"When I see what Constantine did to the Clique—"

"It's not your fault! My God, aren't there disasters enough without your heaping them all on your own shoulders? Goldreich-Tremaine is through! We have to live now! I told you years ago that it couldn't last, and now it's over!" He flung his arms wide. The left one, tugged by gravity, fell limply; the other whirred with smooth precision through a powered arc.

They had been over this a hundred times, and she saw that his nerves were frayed. Under the influence of the treatment his hard-won patience had vanished in a blaze of false youth. He was shouting at her. "You're not God! You're not history! You're not the Ring Council! Don't flatter yourself! You're nothing now, you're a target, a scapegoat! Run, Nora! Sundog it!"

"The Mavrides clan needs me," she said.

"They're better off without you. You're an embarrassment to them now, we both are—"

"And the children?"

He was silent a moment. "I'm sorry for them, more sorry than I can say, but they're adults now and they can take their own chances. They're not the problem here, we are! If we make things easy for the enemy, just slip away, evaporate, we'll be forgotten. We can wait it out."

"And give the fascists their way in everything? The assassins, the killers? How long before the Belt fills up again with Shaper agents, and little wars blaze up in every corner?"

"And who'll stop that? You?"

"What about you, Abelard? Dressed as a stinking Mechanist with stolen Shaper data in that bag! Do you ever think of anyone's life but your own? Why in God's name don't you stand up for the helpless instead of betraying them? Do you think it's easier for me without you? I'll go on fighting, but without you there'll be no heart in me."

He groaned. "Listen. I was a sundog before I met you, you know just how little I had. . . . I don't want that emptiness, no one caring, no one knowing . . . And another betrayal on my conscience. . . . Nora, we had almost forty years! This place was good to us, but it's falling apart on its own! Good times will come again. We have all the time there is! You wanted more life, and I went out and got it for you. Now you want me to throw it away. I won't be a martyr, Nora. Not for anyone."

"You always talked about mortality," she said. "You're different now."

"If I changed it was because you wanted me to."

"Not like this. Not treason."

"We'll die for nothing."

"Like the others," she said, regretting it at once. And there it was before them: the old guilt in all its stark intimacy. Those others, to whom duty was more than life. Those they had abandoned, those they had killed in the Shaper outpost. That was the crime the two of them had struggled to efface, the crime that had bound them together. "Well, that's what you're asking, isn't it? To betray my own people again, for you!"

There. She had said it. Now there was no going back. She waited in pain for the words that would free her from him.

"You were my people," he said. "I should have known I would never have one for long. I'm a sundog, and it's my way, not yours. I knew you wouldn't come." He leaned his head against the bare fingers of his artificial arm. Piercing highlights glinted off the harsh iron. "Stay and fight, then. You could win, I think."

It was the first time he had lied to her. "But I *can* win," she said. "It won't be easy, we won't have all we had, but we're not beaten yet. Stay, Abelard, please. Please! I need you. Ask me for anything except to give up fighting."

"I can't ask you to change," her husband said. "People only change if you give them time. Someday this thing that's haunted us will wear away, if we both live. I think the love is stronger than the guilt. If it is, and someday you feel your obligations no longer need you, then come after me. Find me. . . ."

"I will, I promise it, Abelard. . . . If I'm killed like the others and you live on safely then say you won't forget me."

"Never. I swear it by everything we had between us."

"Goodbye, then." She climbed up into the huge Investor chair to kiss him. She felt his steel hand go around her wrist like a manacle. She kissed him lightly. Then she tugged, and he let go.

# Chapter 6

Lindsay lay on the floor of his cavernous stateroom, breathing deeply. The ozone-charged air of the Investor ship stung his nose, which was sunburned despite his oils. The stateroom walls were blackened metal, studded with armored orifices. From one of them a freshet of distilled water trickled, cascading limply in the heavy gravity.

This stateroom had seen a lot of use. Faint scratches cuneiformed the floor and walls, almost to the ceiling. Humans were not the only passengers to pay Investor fare.

If modern Shaper exosociology was right, the Investors themselves were not the first owners of these starships. Covered in vainglorious mosaics and metal bas-reliefs, each Investor craft looked unique. But close analysis showed the underlying basic structure: blunt hexagons at bow and stern, with six long rectangular sides. Current thought held that the Investors had bought, found, or stolen them.

The ship's Ensign had given him a pallet, a broad flat mattress patterned in brown-and-white hexagons, built for Investors. Its surface was as harsh as burlap. It smelled faintly of Investor scale-oil.

Lindsay had tested the metal wall of his stateroom, wondering about the scratches. Though it felt faintly grainy, the steel zips of his foot-gloves slid on it like glass. Still, it might be softer under extremes of temperature and pressure. A very large taloned beast afloat in a pool of high-pressure liquid ethane, for instance, might have scratched the walls in an attempt to burrow out.

The gravity was painful, but the stateroom lights had been turned down.

The cabin was huge and unfurnished; his scattering of clothes on magnetic hooks seemed like pathetic scraps.

It was odd of the Investors to leave a room empty, even if it doubled as a zoo. Lindsay lay quietly, trying to catch his breath, thinking about it.

The armored hatchway rang, then shunted open. Lindsay levered himself up with the artificial arm, the only limb not sore from gravity. He smiled. "Yes, Ensign? News?"

The Ensign entered the room. He was small for an Ensign, a mere forearm's length taller than Lindsay himself, and his wiry build was accented by his birdlike habit of ducking his head. He looked more like a crewman than an Ensign. Lindsay studied him thoughtfully.

Academics still speculated about the Investor ranking system. The Ship's Commanders were always female, the only females aboard ship. They were twice the size of crewmen, massively built. With their size went a sluggish calm, a laconic assumption of power. Ensigns were second in command, as combination diplomats and ministers. The rest of the crew formed an adoring male harem. The scampering crewmen with their bead-bright eyes weighed three times as much as a man, but around their monstrous commanders they almost seemed to flutter.

The frills were the central kinesic display. The reptilian Investors had long ribbed frills behind their heads, rainbow-tinted translucent skin netted with blood vessels. Frills had evolved for temperature control; they could be spread to absorb sunlight or opened in shade to dispel heat. In civilized Investor life they were a relic, like the human eyebrow, which had evolved to deflect sweat. Like the eyebrow, their social use was now paramount.

The Ensign's frill bothered Lindsay. It flickered too much. Rapid flickering was usually interpreted as a sign of amusement. In human beings, bad laughter kinesics were a sign of deep stress. Lindsay, despite his professional interest, had no desire to be the first to witness an Investor's hysteria. He hoped it was simply a repulsive mannerism. This ship was new to the Solar System and its crew was unused to humanity.

"No news, Artist," the Ensign said in pained trade English. "A further discussion of payment."

"Good business," Lindsay said in Investor. His throat ached from the high-pitched fluting, but he preferred it to the Ensign's eerie attempts to master human language.

This Ensign was not like the first he had met. That Investor had been smooth and urbane, his vocabulary heavy with glib clichés gleaned from human video broadcasts. This new Ensign was visibly struggling.

Clearly the Investors had sent in their best to make first contact. After thirty-seven years, it seemed that the Solar System was now considered safe for Investor fringe elements. "Our Commander wants you on tape," the Ensign said in English.

Lindsay reached automatically for the thin chain around his neck. His video monocle, with its treasured film of Nora, hung there. "I have a tape which is mostly blank. I can't surrender it, but—"

"Our Commander is very fond of her tape. Her tape has many other images but not one of your species. She will study it."

"I'd like another audience with the Commander," Lindsay said. "The first was so brief. I will gladly submit to the tape. You have your camera?"

The Ensign blinked, the lucid nictitating membrane flickering upward over his dark, bulging eyeball. The dimness of the room seemed to upset him. "I have the tape." He opened his over-the-shoulder valise and produced a flat round canister. He grasped the canister with two of his huge toes and set it on the black gunmetal floor. "You will open the canister. You will then make amusing and characteristic movements of your species, which the tape will see. Continue to do this until the tape understands you."

Lindsay wobbled his jaw from side to side in imitation of the Investor nod. The Investor seemed satisfied. "Language is not necessary. The tape does not hear sound." The Investor turned to the door. "I will return for the tape in two of your hours."

Left alone, Lindsay studied the canister. The ridged and gilded metal top was as wide as both outstretched hands. Before opening it he waited a moment, savoring his disgust. It was as much self-directed as aimed at his hosts.

The Investors had not asked to be deified; they had merely pursued their own gain. They had been aware of mankind for centuries. They were much older than mankind, but they had thoughtfully refrained from interfering until they saw that they could wring a decent profit from the species. Seen from an Investor's viewpoint, their actions were straightforward.

Lindsay opened the canister. A spool of iron-gray tape nestled inside, with ten centimeters of off-white leader. Lindsay put the lid aside—the thin metal was heavy as lead in the Investor gravity—and then froze.

The tape rustled in its box. The leader end flicked upward, twisting, and the whole length of it began to uncoil. It rose, whipping and rippling, faint sheens of random color coiling along its length. Within seconds it had formed an open cloud of bright ribbon, supporting itself on a stiff, half-flattened latticework.

Lindsay, still kneeling and moving only his eyes, watched cautiously. The white end-piece was the tape creature's head, he realized. The head moved on a long craned loop, scanning the room for movement.

The tape creature stirred restlessly, stretching itself in a loose-looped open mass of rolling corkscrews. At its loosest, it was a bloated, giddy yarnball as tall as a man, its stiffened support-loops thinly hissing across the floor.

He'd thought it was machinery at first. Dangerous machinery, because the edges of the warping tape were as thin as razors. But there was an unplanned, organic ease to its coiling.

He had not yet moved. It didn't seem able to see him.

He shook his head sharply, and the heavy sunshades on his forehead flew across the room. The tape's head darted after them at once.

The mimicry started from the tail. The tape shrank, crumpling like packing tissue, sketching the sunshades' form in tightly crinkled ribbon. Before it had quite completed the job, the tape seemed to lose interest. It hesitated, watching the inert sunglasses, then fell apart in a loose, whipping mass.

Briefly it mimicked Lindsay's crouching form, looping itself into a gappy man-sized sculpture of rustling tape. Its tinted ribbon quickly matched the rust-on-black tinge of his coveralls. Then the tape head looked elsewhere and it flew to pieces, its colors racing fretfully.

It flickered as Lindsay watched. Its white head scanned slowly, almost surreptitiously. It flashed muddy brown, the color of Investor hide. Slowly, a memory, either biological or cybernetic, took hold of it. It began to bunch and crumple into a new form.

The image of a small Investor took shape. Lindsay was thrilled. No human being had ever seen an infant Investor, and they were supposedly very rare. But soon Lindsay could tell from the proportions that the tape was modeling an adult female. The tape was too small to form a full-scale replica, but the accuracy of the knee-high model astonished him. Tiny blisters on the ribbon reproduced the hard, pebbly skin of the skull and neck; the tiny eyes, two tinted bumps, seemed full of expression.

Lindsay felt a chill. He recognized the individual. And the expression was one of dull animal pain.

The tape was mimicking the Investor Commander. She was gasping, her barrel-like ribs heaving. She squatted awkwardly, one clawed hand spread across each upthrust knee. The mouth opened in spasms, showing poorly mimicked peg teeth and the hollow paper-thin walls of the model's head.

The ship's Commander was sick. No one had ever seen an Investor ill. The strangeness of it, Lindsay thought, must have stuck in the tape's memory. This opportunity was not to be missed. With glacial slowness Lindsay unsnapped his coverall and exposed the video monocle on its chain. He began filming.

The scaled belly tightened and two edges of tape opened at the base of the model's heavy tail. A rounded white mass with the gleam of dampness appeared, a tightly wrapped oblong of tape: an egg.

It was a slow process, a painful one. The egg was leathery; the contractions of the oviduct were compressing it. At last it was free, though still connected to the tape's parent body by a transparent length of ribbon. The Investor captain's image turned, shuffling, then bent to examine the egg with a sick, rapt intensity. Slowly, her huge hand stretched out, scratched the egg, sniffed the fingers. Her frill began to rise stiffly, engorged with blood. Her arms trembled.

She attacked her egg. She bit savagely into the narrow end, shearing into the leathery shell with the badly mimicked teeth. Yellow ribbon showed, a cheeselike yolk.

She feasted, the taped arms flushing yellow with slime. The frill jutted behind her head, stiff with fury. The furtive nastiness of her crime was unmistakable; it crossed the barrier of species easily. As easily as wealth.

Lindsay put his monocle away. The tape, attracted by the movement, unlaced its head and lifted it blankly. Lindsay waved his arms at it and the model fell into tangles. He stood up and began to shuffle back and forth in the heavy gravity. It watched him, coiling and flickering.

## DEMBOWSHA CARTEL: 10-10-'53

Lindsay lurched down the entry ramp, his scuffed foot-gloves skidding. After the blaze aboard the starship the disembarkation mall seemed murky, subaqueous. Dizziness seized him. He might have managed free-fall, but the Dembowska asteroid's feeble gravity made his stomach lurch.

The lobby was sprinkled with travelers from the other Mechanist cartels. He'd never seen so many Mechs in one place, and despite himself the sight alarmed him. Ahead, luggage and passengers entered the scanning racks of customs. Beyond them loomed the glass fronts of the Dembowska duty-free shops.

Lindsay shuddered suddenly. He had never felt air so cold. An icy draft seeped through his thin coveralls and the flexible fabric of his foot-gloves. His breath was steaming. Dazed, he headed for the customs.

A young woman waited just before it, poised easily on one booted foot. She wore dark tights and a fur-collared jacket. "Captain-Doctor?" she said.

Lindsay stopped with difficulty, gripping the carpet with his toes.

"The bag, please?" Lindsay handed her his ancient diplomatic bag, crammed with data lifted from Kosmosity files. She took his arm in a friendly fashion, leading him through an unmarked door past the customs scanners. "I'm Policewife Greta Beatty. Your liaison." They went down a flight of stairs to an office. She handed the bag to a woman in uniform and accepted a stamped envelope in return.

She led him out onto a lower floor of the duty-free mall, prying open the envelope with her lacquered nails. "This holds your new papers," she said. She handed him a credit card. "You are now Auditor Andrew Bela Milosz. Welcome to Dembowska Cartel."

"Thank you, Policewife."

"Greta will do. May I call you Andrew?"

"Call me Bela," Lindsay said. "Who picked the name?"

"His parents. Andrew Milosz died recently, in Bettina Cartel. But you won't find his death in the records; his next of kin sold his identity to the Dembowska Harem Police. All identifying marks in his records have been erased and replaced with yours. Officially, he emigrated here." She smiled. "I'm here to help you over the transition. To keep you happy."

"I'm freezing," Lindsay said.

"We'll see to that at once." She led him past the frosted glass into one of the duty-free shops, a clothier's. When they reemerged Lindsay wore new coveralls, of thicker quilted fabric with inset vertical puckers at wrists and ankles. The tasteful charcoal gray matched his new fur-lined velcro boots. Gloves were clipped to the vest pocket of his flared fuzzplastic jacket. He sported a microphone boutonniere in one creamtone lapel.

"Now your hair," said Greta Beatty. She carried his new zip-up wardrobe bag. "It's in an awful state."

"It was gray," Lindsay said. "The roots grew in black. So I shaved it off. Since then it's been on its own." He looked at her levelly.

"You want to keep the beard?"

"Yes."

"Whatever makes you happy."

After ten minutes under the stylers Lindsay's hair was brushed back from his forehead and temples in slickly brilliantined curves. The beard was trimmed.

Lindsay had been watching his companion's kinesics. There was a calmness, a quietude about her movements that belied her youth. Lindsay felt strained, hypertensive, but Greta's smooth cheerfulness was beginning to affect him through kinesic contamination. He found himself smiling involuntarily.

"Hungry yet?"

"Yes."

"We'll go to the Periscope. You look fine, Bela. You'll get the hang of Dembowska gravity in no time. Stick close by me." She wrapped her arm around his. "I like your antique arm."

"You're staying with me?"

"As long as you like."

"I see. And if I suggest you leave?"

"Do you really think you'll be better off for that?"

Lindsay considered this. "No. Forgive me, Policewife." He felt touchy, obscurely annoyed. His new identity bothered him. He had never had one forced on him before. His old training urged him to take on local coloration, but the years had calcified him.

Greta led him down two flights of stirruped escalators, deeper into the asteroid. The floor and walls were of scuffed and ancient metal, lined with new velcro. The crowd moved in stately, shredding leaps. Overhead, citizens in a hurry flung themselves along with ceiling loops. They followed a very old Dembowskan who was making good time along the wall in a velcro-wheeled prosthetic chair. "We'll have a little something to eat," Greta Beatty said. "You'll feel better."

He considered mimicking her kinesics. He was a little rusty but he thought he could manage it. It might be the smartest thing: to match her easy affability with his own. He didn't want to. He hurt too much.

"Greta, this easy generosity surprises me. Why are you this way?"

"A policewife? Oh, I wasn't involved in security at first. I was a Carnassus wife, a strictly erotic relationship. Promotion came later. I'm not in espionage. I just do liaison work."

"Many others before me?"

"A few. Sundogs mostly. Not ranking Shaper academics."

"You've seen Michael Carnassus?"

She smiled distantly. "Only in the flesh. We're almost there. Harem Police have reserved tables. You'll want one of the windows, I'm sure."

The dim intimacy of the Periscope, to Lindsay's light-blasted eyes, seemed impossibly gloomy. Steam rose off the food on the tables. He put on his left glove. He had never been anywhere so cold.

Cool blue light poured through the bulging, concave windows. Lindsay glanced through the metaglass briefly, saw a rocky cavern half full of water. An observation sphere the size of a house was anchored to the cavern's ceiling. Beside it was a bank of blue spotlights, mounted across the ceiling on arching rails. Lindsay set his boots into the stirrups of a low-grav chair. The seat warmed beneath him; its padded saddle was wired with heating elements.

Greta smiled at him across the table, her blue eyes huge in the dimness. It was a friendly smile without flirtation in it; without, in fact, any subterranean elements at all. No fear, no shyness; nothing but a well-balanced hint of mild benevolence. Her blonde hair was parted in the middle and fell in modish Dembowska fashion to smooth, blunt-cut edges along her ears and cheekbones. The hair looked very clean. He had an abstract urge to run his hand across it, the way he might run his fingers over the spine of a book.

The fiery letters of the menu appeared in the table's dark surface. Lindsay put his gloved hand on the tabletop. Its surface was sticky with adhesive polymers. He pulled his fingers back; the glue held him at first, then released its grip sharply, leaving no trace. He looked at the menu. "No prices."

"The Harem Police will pick it up. We wouldn't want you getting a bad opinion of our cuisine." She nodded across the restaurant. "That gentleman in the biocuirass, at the table to your right—that's Lewis Martinez, with his wife, Lydia. He heads Martinez Corp, his rank is Comptroller. They say she was born on Earth."

"She looks well-preserved." Lindsay stared with frank curiosity at the sinister pair, whose skill as industrial spies was a byword in Shaper Security circles. They were speaking quietly between courses, smiling at one another with unfeigned affection. Lindsay felt a stab of pain.

Greta was still talking. "The man with the tabletop servo is Coordinator Brandt. . . . The group by the next window are Kabuki Intrasolar types. The one in the silly jacket is Wells. . . ."

"Does Ryumin ever dine here?"

"Oh . . . no." She smiled briefly. "He transmits in different circles."

Lindsay rubbed his bearded chin. "He's well, I hope."

She was polite. "I'm not the one to judge. He seems happy. Let me order for you." She punched in orders on the table's keyboard wing.

"Why is it so cold?"

"History. Fashion. Dembowska's an old colony; it suffered an ecobreakdown. There are places where I can show you layers of flashfrozen mold still peeling off the walls. The worst rots have adjusted to a narrow range in temperature. When it's this cold they're dormant. That's not the only reason, though." She gestured at the window. "That has its influence."

Lindsay looked out. "The swimming pool?"

Greta laughed politely. "That's the Extraterrarium, Bela."

"Burn me!" Lindsay stared outward.

The rough-hewn cavity was slopping over with a turgid, rust-tinged liquid. He'd thought it was water at first. "That's where they keep the monsters," he said. "That observation globe—that's the Carnassus Palace, isn't it?"

"Of course."

"It's quite small."

"It's an exact replica of the observatory of the Chaikin Expedition. Of course it's not large. Imagine what the Investors charged them to ship it to the stars. Carnassus lives very modestly, Bela. It's not like Ring Security told you."

Every diplomatic instinct held Lindsay back. With an effort, he broke them. "But he has two hundred wives."

"Think of us as a psychiatric staff, Auditor. Marriage to Carnassus is an arrangement of rank. Dembowska depends on him, and he depends on us."

Lindsay said, "Could I meet Carnassus?"

"That would be up to the Chief of Police. But what's the point? The man can barely speak. It's not like they say in the Rings. Carnassus is a very dazed, very gentle person, who was terribly wounded. When his embassy was failing, he took an experimental drug, PDKL-Ninety-five. It was supposed to help him grasp alien modes of thought, but it shattered him. He was a brave man. We feel pity for him. The sexual aspect is a very minor part of it."

Lindsay considered this. "I see. With two hundred others, some of them favorites, presumably, it must be a rather rare role. . . . Once a year, perhaps?"

She was calm. "Not quite that rare, but you've grasped the basics. I won't disguise the truth, Bela. Carnassus is not our ruler; he's our resource. The Harem rules Dembowska because we surround him and we're the only ones he'll talk to." She smiled. "It's not a matriarchy. We're not mothers. We're the police."

Lindsay looked out the window. A drip fell and rippled. It was liquid ethane. Just beyond the insulated metaglass the sluggish pond was at an instantly lethal 180 degrees below zero Celsius. A man in that reddish pool would freeze in seconds into a bloated mass of rock. The grayish stones of the shores, Lindsay realized suddenly, were water ice.

Something was emerging onto the shoreline. In the dim bluish light, the ethane's surface was pierced by what appeared to be a rack of broken twigs. Even in the feeble gravity the creature's movements were glacial. Lindsay pointed.

"A sea scorpion," Greta said. "Eurypteroid, to give it its formal name. It's attacking that lump on the shoreline. That black slime is vegetation." More of the predator slid with paralytic slowness from the thin liquid. The twigs were now revealed as interlocking basketlike foreclaws that meshed together like saberteeth. "Its prey is gathering energy to leap. That will take a while. By the standards of this ecosystem, this is a lightning attack. Look at the size of its cephalothorax, Bela."

The sea scorpion had heaved its broad, platelike prosoma out of the water; this crablike head-body was half a meter across. Behind the lozenge-shaped compound eyes was the creature's long, tapering abdomen, plated in overlapping horizontal ridges. "It's three meters long," Greta said as a servo delivered the first course. "Longer if you count the tailspike. A nice size for an invertebrate. Have some soup."

"I'm watching this." The extended claws were closing on the prey with the slow deliberation of a hydraulic door. Suddenly the prey-creature flopped wobblingly into the air and landed in the pool with a splash.

"It jumps fast!" Lindsay said.

"There's only one speed for jumping." Greta Beatty smiled. "That's physics. Eat something. Have a breadstick." Lindsay could not tear his eyes from the eurypteroid, which lay with its claw-teeth intermeshed, inert and apparently exhausted. "I pity it," he said.

Greta was patient. "It came here as an egg, Bela. It didn't get that large eating breadsticks. Carnassus takes good care of them. He was the embassy's exobiologist."

Lindsay tried some soup with the sliding trap-bowl of his low-gravity spoon. "You seem to share his expertise."

"Everyone in Dembowska takes an interest in the Extraterrarium. Local pride. Of course, the tourist trade isn't what it was, since the Investor Peace collapsed. We make up for it with refugees."

Lindsay stared moodily into the pool. The food was excellent, but his appetite was off. The eurytpteroid stirred feebly. He thought of the sculpture the Investors had given him and wondered what its droppings looked like.

A burst of laughter came from Well's table. "I want a word with Wells," Lindsay said.

"Leave it to me," she said. "Wells has Shaper contacts. Word might leak back to the Ring Council." She looked grave. "You wouldn't want to risk your cover before it's well established."

"You don't trust Wells?"

She shrugged. "That's not your worry." A new course arrived, borne by a squeaking, velcro-footed robot. "I love the antique servos here, don't you?" She squirted heavy cream sauce over a meat pastry and gave him the plate. "You're under stress, Bela. You need food. Sleep. A sauna. The good things in life. You look edgy. Relax."

"I live on the edge," Lindsay said.

"Not now. You live with me. Eat something so I'll know you feel safe."

To please her, Lindsay bit reluctantly into the pastry. It was delicious. Appetite flooded back into him. "I have things to do," he said, stifling the urge to wolf it down.

"Think you'll do them better without food and sleep?"

"I suppose you have a point." He looked up; she handed him the sauce bulb. As he squeezed on more sauce she passed him a slotted wineglass. "Try the local claret." He sampled it. It was as good as vintage Synchronis, from the Rings. "Someone stole this technology," he said.

"You aren't the first defector. Things are calmer here." She pointed out the window. "Look at that xiphosuran." A lumpy crab was sculling across the pool with intolerable sluggish calm. "It has a lesson for you."

Lindsay stared quietly, thinking.

Greta's domicile was seven levels down. A silver-plated household servo took Lindsay's wardrobe bag. Greta's parlor had a baroque furred couch with sliding stirrups and two anchored chairs upholstered in burgundy velvet. An adhesive coffee table held a flip-top inhaler case and a rack of cassettes.

The bathroom had a sauna compartment and a fold-out suction toilet with a heated elastic rim. The overhead light glowed pink with infrared heat. Standing on the icy tiles, Lindsay dropped his glove. It fell slowly, at a pronounced slant. The room's verticals didn't match the local gravity. This keen touch of avant-garde interior design filled Lindsay with sudden nausea. He leaped up and clung to the ceiling, closing his eyes until the dizziness passed.

Greta called through the door. "You want a sauna?"

"Anything to get warm."

"The controls are on the left."

Lindsay stripped, gasping as the freezing metal of his artificial arm brushed his bare ribs. He held the arm well away as he stepped into the blizzard of steam. In the low gravity the air was thick with flying water. Coughing, he groped for the breathing mask. It was pure oxygen; in moments he felt like a hero. He twisted the controls recklessly, biting back a scream as he was pelted with a sudden sandblast of powdered snow. He twisted back and let himself cook in wet heat, then stepped out. The sauna cycled through the boiling point, sterilizing itself.

He turbaned his damp hair, absently knotting the towel's ends in a Goldreich-Tremaine flourish. He found pajamas his size in the cabinet; royal blue with matching fur-lined mukluks.

Outside, Greta had changed from her fur jacket and tights into a quilted nightrobe with a flaring collar. For the first time he noticed her forearms, both heavily overlaid with Mechanist implants. The right one held some kind of weapon: a series of short parallel tubes mounted above the wrist. There was no sign of a trigger; it probably worked by nerve interaction. From inside the other sleeve he caught a red flicker of readouts from a biomonitor.

Mechs cherished a fanatic interest in biofeedback. It was part of most Mech programs for longevity. He hadn't thought of Greta as a Mechanist. Despite himself, the sight shocked him.

"You're not sleepy?"

He yawned. "A little."

She raised her right arm above her head, absently. A remote control unit leaped across the room into her hand, and she turned on the videowall. It showed an overhead view of the Extraterrarium, taken through one of the monitors in the Carnassus Palace.

Lindsay joined her on the couch, tucking his mukluks into the heated stirrups. "Not that," he said, shivering. She touched a button; the videowall blurred and resolved into the Saturnian surface, crawling in red and amber. Nostalgia flooded him. He turned his face away.

She switched scenes. A craggy landscape appeared; enormous pits next to a blasted, flaking area cut by two huge crevasses. "This is erotica," she said. "Skin at twenty thousand times life size. One of my favorites." She touched buttons and the video raced across the ominous landscape, pulling to a stop by the root of a gigantic scaled spar. "See those domes?"

"Yes."

"Those are bacteria. This is a Mechanist, you see."

"You?"

She smiled. "This is often the hardest part for a Shaper. You can't stay sterile here; we depend on these little creatures. We don't have your internal alterations. We don't want them. You'll have to crawl like the rest of us." She took his left hand. Her hand was warm and faintly moist. "This is contamination. Is it so bad?"

"No."

"Better to get it over with all at once. Do you agree?"

He nodded. She put her hand on the back of his neck and kissed him warmly, her mouth open. Lindsay touched his flannel sleeve to his lips. "That was more than a medical action," he said.

She pulled the knotted towel from his head and tossed it to the household servo. "Nights are cold in Dembowska. A bed is warmer with two."

"I have a wife."

"Monogamy? How quaint." She smiled sympathetically. "Face facts, Bela. Defection broke your contract with the Mavrides gene-line. You're a nonperson now. Except to us."

Lindsay brooded. An image surged up within him: Nora, curled alone in their bed, her eyes wide, her mind racing as her enemies closed in. He shook his head.

Calmly, Greta smoothed his hair. "If you tried a little, you'd recover your appetite. Still, it's wise not to rush things."

She showed the polite disappointment that a hostess might show to a guest who refused dessert. He felt tired. Despite his renewed youth he ached from the Investor gravity.

"I'll show you the bedroom." It was lined in dark fur. The bed's canopy was an overhead videoceiling. The massive headboard was equipped with the latest in slumber technology. He recognized an encephalogram, monitoring jacks for artificial body parts, fluorographs for midnight blood fractionation.

He climbed into the bed, kicking off his mukluks. The sheets rippled, swaddling over him. "Sleep well," Greta said, leaving. Something touched the top of his head; above him the canopy flickered gently into life, sketching out brain rhythms. The waves were complex and annotated cryptically. One of the wave functions was outlined in roseate pink. As he looked at it, relaxing, it began to grow. He intuited suddenly what went on inside his mind to make it larger. He gave in to it and was suddenly asleep.

When he woke next morning Greta was sleeping peacefully beside him, an alarm tiara clamped to her forehead, tied in to the house security. He climbed out of bed. His skin itched ferociously. His tongue felt furred. He was beginning to crawl.

## DEMBOWSHA CARTEL: 24-10-'53

"I never thought I'd see you this way, Fyodor." On Greta's parlor wall across the room from Lindsay, Ryumin's video-manicured face glowed with bogus health. It was a good replica, but to Lindsay's trained eye it was clearly computer-generated; its perfection was frightening. The lips moved accurately with Ryumin's words, but its little idiosyncrasies of movement were eerily off-key. "How long have you been a wirehead?"

"Ten years or so. Time alters under the wires. You know, I can't remember offhand where I left my brain. Someplace unlikely, I'm sure." Ryumin smiled. "It must be in Dembowska Cartel, or there'd be a transmission lag."

"I want to talk privately. How many people do you suppose are listening in on us?"

"Just the police," Ryumin assured him. "You're in a Harem safehouse; their calls are routed directly through the Chief's databanks. In Dembowska this is as private as it gets. Especially for someone whose past is as dubious as yours, Mr. Dze."

Lindsay dabbed at his nose with a kerchief. The new bacteria had hit his sinuses badly; they had already been weakened by the Investors' ozone-charged air. "Things were different in the Zaibatsu. When we were face to face."

"The wires bring changes," Ryumin said. "It all becomes a matter of input, you see. Systems. Data. We tend toward solipsism; it comes with the territory. Please don't resent it if I doubt you."

"How long have you been in Dembowska?"

"Since the Peace began to crumble. I needed a haven. This is the best available."

"So your travels are over, old man?"

"Yes and no, Mr. Dze. With the loss of mobility comes extension of the senses. If I want I can switch out to a probe in Mercurian orbit. Or in the winds of Jupiter. I often do, in fact. Suddenly I'm there, just as fully as I'm ever anywhere these days. The mind isn't what you think, Mr. Dze. When you grip it with wires, it tends to flow. Data seem to bubble up from some deep layer of the mind. This is not exactly living, but it has advantages."

"You've given up Kabuki Intrasolar?"

"With the war heating up, the theatre's glory days are over for a while. The Network takes up most of my time."

"Journalism?"

"Yes. We wireheads—or, rather, Senior Mechanists, to give us a name not tainted by Shaper propaganda—we have our own modes of dataflow. News networks. At its most intense it approaches telepathy. I'm the local stringer for Ceres Datacom Network. I hold citizenship in it, though legally speaking it's sometimes more convenient to be treated as wholly owned depreciable hardware. Our life is information—even money is information. Our money and our life are one and the same."

The Mechanist's synthesized voice was calm, detached, but Lindsay felt alarm. "Are you in danger, old man? Is it something I can help?"

"My boy," Ryumin said, "there's a whole world behind this screen. The lines have blurred so much that mere matters of life and death have to take a back seat. There are those among us whose brains broke down years ago: they totter along on investments and programmed routines. If the fleshies knew, they'd declare them legally dead. But we're not telling." He smiled. "Think of us as angels, Mr. Dze. Spirits on the wires. Sometimes it's easier that way."

"I'm a stranger here. I'd hoped you could help me, as you did once. I need advice. I need your wisdom."

Ryumin sighed precisely. "I knew a Dze once when we were both rogues. I trusted him; I admired his daring. We were men together. That's no longer the case."

Lindsay blew his nose. With a shudder of deep loathing he handed the soiled kerchief to the household servo. "I would have dared anything then. I was ready to die, but I didn't. I kept looking. And I found someone. I had a wife, and there was no pretense between us. We were happy together."

"I'm glad for you, Mr. Dze."

"When danger crowded in on us I broke and ran. Now after almost forty years I'm a sundog again."

"Forty years is a human lifetime, Mr. Dze. Don't force yourself to be human. A time comes when you have to give that up."

Lindsay looked at his prosthetic arm, flexed the fingers slowly. "I still love her. It was the war that parted us. If there were peace again—"

"Those are Détentiste sentiments. They're out of fashion."

"Have you given up hope, Ryumin?"

"I'm too old for passion," Ryumin said. "Don't ask me to take risks. Leave me to my data streams, Mr. Dze, or whoever you are. I'm what I am. There's no going back, no starting over. That's a game for those who still have flesh. Those who can heal."

"I'm sorry," Lindsay said, "but I need allies. Knowledge is power, and I know things others don't. I mean to fight. Not against my enemies. Against the circumstances. Against history. I want my wife back, Ryumin. My Shaper wife. I want her back free and clear, without the shadows on her. If you won't help me, who will?"

Ryumin hesitated. "I have a friend," he said at last. "His name is Wells."

# DEMBOWSKA CARTEL: 31-10-'53

Before the advent of humankind, the Asteroid Belt had arranged itself through the physics of rubble. Fragments were distributed in powers of ten. For every asteroid there were ten others a third its size, from Ceres at a thousand kilometers down to the literal trillions of uncharted boulders following spacetime potentials at relative speeds of five kilometers per second.

Dembowska was of the third rank, two hundred kilometers across. Like other circumsolar bodies, it had paid its homage to the laws of chance. In the time of the dinosaurs, something large had hit Dembowska. The visitor was there and gone in a split second, leaving chunks of its impact-melted pyroxene embedded in the crust as it flew apart in gouts of fire. At the point of impact, Dembowska's silicate matrix had shattered, opening a ragged vertical crevasse twenty kilometers down to the asteroid's nickel-iron core.

Now most of the core was gone, devoured by ever-hungry industry. Dembowska Cartel lived within the crevasse, long plazas dropping level after level into the fading gravity, the gradient shifting until what were formerly walls became floors, until walls and floors vanished altogether into the closest thing to free-fall. At the crevasse's base the world expanded into an enormous cavernous dugout, Dembowska's hollow heart, where generations of mining drones had gnawed at the metal and the ores that held it.

The hole was too large for air. They treated it as space. Within the free-fall vacuum at the asteroid's core were the new heavy industries: the cryonics factories, where hints and memories teased from the blasted mind of Michael Carnassus were translated into a steady rise of Dembowska Cartel stock on the market monitors of a hundred worlds.

Trade secrets were secure within Dembowska's bowels, snug beneath kilometers of rock. Life had forced itself like putty into the fracture in this minor planet: dug out its inert heart and filled it with engines.

Seen from the industrial core, the bottom of the crevasse was the top layer of the outside world. Here Wells had his offices; where twenty-four-hour crews of his employees monitored the datapulses of the Union of Cartels, under the quasinational aegis of Ceres Datacom Network.

The offices were walled in velcro and video, the glowing walls with their ceaseless murmur of news acting as work partitions. Bits of hard copy were velcro-clipped underfoot and overhead; reporters in headsets spoke over audiolines or tapped energetically at keyboards. They looked young; there was a calculated extravagance in their dress. Over the mumble of narrative, the smooth rattle of printouts, the whir of booted datatapes, came faint background music: the brittle keening of synthesizers. The cold air smelled of roses.

A secretary announced them. His hair crisped out from under a loose Mech beret. Its puffiness suggested possible cranial taps. He wore a patriotic lapel tag, showing the wide-eyed face of Michael Carnassus.

Wells's office was more secure than the rest. His videowalls formed a surging mosaic of headlines, interlocking rectangles of data that could be frozen and expanded at will. He wore quilted coveralls with Shaper lace at the throat; the gray fabric was overprinted with stylized eurypteroids in darker gray. His stylish gloves were overlaid with circuit-laden control rings.

"Welcome to CDN, Auditor Milosz. You too, Policewife. May I offer you hot tea?"

Lindsay accepted the warm bulb gratefully. The tea was synthetic but good. Greta took the bulb but drank nothing. She watched Wells with calm wariness.

Wells touched a switch on the sticky surface of his free-fall desk. A large goose-necked lamp swiveled on its coiled neck with subtle, reptilian grace and stared at Lindsay. There were human eyes within the hood, embedded in a smooth matrix of dark flesh. The eyes blinked and shifted from Lindsay to Greta Beatty. Greta bowed her head in recognition.

"This is a monitor outlet for the Chief of Police," Wells told him. "She prefers to see things with her own eyes, when they have as much importance as you claim your news does." He turned to Greta. "The situation is under control, Policewife." The accordioned door shunted open behind her.

Tight-lipped, she bowed again to the lamp, shot a quick look at Lindsay, and kicked her way off the wall and out the door. It slid shut.

"How'd you get stuck with the Zen nun?" Wells said.

"I beg your pardon?" said Lindsay.

"Beatty. She hasn't told you about her cult affiliation? Zen Serotonin?"

"No," Lindsay hesitated. "She seems very self-possessed."

"Odd. I understand the cult is well established in your homeworld. Bettina, wasn't it?"

Lindsay locked eyes with him. "You know me, Wells. Think back. Goldreich-Tremaine."

Wells smirked one-sidedly and squeezed his bulb of tea, firing an amber stream into his mouth. His teeth were strong and square, and the effect was alarmingly feral. "I thought you had a Shaper look about you. If you're a Cataclyst, don't try anything desperate under the eyes of the Chief of Police."

"I was a Cataclyst victim," Lindsay said. "They put me on ice for a month. It broke me out of my routines. And then I defected." He pulled the glove from his right hand.

Wells recognized the antique prosthetic. "Captain-Doctor Mavrides. This is an unexpected pleasure. Rumor said you were hopelessly insane. Frankly, the news had pleased me. Abelard Mavrides, the Investor pet. What's become of your jewels and cables, Captain-Doctor?"

"I travel light these days."

"No more plays?" Wells opened a drawer in his desk and pulled out a humidor. He offered Lindsay a cigarette. Lindsay took it gratefully. "The theatre's out of fashion," he said. They lit up. Lindsay coughed helplessly.

"I must have annoyed you at that wedding party, doctor. When I came in to recruit your students."

"They were the ideologues, Wells, not me. I was afraid for you."

"You needn't have been." Wells blew smoke and smiled. "Your student Besetzny is one of ours now."

"A Détentiste?"

"Our thinking's progressed since then, doctor. The old categories, Mechanist and Shaper—they're a bit outmoded these days, aren't they? Life moves in clades." He smiled. "A clade is a daughter species, a related descendant. It's happened to other successful animals, and now it's humanity's turn. The factions still struggle, but the categories are breaking up. No faction can claim the one true destiny for mankind. Mankind no longer exists."

"You're talking Cataclysm."

"There are others just as crazy. Those who hold power in the Cartels, in the Ring Council. Blinding the Schismatrix with hatred is easier than accepting our potentials. Our missions to the aliens have failed because we can't even deal with the strangers who share our own ancestry. We are breaking up into clades. We have to let go and reunite on a more basic level."

"If humankind flies to pieces, what could possibly unite it?"

Wells glanced at his videowall and froze a piece of news with his finger ring. "Have you ever heard of Prigoginic Levels of Complexity?"

Lindsay's heart sank. "I've never been one for metaphysics, Wells. Your religious beliefs are your own business. I had a woman who loved me and a safe place to sleep. The rest is abstract."

Wells examined his wall. Print blurred by, discussing a scandalous defection on Ceres. "Oh yes, your Colonel-Professor. I can't help you with that. You need a kidnapper to spirit her out. You won't find one here. You should try Ceres or Bettina."

"My wife's a stubborn woman. Like you, she has ideals. Only peace can reunite us. And there's only one source of peace in our world. That's the Investors."

Wells laughed shortly. "Still the same line, Captain-Doctor?" Suddenly he spoke in halting Investor. "The value of your argument has depreciated."

"They have their weaknesses, Wells." His voice rose. "Do you think I'm any less desperate than the Cataclysts? Ask your friend Ryumin if I know weakness when I see it, or if I lack the will to exploit it. The Investor Peace: yes, I had a hand in that. It gave me what I wanted. I was a whole man. You can't know what that meant to me—" He broke off, sweating even in the cold.

Wells looked shocked. Lindsay realized suddenly that his outburst had broken every diplomatic rule. The thought filled him with savage satisfaction. "You know the truth, Wells. We've been Investor pawns for years. It's time we turned the chessboard around."

"You mean to attack the Investors?" Wells said.

"What else, fool? What choice do we have?"

A woman's voice came from the base of the lamp. "Abelard Mavrides, you are under arrest."

•   •   •

The elevator car hissed shut behind him. False gravity hit as they accelerated upward. "Put your hands against the wall, please," Greta said politely. "Move your feet backward."

Lindsay complied, saying nothing. The old-fashioned elevator clacked noisily on rails up the vertical wall of the Dembowska Crevasse. Two kilometers passed. Greta sighed. "You must have done something drastic."

"That's not your worry," Lindsay said.

"To go by the book, I ought to cut the cables on your iron arm. But I'll let it go. This is my fault too, I think. If I'd made you feel more at home you wouldn't have been so fanatic."

"No weapons in my arm," Lindsay said. "Surely you examined it while I slept."

"I don't understand this hard suspicion, Bela. Have I mistreated you somehow?"

"Tell me about Zen Serotonin, Greta."

She straightened slightly. "I'm not ashamed of belonging to the Nonmovement. I would have told you, but we don't proselytize. We win over by example."

"Very laudable, I'm sure."

She frowned. "In your case I should have made an exception. I'm sorry for your pain. I knew pain once." Lindsay said nothing. "I was born on Themis," she said. "I knew some Cataclysts there, one of the Mechanist factions. They were ice assassins. The military found one of their cryocells, where they were enlightening one of my teachers with a one-way ticket to the future. I didn't wait for arrest. I ran to Dembowska.

"When I got here the Harem drafted me. I found out I had to whore to Carnassus. I didn't take to it. But then I found Zen Serotonin."

"Serotonin's a brain chemical," Lindsay said.

"It's a philosophy," she said. "The Shapers, the Mechanists—those aren't philosophies, they're technologies made into politics. The technologies are at the core of it. Science tore the human race to bits. When anarchy hit, people struggled for community. The politicians chose enemies so that they could bind their followers with hate and terror. Community isn't enough when a thousand new ways of life beckon from every circuit and test tube. Without hatred there is no Ring Council, no Union of Cartels. No conformity without the whip."

"Life moves in clades," Lindsay murmured.

"That's Wells with his mishmash of physics and ethics. What we need is nonmovement, calmness, clarity." She stretched out her left arm. "This monitor drip-feeds into my arm. Fear means nothing to me. With this, there's nothing I can't face and analyze. With Zen Serotonin you see life in the light of reason. People turn to us, especially in crisis. Every day the Nonmovement wins more adherents."

Lindsay thought of the brainwaves he had seen in his safehouse bed. "You're in a permanent alpha state, then."

"Of course."

"Do you ever dream?"

"We have our vision. We can see the new technologies that disrupt human life. We throw ourselves into those currents. Perhaps each one of us is no more than a particle. But together we form a sediment that slows the flow. Many innovators are profoundly unhappy. After Zen Serotonin they lose their neurotic urge to meddle."

Lindsay smiled grimly. "It was no accident that you were assigned my case."

"You are a profoundly unhappy man. It's brought this trouble on you. The Nonmovement has a strong voice in the Harem. Join us. We can save you."

"I had happiness once, Greta. You'll never know it."

"Violent emotion isn't our forte, Bela. We're trying to save the human race."

"Good luck," Lindsay said. They had reached the end of the line.

The old acromegalic stepped back to admire his handiwork. "Strap is all right, sundog? You can breathe?"

Lindsay nodded. The kill-clamp dug painfully into the base of his skull.

"It reads the backbrain," the giant said. Growth hormones had distorted his jaw; he had a bulldog's underbite and his voice was slurred. "Remember to shuffle. No sudden movements. Don't think about moving fast, and your head will stay whole."

"How long have you been in this business?" Lindsay said.

"Long enough."

"Are you part of the Harem?"

The giant glared. "Sure, I fuck Carnassus, what do you think?" His enormous hand grasped Lindsay's entire face. "You ever see your own eyeball? Maybe I pull one out. The Chief can graft you a new one."

Lindsay flinched. The giant grinned, revealing poorly spaced teeth. "I see your type before. You are a Shaper antibiotic. Your type tricked me once. Maybe you think you can trick the clamp. Maybe you think you can kill the Chief without moving. Keep in mind you must get by me on the way out." He gripped the top of Lindsay's head and lifted him off the velcro. "Or maybe you think I'm stupid."

Lindsay spoke in trade Japanese. "Save it for the whores, yakuza. Or maybe your excellency would care to take this clamp off and go hand to hand."

The giant laughed, startled, and set Lindsay down carefully. "Sorry, friend. Didn't know you were one of our own."

Lindsay stepped through the airlock. Inside, the air was at blood heat. It reeked of perfumed sweat and the odor of violets. The brittle whine of a synthesizer broke off suddenly.

The room was full of flesh. It was made of it: satiny brown skin, broken here and there by rugs of lustrous black hair and mauve flashes of mucus membrane. Everything was involuted, curved: armchair lounges, a rounded mass like a bed of flesh, studded with mauve holes. Blood thrummed through a pipe-sized artery beneath his feet.

Another hooded lamp-device swiveled up on a sleek-skinned elbowed hinge. Dark eyes observed him. A mouth opened in the sleek rump of a footstool beside him. "Take off those velcro boots, darling. They itch."

Lindsay sat down. "It's you, Kitsune."

"You knew when you saw my eyes in Wells's office," the voice purred from the wall.

"Not till I saw your bodyguard, really. It's been a long time. Sorry about the boots." He sat and pulled them off carefully, masking his shudder at the sensual warmth of the fleshy armchair. "Where are you?"

"All around you. I have eyes and ears everywhere."

"Where's your body?"

"I had it scrapped."

Lindsay was sweating. After four weeks in the Dembowska chill, the heated air was stifling. "You knew it was me?"

"You're the only one I cared to keep who ever left me, darling. I wasn't likely to forget."

"You've done well, Kitsune," Lindsay said, masking his terror under a sudden onrush of half-forgotten discipline. "Thank you for killing the antibiotic."

"It was easy," she said. "I pretended he was you." She hesitated. "The Geisha Bank believed your deception. It was thoughtful of you to take the *yarite*'s head."

"I wanted to make you a parting gift," Lindsay said carefully, "of absolute power." He looked at the sleek masses of flesh. There was no face anywhere. From the walls and floors came the syncopated muffled thumping of half a dozen hearts.

"Were you upset because I wanted power more than you?"

His mind raced. "You've gained in wisdom since those days. Yes, I admit it. The day would have come when you chose between me and your ambitions. And I knew which one you'd choose. Was I wrong to leave?"

There was silence for a moment; then several of the mouths in the room laughed. "You could make anything plausible, darling. That was your gift. No, I've had many favorites since then. You were a good weapon, but I've had others. I forgive you."

"Thank you, Kitsune."

"You may consider yourself no longer under arrest."

"You're very generous."

"Now, what's this craziness about the Investors? Don't you know how the System depends on them now? Any faction that crosses the Investors might as well cut their own throats."

"I had in mind something more subtle. I thought we might persuade them to cross themselves."

"Meaning?"

"Blackmail."

Some of the mouths laughed uneasily. "In what form, darling?"

"Sexual perversion."

The eyes swiveled up on their organic mounting. Lindsay saw the wideness of their pupils, his first kinesic clue, and knew he had struck home. "You have the evidence?"

"I'd hand it over at once," Lindsay said, "but this clamp constrains me."

"Take it off. I've neutralized it."

Lindsay unbuckled the kill-clamp and set it gently on the chair's quivering arm. He walked toward the bed in his socks. He produced the videomonocle from within his shirt.

Dark eyes opened within the headboard. A pair of sleek arms emerged through soft furred slots. An arm took the monocle and placed it over one eye. Lindsay said, "I've set it to the beginning of the sequence."

"But that's not the beginning of the tape."

"The first part is—"

"Yes," she said icily. "I see. Your wife?"

"Yes."

"No matter. If she'd come with you, things might have been different. But now she's crossed Constantine."

"You know him?"

"Of course. He crowded the Zaibatsu with the victims of his purge. The Shapers are proud, in the Ring Council. They'll never believe an unplanned can match them scheme for scheme. Your wife is a dead woman."

"There might be—"

"Forget it. You had your years of peace. The next are his. Ah." She hesitated. "This was taken aboard an Investor starship? The one that brought you here?"

"Yes. I filmed it myself."

"Ahh." The moan was purely sensual. One of the room's huge hearts was under the bed; its pulse had speeded. "It's their queen, their captain. Oh, these Investor women and their harem rule, what a pleasure it is to have beaten one. The filthy creature. Oh, what a joy you are, Lin Dze, Mavrides, Milosz."

Lindsay said, "My name is Abelard Malcolm Tyler Lindsay."

"I know. Constantine told me. And I convinced him you were dead."

"Thank you, Kitsune."

"What do names mean to us? They call me the Chief of Police. The control is what matters, darling, not the front. You fooled the Shapers in the Ring Council. The Mechanists were my prey. I moved to the Cartels. I watched, I waited. Then one day I found Carnassus. The last survivor of his mission."

She laughed lightly, the high-pitched skipping laugh he once had known so well. "The Mechs sent out their best. But they were too strong, too stiff, too brittle. The strangeness of it broke them, and the isolation. Carnassus had to kill the other two, and he still wakes up screaming because of it. Yes, even in this room. His company was bankrupted. I bought him, and all his strange booty, from the wreckage."

"In the Rings they say he rules here."

"Of course they do; that's what I told them. Carnassus belongs to me. My surgeons have been at him. There's not a neuron in him that pleasure hasn't blasted. Life is simple for him, a constant dream of flesh."

Lindsay looked about the room. "And you're his favorite."

"Would I tolerate anything else, darling?"

"You don't mind that other wives practice Zen Serotonin?"

"I don't care what they think or claim they think. They obey me. I'm not concerned with ideology. What concerns me is the future."

"Oh?"

"The day will come when we've squeezed everything we can out of Carnassus. And cryonic products will lose their novelty as the technology spreads."

"That might take years."

"It all takes years," she said. "And it's a question of years. The ship you arrived on has left circumsolar space."

"You're sure?" Lindsay said, stricken.

"That's what my databanks tell me. Who knows when they'll return?"

"It doesn't matter," Lindsay said. "I can wait."

"Twenty years? Thirty?"

"Whatever it takes," Lindsay said, though the thought suffocated him.

"By then Carnassus will be useless. I'll need a new front. And what could be better than an Investor Queen? It's a risk worth taking. You'll work on it for me. You and Wells."

"Of course, Kitsune."

"You'll have the support you need. But don't squander a kilowatt of it trying to save that woman."

"I'll try to think only of the future."

"Carnassus and I will need a safehouse. That will be your priority."

"Depend on it," said Lindsay. *'Carnassus and I,'* he thought.

## DEMBOWSKA CARTEL: 14-2-'58

Lindsay studied the latest papers from the peer review committee. He paged through the data expertly, devouring the abstracts, screen-scanning through paragraphs, highlighting the worst excesses of technical jargon. He worked with driven efficiency.

The credit went to Wells. Wells had placed him in the department chairmanship at the Kosmosity; Wells had put the editorship of the *Journal of Exoarchosaurian Studies* into his hands.

Routine had seized Lindsay. He welcomed the distractions of administration and research, which robbed him of the leisure necessary for pain. Within his office in the Crevasse, in an exurb of the newly completed Kosmosity, he wheeled in his low-grav swivel chair, chasing rumors, coaxing, bribing, trading information. Already the *Journal* was the largest unclassified databank on the

Investors, and its restricted files mushroomed with speculation and espionage. Lindsay was at its core, working with the stamina of youth and the patience of age.

In the five years since Lindsay's arrival in Dembowska, he had watched Wells move from strength to strength. In the absence of a state ideology, the influence of Wells and his Carbon Clique spread throughout the colony, encompassing art, the media, and academic life.

Ambition was an endemic vice among Wells and his group. Lindsay had joined the Clique without much enthusiasm. With proximity, though, he had picked up their plans as if they were local bacteria. And their fashions as well: his hair was slickly brilliantined and his mustache was nicked for a paste-on microphone lip bead. He wore video-control rings on the wrinkled fingers of his left hand.

Work ate the years. Once time had seemed solid to him, dense as lead. Now it flowed through his hands. Lindsay saw that his perception of time was slowly coming to match that of the senior Shapers he'd known in Goldreich-Tremaine. To the truly old, time was as thin as air, a keening and destructive wind that erased their pasts and attacked their memories. Time was accelerating. Nothing could slow it down for him but death. He tasted this truth, and it was bitter as amphetamine.

He returned his attention to the paper; a reassessment of a celebrated Investor scale fragment found among the effects of a failed Mechanist interstellar embassy. Few bits of matter had ever been analyzed so exhaustively. The paper, "Proximo-Distal Gradients in Epidermal Cell Adhesiveness," came from a Shaper defector in Diotima Cartel.

His desk rang. His visitor had arrived.

The unobtrusive guard systems in Lindsay's office showed Wells's characteristic touch. The visitor had been issued a stylish coronet, which had evolved from the much clumsier kill-clamp. A tiny red light, unseen by the guest himself, glowed on the man's forehead. It denoted the potential impact site for armaments, decently concealed in the ceiling.

"Professor Milosz?" The visitor's dress was odd. He wore a white formal suit with a ring-shaped open collar and accordioned elbows and knees.

"You're Dr. Morrissey? From the Concatenation?"

"From the Mare Serenitatis Republic," the man said. "Dr. Pongpianskul sent me."

"Pongpianskul is dead," Lindsay said.

"So they said." Morrissey nodded. "Killed on Chairman Constantine's orders. But the doctor had friends in the Republic. So many that he now controls the nation. His title is Warden, and the nation is reborn as the Neotenic Cultural Republic. I am the harbinger of the Revolution." He hesitated. "Maybe I should let Dr. Pongpianskul tell it."

Lindsay was stunned. "Perhaps you should."

The man produced a videotablet and plugged it into his briefcase. He handed Lindsay the tablet, which flickered into life. It showed a face: Pongpianskul's. Pongpianskul brushed at his braids, disheveling them with leathery, wrinkled hands. "Abelard, how are you?"

"Neville. You're alive?"

"I'm still a tenant of the flesh, yes. Morrissey's briefcase is programmed with an interactive expert system. It ought to carry out a decent conversation with you, in my absence."

Morrissey cleared his throat. "These machines are new to me. I think, though, that I should let the two of you speak privately."

"That might be best."

"I'll wait in the lobby."

Lindsay watched the man's retreating back. Morrissey's clothes amazed him. Lindsay had forgotten that he'd ever dressed like that, in the Republic.

He studied the tablet's screen. "You look well, Neville."

"Thank you. Ross arranged my last rejuvenation. By the Cataclysts. The same group that treated you, Mavrides."

"Treated me? They put me on ice."

"On ice? That's odd. The Cataclysts woke me up. I never felt so alive as when I was here in the Republic, pretending to be dead. It's been a long ten years, Abelard. Eleven, whatever." Pongpianskul shrugged.

Lindsay Looked at the tablet. The image made no response to the Look, and the charm faded. Lindsay spoke slowly. "So you've attacked the Republic? Through the Cataclyst terror networks?"

The tablet smiled Pongpianskul's smile. "The Cataclysts had their part in it, I admit. You would have appreciated this, Mavrides. I played off the youth element. There was a political group called the Preservationists, dating—oh, forty or fifty years back. Constantine used them to seize power, but they detested the Shapers as much as they did the Mechs. What they wanted, really, was a human life, droll as that might seem. Now there's a new generation of them, raised under Shaper influence and hating it. But thanks to Shaper breeding policies, the young hold a majority."

Pongpianskul laughed. "Constantine used the Republic as a storehouse for Shaper militants. He made things here a muddle of subterfuge. When the war heated up, the militants rushed back to the Ring Council and Cataclyst Superbrights hid here instead. Constantine spent too much time in the Rings, and lost touch. . . . The Cataclysts like my notion of a cultural preserve. It's all down in the new Constitution. My messenger will give you a copy."

"Thank you."

"Things haven't gone well with the rest of the Midnight Clique. . . . It's been too long since we've talked. I tracked you down through your ex-wife."

"Alexandrina?"

"What?" The programmed system was confused; the persona flickered for a second's fraction. "It took some doing. Nora's under close surveillance."

"Just a moment." Lindsay rose from his chair and poured himself a drink. A cascade of memories from the Republic had rushed through him, and he'd thought automatically of his first wife, Alexandrina Tyler. But of course she was not in the Republic. She had been a victim of Constantine's purge, shipped out to the Zaibatsu.

He returned to the screen. It said, "Ross left for the cometaries when G-T crumbled. Fetzko has faded. Vetterling's in Skimmers Union, sucking up to the fascists. Ice assassins took Margaret Juliano. She's still awaiting the thaw. I have power here, Mavrides. But that can't make up for what we lost."

"How is Nora?" Lindsay said.

The false Pongpianskul looked grave. "She fights Constantine where he's strongest. If it weren't for her my coup here would have failed; she distracted him. . . . I'd hoped I could lure her here, and you as well. She was always so good to us. Our premier hostess."

"She wouldn't come?"

"She has remarried."

The slotted glass broke in Lindsay's iron hand. Blobs of liqueur drifted toward the floor.

"For political reasons," the screen continued. "She needs every ally she can find. Having you join me would have been difficult in any case. No one over sixty is allowed in the Neotenic Cultural Republic. Except for myself and my officers."

Lindsay yanked the cord from the tablet. He helped the small office servo pick up the shards of glass.

When he called Morrissey in again, much later, the man was diffident. "Are you quite through, sir? I've been instructed to erase the tablet."

"It was kind of you to bring it." Lindsay gestured at a chair. "Thank you for waiting so long."

Morrissey wiped the construct's memory and put the tablet in his briefcase. He studied Lindsay's face. "I hope I haven't brought bad news."

"It's astonishing," Lindsay said. "Maybe we should have a drink to celebrate."

A shadow crossed Morrissey's face.

"Forgive me," Lindsay said. "Perhaps I was tactless." He put the bottle away. There was not much left.

"I'm sixty years old," Morrissey said. He sat uncomfortably. "So they ousted me. They were polite about it." He smiled painfully. "I was a Preservationist once. I was eighteen in the first Revolution. It's ironic, isn't it? Now I'm a sundog."

Lindsay said carefully, "I'm not without power here. And not without funds. Dembowska handles many refugees. I can find you room."

"You're very kind." Morrissey's face was stiff. "I worked as a biologist, on the nation's ecological troubles. Dr. Constantine trained me. But I'm afraid I'm very much behind the times."

"That can be remedied."

"I've brought an article for your *Journal*."

"Ah. You have an interest in Investors, Dr. Morrissey?"

"Yes. I hope my piece meets your standards."

Lindsay forced a smile. "We'll work on it together."

# Chapter 7

He could feel it coming on, creeping across the back of his head in a zone of quivering subepidermal tightness. A fugue state. The scene before him trembled slightly, the crowds below his private box blurring in a frieze of packed heads against dark finery, the rounded stage with actors in costume, dark red, gleaming, a gesture. It slowed—it froze:

Fear . . . no, not even that, exactly . . . a certain sadness now that the die was cast. The waiting was the hell of it . . . He had waited sixty years to resume his old contacts, the wirehead Radical Old of the Republic. . . . Now the wirehead leaders, like him, had worked their way to power in the worlds outside. Sixty years was nothing to a mind on the wires . . . time meant nothing . . . fugue states. . . . They still remembered him quite well, their friend, Philip Khouri Constantine. . . .

It was he who had sprung them loose, purging the middle-aged aristocrats to finance the wirehead defections. . . . Memories went back; they were data, that was all, just as fresh on reels somewhere as the enemy Margaret Juliano was on her bed of Cataclyst ice. . . . Even amid fugue the surge of satisfaction was quick and sharp enough to penetrate into consciousness from his backbrain. . . . That unique sense of warmth that came only from the downfall of a rival. . . .

Now, trailing sluggishly behind his racing thoughts, the slow-motion blooming of a light tingle of fear. . . . Nora Everett, the wife of Abelard Mavrides. . . . She had hurt him seventeen years ago with the coup in the Republic, though he was able to entangle her in charges of treason. . . . The tinpot Republic was of no concern to him now, its willfully ignorant child-citizens flying kites and eating apples under the crazed charlatan gaze of Dr. Pong-pianskul. . . . No problem there, the future would ignore them, they were living fossils, harmless in themselves. . . .

But the Cataclysts . . . the fear was resolving itself now, beginning to flower, its first dim shades of backbrain unease taking on emotional substance now, uncoiling through his consciousness like a drop of ink streaming into a glass of water. . . . He would see to his emotions later when the fugue was over; now he was struggling to shut his eyes . . . focus was lost, dim tear-blur over frozen performers; his eyelids were dropping with nightmare sluggishness, nerve impulses confused by the racing fugue-consciousness. . . . The Cataclysts, though. . . . They took it all as an enormous joke, enjoyed hiding in the Republic disguised as plebes and farmers, the huge panorama interior of the cylindrical world as weird to them as a trace dose of their favorite drug, PDKL-95. . . . The Cataclyst mind-set fed on correspondences and poetic justice, a trip to the human past in the Neotenic Republic the inverse of an ice assassination, with its one-way ticket to the future. . . .

The fugue was about to break. He felt a strange cracking sensation of psychic upheaval, mental crust giving way before the upsurge. In the last microseconds of fugue an eidetic flash seized him, surveyor photos from the surface of Titan, red volcanic shelves of heavy hydrocarbon split by ammonia lava, bursting from the depths . . . from Titan, far below their orbit, prime wall-decor in Skimmers Union. . . .

Gone. Constantine leaned forward in his box seat, clearing his throat. Delayed fear swept over him; he pushed it brusquely away, had a light sniff of acetaminophen to avert migraine. He glanced at his wristwatch through damp lashes. Four seconds of fugue.

He wiped his eyes, became aware of his wife sitting beside him, her finely chiseled Shaper face a study in surprise. Was she aware that he had been sitting rapt for four seconds with his eyes showing only a rim of white? No. She thought he was touched by the play, was startled to see this excess of emotion in her iron-hard husband. Constantine favored her with a smile. Her color heightened; she leaned forward in her seat, her jeweled hands in her lap, studying the play alertly. Later she would try to discuss it with him. Natalie Constantine was young and bright, the scion of a military gene-line. She had grown used to his demands.

Not like his first wife, the treasonous bitch. . . . He had left the old aristocrat in the Republic, having nurtured her vicious streak patiently until his own coup allowed him to turn it against her peers. Now rumor said she was Pongpianskul's lover, won over by fraudulent Shaper charm and degraded senile intimacy. No matter, no matter. Long years had taken the sting from it; tonight's stroke, if it came, was more important than any circumlunar moondock.

His nine-year-old daughter, Vera, leaned in her seat to whisper to Natalie. Constantine gazed at the child he had built. Half her genetics were Vera Kelland's, drawn from skin flakes he had taken before the woman's suicide. For years he had treasured the stolen genes, and when the time was ripe he had brought them to flower in this child. She was his favorite, the first of his progeny. When he thought how his own failure might doom her, he felt the fear again, sharper than before, because it was not for himself.

An extravagant gesture from the stage caught his attention, a brief flurry of stilted action as the deranged Superbright villain clutched his head and fell. Constantine surreptitiously scratched his ankle with the sole of his foot-glove. Over the years his skin virus had improved, limited to dry outbreaks of shingles at his extremities.

The play was one of Zeuner's, and it bored him. Skimmers Union had caught the habit from Goldreich-Tremaine, bolstered by dramatists fleeing the crippled ex-capital. But the modern theatre was lifeless. Fernand Vetterling, for instance, author of *The White Periapsis* and *The Technical Advisor,* languished in sullen silence with his disgraced Mavrides wife. Other artists with Détentiste leanings now paid for their indiscretion with fines or house arrest. Some had defected, others had "gone undertime" to join the Cataclyst action brigades in the graveyard dayshifts.

But the Cataclysts were losing cohesion, becoming mere terrorists. Their Superbright elite was under severe attack. The pogrom on the Superbrights was increasingly thorough as hysteria mounted. Their promoters and educators were now political nonpersons, many having fallen to the twisted vengeance of the Superbrights themselves.

The Superbrights were too brilliant for community; they demanded the world-shattering anarchy of supermen. That could not be tolerated. And Constantine had served that intolerance. Life had never looked better for him: high office, his own Constantine gene-line, a free hand for anti-Mech adventurism, and his own barbed nets poised for disloyalty.

And tonight he had risked it all. Would his news ever come? How would he hear it? From his bodyguards, through the earpiece? Through the stolen Mech implants in his own brain, that opened internal channels to the thin data-whispers of the wireheads? Or—

Something was happening. The banner-waving choreography on the curved stage disintegrated in sudden confusion, the colored corporate logos and gene-line insignia slowing and tangling. The dancers fell back in chaos in response to shouted orders. Someone was floating to the edge of the podium. It was the wretched Charles Vetterling, his aged face bloated with triumph and a lackey's self-importance.

This was it. Vetterling was shouting. The play's leading man gave him a throat mike. Vetterling's voice roared suddenly in thudding feedback.

". . . of the War! Mech markets are in panic! The asteroid Nysa has declared for the Ring Council! I repeat, the Nysa Cartel has abandoned the Mechanist Union! They have asked for admittance as a Ring Council Treaty State! The Council is meeting. . . ." His words were drowned in the roar from the audience, the clatter of buckles as they unstrapped from their seats and rose in confusion.

Vetterling struggled with the mike. Patches of his words broke the din. ". . . capitulation . . . through banks in Skimmers Union . . . industrial . . . new victory!"

It started among the actors. The leading man was pointing above the heads of the audience at Constantine's box, shouting fiercely at the rest of the cast. One of the women began applauding. Then it spread. The whole cast was applauding, their faces alight. Vetterling heard them behind him, turned to look. He grasped things at once, and a stiff smile spread over his face. He pointed dramatically. "Constantine! he shouted. "Ladies and gentlemen, the Chancellor-General!"

Constantine rose to his feet, gripping the iron banister behind the transparent shield. When they saw him the crowd exploded, a free-fall maelstrom of shouts and applause. They knew it was his triumph. The joy of it overwhelmed them, the brief bright release from the dark tension of the War. If he'd failed, they would have hounded him to death with the same passion. But that dark knowledge had been blasted by victory. Because he'd won, now the risk he'd run only sharpened his delight.

He turned to his wife. Her eyes brimmed over with tears of pride. Slowly, not leaving the banister, he extended his hand to her. When their fingers touched he read her face. He saw the truth there. From this night on his dominion over her was total.

She took her place beside him. Vera tugged his sleeve, her eyes wide. He lifted her up, cradling her in his left arm. His lips touched her ear. "Remember this," he whispered fiercely.

The anarchic shouts died down as another rhythm spread. It was the rhythm of applause, the long, cadenced, ritual applause that followed every session of the Ring Council itself, ageless, solemn, overwhelming applause, applause that brooked no dissent. The music of power. Constantine raised his wife's hand above their heads and closed his eyes.

It was the happiest moment of his life.

## DEMBOWSKA CARTEL: 15-5-'75

Lindsay was playing keyboards for the sake of his new arm. It was much more advanced than his old one, and the fine discrimination of its nerve signals confused him. As he ran through the composition, one of Kitsune's, he felt each key click down with a brief muddled sensation of sharp heat.

He rested, rubbing his hands together. A pins-and-needles tingling ran up the wires. The new hand was densely honeycombed with fingertip sensors. They were much more responsive than his old arm's feedback pads.

The change had jarred him. He looked about his desolate apartment. In twenty-two years it had never been anything more to him than a place to camp. The apartment's fashions, its ribbed wallpaper and skeletal chairs, were two decades out of date. Only the security systems, Wells's latest, had any touch of the mode.

Lindsay himself had gone stale. At ninety, grooves marked his eyes and mouth from decades of habitual expression. His hair and beard were sprinkled with gray.

He was improving at the keyboards. He had attacked the problem of music with his usual inhuman steadiness. For years he had worked hard enough to kill himself, but modern biomonitoring technique saw each breakdown coming and averted it months ahead of time. The bed took care of that, feeding him subterranean flashes of intense and blurry dream that left him each morning blank and empty with perfect mental health.

Eighteen years had passed since his wife's remarriage. The pain of it had never fully hit him. He'd known her present husband briefly in the Council: Graham Everett, a colorless Détentiste with powerful clan connections. Nora used Everett's influence to parry the attacks of militants. It was sad: Lindsay didn't remember the man well enough to hate him.

Warnings cut short his playing. Someone had arrived at his entry hall. The scanners there assured him that the visitor, a woman, bore only harmless Mechanist implants: plaque-scraping arterial microbots, old-fashioned teflon kneecaps, plastic knuckles, a porous drug duct in the crook of the left elbow. Much of her hair was artificial, implanted strands of shining optical fibers.

He had his household servo escort the woman in. She had the strange complexion common to many older Mechanist women, smooth unblemished skin like a perfectly form-fitted paper mask. Her red hair was shot through with copper highlights from the fiberoptics. She wore a sleeveless gray suit, furred vest, and elbow-length white thermal gloves. "Auditor Milosz?"

She had a Concatenate accent. He ushered her to the couch. She sat gracefully, her movements honed to precision by age. "Yes, madam. What may I do for you?"

"Forgive me for intruding, Auditor. My name is Tyler. I'm a clerk with Limonov Cryonics. But my business here is personal. I've come to ask your help. I've heard of your friendship with Neville Pongpianskul."

"You're Alexandrina Tyler," Lindsay realized aloud. "From Mare Serenitatis. The Republic."

She looked surprised and lifted her thin, arched brows. "You already know my case, Auditor?"

"You"—Lindsay sat down in the stirruped chair—"would like a drink, perhaps?" She was his first wife. From some deeply buried level of reflex he felt the stirrings of a long-dead persona, the brittle layer of false kinesics he had put between them in their marriage. Alexandrina Tyler, his wife, his mother's cousin.

"No, thank you," she said. She adjusted the fabric over her knees. She'd always had trouble with her knees; she'd had the teflon put in in the Republic.

Her familiar gesture brought it all back to him: the marriage politics of the Republic's aristocrats. She had been fifty years his senior, their marriage a stifling net of strained politeness and grim rebellion. Lindsay was ninety now, older than she had been at their marriage. With a flood of new perspective, he could taste the long-forgotten pain that he had caused her.

"I was born in the Republic," she said. "I lost my citizenship in the Shaper purges, almost fifty years ago. I loved the Republic, Auditor. I've never forgotten it. . . . I came from one of the privileged familes, but I thought, perhaps now, since the new regime there has settled, surely that's all a dead issue?"

"You were Abelard Lindsay's wife."

Her eyes widened. "So you do know my case. You know I've applied to emigrate? I had no response from the Pongpianskul government. I've come to ask for your help, Auditor. I'm not a member of your Carbon Clique, but I know their power. You have influence that works around the laws."

"Life must have been difficult for you, madam. Thrown out without resources into the Schismatrix."

She blinked, china-white lids falling over her eyes like paper shutters. "Things were not so bad once I'd reached the cartels. But I can't pretend I've known happiness. I haven't forgotten home. The trees. The gardens."

Lindsay knotted his hands, ignoring the tingle of confused sensation from his right. "I can't encourage false hopes, madam. Neotenic law is very strict. The Republic has no interest in those our age, those who are estranged in any way from the raw state of humanity. It's true that I've handled some matters for the Neotenic government. Those involve the resettlement of Neotenic citizens who reach the age of sixty. 'Dying out into the world,' they call it. The flow of emigration is strictly one-way. I'm very sorry."

She was silent a moment. "You know the Republic well, Auditor?" Her voice told him that she had accepted defeat. Now she was hunting for memories.

"Well enough to know that the wife of Abelard Lindsay has been defamed. Your late husband is regarded there as a Preservationist martyr. They portray you as a Mechanist collaborator, driving Lindsay into exile and death."

"How terrible." Her eyes filled with tears; she stood up in agitation. "I'm very sorry. May I use your biomonitor?"

"Tears don't alarm me, madam," Lindsay said gently. "I am not a Zen Serotonist."

"My husband," she said. "He was such a bright boy; we thought we'd done well when we scholarshipped him to the Shapers. I never understood what they did to him, but it was horrible. I tried to make our marriage work, but he was so clever, so smooth and plausible, that he could twist anything I said or did to serve some other purpose. He terrified the others. They swore he would rip our world apart. We should never have sent him to the Shapers."

"I'm sure it seemed a wise decision at the time," Lindsay said. "The Republic was already in the Mechanist orbit, and they wanted to redress the balance."

"Then they shouldn't have done it to my cousin's son. There were plenty of plebes to send out, people like Constantine." She put one wrinkled knuckle to her lips. "I'm sorry. That's aristocratic prejudice. Forgive me, Auditor, I'm distraught."

"I understand," Lindsay said. "To those our age, old memories can come with unexpected force. I'm very sorry, madam. You have been treated unjustly."

"Thank you, sir." She accepted a tissue from the household servo. "Your sympathy touches me deeply." She dabbed at her eyes with precise, birdlike movements. "I almost feel that I know you."

"A trick of memory," Lindsay said. "I was married once to a woman much like you."

A slow Look passed between them. A great deal was said, below the level of words. The truth surfaced briefly, was acknowledged, and then vanished beneath the necessity for subterfuge.

"This wife," she said. Her face was flushed. "She did not accompany you on your journey here."

"Marriage in Dembowska is a different situation," Lindsay said.

"I was married here. A five-year contract marriage. Polygamous. It expired last year."

"You are currently unattached?"

She nodded. Lindsay gestured about the room with a whir of his right arm. "Myself as well. You can see the state of my domestic affairs. My career has made my life rather arid."

She smiled tentatively.

"Would you be interested in the management of my household? An Assistant Auditorship would pay rather better than your current position, I think."

"I'm sure it would."

"Shall we say, a six-month probationary period against a five-year joint management contract, standard terms, monogamous? I can have my office print out a contract by tomorrow morning."

"This is quite sudden."

"Nonsense, Alexandrina. At our age, if we put things off, we never accomplish anything. What's five years to us? We have reached the age of discretion."

"May I have that drink?" she said. "It's bad for my maintenance program, but I think I need it." She looked at him nervously, a ghost of strained intimacy waking behind her eyes.

He looked at her smooth paper skin, the brittle precision of her hair. He realized that his gesture of atonement would add another rote to his life, a new form of routine. He restrained a sigh. "I look to you to set our sexuality clause."

## SHIMMERS UNION COUNCIL STATE: 23-6-'83

Constantine looked into the tank. Behind the glass window, below the surface of the water, was the waterlogged head of Paolo Mavrides. The dark, curled hair, a major trait of the Mavrides gene-line, floated soggily around the young man's neck and shoulders. The eyes were open, greenish and bloodshot. Injections had paralyzed his optic nerve. A spinal clamp left him able to feel but not to move. Blind and deaf, numbed by the blood-warmed water, Paolo Mavrides had been in sensory isolation for two weeks.

A tracheal plug fed him oxygen. Intravenous taps kept him from starving.

Constantine touched a black rocker switch on the welded tank, and the jury-rigged speakers came alive. The young assassin was talking to himself, some mumbled litany in different voices. Constantine spoke into the microphone. "Paolo."

"I'm busy," Paolo said. "Come back later."

Constantine chuckled. "Very well." He tapped against the microphone to make the sound of a switch closing.

"No, wait!" Paolo said at once. Constantine smiled at the trace of panic. "Never mind, the performance is ruined anyway. Vetterling's *Shepherd Moons.*"

"Hasn't had a performance in years," Constantine said. "You must have been a mere child then."

"I memorized it when I was nine."

"I'm impressed by your resourcefulness. Still, the Cataclysts believe in that, don't they? Testing the inner world of the will . . . You've been in there quite a while. Quite a while."

There was silence. Constantine waited. "How long?" Mavrides burst out.

"Almost forty-eight hours."

Mavrides laughed shortly.

Constantine joined in. "Of course we know that isn't so. No, it's been almost a year. You'd be surprised how thin you look."

"You should try it sometime. Might help your skin problems."

"Those are the least of my difficulties, young man. I made a tactical error when I chose the best security possible. It made me a challenge. You'd be surprised how many fools have had this tank before you. You made a mistake, young Paolo."

"Tell me something," Paolo said. "Why do you sound like God?"

"That's a technical artifact. My voice has a direct feed to your inner ear. That's why you can't hear your own voice. I'm reading it off the nerves to your larynx."

"I see," Paolo said. "Wirehead work."

"Nothing irreversible. Tell me about yourself, Paolo. What was your brigade?"

"I'm no Cataclyst."

"I have your weapon here." Constantine pulled a small timer-vial from his tailored linen jacket and rolled it between his fingers. "Standard Cataclyst issue. What is it? PDKL-Ninety-five?"

Paolo said nothing.

"Perhaps you know the drug as 'Shatter,' " Constantine said.

Paolo laughed. "I know better than to try to re-form your mind. If I could have entered the same room with you I would have set it for five seconds and we would have both died."

"An aerosol toxin, is it? How rash."

"There are more important things than living, plebe."

"What a quaint insult. I see you've researched my past. Haven't heard the like in years. Next you'll be saying I'm unplanned."

"No need. Your wife tells us that much."

"I beg your pardon?"

"Natalie Constantine, your wife. Ever hear of her? She doesn't take neglect easily. She's become the prime whore of Skimmers Union."

"How distressing."

"How do you think I planned to enter your house? Your wife's a slut. She begs me for it."

Constantine laughed. "You'd like me to strike you, wouldn't you? The pain would give you something to hold on to. No, you should have stayed in Goldreich-Tremaine, young man. In those empty halls and broken-down offices. I'm afraid you've begun to bore me."

"Let me tell you what I regret, before you go. I regret that I set my sights so low. I've had time to think, recently." Hollow laughter. "I fell for your image, your propaganda line. The Nysa asteroid, for instance. It seemed so grand at first. The Ring Council didn't know that Nysa Cartel was a dumping ground for burnt-out wireheads from the moondocks. You were still sucking up to aristocrats from the Republic. With all your rank you're still a cheap informer, Constantine. And a fucking lackey."

Constantine felt a quiver of familiar tension across the back of his head. He touched the plug there and reached in his pocket for the inhaler. No use going into fugue when the boy was starting to babble, at the point of breaking. "Go on," he said.

"The great things you claim you've done are all facades and frauds. You've never built anything of your own. You're small, Constantine. Very small. I know a man who could hide ten of you under his thumbnail."

"Who?" Constantine said. "Your friend Vetterling?"

"Poor Fernand, your victim? Yes, of course he's a thousand times your size, but that's hardly fair, is it? You never had an atom of artistic talent. No, I mean in your own skill. Politics. Espionage."

"Some Cataclyst, then." Constantine was bored.

"No. Abelard Lindsay."

It hit him then. A lightning stroke of migraine raced across his left frontal lobe. The surface of the tank came toward him in slow motion as he fell, a frozen icescape of dull metallic glitter, and he struggled to get his hands up, nerve impulses locked in a high-speed fugue that seemed to last a month. When he came to, his cheek pressed against the cold metal, Mavrides was still babbling. ". . . the whole story from Nora. While you were here holding treason trials for artists, Lindsay was scoring the biggest coup in history. An Investor defector. . . . He has an Investor defector, a starship Queen. In the palm of his hand."

Constantine cleared his throat. "I heard that news. Mech propaganda. It's a farce."

Mavrides laughed hysterically. "You're burned! You're a fucking footnote. Lindsay led the revolution in your nation while you were still swatting bugs in the germs and muck and plotting to seize his credit. You're microscopic! I shouldn't have bothered to kill you, but I've never had any luck."

"Lindsay's dead. He's been dead sixty years."

"Sure, plebe. That's what he wanted you to think." The laughter from the speakers was metallic, drawn straight from the nerve. "I lived in his house, fool. He loved me."

Constantine opened the tank. He twisted the timer on the vial and dropped it into the water, then slammed the tank shut. He turned and walked away. As he reached the doorway he heard a sudden frenzied splashing as the toxin hit.

## CZARINA-KLUSTER PEOPLE'S CORPORATE REPUBLIC: 3-1-'84

The long bright line of welded radiance was the cleanest thing he had ever seen. Lindsay floated in an observation bubble, watching construction robots crawl in vacuum. The Mechanist engines had the long sharp noses of weevils, their white-hot welding tips casting long shadows across the blackened hull of the Czarina's Palace.

They were building a full-sized replica of an Investor starship, a starship without engines, a hulk that would never move under its own power. And black, with no trace of the gaudy arabesques and inlays of a true Investor craft. The other Investors had insisted on it: condemned their pervert Queen to this dark and mocking prison.

After years of research, Lindsay had pieced out the truth about the Commander's crime.

Queens intromitted their eggs into the womblike pouches of their males. The males fertilized the eggs and brought them to term within the pouch. The neuter Ensigns controlled ovulation through a complex hormonal pseudo-copulation.

The criminal Queen had killed her Ensign in a fit of passion and set up a common male in his place. But without a true Ensign, the cycles of her sexuality had become distorted. Lindsay's evidence showed her destroying one of her malformed eggs. To an Investor, it was worse than perversion, worse even than murder: it was bad for business.

Lindsay had presented his evidence in a way that pierced to the core of Investor ethics. Embarrassment was not an emotion native to Investors. They had been stunned. But Lindsay was quick with his remedy: exile. Behind it was the implied threat to spread the evidence, to play out the details of the scandal to every Investor ship and every human faction.

It was bad enough that a select group of wealthy Queens and Ensigns had been apprised of the shocking news. That the impressionable males should learn of it was unthinkable. A bargain was struck.

The Queen never knew what had betrayed her. The approach to her had been even more subtle, stretching Lindsay's talents to the utmost. A timely gift of jewels had helped, distracting her with that overwhelming avidity that was the very breath of life to Investors. Business had been poor on her ship, with its debased crew and wretched eunuch Ensign.

Lindsay came armed with charts from Wells, statistics predicting the wealth to be wrung from a city-state independent of faction. Their exponential curves rose to a clean rake-off of breathtaking riches. He told her that he knew nothing of her disgrace; only that her own species was eager to condemn her. With a large enough hoard, he hinted, she might buy her way back into their good graces.

Patiently, fluently, he helped her see that this was her best chance. What could she accomplish alone, without crew, without Ensign? Why not accept the industrious aid of the small polite strangers? The social instincts of the tiny gregarious mammals drove them to consider her their Queen, in truth, and themselves her subjects. Already a Board of Advisors awaited her whims, each one fluent in Investor and begging leave to heap her with wealth.

Greed would only have taken her so far. It was fear that broke her to his will: fear of the small soft-skinned alien with dark plastic over his pulpy eyes and his answers for everything. He seemed to know her own people better than she did herself.

The announcement had come a week later, and with it a sudden hemorrhage of capital to the newborn place of exile. They called the Queen "Czarina," a nickname given by Ryumin. And her city was Czarina-Kluster: in four months already a boom town, accreting out of nothing on the inner edge of the Belt. The Czarina-Kluster People's Corporate Republic had leaped into sudden concrete existence out of raw potential, in what Wells called a "Prigoginic leap," a "mergence into a higher level of complexity." Now the Board of Advisors was deluged with business, comlines frantic with would-be defectors maneuvering for asylum and a fresh start. The presence of an Investor cast an enormous shadow, a wall of prestige that no Mechanist or Shaper dared to challenge.

Makeshift squatter's digs crowded the Queen's raw Palace: nets of tough Shaper bubble suburbs, "subbles"; sleazy pirate craft copulating in a daisy-chain of accordioned attack tunnels; rough blown-out honeycombs of Mechanist nickel-iron, towed into place; limpetlike construction huts clinging to the skeletal girders of an urban complex scarcely off the drawing board. This city would be a metropolis, a circumsolar free port, the ultimate sundog zone. He had brought it into being. But it was not for him.

"A sight to stir the blood, friend." Lindsay looked to his right. The man once called Wells had arrived in the observation bubble. In the weeks of preparation Wells had vanished into a carefully prepared false identity. He was now Wellspring, two hundred years old, born on Earth, a man of mystery, a maneuverer par excellence, a visionary, even a prophet. Nothing less would do. A coup this size demanded legendry. It demanded fraud.

Lindsay nodded. "Things progress."

"This is where the real work starts. I'm not too happy with that Board of Advisors. They seem a bit too stiff, too Mechanist. Some of them have ambition. They'll have to be watched."

"Of course."

"You wouldn't consider the job? The Coordinator's post is open for you. You're the man for it."

"I like the shadows, Wellspring. A role your size is too close to the footlights for me."

Wellspring hesitated. "I have trouble enough with the philosophy. The myth may be too much for me. I need you and your shadows."

Lindsay looked away, watching two construction robots follow a seam to meet in a white-hot kiss of their welding-beaks. "My wife is dead," he said.

"Alexandrina? I'm sorry. This is a shock."

Lindsay winced. "No, not her. Nora. Nora Mavrides. Nora Everett."

"Ah," Wellspring said. "When did you get the news?"

"I told her," Lindsay said, "that I had a place for us. You remember I mentioned to you that there might be a Ring Council breakaway."

"Yes."

"It was as quiet as I could make it, but not quiet enough. Constantine got word somehow, exposed the breakaway. She was indicted for treason. The trial would have implicated the rest of her clan. So she chose suicide."

"She was courageous."

"It was the only thing to do."

"One supposes so."

"She still loved me, Wellspring. She was going to join me here. She was trying to do it when he killed her."

"I recognize your grief," Wellspring said. "But life is long. You mustn't be blinded to your ultimate aims."

Lindsay was grim. "You know I don't follow that post-Cataclyst line."

"Posthumanist," Wellspring insisted. "Are you on the side of life, or aren't you? If you're not, then you'll let the pain overwhelm you. You'll go against Constantine and die as Nora did. Accept her death, and stay with us. The future belongs to Posthumanism, Lindsay. Not to nation-states, not to factions. It belongs to life, and life moves in clades."

"I've heard your spiel before, Wellspring. If we embrace the loss of our humanity then it means worse differences, worse struggle, worse war."

"Not if the new clades can reach accord as cognitive systems on the Fourth Prigoginic Level of Complexity."

Lindsay, despairing, was silent. Finally he said, "I wish you the best of luck here, sincerely. Protect the damaged, if you can. Maybe it'll come to something."

"There's a universe of potential, Lindsay, think of that. No rules, no limits."

"Not while he lives. Forgive me."

"You'll have to do that for yourself."

## AN INVESTOR TRADE SHIP: 14-2-'86

"This is not the sort of transaction we prefer," the Investor said.

"Have we met before, Ensign?" said Lindsay.

"No. I knew one of your students once. Captain-Doctor Simon Afriel. A very accomplished gentleman."

"I remember Simon well."

"He died on embassy." The Investor stared, his dark eyeballs gleaming with hostility above the white rims of his nictitating membranes. "A pity. I always enjoyed his conversation. Still, he had that urge to meddle, to tamper. You call it curiosity. An urge to value useless data. A being with such a handicap runs a great many unnecessary risks."

"Without a doubt," Lindsay agreed. He had not heard of Afriel's death. The knowledge filled him with bitter pleasure: another fanatic gone, another gifted life wasted. . . .

"Hatred is an easier motive to fathom. Strange that you should fall prey to it, Artist. It makes me doubt my judgment of your species."

"I regret being a source of confusion. Chancellor-General Constantine might explain it better."

"I'll speak to him. He and his party have just come aboard. He is not a fit model, though, for a judgment on human nature. Our scanning reveals that he favors severe alterations."

Many did these days, Lindsay thought. Even the very young. As if the existence of the Neotenic Republic, with its forced humanity, freed the other factions from a stifling pretense. "You find this odd in a spacegoing race?"

"No. Not at all. That's why there are so few of them left."

"Nineteen," Lindsay said.

"Yes. The number of vanished races within our trading realm is larger by an order of magnitude. Their artifacts persist, though, such as the one we plan to lease to you presently." The Investor showed his striated, peglike teeth, a sign of distaste and reluctance. "We'd hoped for truly long-term trade with your species, but we cannot dissuade you from aiming for breakthroughs in questions of metaphysics. We will soon have to put your solar system under quarantine for fear of being caught in your transmutations. In the meantime we must abandon a few scruples to make our local investments worthwhile."

"You alarm me," Lindsay said. He had heard this before: vague warnings from the Investors, intended to freeze humanity at its current level of development. It amused him that Investors should preach Preservationism. "Surely the War is a greater threat."

"No," the Investor said. "We ourselves presented you with evidence. Our interstellar drive showed you that space-time is not what you thought. You must be aware of this, Artist. Consider recent breakthroughs in the mathematical treatment of what you call Hilbert space and the ur-space of the precontinuum. They can't have escaped your attention."

"Mathematics isn't my forte," Lindsay said.

"Nor ours. We only know that these discoveries are danger signs of an imminent transition to another mode of being."

"Imminent?"

"Yes. A matter of mere centuries."

Centuries, Lindsay thought. It was easy to forget how old the Investors were. Their deep disinterest in change gave them a wide but shallow field of view. They had no interest in their own history, no urge to contrast their own lives with those of their dead, because there was no assumption that their lives or motives varied in even the slightest degree. They had vague legends and garbled technical readouts concerning particularly prized objects of booty, but even these fragments of history were lost in a jackdaw scramble of loot.

"Not all the extinct races made the transition," the Ensign said, "and those who invented the Arena probably died violently. We have no data on that: only technical data on their modes of perception, allowing us to make the Arena comprehensible to the human nervous system. In this we had the assistance of the Department of Neurology from the Kosmosity of the Nysa Corporate Treaty State."

Constantine's recruits, Lindsay thought. The Nysa rogue wireheads, Mechanist defectors to the Shaper cause, combining Mech techniques with the fascist structure of the Shaper academic-military complex. "The very men—the very beings, rather, for the job."

"So said the Chancellor-General. His party has assembled now. Shall we join them?"

Constantine's group mingled with Lindsay's in one of the cavernous lounges of the Investor ship. The lounge was crowded with towering rococo furniture: dizzyingly overdecorated settees and slablike tables, supported on curved legs crusted with ribbed domes and stylized scrolls. It was all far too large to be of any conventional use to the score of human visitors, who crouched under the furniture warily, careful not to touch anything. Lindsay saw as he entered the lounge that the alien furnishings had been sprayed with a thick protective lacquer to guard them from oxygen.

He had never seen any of the young Constantine genetics. Constantine had brought ten of them: five women, five men. The Constantine siblings were taller than Constantine and had lighter hair, clearly a percentage cut from some other gene-line.

They had that peculiar Shaper magnetism, an acrobatic smoothness and fluidity. Yet something in the set of their shoulders, their slim, dextrous hands, kinesically displayed Constantine's genetic heritage. They wore outlandish finery: round velvet hats, ruby earrings, and gold-laced brocade coats. They dressed for the sake of Investors, who appreciated a prosperous look in their customers.

One woman had her back to Lindsay, examining the towering legs of the furniture. The others stood calmly, trading meaningless pleasantries with Lindsay's people, a motley group of acedemics and Investor specialists on leave from Czarina-Kluster. His wife Alexandrina was among them; she was talking to Constantine himself, with her usual perfect good breeding. Nothing showed that all of them were seconds at a duel, witnesses present to assure fairness.

It had been a two-year struggle, a matter of prolonged and delicate negotiation, to arrange a meeting between himself and Constantine. At last they had settled on the Investor starship as a suitable battleground, one where treachery would be counterproductive. The Arena itself had remained in Investor hands; the Nysa technicians had worked on data freely available to both parties. The costs were split equitably, with Constantine assuming most of the financing, on an option against possible technological spinoffs. Lindsay had received data through a double-blind in Czarina-Kluster and Dembowska, to confuse possible assassins. Constantine, to his credit, had sent no one.

The mechanics of their duel had been fraught with difficulty. Varying proposals had been debated by an ever-widening circle of those in the know. Physical combat was rejected at once as beneath the dignity of the estranged parties. Those familiar with the social gambling of the Shaper underworld favored a form of gambling for suicide. An appeal to chance, though, presumed equality between the parties, which neither was willing to grant.

A proper duel should assure the triumph of the better man. It was argued that this required a test of alertness, will, and mental flexibility, qualities central to modern life. Objective tests were possible, but it was difficult to ensure that one party would not prepare himself ahead of time or influence the judges. Various forms of direct mind-to-mind struggle existed among the wirehead community, but these often lasted for decades and involved radical alteration of the faculties. They decided to consult the Investors.

At first the Investors had difficulty grasping the concept. Later, characteristically, they suggested economic warfare, with each party granted a stake and offered the opportunity to increase it. After a stated period the poorer man was to be executed.

This was not satisfactory. Another Investor suggestion involved attempts by both parties to read the "literature of the (untranslatable)," but it was suggested that the survivor might repeat something of what he had read and become a hazard to the rest of humanity. At this point the Arena was rediscovered in one of the booty-crammed holds of an Investor craft present in circumsolar space.

Study quickly showed the Arena's advantages. Alien forms of experience challenged even the finest members of society: the emissaries to alien worlds. The extremely high casualty rate among this group proved that the Arena would be a test in itself. Within the Arena's simulated environment, the duelists would battle in two alien bodies of guaranteed equality, thus ensuring that victory would go to the superior strategist.

Constantine stood beneath one of the towering tables, sipping a self-chilling silver goblet of distilled water. Like his gaudily clad congenetics, he wore soft lace-cuffed trousers and a gold-threaded coat, its high collar studded with insignias of rank. His round, delicate eyes gleamed black with soft antiglare lenses. His face, like Lindsay's, was creased where years of habitual expression had worked their way into the muscles.

Lindsay wore a dun-brown jumpsuit without markings. His face was oiled against the blue-white glare, and he wore dark sunshades.

He crossed the room to join Constantine. A hush fell, but Constantine gestured urbanely, and his fellow genetics picked up the tag-ends of their conversations.

"Hello, cousin," Constantine said.

Lindsay nodded. "A fine group of congenetics, Philip. Congratulations on your siblings."

"Good sound stock," Constantine agreed. "They handle the gravity well." He looked pointedly at Lindsay's wife, who had shuffled tactfully toward another group, visibly troubled by pain in her knees.

"I spent a lot of time on gene politics," Lindsay said. "In retrospect it seems like an aristocratic fetish."

Constantine's lids narrowed over the black adhesive lenses. "A little more work on the Mavrides production run might have been in order."

Lindsay felt a surge of cold fury. "Their loyalties betrayed them."

Constantine sighed. "The irony hasn't escaped me, Abelard. If you had only maintained your pledged faith to Vera Kelland years ago, none of these aberrations would have occurred."

"Aberrations?" Lindsay smiled icily. "Decent of you to mop up after me, cousin. To tie up my loose ends."

"Small wonder, when you left so many pernicious ones." Constantine sipped his water. "Appeasement policy, for instance. Détente. It was typical of you to fast-talk a population into disaster and then sundog off when it came to the crunch."

Lindsay showed interest. "Is that the new party line? To blame me for the Investor Peace? How flattering. But is it wise to bring up the past? Why remind them that you lost the Republic?"

Constantine's knuckles whitened on the goblet. "I see that you're still an antiquarian. Odd that you should embrace Wellspring and his cadre of anarchists."

Lindsay nodded. "I know that you'll attack Czarina-Kluster if you have the chance. Your hypocrisy astounds me. You're no Shaper. Not only are you unplanned, but your use of Mech techniques is notorious. You're a living demonstration of the power of détente. You seize advantage wherever you find it but deny it to anyone else."

Constantine smiled. "I'm no Shaper. I'm their guardian. It's been my fate, and I've accepted it. I've been alone all my life, except for you and Vera. We were fools then."

"I was the fool," Lindsay said. "I killed Vera for nothing. You killed her to prove your own power."

"The price was bitter, but the proof was worth it. I've made amends since then." He drained his goblet and stretched out his arm.

Vera Kelland took the cup. Around her neck she wore the gold filigree locket she had worn in the crash, the locket that was meant to guarantee his death.

Lindsay was dumbstruck. He had not seen the girl's face when her back was turned.

She did not meet his eyes.

Lindsay stared at her in icy fascination. The resemblance was strong but not perfect. The girl turned and left. Lindsay forced the words. "She's not a full clone."

"Of course not. Vera Kelland was unplanned."

"You used her genetics?"

"Do I hear envy, cousin? Are you claiming her cells loved you and not me?" Constantine laughed.

Lindsay tore his gaze from the woman. Her grace and beauty wounded him. He felt shell-shocked, panicky. "What will happen to her, when you die here?"

Constantine smiled quietly. "Why not mull that over, while we fight?"

"I'll make you a pledge," Lindsay said. "I swear that if I win I'll spare your congenetics in the years to come."

"My people are loyal to the Ring Council. Your Czarina-Kluster rabble are their enemies. They're bound to come in conflict."

"Surely that will be grim enough without our adding to it."

"You're naive, Abelard. Czarina-Kluster must fall."

Lindsay looked aside, studying Constantine's group. "They don't look stupid, Philip. I wonder if they won't rejoice at your death. They might be swept away in the general celebration."

"Idle speculation always bores me," Constantine said.

Lindsay glared. "Then it's time we put the matter to the proof."

Heavy curtains were spread over one of the huge alien tables, falling to the floor. Beneath the table's sheltering expanse the blazing light was dimmer, and a pair of supportive waterbeds were brought in to combat Investor gravity.

The Arena itself was tiny, a fist-sized dodecahedron, its triangular sides so glossily black that they shimmered with faint pastels. Wire trailed from metal-bound sockets in two opposing poles of the structure. The wires led to two goggle-equipped helmets with flexible neck extensions. The helmets had the blunt utilitarian look of Mechanist manufacture.

Constantine won the toss and took the right-hand helmet. He produced a flat curved lozenge of beige plastic from his gold-threaded coat and hooked an elastic strap to its anchor loops. "A spatial analyzer," he explained. "One of my routines. Permitted?"

"Yes." Lindsay pulled a flesh-colored strip of dotted adhesive disks from his breast pocket. "PDKL Ninety-five," he said. "In doses of two hundred micrograms."

Constantine stared. " 'Shatter.' From the Cataclysts?"

"No," Lindsay said. "This was part of the stock of Michael Carnassus. It's original Mechanist issue, for the embassies. Interested?"

"No," Constantine said. He looked shaken. "I protest. I came here to fight Abelard Lindsay, not a shattered personality."

"That scarcely matters now, does it? This is to the death, Constantine. My humanity would only get in the way."

Constantine shrugged. "Then I win, no matter what."

Constantine attached the spatial analyzer, fitting its custom-made curves against the back of his skull. Its microprongs slid smoothly into the jacks connected to his right hemisphere. With its use, space would assume a fantastic solidity, movement would show with superhuman clarity. Constantine lifted the helmet and caught a glimpse of his own sleeve. Lindsay saw him hesitate, studying the fabric's complex interwoven topology. He seemed fascinated. Then he shuddered briefly and slid his head within the helmet.

Lindsay pressed the first dosage against his wrist and donned his headpiece. He felt the adhesive eye-cusps grip his sockets, then a wash of numbness as local anesthetics took effect and threads of stiffened biogel slid over the eyeballs to penetrate his optic nerves. He heard a faint annihilating ringing as other threads wormed past his eardrums into predetermined chemotactic contact with his neurons.

They both lay back on their waterbeds, waiting as the helmets' neck units soaked through predrilled microholes in the seventh cervical vertebra. The microthreads grew their way harmlessly through the myelin casings of the spinal axons in a self-replicating gelatin web.

Lindsay floated quietly. The PDKL was taking hold. As the spinal cutoff proceeded he felt his body dissolving like wax, each sensory clump of muscle sending a final warm glow of sensation as the neck unit shut it off, a last twinge of humanity too thin to be called pain. The Shatter helped him forget. By rendering everything novel, it was intended to rob everything of novelty. While it broke up preconceptions, it heightened the powers of comprehension so drastically that entire intuitive philosophies boiled up from a single moment of insight.

It was dark. His mouth tasted of cobwebs. He felt a brief wave of vertigo and terror before the Shatter aborted it, leaving him suddenly stranded in an emotional no-man's-land where his fear transmuted itself bizarrely into a crushing sense of physical weight.

He was crouching next to the base of a titanic wall. Before him, dim sheens of radiance gleamed from a colossal arch. Beside it, jutting balustrades of icy stone were shrouded in thin webs of sagging dust-covered cable. He reached out to touch the wall and noted with dulled surprise that his arm had transmuted itself into a pallid claw. The arm was jointed in pale armor. It had two elbows.

He began crawling up the wall. Gravity accompanied him. Looking out with new perspective he saw that bridges had transformed themselves into curved columns; loops of sagging cable were now vicious, stiffened arcs.

Everything was old. Something behind his eyes was opening. He could see time lying on the world like a sheen, a frozen blur of movement chopped out of context and painted onto the surface of the cold stone like alien shellac. Walls became floors, balustrades cold barricades. He realized then that he had too many legs. There were legs where his ribs should have been and the crawling feeling in his stomach was a literal crawling: the sensations from his guts were transmuted into the movement of his second pair of limbs.

He struggled to look at himself. He could not curl forward, but his back arched with fantastic ease and his lidless eyes gazed at armored plates thick with intersegmental fur. A pair of wrinkled organs protruded on stalks from his back: he brushed his muzzle against them and suddenly, dizzyingly, he smelled yellow. He tried to scream, then. He had nothing to scream with.

He flopped back against the cold rock. Instinct seized him, and he scuttled headlong across acres of porous gritty stone toward the safe darkness of a huge jutting cornice and a racklike checkerboard of rust-eaten bars. Proportion left him as he crouched there, wobbling in a hideous burst of intuition, and he realized that he was tiny, infinitesimal, that the titanic mortared blocks that dwarfed him must themselves be small, so small that . . .

He jabbed at the porous stone with a raking flex of his foreclaw. It was solid, solid with a weary durability that had waited out uncaring eons, painted with the feeble dust of huge groaning machinery run past the point of uselessness into an utter exhaustion of grit.

He could smell the age of it, even feel it as a kind of pressure, a kind of dread. It was massive, unyielding, and he thought suddenly of water. Water moving at high speed was as hard as steel. His mind rocketed off, then, and he thought of the identity of speed and substance, the kinetic energy of atoms giving form to hard stone, stone which was empty space. It was all abstract structure, ageless form, level after level, emptiness permeated by disturbances of emptiness, waves, quanta. He became aware of fine detail within the stone, the surface suddenly no more than frozen smoke, a hard fog petrified by captive eons. Below the surface a finer level, detail on obsessive detail in an ever-recessive web. . . .

He was attacked. The enemy was on him. He felt a sudden ghastly rending as claws tore into him from above, the alien pain garbled in translation, cramming his brain with black nausea and dread. He flopped in death-stricken convulsion, his face slid apart in a nightmare extrusion of razored mandibles, and he caught a leg and sheared it off at the joint; he smelled hot hunger and pain and the bright hot radiance of his own juices bursting, and then the cold, the seeping, the bright spark fading to become one with the old stone and the age and the dark. . . .

The exterior microphones of his helmet caught Constantine's voice and fed it through his nerves. "Abelard."

Lindsay's throat was rull of rust. "I hear you."

"You're alive?"

The nerve block in his neck half dissolved and he felt his own body, as insubstantial as warm gas. He groped for the strip of dermadisks beside his hand: the perforated plastic felt as thin as ribbon. He peeled off another disk with his fingers and pressed it raggedly against the base of his thumb. "We must try again."

"What did you see, Abelard? I must know."

"Halls. Walls. Dark stones."

"And gulfs? Black gulfs of nothing, bigger than God?"

"I can't talk." The other dose was hitting him, language was collapsing, a tangle of irrelevant assumptions shattered by sudden doubt, wads of grammar mashed beneath the impact of the drug. "Again."

He was back. He could feel the enemy now, sense his presence as a weak distant tingling. The light was clearer, gigantic radiant washes seeping through masses of stone so rotten with age that they were thin as cloth. Fastidiously, he ran his foreclaws through the polyps around his mouth, cleansing them of damp grime. He felt a sense of hunger so overwhelming that the scales equalized, and he realized that the urge to live and kill was as huge as the vaults around him.

He found the enemy crouched within a cul-de-sac between a harsh decaying bridge and its supporting beams. He smelled the fear.

The enemy's position was wrong. The enemy clung to the wall in a false perspective, perceiving the endless horizon as a shattering abyss. The gulf below was an eternal one, a chaos of walls, chambers, landings, self-replicating, built from nothing, a terrifying ramification of infinity.

He attacked, biting deep into the back plates, the taste of hot ooze driving him into frenzy. The enemy slashed back, digging, pushing, pale claws scraping the rock. His jaws ripped free from the enemy's back. The enemy struggled to push him away, to shove him backward into the horizon. For a moment he was gripped by the enemy's own perspective. He knew suddenly that if he fell he would fall forever. Into the abyss, plunging into his own terror and defeat, endlessly, through the self-spinning labyrinth, mind frozen in boundless anguish, a maze of unending experience, unending fright, implacable walls, halls, steps, ramps, crypts, vaults, passages, always icy, always out of reach.

He skidded back. The enemy was desperate, scrabbling convulsively, galvanized with pain. His own claws were slipping. The stone was rejecting him, becoming slicker. Suddenly the breakthrough came, and he saw the world for what it was. His claws slid in, then, with phantom ease, stone slipping aside like smoke.

Then he was anchored. The enemy pushed at him helplessly, uselessly. He tasted the sudden gush of despair as the enemy turned to flee.

He ran him down at once, caught him, and rended him. A miasma of dust and terror burst from the enemy's flesh. He ripped him free from the wall, held him out in an orgasm of hatred and victory—and flung him into the gulf.

# Part 3

## Moving in Clades

# Chapter 8

## THE NEOTENIC CULTURAL REPUBLIC: 17-6-'91

The dreams were pleasant, dreams of warmth and light, an animal's life, an eternal present.

Consciousness returned in tingling pain, like blood seeping into a leg long numbed. He struggled to unify himself, to assume the burden of being Lindsay again, and the pain of it made him claw the grass, spattering his naked skin with dirt.

Chaos roared around him: reality in its rawest form, a buzzing, blinding confusion. He sprawled on his back in the grass, gasping. Above him the world swam into focus: green light, white light, a brown framework of branches. Solidity returned to the world. He saw a living spray of branching leaves and twigs: a form of such fantastic beauty that he was overwhelmed with awe. He heaved himself over and slithered toward the tree's rough trunk, hauling his naked flesh through the sleek grass. He threw his arms around the tree and pressed his bearded cheek against the bark.

Ecstasy seized him. He pressed his face against the tree, sobbing in frenzy, torn with deep visionary rapture. As his mind coalesced he burned with insight, a smoldering oneness with this living being. Helpless joy pervaded him as he joined its serene integration.

When he called for help, two young Shapers wearing hospital whites answered his broken cries. Taking his arms, they helped him stagger across the lawn through the arched stone doorway of the clinic.

Lindsay was afflicted by language. His thoughts were clear, but the words wouldn't come. He recognized the building. It was the mansion of the Tyler clan. He was back in the Republic. He wanted to speak to the orderlies, ask them how he had returned, but his brain couldn't shuffle his vocabulary into order. The words waited agonizingly on the tip of his tongue, just past his reach.

They took him down an entry hall crowded with blueprints and glass-topped exhibits. The left wing of the mansion, with its suite of bedrooms, had been stripped down to the polished wood and filled with medicinal equipment. Lindsay stared helplessly into the face of the man on his left. He had the smooth grace of a Shaper and the riveting eyes of a Superbright.

"You are—" Lindsay burst out suddenly.

"Relax, friend. You're safe. The doctor's on her way." Smiling, he draped Lindsay in a broad-sleeved hospital gown, tying it behind him in an easy flurry of knots. They seated him under an overhead cerebral scanner. The second orderly handed him an inhaler.

"Whiff up on this, cousin. It's tagged glucose. Radioactive. For the scanner." The Superbright whacked the curved white dome of the machine affectionately. "We've got to look you over. I mean right down to the *core*."

Lindsay sniffed obediently at the inhaler. It smelled sweet. The scanner whirred down its upright track-stand to settle around the top of his head.

A woman entered the room. She carried a wooden instrument case and wore a loose medical tunic, short skirt, and muddied plastic boots. "Has he spoken?" she said.

Lindsay recognized her gene-line. "Juliano," he said with difficulty.

She smiled at him. She opened her wooden case with a squeak of antique hinges. "Yes, Abelard," she said. She gave him a Look.

"Margaret Juliano," Lindsay said. He could not interpret the Look, and the inability filled him with a sudden reviving trickle of energy and fear. "The Cataclysts, Margaret. They put you on ice."

"That's right." She reached inside the case and produced a dark candy in a little creased paper tray. "Have a chocolate?"

Lindsay's mouth flooded with saliva. "Please," he said reflexively. She popped the candy into his mouth. It was cloyingly sweet. He chewed it reluctantly.

"Scarper," Juliano told the two technicians. "I'll handle this." The two Superbrights left, grinning.

Lindsay swallowed.

"Another?" she said.

"Never much canned—never much *cared* for candy," Lindsay said.

"That's a good sign," she said, closing the box. She examined the scanner's screen and pulled a light-pen from the cluster of loose blonde hair at her ear. "Those chocolates were the center of your life for the last five years."

The shock was bad, but he had known it was coming. His throat felt dry. "Five years?"

"You're lucky to have any *you* left," she said. "It's been a long treatment: restoring a brain altered by heavy dosage of PDKL Ninety-five. Complicated by changes in your spatial perception, caused by the Arena artifact. It's been a real challenge. Expensive, too." She studied the screen, nibbling the end of her light-pen. "But that's all right. Your friend Wellspring footed the bills."

She had changed so much that it dizzied him. It was hard to reconcile the disciplined pacifist of the Midnight Clique, Margaret Juliano of Goldreich-Tremaine, with this calm, careless woman with grass stains on her knees and loose, dirty hair.

"Don't try to talk too much at first," she said. "Your right hemisphere is handling language functions through the commissure. We can expect neologisms, poverty of speech, a private idiolect . . . don't be alarmed." She circled something on the display screen and pressed a control key: cross-sections of his brain shuffled past in bright false-color blues and oranges.

"How many people in this room?" she said.

"You and I," Lindsay said.

"No sense of someone behind you, to your left?"

Lindsay twisted to look, scraping his forehead painfully on an inner node of the scanner. "No."

"Good. The commissure approach was the right one, then. In split-brain cases we sometimes get a fragmentation of consciousness, a ghost image over-looking the perceptual self. Let me know if you feel anything of the sort."

"No. But outside I felt—" He wanted to tell her about the moment when waking had come suddenly, his long epiphanic insight into self and life. The vision still blazed within him, but the vocabulary was completely beyond him. He knew suddenly that he would never be able to tell anyone the full truth. It was not something that words could hold.

"Don't struggle," she said. "Let it come easily. There's plenty of time."

"My arm," Lindsay said suddenly. He realized with confusion that his right arm, the metal one, had turned to flesh. He raised the left one. It was metal. Horror overloaded him. He had turned inside out!

"Careful," she said. "You may have some trouble with space perceptions, left and right. It's an artifact of the commissural dominance. And you've had a new rejuvenation. We've done a lot of work on you in the past five years. Just to mark time."

The careless ease of it stunned him. "Are you God?" Lindsay said.

She shrugged. "There've been breakthroughs, Abelard. A lot has changed. Socially, politically, medically—all the same thing nowadays, I know, but think of it as spontaneous self-organization, a social Prigoginic Leap to a new level of complexity—"

"Oh, no," Lindsay said.

She tapped the scanner, and it whirred upward off his head. She sat before him in an antique wooden office chair, curling one leg beneath her. "Sure you don't want a chocolate?"

"No!"

"I'll have one, then." She pulled a candy from the case and bit into it, chewing happily. "They're good. " She spoke unaffectedly, her mouth full. "This is one of the good times, Abelard. It's why they thawed me out, I think."

"You changed."

"Ice assassination does that. They were right, the Cataclysts. Right to put me out. I was calcifying. One moment I was floating through the math hall at the Kosmosity, printouts in my hand, on my way to the office, mind full of little problems, worries, schedules. . . . I was dizzy for a moment. I looked around, and everything was gone. Deserted. Trashed. The printouts were crumbling in my hands, clothes full of dust, Goldreich-Tremaine in ruins, computers down, classes all gone. . . . The world leaped thirty years in a moment; it was total Cataclysm. For three days I chased down news, trying to find our Clique, learning I was history, and then it came over me in a wave. I 'preeked,' Abelard. My preconceptions shattered. The world didn't need me, and everything I'd thought was important was gone. My life was totally futile. And totally free."

"Free," Lindsay said, tasting the word. "Constantine," he said suddenly. "My enemy."

"He's dead, so to speak," Margaret Juliano said, "but it's a question of definition. I have the scans on his condition from his congenetics. The damage is very severe. He fell into a protracted fugue state and suffered an accelerated consciousness that must have lasted for subjective centuries. His consciousness could not maintain itself on the data it received from the Arena device. It lasted so long that his personality was abraded away. Speaking metaphorically, he forgot himself to pieces."

"They told you that? His siblings?"

"Times have changed, Abelard. Détente is back. The Constantine gene-line is in trouble, and we paid them well for the information. Skimmers Union lost the capitalship. Jastrow Station is the capital now, and it's full of Zen Serotonists. They hate excitement."

The news thrilled Lindsay. "Five years," he said. He stood up in agitation. "Well, what's five years to me?" He tried to pace about the room, swinging dizzily. The left-right hemispheric confusion made him clumsy. He drew himself up and tried to get a grip on his kinesics.

He failed.

He turned on Juliano. "My training. My kinesics."

She nodded. "Yes. When we went in we noticed the remnants of it. Early Shaper psychotechnic conditioning. Very clumsy by modern standards. It interfered with your recovery. So, over the years, we chased it down and extinguished it bit by bit."

"You mean it's gone?"

"Oh, yes. We had enough cerebral dichotomy to deal with without your training giving you dual modes of thought. 'Hypocrisy as a second state of consciousness' and all that." She sniffed. "It was a bad idea to begin with."

Lindsay sagged back into the scanning chair. "But all my life. . . . And now you took it away. With feck—" He closed his eyes, struggled for the word. "With technology."

She took another candy. "So what?" she said indistinctly, munching. "Technology put it there in the first place. You have your self back. What more do you want?"

Alexandrina Tyler came through the open doorway with a swish of heavy fabric. She wore the finery of her girlhood: a puffed, floor-length skirt and a stiff cream-colored jacket with embroidered input jacks and a round neck-circling collar. She looked at the floor. "Margaret," she said. "Your feet."

Juliano looked absently at the dried mud flaking from her boots. "Oh, dear. Sorry."

The sudden juxtaposition of the two women filled Lindsay with vertigo. A confused wash of tainted déjá vu bubbled up from some drugged cerebral recess, and for a moment he thought he would pass out. When he revived he could feel that he had improved, as if some paralyzing sludge had trickled out of his head, leaving light and space. "Alexandrina," he said, feeling feebler yet somehow more real. "You've been time? All this here?"

"Abelard," she said, surprised. "You're talking."

"Trying to."

"I heard you were better," she said. "So I brought you clothes. From the Museum wardrobe." She showed him a plastic-wrapped suit, an antique. "You see? This is actually one of your own suits from seventy-five years ago. One of the looters saved it when the Lindsay Mansion was sacked. Try it on, dear."

Lindsay touched the suit's stiff, age-worn fabric. "A museum piece," he said.

"Well, of course."

Margaret Juliano Looked at Alexandrina. "Maybe he'd be more comfortable dressed as an orderly. He could fade into the background. Take on local color."

"No," Lindsay said. "All right. I'll wear it."

"Alexandrina's been looking forward to this," Juliano confided as he struggled into the suit's trousers, ramming his bare feet past the wire-stiffened accordioned knees. "Every day she's come to feed you Tyler apples."

"I brought you here after the duel," Alexandrina said. "Our marriage expired, but I run the Museum now. I have a post here." She smiled. "They sacked the mansions, but the family orchards are still standing. Your Grandaunt Marietta always swore by the family's apples."

A seam gave way in the shoulder as Lindsay pulled on the shirt.

"You wolfed down those apples, seeds, stems, and all," Juliano told him. "It was a wonder."

"You're home, Alexa," Lindsay said. It was what she had wanted. He was glad for her.

"This was the Tyler house," Alexandrina said. "The left wing and the grounds are for the clinic; that's Margaret's work. I'm the Curator. I run the rest. I've gathered up all the mementos of our old way of life—all that was spared by Constantine's reeducation squads." She helped him pull the spacesuit-collared formal jacket over his head. "Come on, I'll show you."

Juliano kicked off her boots and stood in her rumpled socks. "I'll come along. I want to judge his reactions."

The main ballroom had become an exhibit hall, with glass-fronted displays and portraits of early clan founders. An antique pedal-driven ultralight aircraft hung from the ceiling. Five Shapers marveled over a case full of crude assembly tools from the circumlunar's construction. The Shapers' chic low-gravity clothing sagged grotesquely in the Republic's centrifugal spin. Alexandrina took his arm and whispered, "The floor looks nice, doesn't it? I refinished it myself. We don't allow robots here."

Lindsay glanced at one wall and was paralyzed at the sight of his own clan's founder, Malcolm Lindsay. As a child, the dead pioneer's face, leering in ancestral wisdom from the tops of dressers and bookshelves, had filled him with dread. Now he realized with a painful leap of insight how young the man had been. Dead at seventy. The whole habitat had been slammed up in frantic haste by people scarcely more than children. He began laughing hysterically. "It's a joke!" he shouted. The laughter was melting his head, breaking up a logjam of thought in little stabbing pangs.

Alexandrina glanced anxiously at the bemused Shapers. "Maybe this was too early for him, Margaret."

Juliano laughed. "He's right. It is a joke. Ask the Cataclysts." She took Lindsay's arm. "Come on, Abelard. We'll go outside."

"It's a joke," Lindsay said. His tongue was loose now and the words gushed free. "This is unbelievable. These poor fools had no idea. How could they? They were dead before they had a chance to see! What's five years to us, what's ten, a hundred—"

"You're babbling, dear." Juliano walked him down the hall and through the mortared stone archway into dappled sunlight and grass. "Watch where you step," she said. "We have other patients. Not housebroken." Beside the high moss-crusted walls a nude young woman was tearing single-mindedly at the grass, pausing to suck grime from her fingers.

Lindsay was horrified. He seemed to taste the grit on his own tongue. "We'll go outside the grounds," Margaret said. "Pongpianskul won't mind."

"He's letting you stay here, is he? That woman's a Shaper. A Cataclyst? He owed a debt to the Cataclysts. You're taking care of them for him."

"Try not to talk too much, dear. You might hurt something." She opened the iron gateway. "They like it here, the Cataclysts. Something about the view."

"Oh, my God," Lindsay said.

The Republic had run wild. The overarching trees on the Museum grounds had hid the full panorama from him. Now it loomed over and around him in its full five-kilometer range, a stunning expanse of ridged and tangled green, three long panels glowing in triple-crossed shafts of mirror-reflected sunlight. He'd forgotten how bright the sun was in circumlunar space.

"The trees," he gasped. "My God, look at them!"

"They've been growing ever since you left," Juliano said. "Come with me. I want to show you another project."

Lindsay looked up through reflex toward his own former home. Seen from above, the sprawling mansion grounds bordered what had once been a lively tangle of cheap low-class restaurants. Those were in decline, and the Lindsay home was in ruin. He could see yawning holes in the red-tiled roofs of fused lunar slate. The private landing pad atop the mansion's four-story tower was swamped in ivy.

At the northern end of the world, up its sloping walls, a crew of ant-sized workmen tore languidly at the skeletal remains of one of the wirehead hospitals. Shoals of clouds hid the old power grid and the area that had once been the Sours. "It smells different," Lindsay realized. He stumbled on the bicycle path beside the Museum's walls and was forced to watch his feet. They were filthy. "I need a bath," he said.

"Either you crawl or you don't, right? If you've got skin bacteria, what's a little dirt? I like it." She smiled. "It's *big* here, isn't it? Sure, Goldreich-Tremaine's ten times this size, but nothing this open. A big risky world."

"I'm glad Alexandrina found her way back," Lindsay said. Their marriage had been a success, because it had gotten her what she wanted most. At last he had made amends. It had always been a strain. Now he was free.

The Republic had changed so much that it filled him with weird exaltation. Yes, big, he thought, but nowhere near big *enough*. He felt a sense of impatience with it, a fierce longing to grab hold of something, something huge and basic. He had slept for five years. Now he felt every hour of that long rest pressing in on him with uncontainable reviving-energy. His knees buckled, and Juliano caught him with her Shaper-strengthened arms.

"Easy," she said.

"I'm all right." They crossed the openwork bridge over the blazing expanse of metaglass that separated two land panels. Lindsay saw the former site of the Sours beneath a raft of clouds. The once-foul morass had become an oasis of vegetation so blindingly green that it seemed to shine even in the clouds' shadow. A tall gangling boy in baggy clothing was running headlong beside the woven-wire fence surrounding the Sours, tugging a large box kite into flight.

"You're not the first I've cured," Juliano said as they walked toward it. "I always said my Superbright students had promise. Some of them work here. A pilot project. I want to show you what they've done. They've been tackling botany from a perspective of Prigoginic complexity theory. New species, advanced chlorophylls, good solid constructive work."

"Wait," said Lindsay. "I want to talk to this youngster." He had noticed the boy's kite. Its elaborate paint job showed a nude man crammed stiflingly within the rigid planes of the box kite's lifting surfaces.

A woman in mud-smeared corduroy leaned over the woven fence, waving a pair of shears. "Margaret! Come see!"

"I'll be back for you," Juliano said. "Don't go away."

Lindsay ambled unsteadily to where the boy stood, expertly managing his kite. "Hello, old cousin," the boy said. "Got any tapes?"

"What kind?"

"Video, audio, anything from the Ring Council. That's where you're from, right?"

Lindsay reached automatically for his training, for the easy network of spontaneous lies that would show the boy a plausible image. His mind was blank. He gaped. Time was passing. He blurted the first thing that came into his head. "I'm a sundog. From Czarina-Kluster."

"Really? Posthumanism! Prigoginic levels of complexity! Fractal scales, bedrock of space-time, precontinuum ur-space! Have I got it right?"

"I like your kite," Lindsay hedged.

"Old Cataclyst logo," the boy said. "We get a lot of old Cataclysts around here. The kite gets their attention. First time I've caught a Cicada, though."

Cicada, Lindsay thought. A citizen of C-K. Wellspring had always been fond of slang. "You're a local?"

"That's right. My name's Abelard. Abelard Gomez."

"Abelard. That name's not too common."

The boy laughed. "Maybe not in C-K. But every fifth kid in the Republic's named Abelard. After Abelard Lindsay, the big historical cheese. You must have heard of him." The boy hesitated. "He used to dress like you. I've seen pictures."

Lindsay looked at the boy's own clothes. Young Gomez wore a faked-up low-grav outfit which sagged dreadfully. "I can tell I'm out of date," Lindsay said. "They make a big deal out of this Lindsay fellow, do they?"

"You don't know the half of it," Gomez said. "Take school. School's completely antique here. They make us read Lindsay's book. Shakespeare, it's called. Translated into modern English by Abelard Lindsay."

"Is it that bad?" Lindsay said, tingling with déjà vu.

"You're lucky, old man. You don't have to read it. I've looked through the whole thing. Not one word in there about spontaneous self-organization."

Lindsay nodded. "That's a shame."

"Everybody's old in that book. I don't mean fake-old like the Preservationists here. Or weird-old like old Pong."

"You mean Pongpianskul?" Lindsay said.

"The Warden, yeah. No, I mean everybody's used up too fast. All burnt up and cramped and sick. It's depressing."

Lindsay nodded. Things had come full circle, he decided. "You resent the control on your life," he speculated. "You and your friends are radicals. You want things changed."

"Not really," the boy said. "They only have me for sixty years. I've got hundreds, cousin. I mean to do big things. It's going to take a lot of time. I mean *big* things. *Huge.* Not like those little dried-up people in the past."

"What kinds of things?"

"Life-spreading. Planet-ripping. World-building. Terraforming."

"I see," Lindsay said. He was startled to see so much self-possession in one so young. It must be the Cataclyst influence. They'd always favored wild schemes, huge lunacies that in the end boiled down to nothing. "And will that make you happy?"

The boy looked suspicious. "Are you one of those Zen Serotonists? 'Happy.' What kind of scam is that? Burn happiness, cousin. This is the Kosmos talking. Are you on the side of life, or aren't you?"

Lindsay smiled. "Is this political? I don't trust politics."

"Politics? I'm talking biology. Things that live and grow. Organisms. Integrated forms."

"Where do people come in?"

The boy waved his hand irritably and caught the kite as it swooped. "Never mind them. I'm talking *basic* loyalties now. Like that tree. Are you on its side, against the inorganic?"

His recent epiphany was still fresh in Lindsay's mind. The boy's question was genuine. "Yes," he said. "I am."

"You see the point of terraforming, then."

"Terraforming," Lindsay said slowly. "I've seen theories. Speculations. And I suppose that it's possible. But what does it have to do with us?"

"A true commitment to the side of Life demands the moral act of Creation," Gomez said promptly.

"Someone's been teaching you slogans," Lindsay said. He smiled. "Planets are real places, not just grids on a drawing board. The effort would be titanic. All out of human scale."

The boy was impatient. "How big are you? Are you bigger than something inert?"

"But it would take centuries—"

"You think that tree would hesitate? How much time do you have, anyway?"

Lindsay laughed helplessly.

"Fine, then. Are you going to live a squished-down little human life, or are you going to go for the potential?"

"At my age," Lindsay said, "if I were human I'd already be dead."

"Now you're talking. You're as big as your dreams. That's what they say in C-K, right? No rules, no limits. Look at the Mechs and Shapers." The boy was contemptuous. "All the power in the world, and they're chasing each other's tails. Burn their wars and midget ideologies. Posthumanity's bigger than that. Ask the people in there." The boy waved one hand at the woven-wire enclosure. "Ecosystem design. Rebuilding life for new conditions. A little biochemistry, a little statistical physics, you can pick it up here and there, that's where the excitement is. If Abelard Lindsay was alive today that's the sort of thing he'd be working on."

The irony of it stung Lindsay. At Gomez's age, he'd never had any sense, either. He felt a sudden alarm for the boy, an urge to protect him from the disaster that his rhetoric would surely earn him. "You think so?"

"Sure. They say he was a hot Preservationist type, but he sundogged off when the getting was good, didn't he? You didn't see him hanging around here to 'die of old age.' Nobody really does anyway."

"Not even here? In the home of Preservationism?"

"Of course not. Everyone here over forty's on the black market for life extension. When they turn sixty they scarper for Czarina-Kluster. The Cicadas don't care about your history or your genes. They take all clades. Dreams matter more."

Dreams, Lindsay thought. Dreams of Preservationism, turned into a black-market scrabble for immortality. The dream of Investor Peace had rusted and collapsed. The dream of terraforming still had a shine on it. Young Gomez could not know that it too would surely tarnish.

But somehow, Lindsay thought, you had to dream or die. And with new life pouring through him, he knew which choice was his.

Margaret Juliano leaned over the fence. "Abelard! Abelard, over here! You need a look at this."

The boy, startled, began reeling in his kite hand over hand. "Now this is luck! That old psychotech wants to show me something in the compound."

"Go to it," Lindsay said. "You tell her that I said to show you anything you like, understand? And tell her that I've gone off for a little talk with Pongpianskul. All right, cousin?"

The boy nodded slowly. "Thanks, old Cicada. You're one of us."

Pongpianskul's office was a paper wasteland. Musty cloth-bound books of Concatenate law were heaped beside his wooden desk; schedules and production graphs were pinned up at random on the room's ancient paneling. A tortoiseshell cat yawned in one corner and sharpened its claws in the carpet. Lindsay, whose experience with cats was limited, watched it guardedly.

Pongpianskul wore a suit similar to Lindsay's but newer and obviously hand-stitched. He had lost hair since his days in Goldreich-Tremaine, and light gleamed dully on the dusky skin of his scalp. He swept a sheaf of records from the desk and paper-clipped them with skinny, wrinkled fingers.

"Papers," he muttered. "Trying to take everything off computers these days. Don't trust 'em. You use computers and there's always some Mech ready to step in with new software. Thin edge of the wedge, Mavrides. Lindsay, I mean."

"Lindsay is better."

"You must admit it's hard keeping track of you. It was a fine scam you pulled, passing yourself off as a senior genetic in the Rings." He Looked at Lindsay. Lindsay caught part of the Look. The experience of age made up somewhat for his loss of kinesic training.

Pongpianskul said, "How long has it been since we last talked?"

"Hmm. What year is this?"

Pongpianskul frowned. "No matter. You were in Dembowska then, anyway. Things aren't so bad here under Neotenic aegis, eh, Mavrides, you admit? Gone a bit to rack and ruin, but all the better for the tourist trade; those Ring Council types eat it up with a spoon. Tell the truth, we had to go into the old Lindsay mansion and bash it about a bit, make it more romantic. Had some mice installed. You know mice? Bred 'em back to the wild state from lab specimens. You know their eyes weren't pink in the wild? Funny look in those eyes, reminds me of a wife of mine."

Pongpianskul opened one of the drawers in his cavernous desk and tossed in his sheaf of clipped papers. He pulled out a crumbling wad of graphs and started. "What's this? Should have been done weeks ago. No matter. Where were we? Oh, yes, wives. I married Alexandrina, by the way. Alexa's a fine Preservationist. Couldn't risk her slipping away."

"You did well," Lindsay said. His marriage contract had expired; her new marriage was a sound political move. It did not occur to him to feel jealousy; that had not been in the contract. He was glad that she had secured her position.

"Can't have too many wives, it's what life's all about. Take Georgiana for instance, Constantine's first wife. Talked her into a trace of Shatter, no more than twenty mikes, I swear, and it improved her disposition no end. Now she's as sweet as the day is long." He looked at Lindsay seriously. "Can't have too many oldsters around, though. Disturbs the ideology. Bad enough with those pesky Cataclysts and their posthuman schemes. Keep 'em behind wire, in quarantine. Even then kids keep sneaking in."

"It's kind of you to allow them here."

"I need the foreign exchange. C-K finances their research. But they won't amount to much. Those Superbrights can't concentrate on anything for long." He snorted, then snatched up a bill of lading. "I need the money. Look at these carbon-dioxide imports. It's the damn trees, gobbling it up." He sighed. "I need those trees, though. Their mass helps with the orbital dynamics. These circumlunar orbits are hell."

"I'm glad matters are in good hands."

Pongpianskul smiled sadly. "I suppose. Things never work out the way you plan them. Good thing, though, or the Mechs would have taken over long ago." The cat jumped into Pongpianskul's lap, and he scratched its chin. The animal emitted a rumbling sound that Lindsay found oddly soothing. "This is my cat, Saturn," the old Shaper said. "Say hello to Lindsay, Saturn." The cat ignored him.

"I had no idea you liked animals."

"Couldn't stand him at first. Hair just pours off the little beast. Gets into everything. Dirty as a hog, too. Ever seen a hog, by the way? I had a few imported. Incredible creatures, the tourists just marvel."

"I must have a look before I leave."

"Animals in the air these days. Not literally, I mean, though we did have some trouble with loose hogs running off to the free-fall zone. No, I mean this biomorality from Czarina-Kluster. Another Cataclyst fad."

"You think so?"

"Well," the Warden mused, "maybe not. You start trifling with ecology and it's hard to find a place to stop. I've had a slip of this cat's skin shipped off to the

Ring Council. Have to clone off a whole gene-line of them. Because of the mice, you know. Little vermin are overrunning everything."

"A planet might be better," Lindsay said. "More space."

"I don't hold with messing with gravity wells," Pongpianskul said. "It's just more room for error. Don't tell me you've fallen for that, Mavrides."

"The world needs dreams," Lindsay said.

"You're not going to start on about levels of complexity, I hope."

Lindsay smiled. "No."

"Good. When you came in here unwashed and with no shoes on, I concluded the worst."

"They say the hogs and I had a lot in common," Lindsay said.

Pongpianskul stared, then laughed. "Haw. Haw. Glad to see you're not standing on your dignity. Too much dignity cripples a man. Fanatics never laugh. I hope you can still laugh when you're breaking worlds to the leash."

"Surely someone will get a good chuckle out of it."

"Well, you'll need your humor, friend. Because these things never work out as you plan. Reality's a horde of mice, nibbling away in the basement of your dreams. . . . You know what I wanted here, don't you? A preserve for humanity and the human way of life, that's what. Instead I've ended up with a huge stage set full of tourist shills and Cataclyst fry-brains."

"It was worth a try," Lindsay said.

"That's it, break an old man's heart," Pongpianskul said. "A consoling lie wouldn't have hurt."

"Sorry," Lindsay said. "I've lost the skill."

"Better get it back in a hurry, then. It's still a wide wicked Schismatrix out there, détente or no détente." Pongpianskul brooded. "Those fools in Czarina-Kluster. Selling out to aliens. What's to become of the world? I hear some idiot wants to sell Jupiter."

"I beg your pardon?"

"Yes, sell it off to some group of intelligent gasbags. A scandal, isn't it? Some people will do anything to suck up to aliens. Oh, sorry, no offense." He Looked at Lindsay and saw that he was not insulted. "It won't come to anything. Alien embassies never do. Luckily, aliens all seem to have a lot more sense than we do, with the possible exception of the Investors. Investors, indeed. Just a bunch of interstellar pests and nosey-parkers. . . . If aliens show up in force I swear I'll put the whole Republic under the tightest quarantine this side of a Ring Council session. I'll wait till society disintegrates totally. I'll be faded by then, but the locals can move out to pick up the pieces. They'll see then that there was sense in my little game preserve after all."

"I see. Hedging humanity's bets. You were always a clever gambler, Neville."

The Shaper was pleased. He sneezed loudly, and the startled cat leaped from his lap across the desk, clawing papers. "Sorry," he said. "Bacteria and cat hairs, never got used to them."

"I have a favor to ask," Lindsay said. "I'm leaving for Czarina-Kluster and would like to take one of the locals with me."

"Someone 'dying into the world?' You always handled that well in Dembowska. Certainly."

"No, a youngster."

"Out of the question. A terrible precedent. Wait a moment. Is it Abelard Gomez?"

"The very same."

"I see. That boy troubles me. He has Constantine blood, did you know? I've been watching the local genetics. Genius turns up in that line like a bad roll of the dice."

"I'm doing you a favor, then."

"I suppose so. Sorry to see you go, Abelard, but with your current ideological cast you're a bad influence. You're a culture hero here, you know."

"I'm through with the old dreams. My energy's back, and there's a new dream loose in Czarina-Kluster. Even if I can't believe it, at least I can help those who do." He stood up, stepping back prudently as the cat inspected his ankles. "Good luck with the mice, Neville."

"You too, Abelard."

# Chapter 9

The engines of wealth were at full throttle. A torrent of riches was drowning the world. The exponential curves of growth hit with their always deceptive speed, a counterintuitive quickness that stunned the unwary and dazzled the alert.

The circumsolar population stood at 3.2 billion. It had doubled every twenty years and would double again. The four hundred major Mechanist asteroids roiled in a tidal wave of production from an estimated 8 billion self-replicating mining robots and forty thousand full-scale automated factories. The Shaper worlds measured wealth differently, dwarfed by a staggering 20 billion tons of productive biomass.

The primal measurement of Circumsolar Kilobytes soared to an astronomical figure best estimated as $9.45 \times 10^{18}$. World information, estimating only that available in fully open databanks and not counting the huge empires of restricted data, totalled $2.3 \times 10^{27}$ bits, the equivalent of 150 full-length books for every star in every galaxy in the visible universe.

Stern social measures had to be adopted to keep entire populations from disintegrating in an orgy of plenty.

Megawatts of energy sufficient to run entire Council States were joyfully squandered on high-speed transorbital liners. These spacecraft, large enough to provide every comfort to hundreds of passengers, assumed the dignity of nation-states and suffered their own population booms.

None of these material advances matched the social impact of the progress of the sciences. Breakthroughs in statistical physics proved the objective existence of the four Prigoginic Levels of Complexity and postulated the existence of a fifth. The age of the cosmos was calculated to an accuracy value of plus or minus four years, and rarefied attempts were under way to estimate the "quasi-time" consumed by the precontinuum ur-space.

Slower-than-light interstellar travel became physically possible, and five expeditions were launched, manned by star-peering low-mass wireheads. Ultra-long baseline interferometry, beamed from radiotelescopes aboard the wirehead starships, established hard parallaxes for most stars in the Orion Arm of the Galaxy. Examinations of the Perseus and Centaurus Arms showed troubling patches where patterns of stars appeared to have an ominous regularity.

New studies of the galaxies of the Local Supercluster led to refinements in the Hubble Constant. Minor discrepancies caused some visionaries to conclude that the expansion of the universe had been subjected to crude tampering.

Knowledge was power. And in seizing knowledge, humanity had gripped a power as bright and angry as a live wire. At stake were issues vaster than any before: the prospects were more dazzling, the potentials sharper, and the implications more staggering than anything ever faced by humanity or its successors.

Yet the human mind still had its own resources. The gifts for survival were not found only in the sharp perceptions of the Shapers, with their arsenals of brain-stretching biochemicals, or the cybernetic advances of the Mechanists and the relentless logic of their artificial intelligences. The world was kept intact by the fantastic predilection of the human mind for boredom.

Mankind had always been surrounded by the miraculous. Nothing much had ever come of it. Under the shadow of cosmic revelations, life still swathed itself in comforting routine. The breakaway factions were much more bizarre than ever before, but people had grown used to this, and their horror had lessened. Frankly antihuman clades like the Spectral Intelligents, the Lobsters, and the Blood Bathers were somehow incorporated into the repertoire of possibility and even made into jokes.

And yet the strain was everywhere. The new multiple humanities hurtled blindly toward their unknown destinations, and the vertigo of acceleration struck deep. Old preconceptions were in tatters, old loyalties were obsolete. Whole societies were paralyzed by the mind-blasting vistas of absolute possibility.

The strain took different forms. For the Cataclysts, those Superbrights who had been the first to feel it, it was a frenzied embrace of the Infinite, careless of consequences. Even self-destruction eased the unspoken pain. The Zen Serotonists abandoned the potential for the pale bliss of calm and quiet. For others the strain was never explicit: just a tingling of unease at the borders of sleep, or sudden frantic tears when the mind's inhibitions crumbled from drink or drugs.

For Abelard Lindsay the current manifestation involved sitting strapped to a table in the Bistro Marineris, a Czarina-Kluster bar. The Bistro Marineris was a free-fall inflatable sphere at the junction of four long tubeways, a way station amid the sprawling nexus of habitats that made up the campus of Czarina-Kluster Kosmosity-Metasystems.

Lindsay was waiting for Wellspring. He leaned on the dome-shaped table, pressing the sticktite elbow patches of his academic jacket against its velcro top.

Lindsay was a hundred and six years old. His latest rejuvenation had not erased all outward signs of age. Crow's feet webbed his gray eyes, and creases drooped from his nose to the corners of his mouth. Overdeveloped facial muscle ridged his dark, mobile eyebrows. He had a short beard, and jewel-headed pins held his long hair, streaked with white. One hand was heavily wrinkled, its pale skin like waxed parchment. The metal hand was honeycombed with sensor grids.

He watched the walls. The owner of the Marineris had opaqued the inner surface of the Bistro and turned it into a planetarium. All around Lindsay and the dozen other customers spread the racked and desolate landscape of Mars, relayed live from the Martian surface in painfully vivid 360-degree color.

For months the sturdy robot surveyor had been picking its way along the rim of the Valles Marineris, sending its broadcasts. Lindsay sat with his back to the mighty chasm: its titanic scale and air of desolate, lifeless age had painful associations for him. The rubble and foothills projected on the rounded wall before him, huge upthrust blocks and wind-carved yardangs, struck him as an implied reproach. It was new to him to have a sense of responsibility for a planet. After three months in C-K, he was still trying the dream on for size.

Three Kosmosity academics unbuckled themselves and kicked off from a nearby table. As they left, one noticed Lindsay, started, and came his way. "Pardon me, sir. I believe I know you. Professor Bela Milosz, am I right?"

The stranger had that vaguely supercilious air common to many Shaper defectors, a sense of misplaced fanaticism spinning its wheels. "I've gone by that name, yes."

"I'm Yevgeny Navarre."

The name struck a distant echo. "The membrane chemistry specialist? This is an unexpected pleasure." Lindsay had known Navarre in Dembowska, but only through video correspondence. In person, Navarre seemed arid and colorless. As an annoying corollary, Lindsay realized that he himself had been arid and colorless during those years. "Please join me, Professor Navarre."

Navarre strapped in. "Kind of you to remember my article for your *Journal*," he said. " 'Surfactant Vesicles in Exoarchosaurian Colloidal Catalysis.' One of my first."

Navarre exuded well-bred satisfaction and signaled the bistro's servo, which ambled up on multiple plastic legs. The trendy servo was a faithful miniature of the Mars surveyor. Lindsay ordered a liqueur for politeness' sake.

"How long have you been in C-K, Professor Milosz? Your musculature tells me that you've been in heavy gravity. Investor business?"

The heavy spin of the Republic had marked Lindsay. He smiled cryptically. "I'm not free to speak."

"I see." Navarre offered him the grave, confidential look of a fellow man-of-the-world. "I'm pleased to find you here in the Kosmosity's neighborhood. Are you planning to join our faculty?"

"Yes."

"A stellar addition to our Investor researchers."

"Frankly, Professor Navarre, Investor studies have lost their novelty for me. I plan to specialize in terraforming studies."

Navarre smiled incredulously. "Oh dear. I'm sure you can do much better than that."

"Oh?" Lindsay leaned forward in a brief burst of crudely imitative kinesics. His whole facility was gone. The reflex embarrassed him, and he resolved for the hundredth time to give it up.

Navarre said, "The terraforming section's crawling with post-Cataclyst lunatics. You were always a very sound man. Thorough. A good organizer. I'd hate to see you drift into the wrong circles."

"I see. What brought you to C-Kluster, Professor?"

"Well," said Navarre, "the Jastrow Station labs and I had some differences about patenting. Membrane technology, you see. A technique for producing artificial Investor hide, a very fashionable item here; you'll notice for instance that young lady's boots?" A Cicada student in a beaded skirt and bright face paint was sipping a frappé against the desolate backdrop of shattered red terrain. Her boots were miniature Investor feet, toes, claws, and all. Behind her the landscape lurched suddenly as the surveyor moved on. Lindsay grasped the table in vertigo.

Navarre swayed slightly and said, "Czarina-Kluster is more friendly to the entrepreneur. I was taken off the dogs after only eight months."

"Congratulations," Lindsay said.

The Queen's Advisors kept most immigrants under the surveillance dogs for a full two years. Out in the fringe dogtowns there were whole environments where reality was nailed down by camera and everyone was tagged ceaselessly by videodogs. Widespread taps and monitors were part of public life in Czarina-Kluster. But full citizens could escape surveillance in the discreets, C-K's lush citadels of privacy.

Lindsay sipped his drink. "To prevent confusion, I should tell you that these days I use the name Lindsay."

"What? Like Wellspring?"

"I beg your pardon?"

"You weren't aware of Wellspring's true identity?"

"Why, no," Lindsay said. "I understood the records were lost on Earth, where he was born."

Navarre laughed delightedly. "The truth is an open secret among Cicada inner circles. It's the talk of the discreets. Wellspring is a Concatenate. His true name is Abelard Malcolm Tyler Lindsay."

"You astonish me."

"Wellspring plays a very deep game. The Terran business is only a camouflage."

"How odd."

"Speak of the devil," Navarre said. A noisy crowd burst from the tubeway entrance to Lindsay's left. Wellspring had arrived with a claque of Cicada disciples, a dozen students fresh from some party, flush-faced and shouting with laughter. The young Cicadas were a bustle of blues and greens in long, flowing overcoats, slash-cuffed trousers, and glimmering reptile-scaled waistcoats.

Wellspring spotted Lindsay and approached in free-fall. His mane of matted black hair was held by a copper-and-platinum coronet. Over his foliage-printed green coat he wore a tape-deck armband, which emitted a loud quasi-music of rustling boughs and the cries of animals.

"Lindsay!" he shouted. "Lindsay! Good to have you back." He embraced Lindsay roughly and strapped himself to a chair. Wellspring looked drunk. His face was flushed, he had pulled his collar open, and something was crawling in his beard, a small population of what appeared to be iron fleas.

"How was your trip?" Lindsay said.

"The Ring Council is dull! Sorry I wasn't here to meet you." He signaled the servo. "What are you drinking? Fantastic chasm, the Marineris, isn't it? Even the tributaries are the size of the Grand Canyon in Arizona." He pointed past Lindsay's shoulder at a gap between towering canyon walls, where icy winds kicked up thin puffs of ocher dust. "Imagine a cataract there, pealing out in a thunderband of rainbows! A sight to stir the soul to the roots of its complexity."

"Surely," Navarre said, smiling slightly.

Wellspring turned to Lindsay. "I have a little spiritual drill for doubters like Yevgeny. Every day he should recite to himself, 'Centuries . . . centuries . . . centuries.' "

"I'm a pragmatic man," Navarre said, catching Lindsay's eye and lifting one eyebrow significantly. "Life is lived day to day, not in centuries. Enthusiasms don't last that long. Flesh and blood can't bear it." He addressed Wellspring. "Your ambitions are bigger than life."

"Of course. They must be. They encompass it."

"The Queen's Advisors are more practical." Navarre watched Wellspring with half-contemptuous suspicion.

The Queen's Advisors had risen to authority since the early days of C-K. Rather than fighting them for power, Wellspring had stepped aside. Now, while the Queen's Advisors struggled with day-to-day rule in the Czarina's Palace, Wellspring chose to frequent the dogtowns and discreets. Often he vanished for months, to reappear with shadowy posthumans and bizarre recruits from the fringes of society. These actions clearly baffled Navarre.

"I want tenure," Lindsay told Wellspring. "Nothing political."

"I'm sure we could see to that."

Lindsay glanced about him. It came to him in a burst of conviction. "I don't like Mars."

Wellspring looked grave. "You realize that an entire future destiny might accrete around this momentary utterance? It's from just such nuclei of free will that the future grows, in smooth determinism."

Lindsay smiled. "It's too dry," he said. The crowd gasped and shouted as the surveyor scuttled rapidly down a treacherous slope, sending the world reeling. "And it moves too much."

Wellspring was troubled. As he adjusted his collar, Lindsay noted the faint bruise of teethmarks on the skin of his neck. He turned down the forest sound-track on his armband. "One world at a time seems wisest, don't you think?"

Navarre laughed incredulously.

Lindsay ignored him, gazing over Wellspring's shoulder at his claque of followers. A young Shaper in a fuzz-elbowed academic jacket was burying his elegant face in the floating red-blonde curls of a tigerish young woman. She tilted her head back, laughing in delight, and Lindsay saw, half eclipsed behind her, the stricken face of Abelard Gomez. There were two surveillance dogs with Gomez, crouched on the wall behind him, their metal ribs gleaming, their glassy camera faces taping up his life. Pity struck Lindsay, and a sadness for the transient nature of eternal human verities.

Wellspring plunged into impassioned argument, sweeping aside Navarre's wry comments in a torrent of rhetoric. Wellspring waxed eloquent about asteroids; chunks of ice the size of cities, to be dropped in searing arcs onto the surface of Mars, blasting out damp oases in a crust-ripping megatonnage. Creeks would appear at first, then lakes, as steam and volatiles peeled into the starved air and the polar ice caps dissolved into vaporized carbon dioxide. Crater oases would be manned by teams of scientists, biosculpting whole ecosystems into being. For the first time, humanity would be bigger than life: a living world would owe its existence to humankind, and not vice versa. Wellspring saw it as a moral obligation, a repayment of debt. The cost was irrelevant. Money was symbolic. Life was the real.

Navarre broke in. "But it's the human element that must defeat you. Where's the appeal to greed? That's where you erred before. You could have run Czarina-Kluster. Instead you let your control slip, and now the Queen's Advisors, those Mechanist"—Navarre stopped short, noticing the dogs accompanying Gomez—"gentlemen, are running things with their customary efficiency. But politics aside, this nonsense is ruining C-K's ability to do decent science! Real research, that is; the kind that brings new patents to armor C-K against its enemies. Terraforming squanders our resources, while Mech and Shaper militants scheme relentlessly against us. Yes, I admit your dreams are pretty. Yes, they even serve a social use as a relatively harmless state ideology. But in the end they'll collapse and take C-K with them."

Wellspring's eyes glittered. "You're overworked, Yevgeny. You need a new perspective. Take ten years off, and see if time won't change your mind."

Navarre flushed angrily. He turned to Lindsay. "You see? Cataclysm! That remark meant ice assassination, you heard him allude to it! Come, Milosz, surely you can't hold with these boondoggles!"

Lindsay said nothing. There had been a time when he might have twisted the conversation to his advantage. But now his skill was gone. And he no longer wanted it.

Words were useless. He had grown impatient with words. They could no longer hold him.

Suddenly he knew he had to step outside the rules.

He floated out of his chair and began stripping off his clothes.

Navarre left at once, insulted and flustered. Lindsay's clothes drifted off in free-fall, his jacket and trousers pinwheeling slowly over other tables. The customers ducked, laughing. Soon he was naked. The crowd's nervous laughter died down into puzzled unease. They moved away from Gomez's dogs and muttered together in disconcerted awe.

Lindsay ignored them. He folded his legs in midair and gazed at the wall. Wellspring's students deserted the bar, mumbling excuses and glancing back over their shoulders. Even Wellspring was nonplused. When Wellspring left he took the last of the crowd with him.

Lindsay was left alone with the bar servo, young Gomez, and his dogs.

Gomez edged closer. "Czarina-Kluster isn't like I'd thought it was, in the Republic."

Lindsay meditated on the landscape.

"They put these dogs on me. Because supposedly I might be dangerous. You don't mind the dogs, do you? . . . No, I see that you don't." Gomez sighed tremulously. "After three months, the others still keep me at arm's length. They won't initiate me into their Clique. You saw the girl, didn't you? Melanie Omaha, Dr. Omaha from the Kosmosity? Fire, she's fantastic, isn't she? But she doesn't care for men under the dogs; who would, knowing Security's watching? I'd give my right arm for ten minutes in a discreet with her. Oh, sorry." He looked in embarrassment at Lindsay's mechanical arm.

Gomez wiped red streaks of facepaint from his cheeks. "You remember me telling you about Abelard Lindsay? Well, rumor says you're him. And I think I believe it. You are Lindsay. You're him."

Lindsay drew a deeper breath.

"I understand," Gomez said. "You're telling me that it doesn't matter. The only thing that matters is the Cause. But listen to this!" He pulled a notebook from inside his willow-printed coat. He read loudly, desperately. " 'A dissipative self-organizing system evolves along a coherent sequence of space-time structures. We may distinguish between four different dimensional frameworks: autopoiesis, ontogeny, phylogeny, anagenesis.' " He crumpled the paper in anguish. "And this is from my *poetry* class!"

There was a moment's silence. Then Gomez burst out: "Maybe it's the secret of life! But if it is, can we bear it? Can we meet the goals we set ourselves? Over centuries? What about the simple things? How can I find any joy in a single day when the specters of these centuries loom over me. . . . It's all too huge, yes, even you . . . You! You, who brought me here. Why didn't you tell me you were Wellspring's friend? Was it modesty? But you're Lindsay! Lindsay himself! I didn't believe it at first. When I decided it was true, it terrified me. Like hearing your own shadow speak to you."

Gomez hesitated. "All these years you've hidden. But you're coming into the Schismatrix openly now, aren't you? You've come out to do greatness, to dazzle the world. . . . It's frightening to see you in the open. Like seeing the bones of mathematics under the flesh of the world. But even if the principles are true, then what about the flesh? *We* are the flesh! *What about the flesh?*"

Lindsay had nothing to tell him.

"I know what you're thinking," Gomez said at last. " 'Love has broken his heart; it's an old story. Only time can bring him to a better sense of himself.' That's what you're thinking, isn't it? . . . Of course it is."

When Gomez spoke again he was calm, meditative. "Now I begin to see. It isn't something that words can capture, is it? It can only be grasped all at once. Someday I'll have it entirely. Someday when these dogs are long gone. Someday when even Melanie Omaha is only a memory to me." He was sad but exalted. "I heard them talking as you made your—uh, gesture. These so-called sophisticates, these proud Cicadas. They may have the jargon, but the wisdom is yours." Gomez was radiant. "Thank you, sir."

Lindsay waited until Gomez had left. Then he could not hold it back any longer. He thought he would never stop laughing.

# Chapter 10

## DEMBOWSKA CARTEL: 21-2-'01

Despite her role in its foundation, Kitsune had never visited Czarina-Kluster. Like Wellspring, Kitsune had held great power in C-K's pioneer days; unlike him, she had not released it gracefully. While Wellspring had retreated from day-to-day government and pursued his strategy of rule-by-fashion, Kitsune had blatantly challenged the Queen's Advisors.

In the years while Lindsay recuperated, she had had some success. She announced plans to move to C-K, but as years passed she refused to disturb her routines, and her power decayed. It had led to a break, and the destinies of C-K and Dembowska had radically diverged.

Disquieting stories of her transformations had reached Lindsay in C-K. Rumor said she had embraced new technologies, exploiting the laxity that had come with détente. Dembowska was still a member of the Mechanist Union of Cartels but was constantly on the verge of expulsion, tolerated only as a clearinghouse for Ring Council defectors.

Even the Ring Council was appalled by Dembowska's emergent technology of flesh. In the hands of the Zen Serotonists, the Ring Council struggled for stability; as a result, it was falling behind. The cutting edge of genetics technology had been seized by the wild-eyed black surgeons of the cometaries and the Uranian rings, mushrooming posthuman clades like the Metropolarity, the Blood Bathers, and the Endosymbiotics. They had discarded humanity like a caul. Disintegrating microfactions surrounded the Schismatrix like a haze of superheated plasma.

The march of science had become a headlong stampede. The Mechanists and Shapers had become like two opposing armies, whose rank and file, scattering into swamps and thickets, ignore the orders of their aging generals. The emergent philosophies of the age—Posthumanism, Zen Serotonin, Galacticism—were like signal bonfires lit to attract stragglers. Deserters' philosophies.

Lindsay's fire burned brightly, and its glow attracted many. They called Lindsay's group the Lifesiders Clique.

Czarina-Kluster's cliques had the power of minor factions in their own right. The cliques formed a shadow government in C-K, a moral parallel to the distracted formal rule of the Queen's Advisors. Clique elites moved behind the scenes, imitating their paragon Wellspring in deliberate webs of self-spun obfuscation. The forms of power and its realities had been gently disentangled. The social arbiters of the Polycarbon Clique, the Lifesiders, or the Green Camarilla could work wonders with a dropped hint or a lifted eyebrow.

It followed, then, that groups considering defection to C-K consulted the Cicada cliques before formally requesting asylum. Normally this was Wellspring's domain.

In the latest case, however, Wellspring was absent on one of his many recruiting trips. Lindsay, knowing the nature of the case, had agreed to meet the representative of the breakaway group on neutral ground in Dembowska.

His entourage consisted of his chief lieutenant, Gomez; three of his postdoctoral students; and a diplomatic observer from the Queen's Advisors.

Dembowska had changed. When they debarked into customs amid the sparse crowd from the liner. Lindsay was struck by the warmth. The air was at blood heat and smelled faintly of Kitsune's skin. The smell brought seeping memory with it. Lindsay's smile was melancholy. The memories were eighty-five years old, as thin as paper; they seemed to have happened to someone else.

Lindsay's Lifesiders checked their luggage. Two of the graduate students, Mechanist types, murmured first impressions into their lip mikes. Other passengers waited at the scanning booths.

Two Dembowska agents approached their group. Lindsay stepped forward in the faint gravity. "Harem police?" he said.

"Wallchildren," said the first of the pair, a male. He wore a thin, sleeveless kimono; his bare arms were covered with authority tattoos. His face seemed familiar. Lindsay recognized the genetics of Michael Carnassus. He turned to the other, a woman, and saw Kitsune, younger, her hair shorn, her dark arms stenciled in white ink.

"I'm Colonel Martin Dembowska, and this is my Wallsister, Captain Murasaki Dembowska."

"I'm Chancellor Lindsay. These are cliquemembers Abelard Gomez, Jane Murray, Glen Szilard, Colin Szilard, Emma Meyer, and Undersecretary Fidel Nakamura, our diplomatic observer." The Cicadas bowed, each in turn.

"I hope you weren't distressed by the bacterial change aboard ship," Murasaki said. She had Kitsune's voice.

"A minor inconvenience."

"We are forced to take great care with the Wallmother's skin bacteria," the

Colonel explained. "There is a considerable acreage involved. I'm sure you understand."

"Could you offer us exact figures?" asked one of the Szilard brothers, with a Mechanist's dry craving for hard data. "Reports in Czarina-Kluster are clouded."

"At last report the Wallmother massed four hundred thousand, eight hundred and twelve tons." The Colonel was proud. "Have you anything to declare? No? Then follow me."

They followed the Dembowskan into a confidential clearance office, where they left their luggage and were provided with sterilized guest's kimonos. They floated barefoot into the hot air of Dembowska's first mall.

The cavernous duty-free shopping area was paved, walled, and ceilinged in flesh. The Cicadas padded along reluctantly, their toes just brushing the resilient skin. They looked with hidden longing at the shops, safe islands of stone and metal. Lindsay had schooled them to be tactful and was proud of their masked reactions.

Even Lindsay felt a qualm when they entered the first long tunnel; its round, gulletlike design tapped a deep well of unease. The party boarded an openwork sled, propelled by peristaltic twitches from the sinewed tracks beneath it.

The slick wall was studded periodically by sphinctered plugs for predigested pap. Light glowed gently from translucent bladders swollen with white phosphorescence. Gomez, at Lindsay's elbow, studied the architecture with a trancelike intensity. His attention was sharpened to a cutting edge by a drug known in Cicada circles as "Green Rapture."

"They've gone for broke," Gomez said softly. "Could there be personality behind this? It must take half a ton of backbrain to manage all this meat." His eyes narrowed. "Imagine how it must feel."

The Carnassus clone, in the sled's first compartment, touched the controls. A seam parted wetly in the floor, pitching the sled into vertical free-fall. They catapulted down a multitrack elevator shaft, broken periodically by dizzying vistas of plazas and suburbs.

Shops and offices flashed past, embedded in billows of dark satiny skin. The heat and smell of perfumed flesh were everywhere: intimacy on an industrial scale. The crowds were sparse. Many were young children, running naked.

The sled braked to a halt. The group disembarked onto a furred landing. Gomez nudged Lindsay as the empty sled slid back up the rails. "The walls have ears, Chancellor."

They did, and eyes as well.

There was something in the air on this level. The perfume was particularly heady. Gomez grew heavy-lidded suddenly, and the Szilard brothers, who had donned headband cameras, took them off to dab at sweat. Jane Murray and Emma Meyer, puzzled by something they couldn't define, looked about suspiciously. As the two Dembowskans led them off the landing and into the fleshy depths, Lindsay placed it suddenly: sex pheromones. The architecture was aroused.

The group followed a low-grav footpath: toughened skin marked with the massive whorls of endless fingerprints. The ceiling overhead was a waving carpet of lustrous black hair, for traveling hand-over-hand.

This level was clearly a showpiece: the former buildings had been stripped down to mere frameworks, trellises for flesh. Voluptuous organics rose at every side, euclidean corners scrapped for smooth maternal curves. Structures flowed up from the floor to merge in swan's-neck arches into the lustrous ceiling. Buildings were dimpled, hollowed, the sleek pink of sphinctered doors sliding imperceptibly into skin lightly stippled with down.

They stopped on the furred lawn of an elaborate, massive edifice, its dark walls gleaming with ivory mosaic. "Your hostel," the Colonel announced. The building's double doors yawned open on muscular, jawlike hinges.

Jane Murray hesitated as the others entered; she took Lindsay's arm. "That ivory in the walls—it's teeth." She had gone pale under the cool blues and aquamarines of her Cicada face paint.

"Female pheromones in the air," Lindsay said. "They're making you uneasy. It's backbrain response, doctor."

"Jealous of the walls." The postanthropologist smiled. "This place feels like a gigantic discreet."

Despite her bravado, Lindsay saw her fright. She would have preferred even the most notorious of Cicada discreets, with their clandestine games, to this dubious lodging. They stepped inside.

Murasaki addressed the group. "You'll be sharing the hostel with two groups of commercial agents from Diotima and Themis, but you'll have a wing of your own. This way, please."

They followed her along a walkway of flat ivory implants. One of Dembowska's myriad of hearts, an industrial-scale blood-pumping station, thudded behind the ribs of the ceiling. Its double beat set the rhythm to light musical warbling from a wall-set larynx.

Their quarters were a biomechanical mix. Market monitors glowed in the walls, tracing the rise and fall of prominent Mechanist stocks. The furniture was a series of tasteful lumps and hummocks: curved beds of flesh, dressed modestly in iris-printed bedclothes.

The extensive suite was divided by tattooed membranous screens. The Colonel tapped one membrane divider. It wrinkled into the ceiling like an eyelid. He gestured politely at one of the beds. "These furnishings are exemplars of our Wallmother's erototechnology. They exist for your comfort and pleasure. I must inform you, though, that our Wallmother reserves the right to fecundity."

Emma Meyer, who had settled cautiously onto one of the beds, stood up. "I beg your pardon?"

The Colonel frowned. "Male ejaculations become the property of the recipient. This is an ancient feminine principle."

"Oh. I see."

Murasaki pursed her lips. "You consider this odd, doctor?"

"Not at all," Meyer said winningly. "It makes perfect sense."

The Dembowskan girl pressed on. "Any children sired by the men of your group will be full citizens. All Wallchildren are equally beloved. I happen to be a perfect clone, but I've won my post by merit, in the Mother's love. Isn't that so, Martin?"

The Colonel had a firmer grasp of diplomatic niceties. He nodded shortly. "The water of the baths is sterile and contains a minimum of dissolved organics. It may be drunk freely. The plumbing is genitourinary technology, but it is not waste fluid."

Gomez oozed charm. "As a biological designer, I'm delighted by your ingenious architecture. Not merely by its technical adroitness but by its fine aesthetics." He hesitated. "Is there time for a bath before the luggage arrives?"

The Cicadas needed baths. The bacterial changeover had not quite settled in, and the blood heat of the Dembowskan air made them itch.

Lindsay withdrew to one end of the suite and lowered the membrane wall.

At once his tempo changed. Without his young followers, he moved at his own pace.

He didn't need to bathe. His aged skin could no longer support a large population of bacteria.

He sat on the edge of the bed. He was tired. Without volition, his eyes glazed over. A long moment passed in which he was simply empty, thinking nothing at all.

At last, blinking, he came back to himself. He reached reflexively into his jacket pocket and produced an enameled inhaler. Two long whifs of Green Rapture brought interest back into the world. He looked slowly about him and was surprised to see a blue kimono against the wall. Murasaki was wearing it. Her body was camouflaged almost perfectly against the background of skin.

"Captain Murasaki," he said. "I didn't notice you. Forgive me."

"I was—" She'd been standing there in polite silence. She was flustered by his reputation. "I was ordered to—" She gestured at the door, a pucker in the wall.

"You want to take me somewhere?" he said. "My companions can manage without me. I'm at your disposal."

He followed the girl into the ivory and fur of the hall.

In the lobby she stopped and ran her hand along the smooth flesh of the wall. A hole sphinctered open beside her feet, and the two of them dropped gently down one floor.

Below the hostel was a maintenance area. He heard a steady rushing of arteries and an occasional bowel-like gurgle from the naked walls. Biomonitors flickered, set in puckered rims of flesh.

"This is a health center," Murasaki explained. "The Wallmother's health, I mean. She has a mind-link here. She can speak to you here, through me. You mustn't be alarmed." She turned her back to him and lifted the dark fringe of hair at her neck, showing him the stippled interlink at the base of her skull.

Green Rapture washed gently over Lindsay, a tingling wave of curiosity. Green Rapture was the ultimate antiboredom drug, the biochemical basis of wonder boiled down to its complex essence. With enough Green Rapture a man could find a wealth of interest in the lines of his own hands. Lindsay smiled with unfeigned delight. "Marvelous," he said.

Murasaki hesitated and looked at him quizzically.

"You mustn't mind if I stare," Lindsay said. "You remind me so of your mother."

"You're really him, Chancellor? Abelard Lindsay, who was my mother's lover?"

"Kitsune and I have always been friends."

"Am I much like she was?"

"Clones are their own people." He spoke soothingly. "In the Ring Council, I had a family once. My congenetics—my children—were clones. And I loved them."

"You mustn't think I'm a mere piece of the Wall," Murasaki said. "The Wall cells are chromosomally depauperate. Chimeric blastomas. The Wall is not as fully human as Kitsune's original flesh. Or mine." She looked searchingly into his eyes. "You don't mind talking to me first? I'm not boring you?"

"Impossible," Lindsay said.

"We Wallchildren have had trouble before. Some foreigners treat us as monsters." She sighed, relaxing. "The truth is, we're really rather dull."

He was sympathetic. "You find it so?"

"It's not like Czarina-Kluster. Things are exciting there, aren't they? Always something happening. Pirates. Posthumanists. Defectors. Investors. I see tapes from there sometimes. I'd love to have clothes like that."

Lindsay smiled. "Clothes look better at a distance, my dear. Cicadas dress for social status. It can take hours."

"You're only prejudiced, Chancellor Lindsay. You invented social stripping!"

Lindsay winced. Was he always to be dogged by this cliché?

"I saw it in a play," the girl confessed. "Goldreich Intrasolar came through on tour. They showed Fernand Vetterling's *Pity For the Vermin*. The hero strips at the climax."

Lindsay felt chagrin. Vetterling's plays had lost all punch since he had become a Zen Serotonist. Lindsay would have told the girl as much, but he felt too much shadowy guilt at the tragic course of Vetterling's career. Because of politics, Vetterling had spent years as a nonperson. Lindsay could not blame the dramatist for choosing peace at any price. "Stripping's bad form, these days," he said. "It's lost all meaning. People do it just to punctuate a conversation."

"I thought it was marvelous. Though nudity doesn't mean much in Dembowska. . . . I shouldn't tell you about plays. Didn't you start Kabuki Intrasolar?"

"That was Fyodor Ryumin," Lindsay said.

"Who's he?"

"A brilliant playwright. He died some years ago."

"Was he very old?"

"Extremely. More so even than me."

"Oh, I'm sorry." He had embarrassed her. "I'll be going now. You and the Wallmother must have a lot to discuss." She pressed her hand against the wall behind her, then turned to him again. "Thank you for indulging me. It was a very great privilege." A fleshy tentacle extruded from the wall behind her. The splayed clump at the tentacle's end grasped the back of her neck. She lifted her hair aside and adjusted the plug. Her face went slack.

Her knees buckled and she fell slowly in the feeble gravity. Kitsune came on line and caught her before she hit the floor. The body trembled briefly in a palsy of feedback; then Kitsune stretched it and ran her hands along the arms. The face set itself; the body was all grace, electric with an old and ferocious vitality. Only the eyes were dead.

"Hello, Kitsune."

"Do you like this body, darling?" She stretched luxuriously. "Nothing brings memory back like being in a young woman. What do you call yourself these days?"

"Abelard Lindsay. Chancellor of Czarina-Kluster Kosmosity-Metasystems, Jovian Systems Division."

"And Arbiter of the Lifesiders Clique?"

Lindsay smiled. "Positions in social clubs have no legal validity, Kitsune."

"It's a position strong enough to bring a defector here, all the way from Skimmer's Union. . . . She says her name is Vera Constantine. And that name means enough to you to bring you here?"

Lindsay shrugged. "You see me, Kitsune."

"The daughter of your old enemy? And the congenetic of a long-dead woman whose name escapes me?"

"Vera Kelland."

"How well you remember it. Better than you remember our own relationship?"

"We've had more than one, Kitsune. I remember our youth in the Zaibatsu, though not as well as I would like. And I remember my thirty years here in Dembowska, when I held you at arm's length because your form repulsed me and I missed my wife."

"You could not have resisted me in any form, if I had pressed. In those years I only teased you."

"I've changed since then. These days I'm pressed by other things."

"But now I have a better form. Like the old one." She shrugged the girl's body out of its kimono. "Shall we have a go, for old times' sake?"

Lindsay approached the body and ran his wrinkled hand lingeringly along the long flank. "It's very beautiful," he said.

"It's yours," she said. "Enjoy yourself."

Lindsay sighed. He ran his fingers over the splayed tentacular clump at the back of the girl's neck. "In my duel with Constantine, I had something like this installed. The wires lose a lot in translation. You can't feel it like this, Kitsune. Not like you did then."

"Then?" She laughed aloud. The mouth opened, but the face scarcely moved. "I left those limits behind so long ago that I've forgotten them."

"It's all right, Kitsune. I can't feel it in the same way any more, either." He stepped back and sat on the floor. "If it's any consolation, I still feel something for you. Despite all times and changes. I don't have a name for it. But then what we had between us never had a name."

She picked up the sleeveless kimono. "People who waste time naming never have time for living."

They passed a few moments in companionable silence. She put the robe on and sat before him. "How is Michael Carnassus?" he said at last.

"Michael is well. With each rejuvenation we repair a little more Shatter damage. He leaves his Extraterrarium for longer and longer times, these days. He feels safe in my corridors. He can speak now."

"I'm glad for that."

"He loves me, I think."

"Well, that's not to be despised."

"Sometimes, when I think of how much profit I made from him, I have a strange warm feeling. I never had a better bargain. He was so wonderfully malleable. . . . Even though he's useless now, I still feel real satisfaction when I look at him. I've decided that I'll never throw him away."

"Very good."

"For a Mechanist, he was bright, in his day. An ambassador to aliens; he had to be one of the best. He has many children here—congenetics—they are all very satisfactory."

"I noticed that when I met Colonel Martin Dembowska. A very capable officer."

"You think so, truly?"

Lindsay looked judicious. "Well, young, of course. But that can't be helped."

"No. And this one, this chatterbox"—the body pointed a finger at its own chest—"is even younger. Only nineteen. But my Wallchildren must grow up quickly. I mean to make Dembowska my genetic nest. All others must go. And that includes your Shaper friend from Skimmers Union."

"I'll take her off your hands at your convenience."

"It's a trap, Abelard. Constantine's children have no reason to love you. Don't trust her. Like Carnassus, she has been with aliens. They left their mark on her."

"I must confess I'm curious." He smiled. "I suppose it's the drugs."

"Drugs? It can't be vasopressin, your old favorite. Or you'd have a better memory."

"Green Rapture, Kitsune. I have certain long-term plans. . . . Green Rapture keeps my interest up."

"Your terraforming."

"Yes. It's a problem of time and scale, you see. Long-term fanaticism is hard work. Without Green Rapture, the mind gnaws away at the fantastic until it becomes the commonplace."

"I see," she said. "Your fantastic, and my ecstatic. . . . Childbirth is a wonderful thing."

"To bring new life into the world . . . it is the mystery. Truly a Prigoginic event."

"You must be tired, darling. I've reduced you to Cicada platitudes."

"I'm sorry." He smiled. "It comes with the territory."

"You and Wellspring have a clever front. You're both great talkers. I'm sure you can lecture for hours. Or days. But centuries?"

Lindsay laughed. "It seems like a joke sometimes, doesn't it? Two sundogs embracing the ultimate. Wellspring believes, I think. As for me, I do my best."

"Maybe *he* thinks *you* believe."

"Maybe he does. Maybe I do." Lindsay tugged a long lock of hair through his iron fingers. "As dreams go, Posthumanism has merits. The existence of the Four Levels of Complexity has been proven mathematically. I've seen the equations."

"Spare me, darling. Surely we're not so old that we have to discuss equations."

The words bypassed him. Under the influence of Green Rapture, his brain succumbed momentarily to the lure of mathematics, that purest of intellectual pleasures. In his normal state of mind, despite years of study, he found the formulas painful, a brain-numbing mass of symbols. In Rapture he could grasp them, though afterward he remembered only the white joy of comprehension. The feeling was close to faith.

A long moment passed. He snapped out of it. "I'm sorry, Kitsune. You were saying?"

"Do you remember, Abelard. . . . Once I told you that ecstasy was better than being God."

"I remember."

"I was wrong, darling. Being God is better."


Vera Constantine's quarters were a measure of Kitsune's distrust. The young Shaper clanswoman had been under house arrest for weeks. Her lodging was a three-room cell of stone and iron, outside Kitsune's world-consuming embrace.

She sat at an inset Market monitor, studying the flow of tranaction in a three-dimensional grid. She had never dealt in the Market before, but Abelard Gomez, a kindly young Cicada, had given her a financial stake to pass the time. Knowing no better, she applied to the flow of the Market the principles of atmospheric dynamics she'd learned on Fomalhaut IV. Oddly, it seemed to be working. She was clearly gaining.

The door unsealed and shunted open. An old man stepped in, tall and thin in muted Cicada garb: a long coat, dark slash-cuffed trousers, jeweled rings worn over white gloves. His lined face was bearded, and a silvered coronet of patterned leaves accented his white-streaked, shoulder-length hair. Vera rose from her stirrup-chair and bowed, imitating the Cicada flourish. "Chancellor, welcome."

Lindsay's eyes searched the cell, his sinewy brows knitting in puzzlement. He seemed wary, not of her but of something in the room. Then she felt it herself, and knew that the Presence had returned. Despite herself, knowing it was useless, she looked for it quickly. Something flickered in the corner of her eye as it escaped her vision.

Lindsay smiled at her. Then he continued to scan the room. She didn't want to tell him about the Presence. After a while he would give up looking for it, just as all the others did. "Thank you," he said belatedly. "I trust you're well, Captain-Doctor."

"Your friends, Doctor Gomez and Undersecretary Nakamura, have been most attentive. Thank you for the tapes and gifts."

"It was nothing," Lindsay said.

She feared suddenly that she was disappointing him. He had not seen her in the fifteen years since the duel. She had been very young then—only twenty. She still had the Kelland cheekbones and pointed chin, but time had changed her, and her genotype was not pure. She was not Vera Kelland's clone.

Her sleeveless kimono mercilessly showed the changes brought by her years as an alien emissary. Two circulatory ducts dented the flesh of her neck, and her skin still had a peculiar waxiness. Inside the Embassy at Fomalhaut, she had lived in water for years.

Lindsay's gray eyes would not stop wandering. She was convinced that he could feel the Presence, sense its pervasive eeriness. Sooner or later he would attribute that feeling to her, and then her chance to win his favor would be gone. He spoke abstractedly. "I'm sorry that matters can't be resolved more quickly. . . . In matters of defection it's best not to be rash."

She thought she heard a veiled reference to the fate of Nora Mavrides. That chilled her. "I see your point, Chancellor." Vera had no official backing by the Constantine clan, for they could not risk denunciation within the Ring Council. Life was hard in Skimmers Union these days: with the loss of the capitalship had come a vicious struggle for the remaining scraps of power and a hunt for scapegoats. Constantine clan members were prominent victims.

Once, she had been the favorite of their clan founder, showered with gifts and Constantine's strained affection.

But her clan had made too many bad gambles. Philip Constantine had risked their future on the chance to kill Lindsay and had failed. The clan had invested heavily in Vera's ambassadorship, but she had returned without the riches they'd expected. And she had changed in a way that alarmed them. Now, she was expendable.

As the clan's power dwindled, they had lived in terror of Lindsay. He had survived the duel and returned more powerful than ever. He seemed unstoppable, bigger than life. But the attack they'd expected had never come, and it occurred to them that he had weaknesses. Through her, they hoped to prey on his emotions, on the love or guilt he felt for Vera Kelland. It was the latest and most desperate of gambles. With luck they might win sanctuary. Or vengeance. Or both.

"Why come to me?" he said. "There are other places. Life as a Mechanist is not so bad as the Ring Council paints it."

"The Mechs would turn us against our own people. They would break up our clan. No, Czarina-Kluster is best. There's sanctuary in the shadow of your Queen. But not if you work against us."

"I see," Lindsay said. He smiled. "My friends don't trust you. We have very little to gain, you see. C-K already swarms with defectors. Your clan does not share our Posthuman ideology. Worse yet, there are many in C-K who hate the name Constantine. Former Détentistes, Cataclysts, and so on. . . . You understand the difficulties."

"Those days are behind us, Chancellor. We mean no harm to anyone."

Lindsay closed his eyes. "We could babble reassurances until the sun expands," he said—he seemed to be quoting someone—"and never convince each other. Either we trust each other or we don't."

His bluntness filled her with misgivings. She was at a loss. The silence stretched uncomfortably. "I have a present for you," she said. "An ancient heirloom." She crossed the narrow cell to lift a rectangular wire cage, shrouded in peach-colored velvet. She lifted the cage cover and showed him the clan treasure, an albino laboratory rat. It ran back and forth through its cage, mincing along with bizarre, repetitive precision. "It is one of the first creatures ever to attain physical immortality. An ancient lab specimen. It is over three hundred years old."

Lindsay said, "You're very generous." He lifted the cage and examined it. Within it, the rat, its capacity to learn completely exhausted by age, had been reduced to absolute rote behavior. The twitchings of its muzzle, even the movement of its eyes, were utterly stereotyped.

The old man watched it searchingly. She knew he would get no response. There was nothing in the rat's jellied pink eyes, not even the dimmest flicker of animal awareness. "Has it ever been out of the cage?" he said.

"Not in centuries, Chancellor. It's too valuable."

Lindsay opened the cage. Its routines shattered, the rat cowered beside the steel tube of its water drip, its sinewy furred limbs trembling.

Lindsay wiggled his gloved fingers beside the entrance. "Don't be afraid," he told the rat seriously. "There's a whole world out here."

Some ancient, corroded reflex kicked over in the rat's head. With a squeal it launched itself across the cage at Lindsay's hand, clawing and biting in convulsive fury. Vera gasped and leaped forward, shocked at his action, appalled by the rat's response. Lindsay gestured her back and lifted his hand, watching in pity as the rat attacked him. Beneath his torn right glove, hard prosthetic fingers gleamed with black and copper gridwork.

He grasped the squirming animal with gentle firmness, watching to see that it did not crack its teeth. "Prison has set its mind," he said. "It will take a long time to melt the bars behind its eyes." He smiled. "Luckily, time is in great supply."

The rat stopped struggling. It panted in the throes of some rodent epiphany. Lindsay set it gently on the tabletop beside the Market monitor. It struggled to its pink feet and began to pace in agitation, turning in its tracks at the former limits of its cage.

"It can't change," Vera told him. "Its capacities are exhausted."

"Nonsense," Lindsay said. "He merely needs to make a Prigoginic leap to a new level of behavior." The calm assertion of his ideology frightened her. Something must have shown in her face. He tugged the torn glove from his hand. "Hope is our duty," he said. "You must always hope."

"For years we hoped we could heal Philip Constantine," Vera said. "Now we know better. We are ready to trade him to you for our own safe-conduct."

Lindsay looked at her seriously. "This is cruelty," he said.

"He was your enemy," she said. "We wanted to make amends."

"For me, you are that chance."

It was working. He still remembered Vera Kelland.

"Don't deceive yourself," he said. "I don't offer true recompense. Czarina-Kluster must fall someday. Nations don't last in this era. Only people last, only plans and hopes. . . . I can only offer you what I have. I don't have safety. I have freedom."

"Posthumanism," she said. "It's your state ideology. Of course we'll adapt."

"I thought you had your own convictions, Vera. You're a Galacticist."

She ran her fingers lightly, absently, over one of the gill seams in her neck. "I learned my politics in the observation sphere. In Fomalhaut. The Embassy." She hesitated. "Life there changed me more than you could know. There are things I can't explain."

"There's something in this room," he said.

She was stunned. "Yes," she blurted. "You felt it? Not many do."

"What is it? Something from the Fomalhaut aliens? The gasbags?"

"They know nothing about it."

"But you do," he said. "Tell me."

She was in too far to back out. She spoke reluctantly. "I first noticed it in the Embassy. The Embassy floats in the atmosphere of Fomalhaut Four, a gas-giant planet, like Jupiter. . . . We had to live in water there to survive the gravity. We were thrown together, Mechanists and Shapers; we shared the Embassy, there was no choice. Everything was changed; we changed. . . . The Investors came to take a Mechanist contingent back to the Schismatrix. I think the Presence was aboard the Investor ship. Since then the Presence has been with me."

"Is it real?" said Lindsay.

"I think so. Sometimes I almost see it. A kind of flickering. A mirror-colored thing."

"What did the Investors say?"

"They denied everything. They said I was deluded." She hesitated. "And they weren't the last to say so." She regretted confessing it at once. But the burden had eased. She looked at him, daring to hope.

"An alien, then," Lindsay said. "Not one of the nineteen known species."

"You believe me," she said. "You think that it's really here."

"We must believe each other," Lindsay said. "Life is better that way." He looked about the narrow room carefully, as if testing his eyes. "I'd like to lure it into the open."

"It won't come out," the girl said. "Believe me, I've begged it many times."

"We mustn't try it here," Lindsay said. "Any manifestation would alarm Kitsune. She feels secure in this world. We must consider her feelings."

His sincerity startled her. It hadn't occurred to her that her captor might have feelings, or that anyone might relate, in a personal way, to that titanic mass of flesh.

He picked up the rat, which began squealing loudly, with desperate energy. He examined it with such guileless interest that, before she could help herself, she felt a stab of pity for him, an urge to protect him. The feeling surprised and warmed her.

He said, "We'll be leaving soon. You'll be coming with us." He put the rat in the pocket of his long coat. It rested there quietly.

The history of the Schismatrix was one long racking chronicle of change. The population had reached nine billion. Within the Ring Council, power had slipped from the narcotized hands of the Zen Serotonists. After forty years of their reign, new Shaper ideologues embraced the aggressive schemes of visionary Galacticism.

The new creed had spread slowly. It was born in the interstellar embassies, where ambassadors broke human limits in their struggle to grasp alien ways of life. Now the Galacticist prophets stood ready to abandon humanity entirely, to achieve a Galactic consciousness where mere loyalty to species was obsolete.

Once again détente had shattered. The Mechanists and Shapers fought in bitter rivalry for the favor of aliens. Of the nineteen alien races, only five had shown even the vaguest interest in a closer relationship with humankind. The Chondrule Cloud Processors were willing to move in, but only if Venus could be atomized for easier digestion. The Nerve Coral Aquatics expressed mild interest in invading the Earth, but this would mean breaking the sacred tradition of Interdict. The Culture Ghosts were willing to join with anyone who could endure them, but their hideous effects on the Schismatric diplomatic corps had made them objects of genuine horror.

The gasbags of Fomalhaut offered most. It had taken many decades to master their "language," which was best expressed as complex unstable states of atmospheric dynamics. Once true contact had been established, progress was rapid. Fomalhaut was an enormous star with a huge asteroid belt rich in heavy metals.

The asteroid belt was useless to the gasbags, who disliked space travel. They were, however, interested in Jupiter and planned to seed it with aerial krill.

The Investors were willing to handle transportation, though even their huge ships could carry only a handful of surgically deflated gasbags per trip.

Controversy had raged for decades. The Mechanists had their own Galacticist faction, who struggled to grasp the mind-shattering physics of the sinister Hijack Boosters. The Boosters, like the Investors, possessed a technique of faster-than-light travel. The Investors were willing to sell their secret, but only at a crippling price. The Hijack Boosters mocked mankind but were occasionally indiscreet.

An advance into the galactic arm seemed inevitable. One of two strategies would succeed: that of the Shapers, with their diplomatic negotiation, or of the Mechanists, who directly attacked the problem of starflight. Only a major faction could succeed; the minor breakaway groups lacked the wealth, the skilled population, the diplomatic pull. A new, uneasy polarity took shape.

In the meantime, gasbag larvae in their egg-shaped spacecraft painstakingly inspected circumsolar space. Small groups of Shapers and Mechanist renegades mapped the riches of Fomalhaut. One solar system would never again be enough.

The breakdown of détente aroused old hatreds. Brushfire warfare flourished, unrestrained by the faltering Investors. Bizarre new factions sprang up, led by returned diplomats. Their recruits loomed at the edges of society: the Carnivores, the Viral Army, the Coronaspherics.

History's kaleidoscope worked its permutations, its pace ever faster, approaching some unknown cresendo. Patterns changed and warped and flew apart, each chip of light a human life.

## CZARINA-KLUSTER PEOPLE'S CORPORATE REPUBLIC: 13-1-'54

After seventy years of wealth and stability, disaster was loose in Czarina-Kluster. The elite of the Lifesiders Clique met in secret council, to wrestle with crisis.

Aquamarine Discreet was a Lifesider citadel, and its security was absolute. Mosaic blowups of the Jovian moon, Europa, covered the discreet's walls: bright grooved terrain in ice-white and dusky orange, interior seas in blue and indigo. Over the burnished conference table hung a Europan orrery, where jeweled spacecraft representing Lifesider satellites ticked quietly on orbits of silver wire.

Chancellor Abelard Gomez, a vigorous eighty-five-year-old, had taken over management of the Clique's affairs. His chief compatriots were Professor Glen Szilard, Queen's Advisor Fidel Nakamura, and Gomez's current wife, Project Manager Jane Murray. At the far end of the table sat Chancellor Emeritus Abelard Lindsay. The old visionary's lined face showed the quizzical smile associated with a heavy dosage of Green Rapture.

Gomez rapped the table, bringing the meeting to order. They fell silent, except for the loud chattering of the ancient rat on Lindsay's shoulder. "Sorry," Lindsay murmured. He put the rat in his pocket.

Gomez took control. "Fidel, your report?"

"It's true, Chancellor. The Queen has vanished."

The others groaned. Gomez spoke sharply. "Defected or kidnapped?"

Nakamura wiped his brow. "Wellspring took her; only he can answer that. My fellow Advisors are in uproar. The Coordinator is calling out the dogs. He's even brought the tigers out of mothballs. They want Wellspring for high treason. They won't rest until they have him."

"Or until C-K collapses around them," Gomez said. Gloom settled over the chamber. "Tigers," Gomez said. "Tigers are huge machines; they could shred through the walls of this discreet like paper. We mustn't meet again until we have armed ourselves and established secure perimeters."

Szilard spoke up. "Our dogs have this suburb's exits monitored. I stand ready to carry out loyalty tests. We can purge the suburb of unfriendly ideologues and make this our bastion as the Kluster dissolves."

"That's harsh," Jane Murray said.

"It's us or them," Szilard said. "Once the news spreads, the other factions will be holding kangaroo courts, seizing strongholds, stripping dissidents of property. Anarchy is coming. We must defend ourselves."

"What about our allies?" Gomez said.

Nakamura spoke. "According to our Polycarbon Clique contacts, the announcement of Wellspring's coup d'etat will coincide with the first asteroid impact on Mars, in the morning of 4-14-'54. . . . C-K will disintegrate within weeks. Most Czarina-Kluster refugees will flee to Martian orbit. Wellspring holds the Queen there. He will rule. The new Terraforming-Kluster will have a much stronger Posthuman ideology."

"The Mechs and Shapers will tear C-K apart," Jane Murray said. "And our philosophy profits by the destruction. . . . This is high treason, friends. I feel sick."

"People outlive nations," Lindsay said gently. He was breathing with inhuman regularity: a Mechanist biocuirass managed his internal organs. "C-K is doomed. No number of dogs or purges can hold it, without the Queen. We're finished here."

"The Chancellor Emeritus is right," Gomez told them. "Where will we go? We must decide. Do we join the Polycarbon Clique around Mars, to live in the Queen's shadow? Or do we make our move to CircumEuropan orbit and put our own plans into effect?"

"I say Mars," Nakamura said. "In today's climate Posthumanism needs all the help it can get. The Cause demands solidarity."

"Solidarity? Fluidarity, rather," Lindsay said. He sat upright with an effort. "What's one Queen, more or less? There are always more aliens. Posthumanism must find its own orbit someday . . . why not now?"

While the others argued, Gomez looked moodily, through half-shut eyes, at his old mentor. The remnants of old pain gnawed at him. He could not forget his long marriage to Lindsay's favorite, Vera Constantine. There had been too many shadows between himself and Vera.

Once they had put the shadows aside. That was when she'd confessed to Gomez that she had meant to kill Lindsay. Lindsay had made no move to defend himself, and there had been many opportunities, but the time had never quite been right. And years passed. And convictions faltered and became buried in routines and practicalities. The day came when she knew she could not go through with it. She had confessed it to Gomez, because she trusted him. And they had loved each other.

Gomez led her away from vengeance. She embraced Posthumanism. Even her clan had been won over. The Constantine clan were now the Lifesiders' pioneers, working around Europa.

But Gomez himself had not escaped the years. Time had a way of making passion into work. He had what he wanted. He had his dream. He had to live it and breathe it and do its budget. And he had lost Vera, for there had been one shadow left.

Vera had never been entirely sane. For years she had quietly insisted that an alien Presence followed and watched her. It seemed to come and go with her mood swings; for days she would be cheerful, convinced that it was "off somewhere"; then he would find her moody and withdrawn, convinced that it was back.

Lindsay condoned her illness and claimed to believe her. Gomez too believed in the Presence: he believed it was the reflection of his wife's estrangement from reality. It was not for nothing that she had called it "a mirror-colored thing. . . ." Something that could not be pinned down, an incarnation of unverifiable fluidity. . . . When Gomez got to the point where he himself could feel it, even sense it flickering at the corners of his vision, he knew things had gone too far. Their divorce had been amiable, full of cool politeness.

He wondered sometimes if Lindsay had planned it all. Lindsay knew the trap that was human joy, and the strength that came from clawing free of it. Scalded by pain, Gomez had won that strength. . . . Szilard was reeling off facts and figures about the state of CircumEuropa. The future Lifesiders habitat was being blown into shape around the Jovian moon, an orbiting froth of hard-set angles, walls, bubbled topologies.

The flourishing Constantine clan was snaking plumbing through the walls already and booting up the life-support system. But an attempt by the Lifesiders to move there en masse, in their thousands, would stretch resources to the limit.

Their relations with the gasbag colony on Jupiter were good; they had the expertise of Vera and her cadre of trainees. But the Jovian aliens could not protect them from other human factions. They had no such ambition and no prestige to match that of the Cicada Queen.

Jane Murray presented things from a Project perspective. The surface of Europa was the bleakest of prospects: a vacuum-seared wasteland of smooth water ice, so cold that blood and bone would crack like glass, bathed in deadly Jovian radiation. But there were fissures in that ice, dark streaks thousands of kilometers long. . . . Tidal cracks. For beneath the moon's crust was molten ice, a planet-girdling lava ocean of liquid water. The constant tidal energy of Jupiter,

Ganymede, and Io warmed Europa's ocean to blood heat. Beneath the lacelike web of fractures, a sterile ocean washed a bed of geothermal rock.

For years the Lifesiders had planned a series of massive disasters for the inorganic. It would start with algae. They had already bred forms that could survive in the peculiar mix of salts and sulfurs native to European seas. The algae could cluster around fresh cracks where light seeped through, feasting on the strands of heavy hydrocarbons bobbing aimlessly within the sterile sea. Fish would be next; small ones at first, bred from the half-dozen species of commercial fish mankind had brought into space. Ocean arthropods such as "crabs" and "shrimp," known only from ancient textbooks, could be mimicked through skilled manipulation of the genes of insects.

Fault-lines could be shattered from orbit by dropped projectiles, leaving light-flooded patches of pack ice. They could experiment on a dozen cracks at once, adapting rival ecosystems through trial and error.

It would take centuries. Once again, Gomez took the burden of the years upon himself. "Biodesign is still in its infancy," he said. "We must face facts. At least, with the Queen, the Martian Kluster will have wealth and safety for us. There, at least, our only enemies will be the years."

Lindsay lurched forward abruptly and slammed his iron fist into the table. "We must act now! This is the moment of crux, when a single act can crystallize our future. We have our choice: routines or miracles. Demand the miraculous!"

Gomez was stunned. "It's Europa, then, Chancellor?" he said. "Wellspring's plans seem safer."

"Safer?" Lindsay laughed. "Czarina-Kluster seemed safe. But the Cause moved on, and the Queen moved with it, when Wellspring took her. The abstract dream will flourish, but the tangible city will fall. Those who can't dream will die with it. The discreets will be thick with the blood of suicides. Wellspring himself may be killed. Mech agents will annex whole suburbs, Shapers will absorb whole banks and industries. The routines that seemed so solid here will melt like tears. . . . If we embrace them, we melt with them."

"Then what must we do?"

"Wellspring is not the only one whose crimes are secret and ambitious. And he's not the last to vanish."

"You're leaving us, Chancellor?"

"You must handle distress and disaster yourselves. I'm past any use in that capacity."

The others looked stricken. Gomez rallied himself. "The Chancellor Emeritus is right," he said. "I was about to suggest something similar. Our enemies will focus attacks on the Clique's Arbiter; it might be best if he were hidden."

The others protested automatically; Lindsay overruled them. "There can't always be Queens and Wellsprings. You must trust in your own strength. I trust in it."

"Where will you go, Chancellor?"

"Where I'm least expected." He smiled. "This isn't my first crisis. I've seen many. And when they hit, I always ran. I've preached to you for years, asked you to dedicate your lives. . . . And always I knew that this moment would come. I never knew what I would do when the dream faced its crisis. Would I sundog it as I always have, or would I commit myself? The moment's here. I must defy my past, just as you must. I know how to get you your miracle. And I swear to you, I will."

A sudden dread struck Gomez. He had not seen such resolution in Lindsay for years. It occurred to him suddenly that Lindsay meant to die. He did not know Lindsay's plans, but he realized now that they would be the crux of the old man's life. It would be like him to exit at the climax, to fade into the shadows while some unknown glory still shone. "Chancellor," he said, "when may we expect your return?"

"Before I die, we'll be Europa's angels. And I'll see you in Paradise." Lindsay cycled open the sealed door of the discreet; outside, the free-fall corridors were a burst of sudden crowd noise. The door thunked shut. He was gone. Thick silence fell.

The old man's absence left a hollowness behind. The others sat silently, savoring the sense of loss. They looked at one another. Then, as one, they looked to Gomez. The moment passed; the uneasiness dissolved. Gomez smiled. "Well," he said. "It's miracles, then."

Lindsay's rat leaped spryly onto the table. "He's left it behind," Jane Murray said. She stroked its fur, and it chittered loudly.

"The rat will come to order," Gomez said. He rapped the table, and they set to work.

# Chapter 11

## CIRCUMTERRAN ORBIT: 14-4-'54

Three of them waited within the spacecraft: Lindsay, Vera Constantine, and their Lobster navigator, who was known simply as Pilot.

"Final approach," Pilot said. His beautiful synthesized voice emerged from a vocoder unit hooked to his throat.

Strapped in before his control board, the Lobster was a chunk of shadow. He was sealed within a matte-black permanent spacesuit, knobbed with lumps of internal machinery and dotted with shiny gold input jacks. Lobsters were creatures of the vacuum, faceless posthumans, their eyes and ears wired to sensors woven through the suits. Pilot never ate. He never drank. The routines of his body were subsumed within the life-supporting rhythms of his suit.

Pilot did not like being within this spacecraft; Lobsters had a horror of enclosed spaces. Pilot, though, had put up with the discomfort for the thrill of the crime.

Now that they were dropping from orbit, the drugged calm of weeks of travel had broken. Lindsay had never seen Vera so animated. Her open delight filled him with pleasure.

And she had reason for gladness. The Presence was gone. She had not felt it since the three of them had been sealed within the spacecraft. They'd come so far since then that she believed she had escaped it for good. She found as much happiness in this relief as in the fulfillment of their long conspiracy.

Lindsay was happy for her. He had never had true proof of the objective existence of the Presence, but he had agreed to believe in it for her. And similarly, she had never doubted him. It was a contract and a trust between them. He knew she might have killed him, but that trust had saved his life. Long years since then had only strengthened it.

"Looks good," the Lobster sang. The spacecraft began to buck as it hit the entrance window of the Earth's atmosphere. The Lobster emitted a burst of static, then said, "Air. I hate air. I hate it already."

"Steady," Lindsay said. He tightened the straps of his chair and unfolded his videoscreens.

They were coming in over the continent once known as Africa. Its outlines had been radically changed by the rising seas: archipelagos of drowned hills trailed clouds above a soup of weed-choked ocean. Along the dark shore, rivers poured gray topsoil into water streaked red with algal blooms.

The white-hot flare of entry heat obscured his vision, flickering over the diamond-hard hull lens of the forward scanner. Lindsay leaned back in his seat.

It was an odd ship, an uncomfortable one, not of human manufacture. The egg-shaped hull had the off-white sheen of stabilized metallic hydrogen, built only by gasbags. Its naked interior floor and ceiling bore the rounded, scalloped segmentation marks of its former pilot, a gasbag grub. The spacefaring grub had been packed within the hull as tightly as expanding dough.

One of the gasbags had alluded to the astronaut's death in a "conversation" with Vera Constantine. With its keen sensitivity to magnetic flux, the unlucky grub had perceived a solar flare whose shape and substance it found somehow blasphemous. It had expired in despair.

Lindsay had been looking for just such a chance. When Vera told him of the accident, Lindsay acted at once. He recruited the Lobsters through their business contact in Czarina-Kluster, a Lobster they called "the Modem."

A complex deal was worked out, in utter secrecy, with the anarchic Lobsters. One of their lacy, airless spacecraft used Vera's coordinates to track down the dead grub. Lindsay allowed them to dissect it and appropriate its alien engines. In return they outfitted the emptied shell for a furtive attempt to break the Interdict with Earth.

The Interdict had never applied to the gasbags. They had insisted on exploring the entire solar system, and had granted equal rights to the pioneers in Fomalhaut. Their surveying craft had often studied the Earth. They made no attempt to contact the local primitives. They had satisfied themselves that the planet was harmless and had returned in utter disinterest.

With his two companions, Lindsay had assumed his ultimate disguise. He was passing himself off as an alien, in an attempt to deceive the entire Schismatrix.

Excitement and triumph had stripped decades from Lindsay. He had turned up his chest cuirass so that his heart could labor in time with his feelings. The forearm monitor embedded in his arm glowed amber with adrenaline.

The spacecraft skipped above the bloated South Atlantic and sank deep within the atmosphere at the twilight line. Deceleration pressed Lindsay into the straps of his skeletal chair.

The Lobsters had done a quick, primitive job. The three-man crew was

crammed into a ribbed lozenge four meters across. It held two air-frames, a recycler, and three acceleration couches, of black elastic webbing over iron frames
epoxied to the floor. The rest of the craft was taken up by engines and a garage-
like specimen hold. In the hold crouched a surveyor robot, one of the Europan
submarine probes.

The dead astronaut's former orifices had been stripped of tissue and outfitted with cameras and scanning systems. The specimen hold had a hatchway installed, but there was no room for an airlock in the crew's compartment. The
three of them had been welded in.

Pilot hadn't liked it. Pilot could be trusted, though. He cared nothing for
Europa or their plans, but he relished the chance to count coup on the ancestral
gravity well. He had been everywhere, from the turbulent fringes of the solar
corona to the cometary Oort Cloud at the edge of circumsolar space. He was not
human, but for the time being he was one of them.

The scanners began to clear. Deceleration faded into the heavy tug of Earth
gravity. Lindsay slumped in his seat, wheezing as the cuirass pumped his lungs.
"Look what this muck is doing to the stars," Pilot complained melodiously.

Vera reached beside her chair and unfolded her tight-packed accordioned
screens. She straightened the videoboard with a pop and smoothed out the
creases. "Look, Abelard. There's so much air above us that it's blurring the stars.
Think how much air. It's fantastic."

Lindsay stirred himself and examined the view from the aft camera. Behind
them, a wall of thunderheads towered to the limits of the troposphere. Black
roots furred with rain rose to white anvil heads glowing in the last of twilight.
This was one outstretched arm of the storm zone of permanent tempests that girdled the planet's equator.

He expanded the aft view to fill the whole videoboard. What he saw awed
him. "Look aft at the storm clouds," he said. "Huge streaks of fire are leaping
out of them. What could be burning?"

"Chunks of vegetation?" Vera said.

"Wait. No. It's lightning," Lindsay said. "As in the old phrase, 'thunder and
lightning.' " He stared in utter fascination.

"Lightning bolts are supposed to be red, with jagged edges," Vera said.
"These are like thin white branches."

"The disaster must have changed their form," Lindsay said.

The storm vanished over the horizon. "Coastline coming up," Pilot said.

Sunset fell; they switched to infrareds. "This is part of America," Lindsay
concluded. "It was called Mexico, or possibly Texico. The coastline looked different before the ice caps melted. I don't recognize any of this."

Pilot struggled with the controls. Vera said, "We're going faster than the
movement of sound in this atmosphere. Slow down, Pilot."

"Muck," Pilot complained. "Do you really want to see this? What if the locals see us?"

"They're primitives, they don't have infrareds," Vera said.

"You mean they use only the visible spectrum?" Now Pilot himself was stunned.

They studied the landscape below: knots of dense scrubland, shining in the false black-and-white of infrared. The wilderness was striped occasionally by half-obscured dark streaks. "Tectonic faults?" Vera said.

"Roads," Lindsay said. He explained about low-friction surfaces for ground travel in gravity. They had not seen any cities as yet, though there had been suggestive patches here and there where the rioting vegetation seemed thinner.

Pilot took them lower. They pored over the growth at high magnification. "Weeds," Lindsay concluded. "Since the disaster all ecological stability has collapsed. . . . Adventitious species have moved in. This was probably all cropland once."

"It's ugly," Vera said.

"Systems in collapse often are."

"High-energy flux ahead," Pilot said. The spacecraft dipped and hovered over a ridge.

Wildfire swept the hillside, whole kilometers of orange glow in the darkness. Roaring updrafts flung up flakes of glowing ash, reverse cascades of stripped-off leaves and branches. Behind the wall of fire were the twisted, glowing skeletons of weeds grown large as trees, their smoldering trunks thick bundles of woody filaments. They said nothing, stirred to the core by the wonder of it. "Sundog plants," Lindsay said at last.

"What?"

"The weeds are like sundogs. They thrive on disaster. They move in anywhere where systems break down. After this disaster the plants that grow fastest on scorched earth will thrive. . . ."

"More weeds," Vera concluded.

"Yes." They left the fire behind and cruised past the foothills. Lindsay tapped one of the algae frames and ate a mouthful of green paste.

"Aircraft," Pilot said.

For a moment Lindsay thought he was seeing a mutant gasbag, some bizarre example of parallel evolution. Then he realized it was a flying machine: some kind of blimp or zeppelin. Long seamed ridges of sewn balloon skin supported a skeletal gondola. A thin skein of flexible solar-power disks dotted the craft's skin, dappling over its back, fading to a white underbelly. Long mooring lines trailed from its nose, like drooping antennae.

They approached cautiously and saw its mooring-ground: a city.

A gridwork of streets split a checkerboard of white stone shelters. The houses were marshaled around a looming central core: a four-sided masonry pyramid. The zeppelin was moored to the pyramid's apex. The whole city was hemmed in by a high rectangular wall; outside, agriculture fields glowed a ghastly white, manured with ashes.

A ceremony was progressing. A pyre blazed at the masonry plaza at the pyramid's foot. The city's population was drawn up in ranks. They numbered

less than two thousand. Their clothing was bleached by the infrared glow of
their body heat. "What is it?" said Vera. "Why don't they move?"

"A funeral, I think," Lindsay said.

"What's the pyramid, then? A mausoleum? An indoctrination center?"

"Both, maybe. . . . Do you see the cable system? The mausoleum has an information line, the only one in the village. Whoever lives there holds all links to
the outside world." Lindsay thought suddenly of the domed stronghold of the
Nephrine Black Medicals in the circumlunar Zaibatsu. He hadn't thought of it
for years, but he remembered the psychic atmosphere within it, the sense of
paranoid isolation, of fanaticism slowly drifting past the limits through lack of
variety. A world gone stale. "Stability," he said. "The Terrans wanted stability,
that's why they set up the Interdict. They didn't want technology to break them
into pieces, as it's done to us. They blamed technology for the disasters. The war
plagues, the carbon dioxide that melted the ice caps. . . . They can't forget their
dead."

"Surely the whole world isn't like this," Vera said.

"It has to be. Anywhere there is variety there is the risk of change. Change
that can't be tolerated."

"But they have telephones. Aircraft."

"Enforcement technology," Lindsay said.

On their way to the Pacific they saw two more settlements, separated by
miles of festering wilderness. The cities were as identical as circuit chips. They
crouched unnaturally on the landscape; they could have been stamped out from
some hydraulic press and dropped from the air.

Pilot pointed out more of the bloated aircraft. Their full significance became clear to Lindsay. The flying machines were like plague vectors, carrying
the ideological virus of some calcifying cultural disease. The pyramids towered
in the heart of every city, enormous, dwarfing all hope, the strangling monu-
ments of the legions of the dead.

Tears came to him. He wept quietly, holding nothing back. He mourned
mankind, and the blindness of men, who thought that the Kosmos had rules and
limits that would shelter them from their own freedom. There were no shelters.
There were no final purposes. Futility, and freedom, were Absolute.

They slipped beneath the ocean south of the rocky island chain of Baja Cal-
ifornia. Pilot opened the hatchway, flooding the cargo hold with water, and they
began at once to sink.

They were in search of the world's largest single ecosystem, the only biome
man had never touched.

The surface waters had not escaped. Over the drowned lands of the conti-
nental margins, rafts of rotting moss and algae, the ocean's equivalents of weeds,
festered in choking profusion. But the abyssal depths were undisturbed. In the
crushing blackness of the abyss, larger in area than all the continents combined,
conditions scarcely varied from pole to pole. The denizens of this vast realm
were poorly known. No human being had ever invented a way to wring advantage from them.

But in the Schismatrix, man's successors were more clever. The resemblance of this realm to the dark oceans of Europa had not escaped Lindsay. For decades he had searched the ancient databanks for scraps of knowledge. The surviving records of abyssal life were almost useless, dating back to the dawn of biology. But even these crude hints lured Lindsay with their potential for sudden miracle. Europa too had the gloominess, the depths. And the vast drowned ranges of volcanic rifts, oozing geothermal energy.

The abyss had oases. It had always had them. The knowledge had lit a slow, subterranean fire in his imagination. Life: untouched, primeval life, swarmed in boiling splendor at the fiery edges of the Earth's tectonic plates.

An entire ecosystem, older than mankind, clustered there in all its miraculous richness. Life that could be seized, that could be Europa's.

At first he had rejected the idea. The Interdict was sacred: as old as the unspoken guilt of ancestral spacefarers, who had deserted Earth as disaster loomed. In their desertion, they had robbed the planet of the very expertise that might have saved it. Over centuries of life in space, that guilt had sunk into a darkened region of cultural awareness, surfacing only as caricature, as ritual denial and deliberate ignorance.

The parting had come with hatred: with those in space condemned as anti-human thieves, and Earth's emergency government denounced as fascist barbarism. Hatred made things easier: easier for those in space to shrug off all responsibility, easier for Earth to starve its myriad cultures down to a single gray regime of penance and pointless stability.

But life moved in clades. Lindsay knew it as a fact. A successful species always burst into a joyous wave of daughter species, of hopeful monsters that rendered their ancestors obsolete. Denying change meant denying life.

By this token he knew that humanity on Earth had become a relict.

In the long term, the vast biological timescape that had become Lindsay's obsession, rust ate anything that failed to move. Earth's future did not belong to humanity but to the monstrous weeds, grown strange and woody, and whatever small fleet creatures leaped and bred among them. And Lindsay felt justice in it.

They sank into darkness.

Pressure meant nothing to their alien hull. The gasbags flourished at extremes of pressure that made Earth's oceans seem as thin as plasma. Pilot switched controls over to the water jets epoxied to the hull. He kicked in aperture radar, and their videoboards lit up with the clean green contour lines of the abyssal floor.

Lindsay's heart leaped as he saw the familiar geology. "Just like Europa," Vera murmured. They were floating over an extended tension fault, where volcanic basalt had snapped and rifted, harsh blocks jutting upward, the cracked primeval violence untouched by wind or rain. Rectilinear mountains, lightly dusted with organic ooze, dropped in breathtaking precipitous cliffs, where contour lines crowded together like the teeth of a comb.

But here the rift was dead. They saw no sign of thermal energy. "Follow the fault," Lindsay said. "Look for hot spots." He had lived too long for impatience, even now.

"Shall I kick in the main engines?" Pilot said.

"And make the water boil for miles around? We're deep, Pilot. That water is like steel."

"Is it?" Pilot made an electronic churring noise. "Well, I'd rather have no stars at all than blurry ones."

They followed the rift for hours without finding a lava seep. Vera slept; Lindsay dozed briefly, an old man's cat-sleep. Pilot, who slept only on formal occasions, woke them. "A hot spot," he said.

Lindsay examined his board. Infrareds showed sluggish heat from deep within the interior of a jutting cliff. The cliff was extremely odd: a long, tilted plane of euclidian smoothness, rising abruptly from an oozy badlands of jumbled terrain. An angular foothill at the base of the cliff lay strangely distorted, almost crumpled, atop a dome-shaped rise of lava.

"Send out the drone," he said.

Vera pulled the robot's controls from under her seat and slipped on a pair of eyephones. The robot sculled easily out to the anomalous cliff, its lights blazing. Lindsay switched his board over to the robot's optics.

The tilted cliff was painted. There were white stripes on it, long peeling dashes, some kind of dividing line. "It's a wreck," he said suddenly. "It's man-made."

"Can't be," Vera said. "It's the size of a major spacecraft. There'd be room in it for thousands."

But then she found something that settled it. A machine was lashed to the smooth clifflike deck of the enormous ship. Centuries had corroded it, but its winged outlines were clear. "It's an aircraft," Pilot said. "It had jets. This was some kind of watery spaceport. Airport, rather."

"A ratfish!" Lindsay exulted. "After it, Vera!"

The surveyor lunged after the abyssal creature. The long-tailed, blunt-headed fish, the size of a man's forearm, darted for safety along the broad deck of the aircraft carrier. It vanished through a ruptured crevice in the multistory wreckage of the control tower. The robot pulled up short. "Wait," Vera said. "If this is a ship, where did the heat come from?"

Pilot examined his instruments. "It's radioactive heat," he said. "Is that unusual?"

"Fission power," Lindsay said. "It must have sunk with an atomic pile on board." Common decency forbade him to mention the possibility of atomic weapons.

Vera said, "My instruments show dissolved organics. Creatures are huddling up around the pile for warmth." She tore at an ancient bulkhead with the pressure-toughened arms of the drone. The corroded alloy burst easily, gushing rust. "Should I go after it?"

"No," Lindsay said. "I want the primeval."

She returned the drone to its hold. They sputtered onward.

Time passed; terrain scrolled by with a slowness he would have once found dreadful. Lindsay found himself thinking again of Czarina-Kluster. Sometimes it troubled him that the despair, the suffering there, meant so little to him. C-K was dying, its elegance dissolving into squalor, its delicate, sophisticated balance ripped apart, pieces flung like seeds throughout the Schismatrix. Was it evil of him to accept the flower's death, in hope of seeds?

He could not think it was. Human time meant nothing to him any longer. He wanted only for his will to leave its mark, to cast its light down those long eons, in a world awakened, a planet brought to irrevocable life. And then . . . then he could let go.

"Here," Pilot said.

They had found it. The craft descended.

Life rose all around them: a jungle in defiance of the sun. In the robot's lights the steep, abrasive valley walls flushed in a vivid panoply of color: scarlet, chalk-white, sulfur-gold, obsidian. Like stands of bamboo, tubeworms swayed on the hillsides, taller than a man. The rocks were thick with clams, their white shells yawning to show flesh as red as blood. Purple sponges pulsed, abyssal corals spread black branching thickets, their thin arms jeweled with polyps.

The water of life gushed from the depths of the valley. Chimneys slimed with metal oxides spewed hot clouds of energized sulfur. The sea floor boiled, wobbling bubbles of steam glinting through a haze of bacteria. The bacteria were central. They were the food chain's fundamental link. Through chemosynthesis, they drew energy from the sulfur itself, scorning the sun to thrive on the heat of the Earth.

Within the warmth and darkness, the valley seethed with life. The rock itself seemed to live, festooned with porous knobs and slimed crevasses, red-black tubes of cold lava-stone coiling like snakes, phallic chimneys of precipitated minerals gleaming copper-green with verdigris. Pale crabs with legs as long as a man's arm kicked daintily across the slopes. Jet-black abyssal fish, grown fat on unexpected bounty, moved with slick langour through the clustered stalks of the tubeworms. Bright yellow jellies, like severed flowerheads, floated in thick eddies of bacterial soup.

"Everything," Lindsay breathed. "I want it all."

Vera pulled away her eyephones; her eyes were flooded with tears. She slumped back in the seat, shaking. "I can't see," she said, her voice hoarse. She handed him the control box. "Please . . . it should be yours, Abelard."

Lindsay strapped on the phones, slipped his fingers into the control slots. Suddenly he was amid it all, the scanners turning with the movements of his head. He extended the sampling arms, extruding the delicate clockwork of the genetics needles. He advanced on the nearest stand of tubeworms. Above the serried white columns of their wrist-thick trunks, their foliage was rank upon waving rank of arm-long feathered red fronds, sweeping with feminine elegance, combing life from the water. Their white stems clustered with sheltered creatures: barnacles, tiny crabs, fringed worms in sea-green and electric blue, round comb jellies glinting in faint pastels.

A predator emerged from the jungle, flowing sinuously around the trunks: a jet-black abyssal fish, leg-sized and flattened like an eel, its sides studded with serried dots of phosphorescence. It approached fearlessly, fascinated by the light. Gills pulsed behind its huge-eyed head and it opened a pale, glowing mouth bristling with fangs. "So," Lindsay addressed it. "You were pressed past the limits, forced into the abyss where nothing grows. But see what you've found. The fat of the system, sundog. Welcome to Paradise." As he spoke he moved the arm toward it; the long needle leaped out, touched it, and withdrew. The fish glowed out in sudden gold and green and flashed away.

He moved to the forest, touching everything he could see, sampling bacteria with gentle suction filters. In half an hour he had filled all his sample capsules and turned back to the ship for more.

Then he saw something detach itself from the hull of the ship. At first he thought it a trick of the light, a ripple of pure reflection. Then he saw it moving toward him, wobbling, fluttering, shapeless, and formless, a jellied mirror, fluid in a silver bag. He heard Vera cry out.

He wrenched his hands from the controls and tore away the eyephones. She was bent over the videoboard, staring. "The Presence! You see it? The Presence!"

It was swimming, with an amoebalike rippling and stretching, deeper into the grove. Lindsay quickly jammed on the eyephones and took up the controls, following it with the robot's lights. Its formless surface threw washes of reflected brilliance over the clams and coral. Lindsay said, "You see it, Pilot?"

Pilot turned the spacecraft to follow it with tracking systems. "I see something. . . . It reflects in every wavelength. What a strange creature. Take a sample of it, Lindsay."

"It's not native. It came with us. I saw it attached to the hull."

"To the hull? It survived raw space? And entry heat? And the pressure of this water? It can't be."

"No?"

"No," the Lobster said. "Because if it was real, I couldn't bear not to *be* it."

"It's showing itself," Vera exulted. "Because of where we are! You see? You see?" She laughed. "It's dancing!"

The thing floated smoothly above one of the smoking chimneys, flattening itself to bathe in the searing updraft of unthinkable pressure and heat. Hot bubbles seethed beneath it, sliding with frictionless ease off its mirrored undersurface. As they watched, it drew itself together into a rippling globe. Then, liquescing with sudden speed, it poured itself through a thumb-sized crevice into the core of the heat vent. It vanished at once.

"I didn't see that," the Lobster insisted. "I didn't see it vanish into the bowels of the Earth. Should we leave now? I mean, maybe we should try to get away from it."

"No," Vera said.

"You're right," Pilot quavered. "That might make it mad."

Vera marveled. "Did you see it? It was *enjoying* this! Even it knows. It knows this is Paradise!" She was trembling. "Abelard, someday, in Europa, this will all be ours, we can touch it, feel it, breathe the water, smell it, taste it! I want it! I want to be out there, like the Presence is. . . ." She was breathing hard, her face radiant. "Abelard . . . if it weren't for you I'd have never known this. . . . Thank you. Thank you, too, Pilot."

"Right, yes, surely," Pilot fluted uneasily. "Lindsay, the drone. Should you bring it in?"

Lindsay smiled. "Don't be afraid, Pilot. It's done you a favor. You've seen the potential. Now you'll have something to aim for."

"But think of the power it must have. It's like a god. . . ."

"Then it's in good company, with us."

Lindsay guided the drone into the specimen hold and unloaded the genetic capsules into their pressure racks. He reloaded its arms and returned to work.

The Presence emerged, ballooning suddenly from a second chimney, beside the drone. It drifted toward him, watching. He waved a claw, but it made no response and soon drifted out of the drone's lights into darkness and invisibility.

The creatures showed no fear of the drone. Vera took over, gently parting the supple stems of the tubeworms to harvest everything she could find. The drone walked the length of the valley oasis, probing the ooze, prying into crevices.

They had a stroke of luck where a new hot spring had broken open, parboiling a colony of creatures clustered above it on an overhang. They used the dead as bait to attract scavengers; they opened them to sample gut bacteria and the agents of decay.

Their sample could not be complete; the oasis was far too rich for that. But their success was still entire. No creature born to the seas of Earth could live, unaltered, in Europa's alien waters. That was the task of Europa's angels, the Lifesiders, who would inherit this genetic treasure, tease it apart, and rebuild new creatures for the new conditions. The living beings here would be models, archetypes in a new Creation, where art and purpose would take the place of a billion years of evolution.

As they packed the robot away for the last time and lifted ship, they saw no sign of the Presence. But Lindsay had no doubt that it was with them.

He was tired as they ascended slowly toward the surface. More than his Shaper favorite or the armored Mechanist, he felt the burden of his hubris heavy on him. Who was he to have done these things? The light had drawn him, and he had grown toward it as a tree might grow, spreading blind leaves toward an unknown radiance. Now he had come to his life's fruition, and he was glad of it. But a tree dies when its roots are cut, and Lindsay knew his roots were his humanity. He was a thing of flesh and blood, of life and death, not an Immanent Will.

A tree drew strength from light, but it was not light itself. And life was a process of changing, but it was not change itself. That was what death was for.

When they saw sunlight flooding just below the surface, Pilot yowled in electronic glee and kicked in the main engines. Steam blasted out in an explosive cratering rosette as the sea recoiled. They broke Mach 1 in seconds. As acceleration crushed them into their seats, Vera strained to see her videoboard and screamed. "The sky! Blue sky! A wall above the world! Pilot, give us space!"

Below them, the sea absorbed the shock, as it did all things. And they were gone.

# THE NEOTENIC CULTURAL REPUBLIC: 8-8-'86

Life moved in clades.

Terraform-Kluster loomed over Mars, shattering red monotony with white steam, green growth, blue nascent seas.

On Venus, death's back was broken, as honest clouds threw lace across the searing, acid-bitten sky.

Ice ships with freshly minted creatures from the labs splashed into Europa, dissolving deep within blood-warm abysses.

On Jupiter the Great Red Spot was breaking up, sloughing off strange blooming clouds of red krill, tiny creatures gathered into shoals and herds bigger than Earth.

At the Neotenic Cultural Republic, Abelard Lindsay decamped from a monstrous spacecraft.

In the free-fall zone he moved easily, with the unconscious grace of extreme age.

But as he moved down the slope inside the cylindrical world, past the hotels and low-grav tourist shops, he leaned more and more heavily on the squat head of his robot companion. The two of them reached level ground, a loamy wilderness with solemn, ancient ranks of trees. The tub-shaped robot nurse nicked a quick blood sample from the nerveless flesh of Lindsay's leg. As they shuffled along the leaf-strewn footpath, the machine fractionated the blood and mumbled over its data.

The Republic had become a place of towering gloom, silence broken by birdcalls, a canopy of foliage cracking mirrored sunlight into dappled shards. Local Neotenics in studiedly antique clothing lounged on lichen-eaten stone benches, while their charges, senile Shapers and obsolescent Mechs, tottered marveling through the woods.

Lindsay paused, gasping as the cuirass pumped his chest beneath his dark blue coat. The baggy legs of his trousers and his sturdy orthopedic shoes hid the prosthetic framework strapped to his wasted legs. Overhead, at the core of the world, an ultralight aircraft spewed a long trail of gray cremated powder over the rich green treetops.

No one approached him. The embroidered squids and angler fish on his coat-sleeves identified him as a CircumEuropan, but he had come incognito.

Catching his breath, Lindsay walked on toward the Tyler mansion and his meeting with Constantine.

The mansion had expanded. Beyond its ivy-shrouded walls, other estates had sprung up, a complex of asylums and retirement wards. Over the years, despite the Preservationists, the outside world had seeped in irresistibly. The Republic's premier industries were hospitals and funerals; rehabilitation for those who could make it, a quiet transition for those who could not.

Lindsay crossed the courtyard of the first hospital. A group of Blood Bathers basked in the sun, waiting with animal patience for their skins to grow again. Beyond that estate was a second, where two young Patternists were surrounded by guards. They scratched at the dirt with twigs, their lopsided heads almost touching. Lindsay saw one of them look up for a moment: the boy's cold eyes had the chilly logic of utter paranoia.

Neatly dressed Neotenic attendants ushered Lindsay through the gates of the Tyler estate. Margaret Juliano had been dead for years. Lindsay recognized the new Director as one of her Superbright students.

The Superbright met him on the lawn. The man's face had the quiet self-possession of Zen Serotonin. "I've cleared your visit with Warden Pongpianskul," he said.

"That was thoughtful," Lindsay said. Neville Pongpianskul was dead, but it was not polite to refer to the fact. Following Ring Council ritual, Pongpianskul had "faded," leaving behind him a programmed web of speeches, announcements, taped appearances, and random telephone calls. The Neotenics had never bothered to replace him as Warden. It saved a lot of trouble all around.

"May I show you through the Museum, sir?" the Superbright asked. "Our last Curator, Alexandrina Tyler, left an unmatched collection of Lindsaiana."

"Later, perhaps. Is Chancellor-General Constantine receiving visitors?"

Constantine was in the rose garden, lying in a lounge chair beside a beehive, staring up into the sun with flat plastic eyes. The years had not been kind to him, despite the best of care. Long years in natural gravity had left his body knotted with muscle, strange knobs and bulges over his delicate bones.

There was no ultraviolet in the mirrored sunlight of the Republic, but nevertheless Constantine had tanned, his ancient naked skin taking on mottled birthmark tinges of purple and blue. He had lost most of his hair, and there were dimpled callosities at strategic points on his skull. The treatments had been thorough and exhaustive. And at last they had succeeded.

Constantine turned as Lindsay creaked carefully toward him. The pupils of his plastic eyes were of different sizes; they irised visibly, struggling for focus. "Abelard? It's you?"

"Yes, Philip." The robot sank down beside the lounge chair; Lindsay sat comfortably on its soft, pulpy head.

"So. How was your trip?"

"It's an old ship," Lindsay said. "A bit like a flying geriatrics ward. They were having a revival of Vetterling's *The White Periapsis.*"

"Hmm. Not his best work."

"You always had good taste, Philip."

Constantine sat up in his chair. "Should I call for a robe? I've looked better, I know."

Lindsay spread his hands. "If you could see beneath this suit. . . . I haven't wasted much money on rejuvenation lately. I'm going for total transformation when I return. It's Europa for me, Philip. The seas."

"Sundogging out from under human limitations?"

"Yes, you could say that. . . . I've brought the plans with me." Lindsay reached inside his coat and produced a brochure. "I want you to look at them with me."

"All right. To please you." Constantine accepted the pamphlet.

The center pages showed an Angel's portrait: an aquatic posthuman. The skin was smooth and black and slick. The legs and pelvic girdle were gone; the spine extended to long muscular flukes. Scarlet gills trailed from the neck. The ribcage was black openwork, gushing white, feathery nets packed with symbiotic bacteria.

The long black arms were dotted with phosphorescent patches, in red and blue and green, keyed into the nervous system. Along the ribs and flukes were two long lateral lines. The nerve-packed stripes housed a new aquatic sense that could feel the water's trembling, like touch at a distance. The nose led to lung-like sacs packed with chemosensitive cells. The lidless eyes were huge, and the skull had been rebuilt to accommodate them.

Constantine moved the brochure before his eyes, struggling to focus. "Very elegant," he said at last. "No intestines."

"Yes. The white nets filter sulfur for bacteria. Each Angel is self-sufficient, drawing life, warmth, everything from the water."

"I see," Constantine said. "Community with anarchy. . . . Do they speak?"

Lindsay leaned forward, pointing to the phosphorescent lights. "They glow."

"And do they reproduce?"

"There are genetics labs. Aquatic ones. Children can be created. But these creatures can last out centuries."

"But where's the sin, Abelard? The lies, the jealousy, the struggle for power?" He smiled. "I suppose they can commit gauche acts of ecosystem design."

"They don't lack ingenuity, Philip. I'm sure they can find crimes if they try hard enough. But they're not like we were. They're not forced to it."

"Forced to it. . . ." A bee landed on Constantine's face. He brushed it gently away. He said, "I went to see the impact site last month." He meant the spot where Vera Kelland had crashed. "There are trees there that look as old as the world."

"It's been a long time."

"I don't know what I expected. . . . Some kind of golden glow, perhaps, some shimmer to show where my heart was buried. But we're small creatures, and the Kosmos doesn't care. There was no sign of it." He sighed. "I wanted to

measure myself against the world. So I killed the thing that might have held me
back."

"We were different people then."

"No. I thought I could make myself different. . . . I thought that with you
dead, you and Vera, I'd be a clean slate, a machine for pure ambition. . . . A bul-
let fired into the head of history. . . . I tried to seize power over love. I wanted
everything bound in iron. And I tried to bind it. But the iron broke first."

"I understand," Lindsay told him. "I've also learned the power of plans. My
life's ambition awaits me in Europa." He took the brochure. "It could be yours,
too. If you want it."

"I told you in my message that I was ready for death," Constantine said.
"You always want to sidestep things, Abelard. We go back a long way together,
too far for words like 'friend' or 'enemy.' . . . I don't know what to call you, but
I know you. I know you better than anyone, better than you know yourself.
When you face the consummation, you'll step aside. I know you will. You'll
never see Europa."

Lindsay bowed his head.

"It has to end, Abelard. I measured myself against the world, that was why
I lived. And I cast a large shadow. Didn't I?"

"Yes, Philip." Lindsay's voice was choked. "Even when I hated you most, I
was proud of you."

"But to measure myself against life and death, as if I could go on forever. . . .
There's no dignity in that. What are we to life? We're only sparks."

"Sparks that start a bonfire, maybe."

"Yes. Europa is your bonfire, and I envy you that. But if you go to Europa
you will lose yourself in it. And you couldn't bear that."

"But you could do it, Philip. It could be yours. Your people will be there.
The Constantine clan."

"My people. Yes. You co-opted them."

"I needed them. I needed your genius. . . . And they came to me willingly."

"Yes. . . . Death defeats us in the end. But our children are our revenge
against it." He smiled. "I tried not to love them. I wanted them to be like me, all
steel and edge. But I loved them anyway . . . not because they were like me, but
because they were different. And the one most different, I loved the best."

"Vera."

"Yes. I created her from the samples I stole here, in the Republic. Flakes of
skin. Genetics from the ones I loved. . . ." He looked at Lindsay pleadingly.
"What can you tell me of her, Abelard? How is your daughter?"

"My daughter. . . ."

"Yes. You and Vera were a splendid pair. . . . It seemed a shame that death
should make you barren. I loved Vera too; I wanted to guard her child, and the
child of the man she chose. So I created your daughter. Was I wrong to do it?"

"No," Lindsay said. "Life is better."

"I gave her everything I could. How is she?"

Lindsay felt dizzy. Beneath him, the robot slid a needle into his unfeeling leg. "She's in the labs now. She is going through the transformation."

"Ah. Good. She makes her own choices. As we all must." Constantine reached beneath his lounge chair. "I have poison here. The attendants gave it to me. They grant us the right to die."

Lindsay nodded in distraction as the drugs calmed his pounding heart. "Yes," he said. "We all deserve that right."

"We could walk out to the impact site together, you and I. And drink the poison. There's enough for two." Constantine smiled. "It would be good to have company."

"No, Philip. Not yet. I'm sorry."

"Still no commitment, Abelard?" Constantine showed him a glass vial filled with brown liquid. "It's just as well. I have trouble walking. I have trouble with all dimensions, since . . . since the Arena. That's why they gave me new eyes. The eyes see dimensions for me." He twisted the top from the vial with gnarled fingers. "I see life for what it is now. That's why I know I must do this." He put the poison to his lips, and drank it down. "Give me your hands."

Lindsay reached out. Constantine gripped his hands. "Both of them are metal now?"

"I'm sorry, Philip."

"No matter. All our beautiful machines . . ." Constantine shuddered briefly. "Bear with me, this won't take long."

"I'm here, Philip."

"Abelard . . . I'm sorry. For Nora. For the cruelty. . . ."

"Philip, it doesn't . . . I forgive. . . ." It was too late. The man had died.

# CIRCUMEUROPA: 25-12-'86

What was left of life in CircumEuropa was clustered in the labs. When Lindsay disembarked, he found customs deserted. CircumEuropa was through; imports no longer mattered.

He followed a snaking hallway through translucent tilted walls of membrane. The corridors glimmered, painted with all the blue-green tints of seawater. They were almost deserted.

Lindsay glimpsed occasional sundogs and squatters, come for junk and loot. A party of them waved politely as they sawed noisily through a hard-set wall. An Investor ship had docked as well, but there was no sign of its crew.

The movement was all outwards. Giant ice ships, hulled in crystal, were arcing down to the planet's surface, for gentle splashdowns through the new crevasses. Vera, his daughter, was aboard one of them. She had already gone.

The population had shrunk to a final handful, the last for the transformation. CircumEuropa had dwindled to a series of labs, where the last transformees floated in smoky Europan seawater.

Lindsay paused outside an airlock, watching the activity within, through a hall-mounted monitor. Transformed surgeons were assisting at the birth of Angels, tracking the growth of new nerves through the altered flesh. Their glowing arms flickered rapidly in conversation.

He had only to don an aqualung, step through that airlock into blood-warm water, and join the others. Vera had done it. So had Gomez and the rest. They would greet him joyfully. There would be no pain. It would be easy.

The past hung balanced on the moment.

He could not do it.

He turned away.

Then he sensed it. "You're here," he said. "Show yourself."

The Presence flowed down from the tilted, sea-green membrane of the wall. A puddle of mirrors trickled across the floor, seeping into shape.

Lindsay watched it in wonder. The Presence had its own gravity; it clung to the floor as if pulled there. It warped and rippled, taking form to please him. It became a small, fleet thing, poised on four legs, crouching like an animal. Like a weasel, he thought. Like a fox.

"She's gone," Lindsay told it. "And you let her go."

"Relax, citizen," the fox told him. Its voice had no echo; it made no sound. "It's not my business to hold on to things."

"Europa's not to your taste?"

"Aw, hell," it said. "I'm sure it's fabulous there, but I've seen the real thing, remember? On Earth. What about you, sundog? I don't see you going for it."

"I'm old," Lindsay said. "They're young. It should be their world. They don't need me."

The creature stretched, rippling. "I thought you'd say as much. What do you say, then? Now that you have a chance for, ah, reflection?"

Lindsay smiled, seeing his own warped face across the shining film of the Presence. "I'm at loose ends."

"Oh, very good." There was laughter in the unheard voice. "I suppose you'll be dying now."

"Should I?" He hesitated. "It might be premature."

"It might," the Presence agreed. "You'll stay here a few more centuries, then? And await the final transcendance?"

"The Fifth Prigoginic Level of Complexity?"

"You could call it that. The words don't matter. It's as far beyond Life as Life is from inert matter. I've seen it happen, many times before. I can feel it moving here, I can smell it in the wind. People . . . creatures, beings, they're all people to me . . . they ask the Final Questions. And they get the Final Answers, and then it's goodbye. It's the Godhead, or as close as makes no difference to the likes of you and me. Maybe that's what you want, sundog? The Absolute?"

"The Absolute," Lindsay mused. "The Final Answers. . . . What are your answers, then, friend?"

"My answers? I don't have 'em. I don't care what goes on beneath this skin, I want only to see, only to feel. Origins and destinies, predictions and memories, lives and deaths, I sidestep those. I'm too slick for time to grip, you get me, sundog?"

"What do you want then, Presence?"

"I want what I already have! Eternal wonder, eternally fulfilled. . . . Not the eternal, even, just the Indefinite, that's where all beauty is. . . . I'll wait out the heat-death of the Universe to see what happens next! And in the meantime, isn't it something, all of it?"

"Yes," Lindsay said. His heart was hammering in his chest. His robot nurse reached for him with a needle-load of soothing chemicals; he turned it off, then laughed and stretched. "It's all very much something."

"I had a fine time here," the Presence said. "It's quite a place you have here, around this little sun."

"Thank you."

"Hey, the thanks are all yours, citizen. But there are other places waiting." The Presence hesitated. "You want to come along?"

"Yes!"

"Then hold me."

He stretched his arms out toward it. It came over him in a silver wave. Stellar cold, a melting, a release.

And all things were fresh and new.

He saw his clothes floating within the hallway. His arms drifted out of the sleeves, prosthetics trailing leashes of expensive circuitry. Atop its clean white ladder of vertebrae, his empty skull sank grinning into the collar of his coat.

An Investor appeared at the end of the hall, bounding along in free-fall. Reflexively, Lindsay smeared himself out of sight against the wall. The Investor's frill lifted; it pawed with magpie attraction through the tangle of bones, stuffing items of interest into a swollen bag.

"They're always around to pick up the pieces," the Presence commented. "They're useful to us. You'll see."

Lindsay perceived his new self. "I don't have any hands," he said.

"You won't need 'em." The Presence laughed. "C'mon, we'll follow him. They'll be going someplace soon."

They trailed the Investor down the hall. "Where?" Lindsay said.

"It doesn't matter. Somewhere wonderful."

# Shaper/Mechanist
# Stories

# Swarm

"**I will miss** your conversation during the rest of the voyage," the alien said.

Captain-Doctor Simon Afriel folded his jeweled hands over his gold-embroidered waistcoat. "I regret it also, ensign," he said in the alien's own hissing language. "Our talks together have been very useful to me. I would have paid to learn so much, but you gave it freely."

"But that was only information," the alien said. He shrouded his bead-bright eyes behind thick nictitating membranes. "We Investors deal in energy, and precious metals. To prize and pursue mere knowledge is an immature racial trait." The alien lifted the long ribbed frill behind his pinhole-sized ears.

"No doubt you are right," Afriel said, despising him. "We humans are as children to other races, however; so a certain immaturity seems natural to us." Afriel pulled off his sunglasses to rub the bridge of his nose. The starship cabin was drenched in searing blue light, heavily ultraviolet. It was the light the Investors preferred, and they were not about to change it for one human passenger.

"You have not done badly," the alien said magnanimously. "You are the kind of race we like to do business with: young, eager, plastic, ready for a wide variety of goods and experiences. We would have contacted you much earlier, but your technology was still too feeble to afford us a profit."

"Things are different now," Afriel said. "We'll make you rich."

"Indeed," the Investor said. The frill behind his scaly head flickered rapidly, a sign of amusement. "Within two hundred years you will be wealthy enough to buy from us the secret of our starflight. Or perhaps your Mechanist faction will discover the secret through research."

Afriel was annoyed. As a member of the Reshaped faction, he did not appreciate the reference to the rival Mechanists. "Don't put too much stock in mere technical expertise," he said. "Consider the aptitude for languages we

Shapers have. It makes our faction a much better trading partner. To a Mechanist, all Investors look alike."

The alien hesitated. Afriel smiled. He had appealed to the alien's personal ambition with his last statement, and the hint had been taken. That was where the Mechanists always erred. They tried to treat all Investors consistently, using the same programmed routines each time. They lacked imagination.

Something would have to be done about the Mechanists, Afriel thought. Something more permanent than the small but deadly confrontations between isolated ships in the Asteroid Belt and the ice-rich Rings of Saturn. Both factions maneuvered constantly, looking for a decisive stroke, bribing away each other's best talent, practicing ambush, assassination, and industrial espionage.

Captain-Doctor Simon Afriel was a past master of these pursuits. That was why the Reshaped faction had paid the millions of kilowatts necessary to buy his passage. Afriel held doctorates in biochemistry and alien linguistics, and a master's degree in magnetic weapons engineering. He was thirty-eight years old and had been Reshaped according to the state of the art at the time of his conception. His hormonal balance had been altered slightly to compensate for long periods spent in free-fall. He had no appendix. The structure of his heart had been redesigned for greater efficiency, and his large intestine had been altered to produce the vitamins normally made by intestinal bacteria. Genetic engineering and rigorous training in childhood had given him an intelligence quotient of one hundred and eighty. He was not the brightest of the agents of the Ring Council, but he was one of the most mentally stable and the best trusted.

"It seems a shame," the alien said, "that a human of your accomplishments should have to rot for two years in this miserable, profitless outpost."

"The years won't be wasted," Afriel said.

"But why have you chosen to study the Swarm? They can teach you nothing, since they cannot speak. They have no wish to trade, having no tools or technology. They are the only spacefaring race that is essentially without intelligence."

"That alone should make them worthy of study."

"Do you seek to imitate them, then? You would make monsters of yourselves." Again the ensign hesitated. "Perhaps you could do it. It would be bad for business, however."

There came a fluting burst of alien music over the ship's speakers, then a screeching fragment of Investor language. Most of it was too high-pitched for Afriel's ears to follow.

The alien stood, his jeweled skirt brushing the tips of his clawed birdlike feet. "The Swarm's symbiote has arrived," he said.

"Thank you," Afriel said. When the ensign opened the cabin door, Afriel could smell the Swarm's representative; the creature's warm yeasty scent had spread rapidly through the starship's recycled air.

Afriel quickly checked his appearance in a pocket mirror. He touched powder to his face and straightened the round velvet hat on his shoulder-length reddish-blond hair. His earlobes glittered with red impact-rubies, thick as his thumbs' ends, mined from the Asteroid Belt. His knee-length coat and waistcoat were of gold brocade; the shirt beneath was of dazzling fineness, woven with red-gold thread. He had dressed to impress the Investors, who expected and appreciated a prosperous look from their customers. How could he impress this new alien? Smell, perhaps. He freshened his perfume.

Beside the starship's secondary airlock, the Swarm's symbiote was chittering rapidly at the ship's commander. The commander was an old and sleepy Investor, twice the size of most of her crewmen. Her massive head was encrusted in a jeweled helmet. From within the helmet her clouded eyes glittered like cameras.

The symbiote lifted on its six posterior legs and gestured feebly with its four clawed forelimbs. The ship's artificial gravity, a third again as strong as Earth's, seemed to bother it. Its rudimentary eyes, dangling on stalks, were shut tight against the glare. It must be used to darkness, Afriel thought.

The commander answered the creature in its own language. Afriel grimaced, for he had hoped that the creature spoke Investor. Now he would have to learn another language, a language designed for a being without a tongue.

After another brief interchange the commander turned to Afriel. "The symbiote is not pleased with your arrival," she told Afriel in the Investor language. "There has apparently been some disturbance here involving humans, in the recent past. However, I have prevailed upon it to admit you to the Nest. The episode has been recorded. Payment for my diplomatic services will be arranged with your faction when I return to your native star system."

"I thank Your Authority," Afriel said. "Please convey to the symbiote my best personal wishes, and the harmlessness and humility of my intentions. . . ." He broke off short as the symbiote lunged toward him, biting him savagely in the calf of his left leg. Afriel jerked free and leapt backward in the heavy artificial gravity, going into a defensive position. The symbiote had ripped away a long shred of his pants leg; it now crouched quietly, eating it.

"It will convey your scent and composition to its nestmates," said the commander. "This is necessary. Otherwise you would be classed as an invader, and the Swarm's warrior caste would kill you at once."

Afrial relaxed quickly and pressed his hand against the puncture wound to stop the bleeding. He hoped that none of the Investors had noticed his reflexive action. It would not mesh well with his story of being a harmless researcher.

"We will reopen the airlock soon," the commander said phlegmatically, leaning back on her thick reptilian tail. The symbiote continued to munch the shred of cloth. Afriel studied the creature's neckless segmented head. It had a mouth and nostrils; it had bulbous atrophied eyes on stalks; there were hinged slats that might be radio receivers, and two parallel ridges of clumped wriggling antennae, sprouting among three chitinous plates. Their function was unknown to him.

The airlock door opened. A rush of dense, smoky aroma entered the departure cabin. It seemed to bother the half-dozen Investors, who left rapidly. "We will return in six hundred and twelve of your days, as by our agreement," the commander said.

"I thank Your Authority," Afriel said.

"Good luck," the commander said in English. Afriel smiled.

The symbiote, with a sinuous wriggle of its segmented body, crept into the airlock. Afriel followed it. The airlock shut behind them. The creature said nothing to him but continued munching loudly. The second door opened, and the symbiote sprang through it, into a wide, round stone tunnel. It disappeared at once into the gloom.

Afriel put his sunglasses into a pocket of his jacket and pulled out a pair of infrared goggles. He strapped them to his head and stepped out of the airlock. The artificial gravity vanished, replaced by the almost imperceptible gravity of the Swarm's asteroid nest. Afriel smiled, comfortable for the first time in weeks. Most of his adult life had been spent in free-fall, in the Shapers' colonies in the Rings of Saturn.

Squatting in a dark cavity in the side of the tunnel was a disk-headed furred animal the size of an elephant. It was clearly visible in the infrared of its own body heat. Afriel could hear it breathing. It waited patiently until Afriel had launched himself past it, deeper into the tunnel. Then it took its place in the end of the tunnel, puffing itself up with air until its swollen head securely plugged the exit into space. Its multiple legs sank firmly into sockets in the walls.

The Investors' ship had left. Afriel remained here, inside one of the millions of planetoids that circled the giant star Betelgeuse in a girdling ring with almost five times the mass of Jupiter. As a source of potential wealth it dwarfed the entire solar system, and it belonged, more or less, to the Swarm. At least, no other race had challenged them for it within the memory of the Investors.

Afriel peered up the corridor. It seemed deserted, and without other bodies to cast infrared heat, he could not see very far. Kicking against the wall, he floated hesitantly down the corridor.

He heard a human voice. "Dr. Afriel!"

"Dr. Mirny!" he called out. "This way!"

He first saw a pair of young symbiotes scuttling toward him, the tips of their clawed feet barely touching the walls. Behind them came a woman wearing goggles like his own. She was young, and attractive in the trim, anonymous way of the genetically reshaped.

She screeched something at the symbiotes in their own language, and they halted, waiting. She coasted forward, and Afriel caught her arm, expertly stopping their momentum.

"You didn't bring any luggage?" she said anxiously.

He shook his head. "We got your warning before I was sent out. I have only the clothes I'm wearing and a few items in my pockets."

She looked at him critically. "Is that what people are wearing in the Rings these days? Things have changed more than I thought."

Afriel glanced at his brocaded coat and laughed. "It's a matter of policy. The Investors are always readier to talk to a human who looks ready to do business on a large scale. All the Shapers' representatives dress like this these days. We've stolen a jump on the Mechanists; they still dress in those coveralls."

He hesitated, not wanting to offend her. Galina Mirny's intelligence was rated at almost two hundred. Men and women that bright were sometimes flighty and unstable, likely to retreat into private fantasy worlds or become enmeshed in strange and inpenetrable webs of plotting and rationalization. High intelligence was the strategy the Shapers had chosen in the struggle for cultural dominance, and they were obliged to stick to it, despite its occasional disadvantages. They had tried breeding the Superbright—those with quotients over two hundred—but so many had defected from the Shapers' colonies that the faction had stopped producing them.

"You wonder about my own clothing," Mirny said.

"It certainly has the appeal of novelty," Afriel said with a smile.

"It was woven from the fibers of a pupa's cocoon," she said. "My original wardrobe was eaten by a scavenger symbiote during the troubles last year. I usually go nude, but I didn't want to offend you by too great a show of intimacy."

Afriel shrugged. "I often go nude myself, I never had much use for clothes except for pockets. I have a few tools on my person, but most are of little importance. We're Shapers, our tools are here." He tapped his head. "If you can show me a safe place to put my clothes. . . ."

She shook her head. It was impossible to see her eyes for the goggles, which made her expression hard to read. "You've made your first mistake, Doctor. There are no places of our own here. It was the same mistake the Mechanist agents made, the same one that almost killed me as well. There is no concept of privacy or property here. This is the Nest. If you seize any part of it for yourself—to store equipment, to sleep in, whatever—then you become an intruder, an enemy. The two Mechanists—a man and a woman—tried to secure an empty chamber for their computer lab. Warriors broke down their door and devoured them. Scavengers ate their equipment, glass, metal, and all."

Afriel smiled coldly. "It must have cost them a fortune to ship all that material here."

Mirny shrugged. "They're wealthier than we are. Their machines, their mining. They meant to kill me, I think. Surreptitiously, so the warriors wouldn't be upset by a show of violence. They had a computer that was learning the language of the springtails faster than I could."

"But you survived," Afriel pointed out. "And your tapes and reports—especially the early ones, when you still had most of your equipment—were of tremendous interest. The Council is behind you all the way. You've become quite a celebrity in the Rings, during your absence."

"Yes, I expected as much," she said.

Afriel was nonplused. "If I found any deficiency in them," he said carefully, "it was in my own field, alien linguistics." He waved vaguely at the two symbiotes who accompanied her. "I assume you've made great progress in communicating with the symbiotes, since they seem to do all the talking for the Nest."

She looked at him with an unreadable expression and shrugged. "There are at least fifteen different kinds of symbiotes here. Those that accompany me are called the springtails, and they speak only for themselves. They are savages, Doctor, who received attention from the Investors only because they can still talk. They were a spacefaring race once, but they've forgotten it. They discovered the Nest and they were absorbed, they became parasites." She tapped one of them on the head. "I tamed these two because I learned to steal and beg food better than they can. They stay with me now and protect me from the larger ones. They are jealous, you know. They have only been with the Nest for perhaps ten thousand years and are still uncertain of their position. They still think, and wonder sometimes. After ten thousand years there is still a little of that left to them."

"Savages," Afriel said. "I can well believe that. One of them bit me while I was still aboard the starship. He left a lot to be desired as an ambassador."

"Yes, I warned him you were coming," said Mirny. "He didn't much like the idea, but I was able to bribe him with food. . . . I hope he didn't hurt you badly."

"A scratch," Afriel said. "I assume there's no chance of infection."

"I doubt it very much. Unless you brought your own bacteria with you."

"Hardly likely," Afriel said, offended. "I have no bacteria. And I wouldn't have brought microorganisms to an alien culture anyway."

Mirny looked away. "I thought you might have some of the special genetically altered ones. . . . I think we can go now. The springtail will have spread your scent by mouth-touching in the subsidiary chamber, ahead of us. It will be spread throughout the Nest in a few hours. Once it reaches the Queen, it will spread very quickly."

She jammed her feet against the hard shell of one of the young springtails and launched herself down the hall. Afriel followed her. The air was warm and he was beginning to sweat under his elaborate clothing, but his antiseptic sweat was odorless.

They exited into a vast chamber dug from the living rock. It was arched and oblong, eighty meters long and about twenty in diameter. It swarmed with members of the Nest.

There were hundreds of them. Most of them were workers, eight-legged and furred, the size of Great Danes. Here and there were members of the warrior caste, horse-sized furry monsters with heavy fanged heads the size and shape of overstuffed chairs.

A few meters away, two workers were carrying a member of the sensor caste, a being whose immense flattened head was attached to an atrophied body that was mostly lungs. The sensor had great platelike eyes, and its furred chitin sprouted long coiled antennae that twitched feebly as the workers bore it along. The workers clung to the hollowed rock of the chamber walls with hooked and suckered feet.

A paddle-limbed monster with a hairless, faceless head came sculling past them, through the warm reeking air. The front of its head was a nightmare of sharp grinding jaws and blunt armored acid spouts. "A tunneler," Mirny said. "It can take us deeper into the Nest—come with me." She launched herself toward it and took a handhold on its furry, segmented back. Afriel followed her, joined by the two immature springtails, who clung to the thing's hide with their forelimbs. Afriel shuddered at the warm, greasy feel of its rank, damp fur. It continued to scull through the air, its eight fringed paddle feet catching the air like wings.

"There must be thousands of them," Afriel said.

"I said a hundred thousand in my last report, but that was before I had fully explored the Nest. Even now there are long stretches I haven't seen. They must number close to a quarter of a million. This asteroid is about the size of the Mechanists' biggest base—Ceres. It still has rich veins of carbonaceous material. It's far from mined out."

Afriel closed his eyes. If he was to lose his goggles, he would have to feel his way, blind, through these teeming, twitching, wriggling thousands. "The population's still expanding, then?"

"Definitely," she said. "In fact, the colony will launch a mating swarm soon. There are three dozen male and female alates in the chambers near the Queen. Once they're launched, they'll mate and start new Nests. I'll take you to see them presently." She hesitated. "We're entering one of the fungal gardens now."

One of the young springtails quietly shifted position. Grabbing the tunneler's fur with its forelimbs, it began to gnaw on the cuff of Afriel's pants. Afriel kicked it soundly, and it jerked back, retracting its eyestalks.

When he looked up again, he saw that they had entered a second chamber, much larger than the first. The walls around, overhead, and below were buried under an explosive profusion of fungus. The most common types were swollen barrellike domes, multibranched massed thickets, and spaghettilike tangled extrusions that moved very slightly in the faint and odorous breeze. Some of the barrels were surrounded by dim mists of exhaled spores.

"You see those caked-up piles beneath the fungus, its growth medium?" Mirny said.

"Yes."

"I'm not sure whether it is a plant form or just some kind of complex biochemical sludge," she said. "The point is that it grows in sunlight, on the outside of the asteroid. A food source that grows in naked space! Imagine what that would be worth, back in the Rings."

"There aren't words for its value," Afriel said.

"It's inedible by itself," she said. "I tried to eat a very small piece of it once. It was like trying to eat plastic."

"Have you eaten well, generally speaking?"

"Yes. Our biochemistry is quite similar to the Swarm's. The fungus itself is perfectly edible. The regurgitate is more nourishing, though. Internal fermentation in the worker hindgut adds to its nutritional value."

Afriel stared. "You grow used to it," Mirny said. "Later I'll teach you how to solicit food from the workers. It's a simple matter of reflex tapping—it's not controlled by pheromones, like most of their behavior." She brushed a long lock of clumped and dirty hair from the side of her face. "I hope the pheromonal samples I sent back were worth the cost of transportation."

"Oh, yes," said Afriel. "The chemistry of them was fascinating. We managed to synthesize most of the compounds. I was part of the research team myself." He hesitated. How far did he dare trust her? She had not been told about the experiment he and his superiors had planned. As far as Mirny knew, he was a simple, peaceful researcher, like herself. The Shapers' scientific community was suspicious of the minority involved in military work and espionage.

As an investment in the future, the Shapers had sent researchers to each of the nineteen alien races described to them by the Investors. This had cost the Shaper economy many gigawatts of precious energy and tons of rare metals and isotopes. In most cases, only two or three researchers could be sent; in seven cases, only one. For the Swarm, Galina Mirny had been chosen. She had gone peacefully, trusting in her intelligence and her good intentions to keep her alive and sane. Those who had sent her had not known whether her findings would be of any use or importance. They had only known that it was imperative that she be sent, even alone, even ill-equipped, before some other faction sent their own people and possibly discovered some technique or fact of overwhelming importance. And Dr. Mirny had indeed discovered such a situation. It had made her mission into a matter of Ring security. That was why Afriel had come.

"You synthesized the compounds?" she said. "Why?"

Afriel smiled disarmingly. "Just to prove to ourselves that we could do it, perhaps."

She shook her head. "No mind-games, Dr. Afriel, please. I came this far partly to escape from such things. Tell me the truth."

Afriel stared at her, regretting that the goggles meant he could not meet her eyes. "Very well," he said. "You should know then, that I have been ordered by the Ring Council to carry out an experiment that may endanger both our lives."

Mirny was silent for a moment. "You're from Security, then?"

"My rank is captain."

"I knew it. . . . I knew it when those two Mechanists arrived. They were so polite, and so suspicious—I think they would have killed me at once if they hadn't hoped to bribe or torture some secret out of me. They scared the life out of me, Captain Afriel. . . . You scare me, too."

"We live in a frightening world, Doctor. It's a matter of faction security."

"Everything's a matter of faction security with your lot," she said. "I shouldn't take you any farther, or show you anything more. This Nest, these creatures—they're not *intelligent,* Captain. They can't think, they can't learn. They're innocent, primordially innocent. They have no knowledge of good and evil. They had no knowledge of *anything.* The last thing they need is to become pawns in a power struggle within some other race, light-years away."

The tunneler had turned into an exit from the fungal chambers and was paddling slowly along in the warm darkness. A group of creatures like gray, flattened basketballs floated by from the opposite direction. One of them settled on Afriel's sleeve, clinging with frail whiplike tentacles. Afriel brushed it gently away, and it broke loose, emitting a stream of foul reddish droplets.

"Naturally I agree with you in principle, Doctor," Afriel said smoothly. "But consider these Mechanists. Some of their extreme factions are already more than half machine. Do you expect humanitarian motives from them? They're cold, Doctor—cold and soulless creatures who can cut a living man or woman to bits and never feel their pain. Most of the other factions hate us. They call us racist supermen. Would you rather that one of these cults do what we must do, and use the results against us?"

"This is double-talk." She looked away. All around them workers laden down with fungus, their jaws full and guts stuffed with it, were spreading out into the Nest, scuttling alongside them or disappearing into branch tunnels departing in every direction, including straight up and straight down. Afriel saw a creature much like a worker, but with only six legs, scuttle past in the opposite direction, overhead. It was a parasite mimic. How long, he wondered, did it take a creature to evolve to look like that?"

"It's no wonder that we've had so many defectors, back in the Rings," she said sadly. "If humanity is so stupid as to work itself into a corner like you describe, then it's better to have nothing to do with them. Better to live alone. Better not to help the madness spread."

"That kind of talk will only get us killed," Afriel said. "We owe an allegiance to the faction that produced us."

"Tell me truly, Captain," she said. "Haven't you ever felt the urge to leave everything—everyone—all your duties and constraints, and just go somewhere to think it all out? Your whole world, and your part in it? We're trained so hard, from childhood, and so much is demanded from us. Don't you think it's made us lose sight of our goals, somehow?"

"We live in space," Afriel said flatly. "Space is an unnatural environment, and it takes an unnatural effort from unnatural people to prosper there. Our minds are our tools, and philosophy has to come second. Naturally I've felt those urges you mention. They're just another threat to guard against. I believe in an ordered society. Technology has unleashed tremendous forces that are ripping society apart. Some one faction must arise from the struggle and integrate things. We Shapers have the wisdom and restraint to do it humanely. That's why I do the work I do." He hesitated. "I don't expect to see our day of triumph. I expect to die in some brush-fire conflict, or through assassination. It's enough that I can foresee that day."

"But the arrogance of it, Captain!" she said suddenly. "The arrogance of your little life and its little sacrifice! Consider the Swarm, if you really want your humane and perfect order. Here it is! Where it's always warm and dark, and it smells good, and food is easy to get, and everything is endlessly and perfectly recycled. The only resources that are ever lost are the bodies of the mating swarms, and a little air. A Nest like this one could last unchanged for hundreds of thousands of years. Hundreds . . . of thousands . . . of years. Who, or what, will remember us and our stupid faction in even a thousand years?"

Afriel shook his head. "That's not a valid comparison. There is no such long view for us. In another thousand years we'll be machines, or gods." He felt the top of his head; his velvet cap was gone. No doubt something was eating it by now.

The tunneler took them deeper into the asteroid's honeycombed free-fall maze. They saw the pupal chambers, where pallid larvae twitched in swaddled silk; the main fungal gardens; the graveyard pits, where winged workers beat ceaselessly at the soupy air, feverishly hot from the heat of decomposition. Corrosive black fungus ate the bodies of the dead into coarse black powder, carried off by blackened workers themselves three-quarters dead.

Later they left the tunneler and floated on by themselves. The woman moved with the ease of long habit; Afriel followed her, colliding bruisingly with squeaking workers. There were thousands of them, clinging to ceiling, walls, and floor, clustering and scurrying at every conceivable angle.

Later still they visited the chamber of the winged princes and princesses, an echoing round vault where creatures forty meters long hung crooked-legged in midair. Their bodies were segmented and metallic, with organic rocket nozzles on their thoraxes, where wings might have been. Folded along their sleek backs were radar antennae on long sweeping booms. They looked more like interplanetary probes under construction than anything biological. Workers fed them ceaselessly. Their bulging spiracled abdomens were full of compressed oxygen.

Mirny begged a large chunk of fungus from a passing worker, deftly tapping its antennae and provoking a reflex action. She handed most of the fungus to the two springtails, which devoured it greedily and looked expectantly for more.

Afriel tucked his legs into a free-fall lotus position and began chewing with determination on the leathery fungus. It was tough, but tasted good, like smoked meat—a delicacy he had tasted only once. The smell of smoke meant disaster in a Shaper's colony.

Mirny maintained a stony silence. "Food's no problem," Afriel said. "Where do we sleep?"

She shrugged. "Anywhere . . . there are unused niches and tunnels here and there. I suppose you'll want to see the Queen's chamber next."

"By all means."

"I'll have to get more fungus. The warriors are on guard there and have to be bribed with food."

She gathered an armful of fungus from another worker in the endless stream, and they moved on. Afriel, already totally lost, was further confused in the maze of chambers and tunnels. At last they exited into an immense lightless cavern, bright with infrared heat from the Queen's monstrous body. It was the colony's central factory. The fact that it was made of warm and pulpy flesh did not conceal its essentially industrial nature. Tons of predigested fungal pap went into the slick blind jaws at one end. The rounded billows of soft flesh digested and processed it, squirming, sucking, and undulating, with loud machinelike churnings and gurglings. Out of the other end came an endless conveyorlike blobbed stream of eggs, each one packed in a thick hormonal paste of lubrication. The workers avidly licked the eggs clean and bore them off to nurseries. Each egg was the size of a man's torso.

The process went on and on. There was no day or night here in the lightless center of the asteroid. There was no remnant of a diurnal rhythm in the genes of these creatures. The flow of production was as constant and even as the working of an automated mine.

"This is why I'm here," Afriel murmured in awe. "Just look at this, Doctor. The Mechanists have cybernetic mining machinery that is generations ahead of ours. But here—in the bowels of this nameless little world, is a genetic technology that feeds itself, maintains itself, runs itself, efficiently, endlessly, mindlessly. It's the perfect organic tool. The faction that could use these tireless workers could make itself an industrial titan. And our knowledge of biochemistry is unsurpassed. We Shapers are just the ones to do it."

"How do you propose to do that?" Mirny asked with open skepticism. "You would have to ship a fertilized queen all the way to the solar system. We could scarcely afford that, even if the Investors would let us, which they wouldn't."

"I don't need an entire Nest," Afriel said patiently. "I only need the genetic information from one egg. Our laboratories back in the Rings could clone endless numbers of workers."

"But the workers are useless without the Nest's pheromones. They need chemical cues to trigger their behavior modes."

"Exactly," Afriel said. "As it so happens, I possess those pheromones, synthesized and concentrated. What I must do now is test them. I must prove that I can use them to make the workers do what I choose. Once I've proven it's possible, I'm authorized to smuggle the genetic information necessary back to the Rings. The Investors won't approve. There are, of course, moral questions involved, and the Investors are not genetically advanced. But we can win their approval back with the profits we make. Best of all, we can beat the Mechanists at their own game."

"You've carried the pheromones here?" Mirny said. "Didn't the Investors suspect something when they found them?"

"Now it's you who has made an error," Afriel said calmly. "You assume that the Investors are infallible. You are wrong. A race without curiosity will never explore every possibility, the way we Shapers did." Afriel pulled up his pants cuff and extended his right leg. "Consider this varicose vein along my shin. Circulatory problems of this sort are common among those who spend a lot of time in free-fall. This vein, however, has been blocked artificially and treated to reduce osmosis. Within the vein are ten separate colonies of genetically altered bacteria, each one specially bred to produce a different Swarm pheromone."

He smiled. "The Investors searched me very thoroughly, including X-rays. But the vein appears normal to X-rays, and the bacteria are trapped within compartments in the vein. They are indetectable. I have a small medical kit on my person. It includes a syringe. We can use it to extract the pheromones and test them. When the tests are finished—and I feel sure they will be successful, in fact I've staked my career on it—we can empty the vein and all its compartments. The bacteria will die on contact with air. We can refill the vein with the yolk from a developing embryo. The cells may survive during the trip back, but even if they die, they can't rot inside my body. They'll never come in contact with any agent of decay. Back in the Rings, we can learn to activate and suppress different genes to produce the different castes, just as is done in nature. We'll have millions of workers, armies of warriors if need be, perhaps even organic rocketships, grown from altered alates. If this works, who do you think will remember me then, eh? Me and my arrogant little life and little sacrifice?"

She stared at him; even the bulky goggles could not hide her new respect and even fear. "You really mean to do it, then."

"I made the sacrifice of my time and energy. I expect results, Doctor."

"But it's kidnapping. You're talking about breeding a slave race."

Afriel shrugged, with contempt. "You're juggling words, Doctor. I'll cause this colony no harm. I may steal some of its workers' labor while they obey my own chemical orders, but that tiny theft won't be missed. I admit to the murder of one egg, but that is no more a crime than a human abortion. Can the theft of one strand of genetic material be called 'kidnapping'? I think not. As for the scandalous idea of a slave race—I reject it out of hand. These creatures are genetic robots. They will no more be slaves than are laser drills or cargo tankers. At the very worst, they will be our domestic animals."

Mirny considered the issue. It did not take her long. "It's true. It's not as if a common worker will be staring at the stars, pining for its freedom. They're just brainless neuters."

"Exactly, Doctor."

"They simply work. Whether they work for us or the Swarm makes no difference to them."

"I see that you've seized on the beauty of the idea."

"And if it worked," Mirny said, "if it worked, our faction would profit astronomically."

Afriel smiled genuinely, unaware of the chilling sarcasm of his expression. "And the personal profit, Doctor . . . the valuable expertise of the first to exploit the technique." He spoke gently, quietly. "Ever see a nitrogen snowfall on Titan? I think a habitat of one's own there—larger, much larger than anything possible before. . . . A genuine city, Galina, a place where a man can scrap the rules and discipline that madden him. . . ."

"Now it's you who are talking defection, Captain-Doctor."

Afriel was silent for a moment, then smiled with an effort. "Now you've ruined my perfect reverie," he said. "Besides, what I was describing was the well-earned retirement of a wealthy man, not some self-indulgent hermitage . . . there's a clear difference." He hesitated. "In any case, may I conclude that you're with me in this project?"

She laughed and touched his arm. There was something uncanny about the small sound of her laugh, drowned by a great organic rumble from the Queen's monstrous intestines. . . . "Do you expect me to resist your arguments for two long years? Better that I give in now and save us friction."

"Yes."

"After all, you won't do any harm to the Nest. They'll never know anything has happened. And if their genetic line is successfully reproduced back home, there'll never be any reason for humanity to bother them again."

"True enough," said Afriel, though in the back of his mind he instantly thought of the fabulous wealth of Betelgeuse's asteroid system. A day would come, inevitably, when humanity would move to the stars en masse, in earnest. It would be well to know the ins and outs of every race that might become a rival.

"I'll help you as best I can," she said. There was a moment's silence. "Have you seen enough of this area?"

"Yes." They left the Queen's chamber.

"I didn't think I'd like you at first," she said candidly. "I think I like you better now. You seem to have a sense of humor that most Security people lack."

"It's not a sense of humor," Afriel said sadly. "It's a sense of irony disguised as one."

There were no days in the unending stream of hours that followed. There were only ragged periods of sleep, apart at first, later together, as they held each other in free-fall. The sexual feel of skin and body became an anchor to their common humanity, a divided, frayed humanity so many light-years away that the concept no longer had any meaning. Life in the warm and swarming tunnels was the here and now; the two of them were like germs in a bloodstream, moving ceaselessly with the pulsing ebb and flow. Hours stretched into months, and time itself grew meaningless.

The pheromonal tests were complex, but not impossibly difficult. The first of the ten pheromones was a simple grouping stimulus, causing large numbers of workers to gather as the chemical was spread from palp to palp. The workers then waited for further instructions; if none were forthcoming, they dispersed. To work effectively, the pheromones had to be given in a mix, or series, like computer commands; number one, grouping, for instance, together with the third pheromone, a transferral order, which caused the workers to empty any given chamber and move its effects to another. The ninth pheromone had the best industrial possibilities; it was a building order, causing the workers to gather tunnelers and dredgers and set them to work. Others were annoying; the tenth pheromone provoked grooming behavior, and the workers' furry palps stripped off the remaining rags of Afriel's clothing. The eighth pheromone sent the workers off to harvest material on the asteroid's surface, and in their eagerness to observe its effects the two explorers were almost trapped and swept off into space.

The two of them no longer feared the warrior caste. They knew that a dose of the sixth pheromone would send them scurrying off to defend the eggs, just as it sent the workers to tend them. Mirny and Afriel took advantage of this and secured their own chambers, dug by chemically hijacked workers and defended by a hijacked airlock guardian. They had their own fungal gardens to refresh the air, stocked with the fungus they liked best, and digested by a worker they kept drugged for their own food use. From constant stuffing and lack of exercise the worker had swollen up into its replete form and hung from one wall like a monstrous grape.

Afriel was tired. He had been without sleep recently for a long time; how long, he didn't know. His body rhythms had not adjusted as well as Mirny's, and he was prone to fits of depression and irritability that he had to repress with an effort. "The Investors will be back sometime," he said. "Sometime soon."

Mirny was indifferent. "The Investors," she said, and followed the remark with something in the language of the springtails, which he didn't catch. Despite his linguistic training, Afriel had never caught up with her in her use of the springtails' grating jargon. His training was almost a liability; the springtail language had decayed so much that it was a pidgin tongue, without rules or regularity. He knew enough to give them simple orders, and with his partial control of the warriors he had the power to back it up. The springtails were afraid of him, and the two juveniles that Mirny had tamed had developed into fat, overgrown tyrants that freely terrorized their elders. Afriel had been too busy to seriously study the springtails or the other symbiotes. There were too many practical matters at hand.

"If they come too soon, I won't be able to finish my latest study," she said in English.

Afriel pulled off his infrared goggles and knotted them tightly around his neck. "There's a limit, Galina," he said, yawning. "You can only memorize so much data without equipment. We'll just have to wait quietly until we can get back. I hope the Investors aren't shocked when they see me. I lost a fortune with those clothes."

"It's been so dull since the mating swarm was launched. If it weren't for the new growth in the alates' chamber, I'd be bored to death." She pushed greasy hair from her face with both hands. "Are you going to sleep?"

"Yes, if I can."

"You won't come with me? I keep telling you that this new growth is important. I think it's a new caste. It's definitely not an alate. It has eyes like an alate, but it's clinging to the wall."

"It's probably not a Swarm member at all, then," he said tiredly, humoring her. "It's probably a parasite, an alate mimic. Go on and see it, if you want to. I'll be waiting for you."

He heard her leave. Without his infrareds on, the darkness was still not quite total; there was a very faint luminosity from the steaming, growing fungus in the chamber beyond. The stuffed worker replete moved slightly on the wall, rustling and gurgling. He fell asleep.

• • •

When he awoke, Mirny had not yet returned. He was not alarmed. First, he visited the original airlock tunnel, where the Investors had first left him. It was irrational—the Investors always fulfilled their contracts—but he feared that they would arrive someday, become impatient, and leave without him. The Investors would have to wait, of course. Mirny could keep them occupied in the short time it would take him to hurry to the nursery and rob a developing egg of its living cells. It was best that the egg be as fresh as possible.

Later he ate. He was munching fungus in one of the anterior chambers when Mirny's two tamed springtails found him. "What do you want?" he asked in their language.

"Food-giver no good," the larger one screeched, waving its forelegs in brainless agitation. "Not work, not sleep."

"Not move," the second one said. It added hopefully, "Eat it now?"

Afriel gave them some of his food. They ate it, seemingly more out of habit than real appetite, which alarmed him.

"Take me to her," he told them.

The two springtails scurried off; he followed them easily, adroitly dodging and weaving through the crowds of workers. They led him several miles through the network, to the alates' chamber. There they stopped, confused. "Gone," the large one said.

The chamber was empty. Afriel had never seen it empty before, and it was very unusual for the Swarm to waste so much space. He felt dread. "Follow the food-giver," he said. "Follow the smell."

The springtails snuffled without much enthusiasm along one wall; they knew he had no food and were reluctant to do anything without an immediate reward. At last one of them picked up the scent, or pretended to, and followed it up across the ceiling and into the mouth of a tunnel.

It was hard for Afriel to see much in the abandoned chamber; there was not enough infrared heat. He leapt upward after the springtail.

He heard the roar of a warrior and the springtail's choked-off screech. It came flying from the tunnel's mouth, a spray of clotted fluid bursting from its ruptured head. It tumbled end over end until it hit the far wall with a flaccid crunch. It was already dead.

The second springtail fled at once, screeching with grief and terror. Afriel landed on the lip of the tunnel, sinking into a crouch as his legs soaked up momentum. He could smell the acrid stench of the warrior's anger, a pheromone so thick that even a human could scent it. Dozens of other warriors would group here within minutes, or seconds. Behind the enraged warrior he could hear workers and tunnelers shifting and cementing rock.

He might be able to control one enraged warrior, but never two, or twenty. He launched himself from the chamber wall and out an exit.

He searched for the other springtail—he felt sure he could recognize it, since it was so much bigger than the others—but he could not find it. With its keen sense of smell, it could easily avoid him if it wanted to.

Mirny did not return. Uncountable hours passed. He slept again. He re-

turned to the alates' chamber; there were warriors on guard there, warriors that
were not interested in food and brandished their immense serrated fangs when
he approached. They looked ready to rip him apart; the faint reek of aggressive
pheromones hung about the place like a fog. He did not see any symbiotes of
any kind on the warriors' bodies. There was one species, a thing like a huge tick,
that clung only to warriors, but even the ticks were gone.

He returned to his chambers to wait and think. Mirny's body was not in the
garbage pits. Of course, it was possible that something else might have eaten
her. Should he extract the remaining pheromone from the spaces in his vein and
try to break into the alates' chamber? He suspected that Mirny, or whatever was
left of her, was somewhere in the tunnel where the springtail had been killed. He
had never explored the tunnel himself. There were thousands of tunnels he had
never explored.

He felt paralyzed by indecision and fear. If he was quiet, if he did nothing,
the Investors might arrive at any moment. He could tell the Ring Council anything he wanted about Mirny's death; if he had the genetics with him, no one
would quibble. He did not love her; he respected her, but not enough to give up
his life, or his faction's investment. He had not thought of the Ring Council in a
long time, and the thought sobered him. He would have to explain his
decision. . . .

He was still in a brown study when he heard a whoosh of air as his living
airlock deflated itself. Three warriors had come for him. There was no reek of
anger about them. They moved slowly and carefully. He knew better than to try
to resist. One of them seized him gently in its massive jaws and carried him off.

It took him to the alates' chamber and into the guarded tunnel. A new, large
chamber had been excavated at the end of the tunnel. It was filled almost to
bursting by a black-spattered white mass of flesh. In the center of the soft speckled mass were a mouth and two damp, shining eyes, on stalks. Long tendrils like
conduits dangled, writhing, from a clumped ridge above the eyes. The tendrils
ended in pink, fleshy pluglike clumps.

One of the tendrils had been thrust through Mirny's skull. Her body hung in
midair, limp as wax. Her eyes were open, but blind.

Another tendril was plugged into the braincase of a mutated worker. The
worker still had the pallid tinge of a larva; it was shrunken and deformed, and its
mouth had the wrinkled look of a human mouth. There was a blob like a tongue
in the mouth, and white ridges like human teeth. It had no eyes.

It spoke with Mirny's voice. "Captain-Doctor Afriel . . ."

"Galina . . ."

"I have no such name. You may address me as Swarm."

Afriel vomited. The central mass was an immense head. Its brain almost
filled the room.

It waited politely until Afriel had finished.

"I find myself awakened again," Swarm said dreamily. "I am pleased to see
that there is no major emergency to concern me. Instead it is a threat that has become almost routine." It hesitated delicately. Mirny's body moved slightly in

midair; her breathing was inhumanly regular. The eyes opened and closed. "Another young race."

"What are you?"

"I am the Swarm. That is, I am one of its castes. I am a tool, an adaptation;
my specialty is intelligence. I am not often needed. It is good to be needed
again."

"Have you been here all along? Why didn't you greet us? We'd have dealt
with you. We meant no harm."

The wet mouth on the end of the plug made laughing sounds. "Like yourself, I enjoy irony," it said. "It is a pretty trap you have found yourself in, Captain-Doctor. You meant to make the Swarm work for you and your race. You
meant to breed us and study us and use us. It is an excellent plan, but one we hit
upon long before your race evolved."

Stung by panic, Afriel's mind raced frantically. "You're an intelligent
being," he said. "There's no reason to do us any harm. Let us talk together. We
can help you."

"Yes," Swarm agreed. "You will be helpful. Your companion's memories
tell me that this is one of those uncomfortable periods when galactic intelligence
is rife. Intelligence is a great bother. It makes all kinds of trouble for us."

"What do you mean?"

"You are a young race and lay great stock by your own cleverness," Swarm
said. "As usual, you fail to see that intelligence is not a survival trait."

Afriel wiped sweat from his face. "We've done well," he said. "We came to
you, and peacefully. You didn't come to us."

"I refer to exactly that," Swarm said urbanely. "This urge to expand, to explore, to develop, is just what will make you extinct. You naively suppose that
you can continue to feed your curiosity indefinitely. It is an old story, pursued by
countless races before you. Within a thousand years—perhaps a little
longer . . . your species will vanish."

"You intend to destroy us, then? I warn you it will not be an easy task—"

"Again you miss the point. Knowledge is power! Do you suppose that frag-
ile little form of yours—your primitive legs, your ludicrous arms and hands,
your tiny, scarcely wrinkled brain—can *contain* all that power? Certainly not!
Already your race is flying to pieces under the impact of your own expertise.
The original human form is becoming obsolete. Your own genes have been altered, and you, Captain-Doctor, are a crude experiment. In a hundred years you
will be a relic. In a thousand years you will not even be a memory. Your race
will go the same way as a thousand others."

"And what way is that?"

"I do not know." The thing on the end of the Swarm's arm made a chuck-
ling sound. "They have passed beyond my ken. They have all discovered something, learned something, that has caused them to transcend my understanding. It
may be that they even transcend *being*. At any rate, I cannot sense their presence
anywhere. They seem to do nothing, they seem to interfere in nothing; for all in-

tents and purposes, they seem to be dead. Vanished. They may have become gods, or ghosts. In either case, I have no wish to join them."

"So then—so then you have—"

"Intelligence is very much a two-edged sword, Captain-Doctor. It is useful only up to a point. It interferes with the business of living. Life, and intelligence, do not mix very well. They are not at all closely related, as you childishly assume."

"But you, then—you are a rational being—"

"I am a tool, as I said." The mutated device on the end of its arm made a sighing noise. "When you began your pheromonal experiments, the chemical imbalance became apparent to the Queen. It triggered certain genetic patterns within her body, and I was reborn. Chemical sabotage is a problem that can best be dealt with by intelligence. I am a brain replete, you see, specially designed to be far more intelligent than any young race. Within three days I was fully self-conscious. Within five days I had deciphered these markings on my body. They are the genetically encoded history of my race . . . within five days and two hours I recognized the problem at hand and knew what to do. I am now doing it. I am six days old."

"What is it you intend to do?"

"Your race is a very vigorous one. I expect it to be here, competing with us, within five hunded years. Perhaps much sooner. It will be necessary to make a thorough study of such a rival. I invite you to join our community on a permanent basis."

"What do you mean?"

"I invite you to become a symbiote. I have here a male and a female, whose genes are altered and threfore without defects. You make a perfect breeding pair. It will save me a great deal of trouble with cloning."

"You think I'll betray my race and deliver a slave species into your hands?"

"Your choice is simple, Captain-Doctor. Remain an intelligent, living being, or become a mindless puppet, like your partner. I have taken over all the functions of her nervous system; I can do the same to you."

"I can kill myself."

"That might be troublesome, because it would make me resort to developing a cloning technology. Technology, though I am capable of it, is painful to me. I am a genetic artifact; there are fail-safes within me that prevent me from taking over the Nest for my own uses. That would mean falling into the same trap of progress as other intelligent races. For similar reasons, my life span is limited. I will live for only a thousand years, until your race's brief flurry of energy is over and peace resumes once more."

"Only a thousand years?" Afriel laughed bitterly. "What then? You kill off my descendants, I assume, having no further use for them."

"No. We have not killed any of the fifteen other races we have taken for defensive study. It has not been necessary. Consider that small scavanger floating by your head, Captain-Doctor, that is feeding on your vomit. Five hundred million years ago its ancestors made the galaxy tremble. When they attacked us, we unleashed their own kind upon them. Of course, we altered our side, so that they were smarter, tougher, and, naturally, totally loyal to us. Our Nests were the only world they knew, and they fought with a valor and inventiveness we never could have matched. . . . Should your race arrive to exploit us, we will naturally do the same."

"We humans are different."

"Of course."

"A thousand years here won't change us. You will die and our descendants will take over this Nest. We'll be running things, despite you, in a few generations. The darkness won't make any difference."

"Certainly not. You don't need eyes here. You don't need anything."

"You'll allow me to stay alive? To teach them anything I want?"

"Certainly, Captain-Doctor. We are doing you a favor, in all truth. In a thousand years your descendants here will be the only remnants of the human race. We are generous with our immortality; we will take it upon ourselves to preserve you."

"You're wrong, Swarm. You're wrong about intelligence, and you're wrong about everything else. Maybe other races would crumble into parasitism, but we humans are different."

"Certainly. You'll do it, then?"

"Yes. I accept your challenge. And I will defeat you."

"Splendid. When the Investors return here, the springtails will say that they have killed you, and will tell them to never return. They will not return. The humans should be the next to arrive."

"If I don't defeat you, they will."

"Perhaps." Again it sighed. "I'm glad I don't have to absorb you. I would have missed your conversation."

# Spider Rose

**Nothing was what** Spider Rose felt, or almost nothing. There had been some feelings there, a nexus of clotted two-hundred-year-old emotions, and she had mashed it with a cranial injection. Now what was left of her feelings was like what is left of a roach when a hammer strikes it.

Spider Rose knew about roaches; they were the only native animal life in the orbiting Mechanist colonies. They had plagued spacecraft from the beginning, too tough, prolific, and adaptable to kill. Of necessity, the Mechanists had used genetic techniques stolen from their rivals the Shapers to turn the roaches into colorful pets. One of Spider Rose's special favorites was a roach a foot long and covered with red and yellow pigment squiggles against shiny black chitin. It was clinging to her head. It drank sweat from her perfect brow, and she knew nothing, for she was elsewhere, watching for visitors.

She watched through eight telescopes, their images collated and fed into her brain through a nerve-crystal junction at the base of her skull. She had eight eyes now, like her symbol, the spider. Her ears were the weak steady pulse of radar, listening, listening for the weird distortion that would signal the presence of an Investor ship.

Rose was clever. She might have been insane, but her monitoring techniques established the chemical basis of sanity and maintained it artificially. Spider Rose accepted this as normal.

And it was normal; not for human beings, but for a two-hundred-year-old Mechanist, living in a spinning web of a habitat orbiting Uranus, her body seething with youth hormones, her wise old-young face like something pulled fresh from a plaster mold, her long white hair a rippling display of implanted fiber-optic threads with tiny beads of light oozing like microscopic gems from their slant-cut tips. . . . She was old, but she didn't think about that. And she was lonely, but she had crushed those feelings with drugs. And she had something that the Investors wanted, something that those reptilian alien traders would give their eye-fangs to possess.

Trapped in her polycarbon spiderweb, the wide-stretched cargo net that had given her her name, she had a jewel the size of a bus.

And so she watched, brain-linked to her instruments, tireless, not particularly interested but certainly not bored. Boredom was dangerous. It led to unrest, and unrest could be fatal in a space habitat, where malice or even plain carelessness could kill. The proper survival behavior was this: to crouch in the center of the mental web, clean euclidean weblines of rationality radiating out in all directions, hooked legs alert for the slightest tremble of troubling emotion. And when she sensed that feeling tangling the lines, she rushed there, gauged it, shrouded it neatly, and pierced it cleanly and lingeringly with a spiderfang hypodermic. . . .

*There it was.* Her octuple eyes gazed a quarter of a million miles into space and spotted the star-rippling warp of an Investor ship. The Investor ships had no conventional engines, and radiated no detectable energies; the secret of their star drive was cloesly guarded. All that any of the factions (still loosely called "humanity" for lack of a better term) knew for sure about the Investor drive was that it sent long parabolic streamers of distortion from the sterns of ships, causing a rippling effect against the background of stars.

Spider Rose came partially out of her static observation mode and felt herself in her body once more. The computer signals were muted now, overlaid behind her normal vision like a reflection of her own face on a glass window as she gazed through it. Touching a keyboard, she pinpointed the Investor ship with a communications laser and sent it a pulse of data: a business offer. (Radio was too chancy; it might attract Shaper pirates, and she had had to kill three of them already.)

She knew she had been heard and understood when she saw the Investor ship perform a dead stop and an angled acceleration that broke every known law of orbital dynamics. While she waited, Spider Rose loaded an Investor translator program. It was fifty years old, but the Investors were a persistent lot, not so much conservative as just uninterested in change.

When it came too close to her station for star-drive maneuvers, the Investor ship unfurled a decorated solar sail with a puff of gas. The sail was big enough to gift-wrap a small moon and thinner than a two-hundred-year-old memory. Despite its fantastic thinness, there were molecule-thin murals worked onto it: titanic scenes of Investor argosies where wily Investors had defrauded pebbly bipeds and gullible heavy-planet gasbags swollen with wealth and hydrogen. The great jewel-laden queens of the Investor race, surrounded by adoring male harems, flaunted their gaudy sophistication above miles-high narratives of Investor hieroglyphs, placed on a musical grid to indicate the proper pitch and intonation of their half-sung language.

There was a burst of static on the screen before her and an Investor face appeared. Spider Rose pulled the plug from her neck. She studied the face: its great glassy eyes half-shrouded behind nictitating membranes, rainbow frill behind pinhole-sized ears, bumpy skin, reptile grin with peg-sized teeth. It made noises: "Ship's ensign here," her computer translated. "Lydia Martinez?"

"Yes," Spider Rose said, not bothering to explain that her name had changed. She had had many names.

"We had profitable dealings with your husband in the past," the Investor said with interest. "How does he fare these days?"

"He died thirty years ago," Spider Rose said. She had mashed the grief. "Shaper assassins killed him."

The Investor officer flickered his frill. He was not embarrassed. Embarrassment was not an emotion native to Investors. "Bad for business," he opined. "Where is this jewel you mentioned?"

"Prepare for incoming data," said Spider Rose, touching her keyboard. She watched the screen as her carefully prepared sales spiel unrolled itself, its communication beam shielded to avoid enemy ears.

It has been the find of a lifetime. It had started existence as part of a glacier-like ice moon of the protoplanet Uranus, shattering, melting, and recrystallizing in the primeval eons of relentless bombardment. It had cracked at least four different times, and each time mineral flows had been forced within its fracture zones under tremendous pressure: carbon, manganese silicate, beryllium, aluminum oxide. When the moon was finally broken up into the famous Ring complex, the massive ice chunk had floated for eons, awash in shock waves of hard radiation, accumulating and losing charge in the bizarre electromagnetic flickerings typical of all Ring formations.

And then one crucial moment some millions of years ago it had been ground-zero for a titanic lightning flash, one of those soundless invisible gouts of electric energy, dissipating charges built up over whole decades. Most of the ice-chunk's outer envelope had flashed off at once as a plasma. The rest was . . . changed. Mineral occlusions were now strings and veins of beryl, shading here and there into lumps of raw emerald big as Investors' heads, crisscrossed with nets of red corundum and purple garnet. There were lumps of fused diamond, weirdly colored blazing diamond that came only from the strange quantum states of metallic carbon. Even the ice itself had changed into something rich and unique and therefore by definition precious.

"You intrigue us," the Investor said. For them, this was profound enthusiasm. Spider Rose smiled. The ensign continued: "This is an unusual commodity and its value is hard to establish. We offer you a quarter of a million gigawatts."

Spider Rose said, "I have the energy I need to run my station and defend myself. It's generous, but I could never store that much."

"We will also give you a stabilized plasma lattice for storage." This unexpected and fabulous generosity was meant to overwhelm her. The construction of plasma lattices was far beyond human technology, and to own one would be a ten years' wonder. It was the last thing she wanted. "Not interested," she said.

The Investor lifted his frill. "Not interested in the basic currency of galactic trade?"

"Not when I can spend it only with you."

"Trade with young races is a thankless lot," the Investor observed. "I suppose you want information, then. You young races always want to trade in technology. We have some Shaper techniques for trade within their faction—are you interested in those?"

"Industrial espionage?" Spider Rose said. "You should have tried me eighty years ago. No, I know you Investors too well. You would only sell Mechanist techniques to them to maintain the balance of power."

"We like a competitive market," the Investor admitted. "It helps us avoid painful monopoly situations like the one we face now, dealing with you."

"I don't want power of any kind. Status means nothing to me. Show me something new."

"No status? What will your fellows think?"

"I live alone."

The Investor hid his eyes behind nictitating membranes. "Crushed your gregarious instincts? An ominous development. Well, I will take a new tack. Will you consider weaponry? If you will agree to various conditions regarding their use, we can give you unique and powerful armaments."

"I manage already."

"You could use our political skills. We can strongly influence the major Shaper groups and protect you from them by treaty. It would take ten or twenty years, but it could be done."

"It's up to them to be afraid of me," Spider Rose said, "not vice versa."

"A new habitat, then." The Investor was patient. "You can live within solid gold."

"I like what I have."

"We have some artifacts that might amuse you," the Investor said. "Prepare for incoming data."

Spider Rose spent eight hours examining the various wares. There was no hurry. She was too old for impatience, and the Investors lived to bargain.

She was offered colorful algae cultures that produced oxygen and alien perfumes. There were metafoil structures of collapsed atoms for radiation shielding and defense. Rare techniques that transmuted nerve fibers to crystal. A smooth black wand that made iron so malleable that you could mold it with your hands and set it in shape. A small luxury submarine for the exploration of ammonia and methane seas, made of transparent metallic glass. Self-replicating globes of patterned silica that, as they grew, played out a game simulating the birth, growth, and decline of an alien culture. A land-sea-and-aircraft so tiny that you buttoned it on like a suit. "I don't care for planets," Spider Rose said. "I don't like gravity wells."

"Under certain circumstances we could make a gravity generator available," the Investor said. "It would have to be tamper-proof, like the wand and the weapons, and loaned rather than sold outright. We must avoid the escape of such a technology."

She shrugged. "Our own technologies have shattered us. We can't assimilate what we already have. I see no reason to burden myself with more."

"This is all we can offer you that's not on the interdicted list," he said. "This ship in particular has a great many items suitable only for races that live at very low temperature and very high pressure. And we have items that you would probably enjoy a great deal, but they would kill you. Or your whole species. The literature on the [untranslatable], for instance."

"I can read the literature of Earth if I want an alien viewpoint," she said.

"[Untranslatable] is not really a literature," the Investor said benignly. "It's really a kind of virus."

A roach flew onto her shoulder. "Pets!" he said. "Pets! You enjoy them?"

"They are my solace," she said, letting it nibble the cuticle of her thumb.

"I should have thought," he said. "Give me twelve hours."

She went to sleep. After she woke, she studied the alien craft through her telescope while she waited. All Investor ships were covered with fantastic designs in hammered metal: animal heads, metal mosaics, scenes and inscriptions in deep relief, as well as cargo bays and instruments. But experts had pointed out that the basic shape beneath the ornamentation was always the same: a simple octahedron with six long rectangular sides. The Investors had gone to some pains to disguise this fact; and the current theory held that the ships had been bought, found, or stolen from a more advanced race. Certainly the Investors, with their whimsical attitude toward science and technology, seemed incapable of building them themselves.

The ensign reopened contact. His nictitating membranes looked whiter than usual. He held up a small winged reptilian being with a long spiny crest the color of an Investor's frill. "This is our Commander's mascot, called 'Little Nose for Profits.' Beloved by us all! It costs us a pang to part from him. We had to choose between losing face in this business deal or losing his company." He toyed with it. It grasped his thick digits with little scaly hands.

"He's . . . cute," she said, finding a half-forgotten word from her childhood and pronouncing it with a grimace of distaste. "But I'm not going to trade my find for some carnivorous lizardkin."

"And think of us!" the Investor lamented. "Condemning our little Nose to an alien lair swarming with bacteria and giant vermin. . . . However, this can't be helped. Here's our proposal. You take our mascot for seven hundred plus or minus five of our days. We will return here on our way out of your system. You can choose then between owning him or keeping your prize. In the meantime you must promise not to sell the jewel or inform anyone else of its existence."

"You mean that you will leave me your pet as a kind of earnest money on the transaction."

The Investor covered his eyes with the nictitating membranes and squeezed his pebbly lids half-shut. It was a sign of acute distress. "He is a hostage to your cruel indecision, Lydia Martinez. Frankly we doubt that we can find anything in this system that can satisfy you better than our mascot can. Except perhaps some novel mode of suicide."

Spider Rose was surprised. She had never seen an Investor become so emotionally involved. Generally they seemed to take a detached view of life, even showing on occasion behavior patterns that resembled a sense of humor.

She was enjoying herself. She was past the point when any of the Investor's normal commodities could have tempted her. In essence, she was trading her jewel for an interior mindstate: not an emotion, because she mashed those, but for a paler and cleaner feeling: interestedness. She wanted to be interested, to find something to occupy herself besides dead stones and space. And this looked intriguing.

"All right," she said. "I agree. Seven hundred plus or minus five days. And I keep silence." She smiled. She hadn't spoken to another human in five years and was not about to start.

"Take good care of our Little Nose for Profits," the Investor said, half pleading, half warning, accenting those nuances so that her computer would be sure to pick them up. "We will still want him, even if, through some utter corrosion of the spirit, you do not. He is valuable and rare. We will send you instructions on his care and feeding. Prepare for incoming data."

They fired the creature's cargo capsule into the tight-stretched polycarbon web of her spider habitat. The web was built on a framework of eight spokes, and these spokes were pulled taut by centrifugal force from the wheeling rotation of eight teardrop-shaped capsules. At the impact of the cargo shot, the web bowed gracefully and the eight massive metal teardrops were pulled closer to the web's center in short, graceful free-fall arcs. Wan sunlight glittered along the web as it expanded in recoil, its rotation slowed a little by the energy it had spent in absorbing the inertia. It was a cheap and effective docking technique, for a rate of spin was much easier to manage than complex maneuvering.

Hook-legged industrial robots ran quickly along the polycarbon fibers and seized the mascot's capsule with clamps and magnetic palps. Spider Rose ran the lead robot herself, feeling and seeing through its grips and cameras. The robots hustled the cargo craft to an airlock, dislodged its contents, and attached a small parasitic rocket to boost it back to the Investor mother ship. After the small rocket had returned and the Investor ship had left, the robots trooped back to their teardrop garages and shut themselves off, waiting for the next tremor of the web.

Spider Rose disconnected herself and opened the airlock. The mascot flew into the room. It had seemed tiny compared to the Investor ensign, but the Investors were huge. The mascot was as tall as her knee and looked like it weighed close to twenty pounds. Wheezing musically on the unfamiliar air, it flew around the room, ducking and darting unevenly.

A roach launched itself from the wall and flew with a great clatter of wings. The mascot hit the deck with a squawk of terror and lay there, comically feeling its spindly arms and legs for damage. It half-closed its rough eyelids. Like the eyes of an Investor baby, Spider Rose thought suddenly, though she had never seen a young Investor and doubted if anyone human ever had. She had a dim memory of something she had heard a long time before—something about pets and babies, their large heads, their large eyes, their softness, their dependence.

She remembered scoffing at the idea that the sloppy dependence of, say, a "dog" or "cat" could rival the clean economy and efficiency of a roach.

The Investor mascot had recovered its composure and was crouching bent-kneed on the algae carpet, warbling to itself. There was a sort of sly grin on its miniature dragon face. Its half-slitted eyes were alert and its matchstick ribs moved up and down with each breath. Its pupils were huge. Spider Rose imagined that it must find the light very dim. The lights in Investor ships were like searing blue arc-lamps, drenched in ultraviolet.

"We have to find a new name for you," Spider Rose said. "I don't speak Investor, so I can't use the name they gave you."

The mascot fixed her with a friendly stare, and it arched little half-transparent flaps over its pinhole ears. Real Investors had no such flaps, and she was charmed at this further deviation from the norm. Actually, except for the wings, it looked altogether too much like a tiny Investor. The effect was creepy.

"I'll call you Fuzzy," she said. It had no hair. It was a private joke, but all her jokes were private.

The mascot bounced across the floor. The false centrifugal gravity was lighter here, too, than the 1.3 g's that the massive Investors used. It embraced her bare leg and licked her kneecap with a rough sandpaper tongue. She laughed, more than a little alarmed, but she knew the Investors were strictly non-aggressive. A pet of theirs would not be dangerous.

It made eager chirping sounds and climbed onto her head, clutching handfuls of glittering optic fibers. She sat at her data console and called up the care and feeding instructions.

Clearly the Investors had not expected to trade their pet, because their instructions were almost indecipherable. They had the air of a second-or third-hand translation from some even more profoundly alien language. However, true to Investor tradition, the blandly pragmatic aspects had been emphasized.

Spider Rose relaxed. Apparently the mascots would eat almost anything, though they preferred dextrorotatory proteins and required certain easily acquired trace minerals. They were extremely resistant to toxins and had no native intestinal bacteria. (Neither did the Investors themselves, and they regarded races who did as savages.)

She looked for its respiratory requirements as the mascot leapt from her head and capered across the control board, almost aborting the program. She shooed it off, hunting for something she could comprehend amid dense clusters of alien graphs and garbled technical material. Suddenly she recognized something from her old days in technical espionage: a genetics chart.

She frowned. It seemed she had run past the relevant sections and on to another treatise entirely. She advanced the data slightly and discovered a three-dimensional illustration of some kind of fantastically complex genetic construct, with long helical chains of alien genes marked out in improbable colors. The gene chains were wrapped around long spires or spicules that emerged radially from a dense central knot. Further chains of tightly wound helices connected spire to spire. Apparently these chains activated different sections of genetic material from their junctions on the spires, for she could see ghost chains of slave proteins peeling off from some of the activated genes.

Spider Rose smiled. No doubt a skilled Shaper geneticist could profit spectacularly from these plans. It amused her to think that they never would. Obviously this was some kind of alien industrial genetic complex, for there was more genetic hardware there than any actual living animal could ever possibly need.

She knew that the Investors themselves never tampered with genetics. She wondered which of the nineteen known intelligent races had originated this thing. It might even have come from outside the Investor's economic realm, or it might be a relic from one of the extinct races.

She wondered if she ought to erase the data. If she died, it might fall into the wrong hands. As she thought of her death, the first creeping shades of a profound depression disturbed her. She allowed the sensation to build for a moment while she thought. The Investors had been careless to leave her with this information; or perhaps they underestimated the genetic abilities of the smooth and charismatic Shapers with their spectacularly boosted IQs.

There was a wobbling feeling inside her head. For a dizzying moment the chemically repressed emotions gushed forth with all their pent-up force. She felt an agonized envy for the Investors, for the dumb arrogance and confidence that allowed them to cruise the stars screwing their purported inferiors. She wanted to be with them. She wanted to get aboard a magic ship and feel alien sunlight burn her skin in some place light-years from human weakness. She wanted to scream and feel like a little girl had screamed and felt one hundred and ninety-three years ago on a roller coaster in Los Angeles, screaming in total pure intensity of feeling, in swept-away sensation like she had felt in the arms of her husband, her man dead now thirty years. Dead . . . Thirty years . . .

Her hands trembling, she opened a drawer beneath the control board. She smelled the faint medicinal reek of ozone from the sterilizer. Blindly she pushed her glittering hair from the plastic duct into her skull, pressed the injector against it, inhaled once, closed her eyes, inhaled twice, pulled the hypo away. Her eyes glazed over as she refilled the hypo and slipped it back into its velcro holster in the drawer.

She held the bottle and looked at it blankly. There was still plenty left. She would not have to synthesize more for months. Her brain felt like someone had stepped on it. It was always like this right after a mash. She shut off the Investor data and filed it absently in an obscure corner of computer memory. From its stand on the laser-com interface the mascot sang briefly and groomed its wing.

Soon she was herself again. She smiled. These sudden attacks were something she took for granted. She took an oral tranquilizer to stop the trembling of her hands and antacid for the stress on her stomach.

Then she played with the mascot until it grew tired and went to sleep. For four days she fed it carefully, being especially careful not to overfeed it, for like its models the Investors, it was a greedy little creature and she was afraid it would hurt itself. Even despite its rough skin and cold-bloodedness she was growing fond of it. When it grew tired of begging for food, it would play with string for hours or sit on her head watching the screen as she monitored the mining robots she had out in the Rings.

On the fifth day she found on awakening that it had killed and eaten her four largest and fattest roaches. Filled with a righteous anger she did nothing to blunt, she hunted for it throughout the capsule.

She did not find it. Instead, after hours of search, she found a mascot-sized cocoon wedged under the toilet.

It had gone into some sort of hibernation. She forgave it for eating the roaches. They were easy to replace, anyway, and rivals for her affections. In a way it was flattering. But the sharp pang of worry she felt overrode that. She examined the cocoon closely. It was made of overlapping sheets of some brittle translucent substance—dried mucus?—that she could chip easily with her fingernail. The cocoon was not perfectly rounded; there were small vague lumps that might have been its knees and elbows. She took another injection.

The week it spent in hibernation was a period of acute anxiety for her. She pored over the Investor tapes, but they were far too cryptic for her limited expertise. At least she knew it was not dead, for the cocoon was warm to the touch and the lumps within it sometimes stirred.

She was asleep when it began to break free of the cocoon. She had set up monitors to warn her, however, and she rushed to it at the first alarm.

The cocoon was splitting. A rent appeared in the brittle overlapping sheets, and a warm animal reek seeped out into the recycled air.

Then a paw emerged: a tiny five-fingered paw covered in glittering fur. A second paw poked through, and the two paws gripped the edges of the rent and ripped the cocoon away. It stepped out into the light, kicking the husk aside with a little human shuffle, and it grinned.

It looked like a little ape, small and soft and glittering. There were tiny human teeth behind the human lips of its grin. It had small soft baby's feet on the ends of its round springy legs, and it had lost its wings. Its eyes were the color of her eyes. The smooth mammalian skin of its round little face had the faint rosy flush of perfect health.

It jumped into the air, and she saw the pink of its tongue as it babbled aloud in human syllables.

It skipped over and embraced her leg. She was frightened, amazed, and profoundly relieved. She petted the soft perfect glittering fur on its hard little nugget of a head.

"Fuzzy," she said. "I'm glad. I'm very glad."

"Wa wa wa," it said, mimicking her intonation in its piping child's voice. Then it skipped back to its cocoon and began to eat it by the double handful, grinning.

She understood now why the Investors had been so reluctant to offer their mascot. It was a trade item of fantastic value. It was a genetic artifact, able to judge the emotional wants and needs of an alien species and adapt itself to them in a matter of days.

She began to wonder why the Investors had given it away at all; if they fully understood the capabilities of their pet. Certainly she doubted that they had understood the complex data that had come with it. Very likely, they had acquired the mascot from other Investors, in its reptilian form. It was even possible (the thought chilled her) that it might be older than the entire Investor race.

She stared at it: at its clear, guileless, trusting eyes. It gripped her fingers with small warm sinewy hands. Unable to resist, she hugged it to her, and it babbled with pleasure. Yes, it could easily have lived for hundreds or thousands of years, spreading its love (or equivalent emotions) among dozens of differing species.

And who would harm it? Even the most depraved and hardened of her own species had secret weaknesses. She remembered stories of guards in concentration camps who butchered men and women without a qualm, but meticulously fed hungry birds in the winter. Fear bred fear and hatred, but how could anyone feel fear or hatred toward this creature, or resist its brilliant powers?

It was not intelligent; it didn't need intelligence. It was sexless as well. An ability to breed would have ruined its value as a trade item. Besides, she doubted that anything so complex could have grown in a womb. Its genes would have to be built, spicule by spicule, in some unimaginable lab.

Days and weeks reeled by. Its ability to sense her moods was little short of miraculous. When she needed it, it was always there, and when she didn't it vanished. Sometimes she would hear it chattering to itself as it capered in strange acrobatics or chased and ate roaches. It was never mischievous, and on the odd occasions where it spilled food or upset something, it would unobtrusively clean up after itself. It dropped its small inoffensive fecal pellets into the same recycler she used.

These were the only signs it showed of patterns of thought that were more than animal. Once, and only once, it had mimicked her, repeating a sentence letter-perfect. She had been shocked, and it had sensed her reaction immediately. It never tried to parrot her again.

They slept in the same bed. Sometimes while she slept she would feel its warm nose snuffling lightly along the surface of her skin, as if it could smell her suppressed moods and feelings through the pores. Sometimes it would rub or press with its small firm hands against her neck or spine, and there was always a tightened muscle there that relaxed in gratitude. She never allowed this in the day, but at night, when her discipline was half-dissolved in sleep, there was a conspiracy between them.

The Investors had been gone over six hundred days. She laughed when she thought of the bargain she was getting.

The sound of her own laughter no longer startled her. She had even cut back on her dosages of suppressants and inhibitors. Her pet seemed so much happier when she was happy, and when it was at hand her ancient sadness seemed easier to bear. One by one she began to face old pains and traumas, holding her pet close and shedding healing tears into its glittering fur. One by one it licked her tears, tasting the emotional chemicals they contained, smelling her breath and skin, holding her as she was racked with sobbing. There were so many memories. She felt old, horribly old, but at the same time she felt a new sense of wholeness that allowed her to bear it. She had done things in the past—cruel things—and she had never put up with the inconvenience of guilt. She had mashed it instead.

Now for the first time in decades she felt the vague reawakening of a sense of purpose. She wanted to see people again—dozens of people, hundreds of people, all of whom would admire her, protect her, find her precious, whom she could care for, who would keep her safer than she was with only one companion. . . .

Her web station entered the most dangerous part of its orbit, where it crossed the plane of the Rings. Here she was busiest, accepting the drifting chunks of raw materials—ice, carbonaceous chondrites, metal ores—that her telepuppet mining robots had discovered and sent her way. There were killers in these Rings: rapacious pirates, paranoid settlers anxious to lash out.

In her normal orbit, far off the plane of the ecliptic, she was safe. But here there were orders to be broadcasted, energies to be spent, the telltale traces of powerful mass drivers hooked to the captive asteroids she claimed and mined. It was an unavoidable risk. Even the best-designed habitat was not a completely closed system, and hers was big, and old.

They found her.

Three ships. She tried bluffing them off at first, sending them a standard interdiction warning routed through a telepuppet beacon. They found the beacon and destroyed it, but that gave her their location and some blurry data through the beacon's limited sensors.

Three sleek ships, iridescent capsules half-metal, half-organic, with long ribbed insect-tinted sun-wings thinner than the scum of oil on water. Shaper spacecraft, knobbed with the geodesics of sensors, the spines of magnetic and optical weapons systems, long cargo manipulators folded like the arms of mantises.

She sat hooked into her own sensors, studying them, taking in a steady trickle of data: range estimation, target probabilities, weapons status. Radar was too risky; she sighted them optically. This was fine for lasers, but her lasers were not her best weapons. She might get one, but the others would be on her. It was better that she stay quiet while they prowled the Rings and she slid silently off the ecliptic.

But they had found her. She saw them fold their sails and activate their ion engines.

They were sending radio. She entered it on screen, not wanting the distraction filling her head. A Shaper's face appeared, one of the Oriental-based gene lines, smooth raven hair held back with jeweled pins, slim black eyebrows arched over dark eyes with the epicanthic fold, pale lips slightly curved in a charismatic smile. A smooth, clean actor's face with the glittering ageless eyes of a fanatic. "Jade Prime," she said.

"*Colonel-Doctor* Jade Prime," the Shaper said, fingering a golden insignia of rank in the collar of his black military tunic. "Still calling yourself 'Spider Rose' these days, Lydia? Or have you wiped that out of your brain?"

"Why are you a soldier instead of a corpse?"

"Times change, Spider. The bright young lights get snuffed out, by your old friends, and those of us with long-range plans are left to settle old debts. You remember old debts, Spider?"

"You think you're going to survive this meeting, don't you, Prime?" She felt the muscles of her face knotting with a ferocious hatred she had no time to kill. "Three ships manned with your own clones. How long have you holed up in that rock of yours, like a maggot in an apple? Cloning and cloning. When was the last time a woman let you touch her?"

His eternal smile twisted into a leer with bright teeth behind it. "It's no use, Spider. You've already killed *thirty-seven* of me, and I just keep coming back, don't I? You pathetic old bitch, what the hell is a maggot, anyway? Something like that mutant on your shoulder?"

She hadn't even known the pet was there, and her heart was stabbed with fear for it. "You've come too close!"

"Fire, then! Shoot me, you germy old cretin! Fire!"

"You're not him!" she said suddenly. "You're not the First Jade! Hah! He's dead, isn't he?"

The clone's face twisted with rage. Lasers flared, and three of her habitats melted into slag and clouds of metallic plasma. A last searing pulse of intolerable brightness flashed in her brain from three melting telescopes.

She cut loose with a chugging volley of magnetically accelerated iron slugs. At four hundred miles per second they riddled the first ship and left it gushing air and brittle clouds of freezing water.

Two ships fired. They used weapons she had never seen before, and they crushed two habitats like a pair of giant fists. The web lurched with the impact, its equilibrium gone. She knew instantly which weapons systems were left, and she returned fire with metal-jacketed pellets of ammonia ice. They punched through the semiorganic sides of a second Shaper craft. The tiny holes sealed instantly, but the crew was finished; the ammonia vaporized inside, releasing instantly lethal nerve toxins.

The last ship had one chance in three to get her command center. Two hundred years of luck ran out for Spider Rose. Static stung her hands from the controls. Every light in the habitat went out, and her computer underwent a total crash. She screamed and waited for death.

Death did not come.

Her mouth gushed with the bile of nausea. She opened the drawer in the darkness and filled her brain with liquid tranquillity. Breathing hard, she sat back in her console chair, her panic mashed. "Electromagnetic pulse," she said. "Stripped everything I had."

The pet warbled a few syllables. "He would have finished us by now if he could," she told her pet. "The defenses must have come through from the other habitats when the mainframe crashed."

She felt a thump as the pet jumped into her lap, shivering with terror. She hugged it absently, rubbing its slender neck. "Let's see," she said into the darkness. "The ice toxins are down, I had them overridden from here." She pulled the useless plug from her neck and plucked her robe away from her damp ribs. "It was the spray, then. A nice, thick cloud of hot ionized metallic copper. Blew every sensor he had. He's riding blind in a metallic coffin. Just like us."

She laughed. "Except Old Rose has a trick left, baby. The Investors. They'll be looking for me. There's nobody left to look for him. And I still have my rock."

She sat silently, and her artificial calmness allowed her to think the unthinkable. The pet stirred uneasily, sniffing at her skin. It had calmed a little under her caresses, and she didn't want it to suffer.

She put her free hand over its mouth and twisted its neck till it broke. The centrifugal gravity had kept her strong, and it had no time to struggle. A final tremor shook its limbs as she held it up in the darkness, feeling for a heartbeat. Her fingertips felt the last pulse behind its frail ribs.

"Not enough oxygen," she said. Mashed emotions tried to stir, and failed. She had plenty of suppressor left. "The carpet algae will keep the air clean a few weeks, but it dies without light. And I can't eat it. Not enough food, baby. The gardens are gone, and even if they hadn't been blasted, I couldn't get food in here. Can't run the robots. Can't even open the airlocks. If I live long enough, they'll come and pry me out. I have to improve my chances. It's the sensible thing. When I'm like this I can only do the sensible thing."

When the roaches—or at least all those she could trap in the darkness—were gone, she fasted for a long dark time. Then she ate her pet's undecayed flesh, half hoping even in her numbness that it would poison her.

When she first saw the searing blue light of the Investors glaring through the shattered airlock, she crawled back on bony hands and knees, shielding her eyes.

The Investor crewman wore a spacesuit to protect himself from bacteria. She was glad he couldn't smell the reek of her pitch-black crypt. He spoke to her in the fluting language of the Investors, but her translator was dead.

She thought then for a moment that they would abandon her, leave her there starved and blinded and half-bald in her webs of shed fiber-hair. But they took her aboard, drenching her with stinging antiseptics, scorching her skin with bacterial ultraviolet rays.

They had the jewel, but that much she already knew. What they wanted—(this was difficult)—what they wanted to know was what had happened to their mascot. It was hard to understand their gestures and their pidgin scraps of human language. She had done something bad to herself, she knew that. Overdoses in the dark. Struggling in the darkness with a great black beetle of fear that broke the frail meshes of her spider's web. She felt very bad. There was something wrong inside of her. Her malnourished belly was as tight as a drum, and her lungs felt crushed. Her bones felt wrong. Tears wouldn't come.

They kept at her. She wanted to die. She wanted their love and understanding. She wanted—

Her throat was full. She couldn't talk. Her head tilted back, and her eyes shrank in the searing blaze of the overhead lights. She heard painless cracking noises as her jaws unhinged.

Her breathing stopped. It came as a relief. Antiperistalsis throbbed in her gullet, and her mouth filled with fluid.

A living whiteness oozed from her lips and nostrils. Her skin tingled at its touch, and it flowed over her eyeballs, sealing and soothing them. A great coolness and lassitude soaked into her as wave after wave of translucent liquid swaddled her, gushing over her skin, coating her body. She relaxed, filled with a sensual, sleepy gratitude. She was not hungry. She had plenty of excess mass.

In eight days she broke from the brittle sheets of her cocoon and fluttered out on scaly wings, eager for the leash.

# Cicada Queen

**It began the** night the Queen called off her dogs. I'd been under the dogs for two years, ever since my defection.

My initiation, and my freedom from the dogs, were celebrated at the home of Arvin Kulagin. Kulagin, a wealthy Mechanist, had a large domestic-industrial complex on the outer perimeter of a midsized cylindrical suburb.

Kulagin met me at his door and handed me a gold inhaler. The party was already roaring. The Polycarbon Clique always turned out in force for an initiation.

As usual, my entrance was marked by a subtle freezing up. It was the dogs' fault. Voices were raised to a certain histrionic pitch, people handled their inhalers and drinks with a slightly more studied elegance, and every smile turned my way was bright enough for a team of security experts.

Kulagin smiled glassily. "Landau, it's a pleasure. Welcome. I see you've brought the Queen's Percentage." He looked pointedly at the box on my hip.

"Yes," I said. A man under the dogs had no secrets. I had been working off and on for two years on the Queen's gift, and the dogs had taped everything. They were still taping everything. Czarina-Kluster Security had designed them for that. For two years they'd taped every moment of my life and everything and everyone around me.

"Perhaps the Clique can have a look," Kulagin said. "Once we've whipped these dogs." He winked into the armored camera face of the watchdog, then looked at his timepiece. "Just an hour till you're out from under. Then we'll have some fun." He waved me on into the room. "If you need anything, use the servos."

Kulagin's place was spacious and elegant, decorated classically and settled by gigantic suspended marigolds. His suburb was called the Froth and was the Clique's favorite neighborhood. Kulagin, living at the suburb's perimeter, profited by the Froth's lazy spin and had a simulated tenth of a gravity. His walls were striped to provide a vertical referent, and he had enough space to affect such luxuries as "couches," "tables," "chairs," and other forms of gravity-oriented furniture. The ceiling was studded with hooks, from which were suspended a dozen of his favorite marigolds, huge round explosions of reeking greenery with blossoms the size of my head.

I walked into the room and stood behind a couch, which partially hid the two offensive dogs. I signaled one of Kulagin's spidery servos and took a squeezebulb of liquor to cut the speedy intensity of the inhaler's phenethylamine.

I watched the party, which had split into loose subcliques. Kulagin was near the door with his closest sympathizers, Mechanist officers from Czarina-Kluster banks and quiet Security types. Nearby, faculty from the Kosmosity-Metasystem campus talked shop with a pair of orbital engineers. On the ceiling, Shaper designers talked fashion, clinging to hooks in the feeble gravity. Below them a manic group of C-K folk, "Cicadas," spun like clockwork through gravity dance steps.

At the back of the room, Wellspring was holding forth amid a herd of spindly-legged chairs. I leapt gently over the couch and glided toward him. The dogs sprang after me with a whir of propulsive fans.

Wellspring was my closest friend in C-K. He had encouraged my defection when he was in the Ring Council, buying ice for the Martian terraforming project. The dogs never bothered Wellspring. His ancient friendship with the Queen was well known. In C-K, Wellspring was a legend.

Tonight he was dressed for an audience with the Queen. A coronet of gold and platinum circled his dark, matted hair. He wore a loose blouse of metallic brocade with slashed sleeves that showed a black underblouse shot through with flickering pinpoints of light. This was complemented by an Investor-style jeweled skirt and knee-high scaled boots. The jeweled cables of the skirt showed Wellspring's massive legs, trained to the heavy gravity favored by the reptilian Queen. He was a powerful man, and his weaknesses, if he had any, were hidden within his past.

Wellspring was talking philosophy. His audience, mathematicians and biologists from the faculty of C-K K-M, made room for me with strained smiles. "You asked me to define my terms," he said urbanely. "By the term *we,* I don't mean merely you Cicadas. Nor do I mean the mass of so-called humanity. After all, you Shapers are constructed of genes patented by Reshaped genetics firms. You might be properly defined as industrial artifacts."

His audience groaned. Wellspring smiled. "And conversely, the Mechanists are slowly abandoning human flesh in favor of cybernetic modes of existence. So. It follows that my term, *we,* can be attributed to any cognitive metasystem on the Fourth Prigoginic Level of Complexity."

A Shaper professor touched his inhaler to the painted line of his nostril and said, "I have to take issue with that, Wellspring. This occult nonsense about levels of complexity is ruining C-K's ability to do decent science."

"That's a linear causative statement," Wellspring riposted. "You conservatives are always looking for certainties outside the level of the cognitive meta-system. Clearly every intelligent being is separated from every lower level by a Prigoginic event horizon. It's time we learned to stop looking for solid ground to stand on. Let's place *ourselves* at the center of things. If we need something to stand on, we'll have it orbit us."

He was applauded. He said. "Admit it, Yevgeny. C-K is blooming in a new moral and intellectual climate. It's unquantifiable and unpredictable, and, as a scientist, that frightens you. Posthumanism offers fluidity and freedom, and a metaphysic daring enough to think a whole world into life. It enables us to take up economically absurd projects such as the terraforming of Mars, which your pseudopragmatic attitude could never dare to attempt. And yet think of the gain involved."

"Semantic tricks," smiffed the professor. I had never seen him before. I suspected that Wellspring had brought him along for the express purpose of baiting him.

I myself had once doubted some aspects of C-K's Posthumanism. But its open abandonment of the search for moral certainties had liberated us. When I looked at the eager, painted faces of Wellspring's audience, and compared them to the bleak strain and veiled craftiness that had once surrounded me, I felt as if I would burst. After twenty-four years of paranoid discipline under the Ring Council, and then two more years under the dogs, tonight I would be explosively released from pressure.

I sniffed at the phenethylamine, the body's own "natural" amphetamine. I felt suddenly dizzy, as if the space inside my head were full of the red-hot Ur-space of the primordial de Sitter cosmos, ready at any moment to make the Prigoginic leap into the "normal" space-time continuum, the Second Prigoginic Level of Complexity. . . . Posthumanism schooled us to think in terms of fits and starts, of structures accreting along unspoken patterns, following the lines first suggested by the ancient Terran philosopher Ilya Prigogine. I directly understood this, since my own mild attraction to the dazzling Valery Korstad had coalesced into a knotted desire that suppressants could numb but not destroy.

She was dancing across the room, the jeweled strings of her Investor skirt twisting like snakes. She had the anonymous beauty of the Reshaped, overlaid with the ingenious, enticing paint of C-K. I had never seen anything I wanted more, and from our brief and strained flirtations I knew that only the dogs stood between us.

Wellspring took me by the arm. His audience had dissolved as I stood rapt, lusting after Valery. "How much longer, son?"

Startled, I looked at the watch display on my forearm. "Only twenty minutes, Wellspring."

"That's fine, son." Wellspring was famous for his use of archaic terms like *son.* "Once the dogs are gone, it'll be your party, Hans. I won't stay here to eclipse you. Besides, the Queen awaits me. You have the Queen's Percentage?"

"Yes, just as you said." I unpeeled the box from the stick-tight patch on my hip and handed it over.

Wellspring lifted its lid with his powerful fingers and looked inside. Then he laughed aloud. "Jesus! It's beautiful!"

Suddenly he pulled the open box away and the Queen's gift hung in midair, glittering above our heads. It was an artificial gem the size of a child's face, its chiseled planes glittering with the green and gold of endolithic lichen. As it spun it threw tiny glints of fractured light across our faces.

As it fell, Kulagin appeared and caught it on the points of four extended fingertips. His left eye, an artificial implant, glistened darkly as he examined it.

"Eisho Zaibatsu?" he asked.

"Yes," I said. "They handled the synthesizing work; the lichen is a special variety of my own." I saw that a curious circle was gathering and said aloud, "Our host is a connoisseur."

"Only of finance," Kulagin said quietly, but with equal emphasis. "I understand now why you patented the process in your own name. It's a dazzling accomplishment. How could any Investor resist the lure of a living jewel, friends? Someday soon our initiate will be a wealthy man."

I looked quickly at Wellspring, but he unobtrusively touched one finger to his lips. "And he'll need that wealth to bring Mars to fruition," Wellspring said loudly. "We can't depend forever on the Kosmosity for funding. Friends, rejoice that you too will reap the profits of Landau's ingenious genetics." He caught the jewel and boxed it. "And tonight I have the honor of presenting his gift to the Queen. A double honor, since I recruited its creator myself." Suddenly he leapt toward the exit, his powerful legs carrying him quickly above our heads. As he flew he shouted, "Goodbye, son! May another dog never darken your doorstep!"

With Wellspring's exit, the non-Polycarbon guests began leaving, forming a jostling knot of hat-fetching servos and gossiping well-wishers. When the last was gone, the Clique grew suddenly quiet.

Kulagin had me stand at a far corner of his studio while the Clique formed a long gauntlet for the dogs, arming themselves with ribbons and paint. A certain dark edge of smoldering vengeance only added a tang to their enjoyment. I took a pair of paint balloons from one of Kulagin's scurrying servos.

The time was almost on me. For two long years I'd schemed to join the Polycarbon Clique. I needed them. I felt they needed me. I was tired of suspicion, of strained politeness, of the glass walls of the dogs' surveillance. The keen edges of my long discipline suddenly, painfully, crumbled. I began shaking uncontrollably, unable to hold it back.

The dogs were still, taping steadily to the last appointed instant. The crowd began to count down. Exactly at the count of zero the two dogs turned to go.

They were barraged with paint and tangled streamers. A moment earlier they would have turned savagely on their tormentors, but now they had reached the limits of their programming, and at long last they were helpless. The Clique's aim was deadly, and with every splattering hit they split the air with screams of laughter. They knew no mercy, and it took a full minute before the humiliated dogs could hop and stagger, blinded, to the door.

I was overcome with mob hysteria. Screams escaped my clenched teeth. I had to be grappled back from pursuing the dogs down the hall. As firm hands pulled me back within the room I turned to face my friends, and I was chilled at the raw emotion of their faces. It was as if they had been stripped of skin and watched me with live eyes in slabs of meat.

I was picked up bodily and passed from hand to hand around the room. Even those that I knew well seemed alien to me now. Hands tore at my clothing until I was stripped; they even took my computer gauntlet, then stood me in the middle of the room.

As I stood shivering within the circle, Kulagin approached me, his arms rigid, his face stiff and hieratic. His hands were full of loose black cloth. He held the cloth over my head, and I saw that it was a black hood. He put his lips close to my ear and said softly, "Friend, go the distance." Then he pulled the hood over my head and knotted it.

The hood had been soaked in something; I could smell that it reeked. My hands and feet began to tingle, then go numb. Slowly, warmth crept like bracelets up my arms and legs. I could hear nothing, and my feet could no longer feel the floor. I lost all sense of balance, and suddenly I fell backward, into the infinite.

My eyes opened, or my eyes closed, I couldn't tell. But at the limits of vision, from behind some unspoken fog, emerged pinpoints of cold and piercing brightness. It was the Great Galactic Night, the vast and pitiless emptiness that lurks just beyond the warm rim of every human habitat, emptier even than death.

I was naked in space, and it was so bitterly cold that I could taste it like poison in every cell I had. I could feel the pale heat of my own life streaming out of me like plasma, ebbing away in aurora sheets from my fingertips. I continued to fall, and as the last rags of warmth pulsed off into the devouring chasm of space, and my body grew stiff and white and furred with frost from every pore, I faced the ultimate horror: that I would not die, that I would fall forever backward into the unknown, my mind shriveling into a single frozen spore of isolation and terror.

Time dilated. Eons of silent fear telescoped into a few heartbeats and I saw before me a single white blob of light, like a rent from this cosmos into some neighboring realm full of alien radiance. This time I faced it as I fell toward it, and through it, and then, finally, jarringly, I was back behind my own eyes, within my own head, on the soft floor of Kulagin's studio.

The hood was gone. I wore a loose black robe, closed with an embroidered belt. Kulagin and Valery Korstad helped me to my feet. I wobbled, brushing away tears, but I managed to stand, and the Clique cheered.

Kulagin's shoulder was under my arm. He embraced me and whispered, "Brother, remember the cold. When we your friends need warmth, be warm, remembering the cold. When friendship pains you, forgive us, remembering the cold. When selfishness tempts you, renounce it, remembering the cold. For you have gone the distance, and returned to us renewed. Remember, remember the cold." And then he gave me my secret name, and pressed his painted lips to mine.

I clung to him, choked with sobs. Valery embraced me and Kulagin pulled away gently, smiling.

One by one the Clique took my hands and pressed their lips quickly to my face, murmuring congratulations. Still unable to speak, I could only nod. Meanwhile Valery Korstad, clinging to my arm, whispered hotly in my ear, "Hans, Hans, Hans Landau, there still remains a certain ritual, which I have reserved to myself. Tonight the finest chamber in the Froth belongs to us, a sacred place where no glassy-eyed dog has ever trespassed. Hans Landau, tonight that place belongs to you, and so do I."

I looked into her face, my eyes watering. Her eyes were dilated, and a pink flush had spread itself under her ears and along her jawline. She had dosed herself with hormonal aphrodisiacs. I smelled the antiseptic sweetness of her perfumed sweat and I closed my eyes, shuddering.

Valery led me into the hall. Behind us, Kulagin's door sealed shut, cutting the hilarity to a murmur. Valery helped me slip on my air fins, whispering soothingly.

The dogs were gone. Two chunks of my reality had been edited like tape. I still felt dazed. Valery took my hand, and we threaded a corridor upward toward the center of the habitat, kicking along with our air fins. I smiled mechanically at the Cicadas we passed in the halls, members of another day crowd. They were soberly going about their day shift's work while the Polycarbon Clique indulged in bacchanalia.

It was easy to lose yourself within the Froth. It had been built in rebellion against the regimented architecture of other habitats, in C-K's typical defiance of the norm. The original empty cylinder had been packed with pressurized plastic, which had been blasted to foam and allowed to set. It left angular bubbles whose tilted walls were defined by the clean topologies of close packing and surface tension. Halls had been snaked through the complex later, and the doors and airlocks cut by hand. The Froth was famous for its delirious and welcome spontaneity.

And its discreets were notorious. C-K showed its civic spirit in the lavish appointments of these citadels against surveillance. I had never been in one before. People under the dogs were not allowed across the boundaries. But I had heard rumors, the dark and prurient scandal of bars and corridors, those scraps of licentious speculation that always hushed at the approach of dogs. Anything, anything at all, could happen in a discreet, and no one would know of it but the lovers or survivors who returned, hours later, to public life. . . .

As the centrifugal gravity faded we began floating, Valery half-towing me. The bubbles of the Froth had swollen near the axis of rotation, and we entered a neighborhood of the quiet industrial domiciles of the rich. Soon we had floated to the very doorstep of the infamous Topaz Discreet, the hushed locale of unnumbered elite frolics. It was the finest in the Froth.

Valery looked at her timepiece, caressing away a fine film of sweat that had formed on the flushed and perfect lines of her face and neck. We hadn't long to wait. We heard the mellow repeated bonging of the discreet's time alarm, warning the present occupant that his time was up. The door's locks unsealed. I wondered just what member of C-K's inner circle would emerge. Now that I was free of the dogs, I longed to boldly meet his eyes.

Still we waited. Now the discreet was ours by right and every moment lost pained us. To overstay in a discreet was the height of rudeness. Valery grew angry, and pushed open the door.

The air was full of blood. In free-fall, it floated in a thousand clotting red blobs.

Near the center of the room floated the suicide, his flaccid body still wheeling slowly from the gush of his severed throat. A scalpel glittered in the mechanically clenched fingers of the cadaver's outstretched hand. He wore the sober black overalls of a conservative Mechanist.

The body spun, and I saw the insignia of the Queen's Advisers stitched on his breast. His partially metallic skull was sticky with his own blood; the face was obscured. Long streamers of thickened blood hung from his throat like red veils.

We had cometaried into something very much beyond us. "I'll call Security," I said.

She said two words. "Not yet." I looked into her face. Her eyes were dark with fascinated lust. The lure of the forbidden had slid its hooks into her in a single moment. She kicked languidly across one tessellated wall, and a long streak of blood splattered and broke along her hip.

In discreets one met the ultimates. In a room with so many hidden meanings, the lines had blurred. Through constant proximity pleasure had wedded with death. For the woman I adored, the private rites transpiring there had become of one unspoken piece.

"Hurry," she said. Her lips were bitter with a thin grease of aphrodisiacs. We interlaced our legs to couple in free-fall while we watched his body twist.

That was the night the Queen called off her dogs.

It had thrilled me in a way that made me sick. We Cicadas lived in the moral equivalent of de Sitter space, where no ethos had validity unless it was generated by noncausative free will. Every level of Prigoginic Complexity was based on a self-dependent generative catalyst: space existed because space existed, life was because it had come to be, intelligence was because it is. So it was possible for an entire moral system to accrete around a single moment of profound disgust. . . . Or so Posthumanism taught. After my blighted consummation with Valery I withdrew to work and think.

I lived in the Froth, in a domestic-industrial studio that reeked of lichen and was much less chic than Kulagin's.

On the second day-shift of my meditation I was visited by Arkadya Sorienti, a Polycarbon friend and one of Valery's intimates. Even without the dogs there were elements of a profound strain between us. It seemed to me that Arkadya was everything that Valery was not: blonde where Valery was dark, covered with Mechanist gimmickry where Valery had the cool elegance of the genetically Reshaped, full of false and brittle gaiety where Valery was prey to soft and melancholy gloom. I offered her a squeezebulb of liqueur; my apartment was too close to the axis to use cups.

"I haven't seen your apartment before," she said. "I love your airframes, Hans. What kind of algae is it?"

"It's lichen," I said.

"They're beautiful. One of your special kinds?"

"They're all special," I said. "Those have the Mark III and IV varieties for the terraforming project. The others have some delicate strains I was working on for contamination monitors. Lichen are very sensitive to pollution of any sort." I turned up the air ionizer. The intestines of Mechanists seethed with bacteria, and their effects could be disastrous.

"Which one is the lichen of the Queen's jewel?"

"It's locked away," I said. "Outside the environs of a jewel its growth becomes very distorted. And it smells." I smiled uneasily. It was common talk among Shapers that Mechanists stank. It seemed to me that I could already smell the reek of her armpits.

Arkadya smiled and nervously rubbed the skin-metal interface of a silvery blob of machinery grafted along her forearm. "Valery's in one of her states," she said. "I thought I'd come see how you were."

In my mind's eye flickered the nightmare image of our naked skins slicked with blood. I said, "It was . . . unfortunate."

"C-K's full of talk about the Comptroller's death."

"It was the Comptroller?" I said. "I haven't seen any news."

Slyness crept into her eyes. "You saw him there," she said.

I was shocked that she should expect me to discuss my stay in a discreet. "I have work," I said. I kicked my fins so that I drifted off our mutual vertical. Facing each other sideways increased the social distance between us.

She laughed quietly. "Don't be a prig, Hans. You act as if you were still under the dogs. You have to tell me about it if you want me to help the two of you."

I stopped my drift. She said, "And I want to help. I'm Valery's friend. I like the way you look together. It appeals to my sense of aesthetics."

"Thanks for your concern."

"I *am* concerned. I'm tired of seeing her on the arm of an old lecher like Wellspring."

"You're telling me they're lovers?" I said.

She fluttered her metal-clad fingers in the air. "You're asking me what the two of them do in his favorite discreet? Maybe they play chess." She rolled her eyes under lids heavy with powdered gold. "Don't look so shocked, Hans. You should know his power as well as anyone. He's old and rich; we Polycarbon women are young and not too terribly principled." She looked quickly up and away from beneath long lashes. "I've never heard that he took anything from us that we weren't willing to give." She floated closer. "Tell me what you saw, Hans. C-K's crazy with the news, and Valery does nothing but mope."

I opened the refrigerator and dug among Petri dishes for more liqueur. "It strikes me that you should be doing the talking, Arkadya."

She hesitated, then shrugged and smiled. "Now you're showing some sense, my friend. Open eyes and ears can take you a long way in C-Kluster." She took a stylish inhaler from a holster on her enameled garter. "And speaking of eyes and ears, have you had your place swept for bugs yet?"

"Who'd bug me?"

"Who wouldn't?" She looked bored. "I'll stick to what's common knowledge, then. Hire us a discreet sometime, and I'll give you all the rest." She fired a stream of amber liqueur from arm's length and sucked it in as it splashed against her teeth. "Something big is stirring in C-K. It hasn't reached the rank and file yet, but the Comptroller's death is a sign of it. The other Advisers are treating it like a personal matter, but it's clear that he wasn't simply tired of life. He left his affairs in disorder. No, this is something that runs back to the Queen herself. I'm sure of it."

"You think the Queen ordered him to take his own life?"

"Maybe. She's getting erratic with age. Wouldn't you, though, if you had to spend your life surrounded by aliens? I feel for the Queen, I really do. If she needs to kill a few stuffy rich old bastards for her own peace of mind, it's perfectly fine by me. In fact, if that's all there was to it, I'd sleep easier."

I thought about this, my face impassive. The entire structure of Czarina-Kluster was predicated on the Queen's exile. For seventy years, defectors, malcontents, pirates, and pacifists had accreted around the refuge of our alien Queen. The powerful prestige of her fellow Investors protected us from the predatory machinations of Shaper fascists and dehumanized Mechanist sects. C-K was an oasis of sanity amid the vicious amorality of humanity's warring factions. Our suburbs spun in webs around the dark hulk of the Queen's blazing, jeweled environment.

She was all we had. There was a giddy insecurity under all our success. C-K's famous banks were backed by the Cicada Queen's tremendous wealth. The academic freedom of C-K's teaching centers flourished only under her shadow.

And we did not even know why she was disgraced. Rumors abounded, but only the Investors themselves knew the truth. Were she ever to leave us, Czarina-Kluster would disintegrate overnight.

I said offhandedly, "I've heard talk that she's not happy. It seems these rumors spread, and they raise her Percentage for a while and panel a new room with jewels, and then the rumors fade."

"That's true. . . . She and our sweet Valery are two of a kind where these dark moods are concerned. It's clear, though, that the Comptroller was left no choice but suicide. And that means disaster is stirring at the heart of C-K."

"It's only rumors," I said. "The Queen is the heart of C-K, and who knows what's going on in that huge head of hers?"

"Wellspring would know," Arkadya said intently.

"But he's not an Adviser," I said. "As far as the Queen's inner circle is concerned, he's little better than a pirate."

"Tell me what you saw in Topaz Discreet."

"You'll have to allow me some time," I said. "It's rather painful." I wondered what I should tell her, and what she was willing to believe. The silence began to stretch.

I put on a tape of Terran sea sounds. The room began to surge ominously with the roar of alien surf.

"I wasn't ready for it," I said. "In my crèche we were taught to guard our feelings from childhood. I know how the Clique feels about distance. But that kind of raw intimacy, from a woman I really scarcely know—especially under that night's circumstances—it wounded me." I looked searchingly into Arkadya's face, longing to reach through her to Valery. "Once it was over, we were further apart than ever."

Arkadya tilted her head to the side and winced. "Who composed this?"

"What? You mean the music? It's a background tape—sea sounds from Earth. It's a couple of centuries old."

She looked at me oddly. "You're really absorbed by the whole planetary thing, aren't you? 'Sea sounds.'"

"Mars will have seas someday. That's what our whole Project is about, isn't it?"

She looked disturbed. "Sure . . . We're working at it, Hans, but that doesn't mean we have to live there. I mean, that's centuries from now, isn't it? Even if we're still alive, we'll be different people by then. Just think of being trapped down a gravity well. I'd choke to death."

I said quietly, "I don't think of it as being for the purposes of settlement. It's a clearer, more ideal activity. The instigation by Fourth-Level cognitive agents of a Third-Level Prigoginic Leap. Bringing life itself into being on the naked bedrock of space-time. . . ."

But she was shaking her head and backpedaling toward the door. "I'm sorry, Hans, but those sounds, they're just . . . getting into my blood somehow. . . ." She shook herself, shuddering, and the filigree beads woven into her blonde hair clattered loudly. "I can't bear it."

"I'll turn it off."

But she was already leaving. "Goodbye, goodbye . . . We'll meet again soon."

She was gone. I was left to steep in my own isolation, while the roaring surf gnawed and mumbled at its shore.

One of Kulagin's servos met me at his door and took my hat. Kulagin was seated at a workplace in a screened-off corner of his marigold-reeking domicile, watching stock quotations scroll down a display screen. He was dictating orders into a microphone on his forearm gauntlet. When the servo announced me he unplugged the jack from his gauntlet and stood, shaking my hand with both of his. "Welcome, friend, welcome."

"I hope I haven't come at a bad time."

"No, not at all. Do you play the Market?"

"Not seriously," I said. "Later, maybe, when the royalties from Eisho Zaibatsu pile up."

"You must allow me to guide your eyes, then. A good Posthumanist should have a wide range of interests. Take that chair, if you would."

I sat beside Kulagin as he sat before the console and plugged in. Kulagin was a Mechanist, but he kept himself rigorously antiseptic. I liked him.

He said, "Odd how these financial institutions tend to drift from their original purpose. In a way, the Market itself has made a sort of Prigoginic Leap. On its face, it's a commercial tool, but it's become a game of conventions and confidences. We Cicadas eat, breathe, and sleep rumors, so the Market is the perfect expression of our zeitgeist."

"Yes," I said. "Frail, mannered, and based on practically nothing tangible."

Kulagin lifted his plucked brows. "Yes, my young friend, exactly like the bedrock of the cosmos itself. Every level of complexity floats freely on the last, supported only by abstractions. Even natural laws are only our attempts to strain our vision through the Prigoginic event horizon. . . . If you prefer a more primal metaphor, we can compare the Market to the sea. A sea of information, with a few blue-chip islands here and there for the exhausted swimmer. Look at this."

He touched buttons, and a three-dimensional grid display sprang into being. "This is Market activity in the past forty-eight hours. It looks rather like the waves and billows of a sea, doesn't it? Note these surges of transaction." He touched the screen with the light pen implanted in his forefinger, and gridded areas flushed from cool green to red. "That was when the first rumors of the iceteroid came in—"

"What?"

"The asteroid, the ice-mass from the Ring Council. Someone has bought it and is mass-driving it out of Saturn's gravity well right now, bound for Martian impact. Someone very clever, for it will pass within a few thousands of klicks from C-K. Close enough for naked-eye view."

"You mean they've really done it?" I said, caught between shock and joy.

"I heard it third-, fourth-, maybe tenth-hand, but it fits in well with the parameters the Polycarbon engineers have set up. A mass of ice and volatiles, well over three klicks across, targeted for the Hellas Depression south of the equator at sixty-five klicks a second, impact expected at UT 20:14:53, 14-4-'54. . . . That's dawn, local time. Local Martian time, I mean."

"But that's months from now," I said.

Kulagin smirked. "Look, Hans, you don't push a three-klick ice clump with your thumbs. Besides, this is just the first of dozens. It's more of a symbolic gesture."

"But it means we'll be moving out! To Martian orbit!"

Kulagin looked skeptical. "That's a job for drones and monitors, Hans. Or maybe a few rough and tough pioneer types. Actually, there's no reason why you and I should have to leave the comforts of C-K."

I stood up, knotting my hands. "You want to *stay*? And miss the Prigoginic catalyst?"

Kulagin looked up with a slight frown. "Cool off, Hans, sit down, they'll be looking for volunteers soon enough, and if you really mean to go I'm sure you can manage somehow. . . . The point is that the effect on the Market has been spectacular. . . . It's been fairly giddy ever since the Comptroller's death, and now some very big fish indeed is rising for the kill. I've been following his movements for three day-shifts straight, hoping to feast on his scraps, so to speak. . . . Care for an inhale?"

"No, thanks."

Kulagin helped himself to a long pull of stimulant. He looked ragged. I'd never seen him without his face paint before. He said, "I don't have the feeling for mob psychology that you Shapers have, so I have to make do with a very, very good memory. . . . The last time I saw something like this was thirteen years ago. Someone spread the rumor that the Queen had tried to leave C-K, and the Advisers had restrained her by force. The upshot of that was the Crash of 'Forty-one, but the real killing came in the Rally that followed. I've been reviewing the tapes of the Crash, and I recognize the fins and flippers and big sharp teeth of an old friend. I can read his style in his maneuvering. It's not the slick guile of a Shaper. It's not the cold persistence of a Mechanist, either."

I considered. "Then you must mean Wellspring."

Wellspring's age was unknown. He was well over two centuries old. He claimed to have been born on Earth in the dawn of the Space Age, and to have lived in the first generation of independent space colonies, the so-called Concatenation. He had been among the founders of Czarina-Kluster, building the Queen's habitat when she fled in disgrace from her fellow Investors.

Kulagin smiled. "Very good, Hans. You may live in moss, but there's none on you. I think Wellspring engineered the Crash of 'Forty-one for his own profit."

"But he lives very modestly."

"As the Queen's oldest friend, he was certainly in a perfect position to start rumors. He even engineered the parameters of the Market itself, seventy years ago. And it was after the Rally that the Kosmosity-Metasystems Department of Terraformation was set up. Through anonymous donations, of course."

"But contributions came in from all over the system," I objected. "Almost all the sects and factions think that terraforming is humanity's sublimest effort."

"To be sure. Though I wonder just how that idea became so widely spread. And to whose benefit. Listen, Hans. I love Wellspring. He's a *friend,* and I remember the cold. But you have to realize just what an anomaly he is. He's not one of us. He wasn't even born in space." He looked at me narrowly, but I took no offense at his use of the term *born.* It was a deadly insult against Shapers, but I considered myself a Polycarbon first and Cicada second, with Shaperism a distant third.

He smiled briefly. "To be sure, Wellspring has a few Mechanist knick-knacks implanted, to extend his life span, but he lacks the whole Mech style. In fact he actually *predates* it. I'd be the last to deny the genius of you Shapers, but in a way it's an artificial genius. It works out well enough on IQ tests, but it

somehow lacks that, well, primeval quality that Wellspring has, just as we
Mechanists can use cybernetic modes of thinking but we can never be actual
machines. . . . Wellspring simply is one of those people at the farthest reaches of
the bell curve, one of those titans that spring up only once a generation. I mean,
think what's become of his normal human contemporaries."

I nodded. "Most of them have become Mechs."

Kulagin shook his head fractionally, staring at the screen. "I was born here
in C-K. I don't know that much about the old-style Mechs, but I do know that
most of the first ones are dead. Outdated, crowded out. Driven over the edge by
future shock. A lot of the first life-extension efforts failed, too, in very ugly
ways. . . . Wellspring survived that, too, from some innate knack he has. Think
of it, Hans. Here we sit, products of technologies so advanced that they've
smashed society to bits. We trade with aliens. We can even hitchhike to the stars,
if we pay the Investors' fare. And Wellspring not only holds his own, he rules us.
We don't even know his real name."

I considered what Kulagin had said while he switched to a Market update. I
felt bad. I could hide my feelings, but I couldn't shake them off. "You're right,"
I said. "But I trust him."

"I trust him too, but I know we're cradled in his hands. In fact, he's protect-
ing us right now. This terraforming project has cost megawatt after megawatt.
All those contributions were anonymous, supposedly to prevent the factions
from using them for propaganda. But I think it was to hide the fact that most of
them were from Wellspring. Any day now there's going to be an extended Market crash. Wellspring will make his move, and that will start the rally. And every
kilowatt of his profits will go to us."

I leaned forward in my chair, interlacing my fingers. Kulagin dictated a series of selling orders into his microphone. Suddenly I laughed.

Kulagin looked up. "That's the first time I've ever heard you laugh like you
meant it, Hans."

"I was just thinking. . . . You've told me all this, but I came here to talk
about Valery."

Kulagin looked sad. "Listen, Hans. What I know about women you could
hide under a microchip, but, as I said, my memory is excellent. The Shapers
blundered when they pushed things to the limits. The Ring Council tried to
break the so-called Two-Hundred Barrier last century. Most of the so-called Superbrights went mad, defected, turned against their fellows, or all three. They've
been hunted down by pirates and mercenaries for decades now.

"One group found out somehow that there was an Investor Queen living in
exile, and they managed to make it to her shadow, for protection. And someone—you can imagine who—talked the Queen into letting them stay, if they
paid a certain tax. That tax became the Queen's Percentage, and the settlement
became Czarina-Kluster. Valery's parents—yes, parents; it was a natural birth—
were among those Superbrights. She didn't have the schooling Shapers use, so
she ranks in at only one forty-five or so.

"The problem is those mood cycles of hers. Her parents had them, she's had them since she was a child. She's a dangerous woman, Hans. Dangerous to herself, to all of us. She should be under the dogs, really. I've suggested that to my friends in Security, but someone stands in my way. I have my ideas who."

"I'm in love with her. She won't speak to me."

"I see. Well, I understand she's been full of mood suppressants lately; that probably accounts for her reticence. . . . I'll speak frankly. There's an old saying, Hans, that you should never enter a discreet with someone crazier than you are. And it's good advice. You can't trust Valery."

He held up his hand. "Hear me out. You're young. You've just come out from under the dogs. This woman has enchanted you, and admittedly she has the famous Shaper charm in full measure. But a liaison with Valery is like an affair with five women, three of whom are crazy. C-K is full to bursting with the most beautiful women in human history. Admittedly you're a bit stiff, a bit of an obsessive perhaps, but you have a certain idealistic charm. And you have that Shaper intensity, fanaticism even, if you don't mind my saying so. Loosen up a little, Hans. Find some woman who'll rub the rough edges off of you. Play the field. It's a good way to recruit new friends to the Clique."

"I'll keep what you said in mind," I said.

"Right. I knew it was wasted effort." He smiled ironically. "Why should I blight the purity of your emotions? A tragic first love may become an asset to you, fifty or a hundred years from now." He turned his attention back to the screen. "I'm glad we had this talk, Hans. I hope you'll get in touch again when the Eisho Zaibatsu money comes through. We'll have some fun with it."

"I'd like that," I said, though I knew already that every kilowatt not spent on my own research would go—anonymously—to the terraforming fund. "And I don't resent your advice. It's just that it's of no use to me."

"Ah, youth," Kulagin said. I left.

Back to the simple beauty of the lichens. I had been trained for years to specialize in them, but they had taken on beauty and meaning for me only after my Posthumanist enlightenment. Viewed through C-K's philosophies, they stood near the catalysis point of the Prigoginic Leap that brought life itself into being.

Alternately, a lichen could be viewed as an extended metaphor for the Polycarbon Clique: a fungus and an alga, potential rivals, united in symbiosis to accomplish what neither could do alone, just as the Clique united Mechanist and Shaper to bring life to Mars.

I knew that many viewed my dedication as strange, even unhealthy. I was not offended by their blindness. Just the names of my genetic stocks had a rolling majesty: *Alectoria nigricans, Mastodia tessellata, Ochrolechia frigida, Stereocaulon alpinum.* They were humble but powerful: creatures of the cold desert whose roots and acids could crumble naked, freezing rock.

My gel frames seethed with primal vitality. Lichens would drench Mars in one green-gold tidal wave of life. They would creep irresistibly from the moist craters of the iceteroid impacts, proliferating relentlessly amid the storms and earthquakes of terraformation, surviving the floods as permafrost melted. Gushing oxygen, fixing nitrogen.

They were the best. Not because of pride or show. Not because they trumpeted their motives, or threatened the cold before they broke it. But because they were silent, and the first.

My years under the dogs had taught me the value of silence. Now I was sick of surveillance. When the first royalty payment came in from Eisho Zaibatsu, I contacted one of C-K's private security firms and had my apartment swept for bugs. They found four.

I hired a second firm to remove the bugs left by the first.

I strapped myself in at a floating workbench, turning the spy eyes over and over in my hands. They were flat videoplates, painted with one-way colorshifting polymer camouflage. They would fetch a nice price on the unofficial market.

I called a post office and hired a courier servo to take the bugs to Kulagin. While I awaited the servo's arrival, I turned off the bugs and sealed them into a biohazard box. I dictated a note, asking Kulagin to sell them and invest the money for me in C-K's faltering Market. The Market looked as if it could use a few buyers.

When I heard the courier's staccato knock, I opened my door with a gauntlet remote. But it was no courier that whirred in. It was a guard dog.

"I'll take that box, if you please," said the dog.

I stared at it as if I had never seen a dog before. This dog was heavily armored in silver. Thin powerful limbs jutted from its silver-seamed black-plastic torso, and its swollen head bristled with spring-loaded taser darts and the blunt nozzles of restraint webs. Its swiveling antenna tail showed that it was under remote control.

I spun my workbench so that it stood between me and the dog. "I see you have my comm lines tapped as well," I said. "Will you tell me where the taps are, or do I have to take my computer apart?"

"You sniveling little Shaper upstart," commented the dog, "do you think your royalties can buy you out from under everyone? I could sell you on the open market before you could blink."

I considered this. On a number of occasions, particularly troublesome meddlers in C-K had been arrested and offered for sale on the open market by the Queen's Advisers. There were always factions outside C-K willing to pay good prices for enemy agents. I knew that the Ring Council would be overjoyed to make an example of me. "You're claiming to be one of the Queen's Advisers, then?"

"*Of course* I'm an Adviser! Your treacheries haven't lured us all to sleep. Your friendship with Wellspring is notorious!" The dog whirred closer, its clumped camera eyes clicking faintly. "What's inside that freezer?"

"Lichen racks," I said impassively. "You should know that well enough."

"Open it."

I didn't move. "You're going beyond the bounds of normal operations," I said, knowing that this would trouble any Mechanist. "My Clique has friends among the Advisers. I've done nothing wrong."

"Open it, or I'll web you and open it myself, with this dog."

"Lies," I said. "You're no Adviser. You're an industrial spy, trying to steal my gemstone lichen. Why would an Adviser want to look into my freezer?"

"Open it! Don't involve yourself more deeply in things you don't understand."

"You've entered my domicile under false pretense and threatened me," I said. "I'm calling Security."

The dog's chromed jaws opened. I twisted myself free of the workbench, but a thready spray of white silk from one of the dog's facial nozzles caught me as I dodged. The filaments clung and hardened instantly, locking my arms in place where I had instinctively raised them to block the spray. A second blast caught my legs as I struggled uselessly, bouncing off a tilted Froth-wall.

"Troublemaker," muttered the dog. "Everything would have gone down smooth without you Shapers quibbling. We had the soundest banks, we had the Queen, the Market, everything. . . . You parasites gave C-K nothing but your fantasies. Now the system's crumbling. Everything will crash. Everything. I ought to kill you."

I gasped for breath as the spray rigidified across my chest. "Life isn't banks," I wheezed.

Motors whined as the dog flexed its jointed limbs. "If I find what I expect in that freezer, you're as good as dead."

Suddenly the dog stopped in midair. Its fans whirred as it wheeled to face the door. The door clicked convulsively and began to slide open. A massive taloned forelimb slammed through the opening.

The watchdog webbed the door shut. Suddenly the door shrieked and buckled, its metal peeling back like foil. The goggling head and spiked legs of a tiger crunched and thrashed through the wreckage. "Treason!" the tiger roared.

The dog whirred backward, cringing, as the tiger pulled its armored hindquarters into the room. The jagged wreckage of the door didn't even scratch it. Armored in black and gold, it was twice the size of the watchdog. "Wait," the dog said.

"The Council warned you against vigilante action," the tiger said heavily. "I warned you myself."

"I had to make a choice, Coordinator. It's *his* doing. He turned us against one another, you have to see that."

"You have only one choice left," the tiger said. "Choose your discreet, Councilman."

The dog flexed its limbs indecisively. "So I'm to be the second," he said. "First the Comptroller, now myself. Very well, then. Very well. He has me. I can't retaliate." The dog seemed to gather itself up for a rush. "But I can destroy his favorite!"

The dog's legs shot open like telescopes, and it sprang off a wall for my throat. There was a terrific flash with the stench of ozone, and the dog slammed bruisingly into my chest. It was dead, its circuits stripped. The lights flickered and went out as my home computer faltered and crashed, its programming scrambled by incidental radiation from the tiger's electromagnetic pulse.

Flanges popped open on the tiger's bulbous head, and two spotlights emerged. "Do you have any implants?" it said.

"No," I said. "No cybernetic parts. I'm all right. You saved my life."

"Close your eyes," the tiger commanded. It washed me with a fine mist of solvent from its nostrils. The web peeled off in its talons, taking my clothing with it.

My forearm gauntlet was ruined. I said, "I've committed no crime against the state, Coordinator. I love C-K."

"These are strange days," the tiger rumbled. "Our routines are in decay. No one is above suspicion. You picked a bad time to make your home mimic a discreet, young man."

"I did it openly," I said.

"There are no rights here, Cicada. Only the Queen's graces. Dress yourself and ride the tiger. We need to talk. I'm taking you to the Palace."

The Palace was like one gigantic discreet. I wondered if I would ever leave its mysteries alive.

I had no choice.

I dressed carefully under the tiger's goggling eyes, and mounted it. It smelled of aging lubrication. It must have been in storage for decades. Tigers had not been seen at large in C-K for years.

The halls were crowded with Cicadas going on and off their day shifts. At the tiger's approach they scattered in terror and awe.

We exited the Froth at its cylinder end, into the gimbaling cluster of interurban tube roads.

The roads were transparent polycarbon conduits, linking C-K's cylindrical suburbs in an untidy web. The sight of these shining habitats against the icy background of the stars gave me a sharp moment of vertigo. I remembered the cold.

We passed through a thickened knot along the web, a swollen intersection of tube roads where one of C-K's famous highway bistros had accreted itself into being. The lively gossip of its glittering habitués froze into a stricken silence as I rode by, and swelled into a chorus of alarm as I left. The news would permeate C-K in minutes.

The Palace imitated an Investor starship: an octahedron with six long rectangular sides. Genuine Investor ships were crusted with fantastic designs in hammered metal, but the Queen's was an uneven dull black, reflecting her unknown shame. With the passage of time it had grown by fits and starts, and now it was lumped and flanged with government offices and the Queen's covert hideaways. The ponderous hulk spun with dizzying speed.

We entered along one axis into a searing bath of blue-white light. My eyes shrank painfully and began oozing tears.

The Queen's Advisers were Mechanists, and the halls swarmed with servos.

They passively followed their routines, ignoring the tiger, whose chromed and plated surfaces gleamed viciously in the merciless light.

A short distance from the axis the centrifugal force seized us and the tiger sank creaking onto its massive legs. The walls grew baroque with mosaics and spun designs in filamented precious metals. The tiger stalked down a flight of stairs. My spine popped audibly in the increasing gravity, and I sat erect with an effort.

Most of the halls were empty. We passed occasional clumps of jewels in the walls that blazed like lightning. I leaned against the tiger's back and locked my elbows, my heart pounding. More stairs. Tears ran down my face and into my mouth, a sensation that was novel and disgusting. My arms trembled with fatigue.

The Coordinator's office was on the perimeter. It kept him in shape for audiences with the Queen. The tiger stalked creaking through a pair of massive doors, built to Investor scale.

Everything in the office was in Investor scale. The ceilings were more than twice the height of a man. A chandelier overhead gushed a blistering radiance over two immense chairs with tall backs split by tail holes. A fountain surged and splattered feebly, exhausted by strain.

The Coordinator sat behind a keyboarded business desk. The top of the desk rose almost to his armpits, and his scaled boots dangled far above the floor. Beside him a monitor scrolled down the latest Market reports.

I heaved myself, grunting, off the tiger's back and up into the scratchy plush of an Investor chair seat. Built for an Investor's scaled rump, it pierced my trousers like wire.

"Have some sun shades," the Coordinator said. He opened a cavernous desk drawer, fished elbow-deep for a pair of goggles, and hurled them at me. I reached high, and they hit me in the chest.

I wiped my eyes and put on the goggles, groaning with relief. The tiger crouched at the foot of my chair, whirring to itself.

"Your first time in the Palace?" the Coordinator said.

I nodded with an effort.

"It's horrible, I know. And yet, it's all we have. You have to understand that, Landau. This is C-K's Prigoginic catalyst."

"You know the philosophy?" I said.

"Surely. Not all of us are fossilized. The Advisers have their factions. That's common knowledge." The Coordinator pushed his chair back. Then he stood up in its seat, climbed up onto his desk top, and sat on its forward edge facing me, his scaled boots dangling.

He was a blunt, stocky, powerfully muscled man, moving easily in the force that flattened me. His face was deeply and ferociously creased with two centuries of seams and wrinkles. His black skin gleamed dully in the searing light. His eyeballs had the brittle look of plastic. He said, "I've seen the tapes the dogs made, and I feel I understand you, Landau. Your sin is distance."

He sighed. "And yet you are less corrupt than others. . . . There is a certain threshold, an intensity of sin and cynicism, beyond which no society can survive. . . . Listen. I know about Shapers. The Ring Council. Stitched together by black fear and red greed, drawing power from the momentum of its own collapse. But C-K's had hope. You've lived here, you must have at least seen it, if you can't feel it directly. You must know how precious this place is. Under the Cicada Queen, we've drawn survival from a state of mind. Belief counts, confidence is central." The Comptroller looked at me, his dark face sagging. "I'll tell you the truth. And depend on your goodwill. For the proper response."

"Thank you."

"C-K is in crisis. Rumors of the Queen's disaffection have brought the Market to the point of collapse. This time they're more than rumors, Landau. The Queen is on the point of defection from C-K."

Stunned, I slumped suddenly into my chair. My jaw dropped. I closed it with a snap.

"Once the Market collapses," the Coordinator said, "it means the end of all we had. The news is already spreading. Soon there will be a run against the Czarina-Kluster banking system. The system will crash, C-K will die."

"But . . . ," I said. "If it's the Queen's own doing. . . ." I was having trouble breathing.

"It's *always* the doing of the Investors, Landau; it's been that way ever since they first swept in and made our wars into an institution. . . . We Mechanists had you Shapers at bay. We ruled the entire system while you hid in terror in the Rings. It was your trade with the Investors that got you on your feet again. In fact, they deliberately built you up, so that they could maintain a competitive trade market, pit the human race against itself, to their own profit. . . . Look at C-K. We live in harmony here. That could be the case everywhere. It's their doing."

"Are you saying," I said, "that the history of C-K is an Investor scheme? That the Queen was never really in disgrace?"

"They're not infallible," the Coordinator said. "I can save the Market, and C-K, if I can exploit their own greed. It's your jewels, Landau. Your jewels. I saw the Queen's reaction when her . . . damned lackey Wellspring presented your gift. You learn to know their moods, these Investors. She was livid with greed. Your patent could catalyze a major industry."

"You're wrong about Wellspring," I said. "The jewel was his idea. I was working with endolithic lichens. 'If they can live within stones they can live within jewels,' he said. I only did the busywork."

"But the patent's in your name." The Coordinator looked at the toes of his scaled boots. "With one catalyst, I could save the Market. I want you to transfer your patent from Eisho Zaibatsu to me. To the Czarina-Kluster People's Corporate Republic."

I tried to be tactful. "The situation does seem desperate," I said, "but no one within the Market really wants it destroyed. There are other powerful forces preparing for a rebound. Please understand—it's not for any personal gain that I must keep my patent. The revenue is already pledged. To terraforming."

A sour grimace deepened the crevasses in the Coordinator's face. He leaned forward, and his shoulders tightened with a muffled creaking of plastic. "Terraforming! Oh, yes, I'm familiar with the so-called moral arguments. The cold abstractions of bloodless ideologues. What about respect? Obligation? Loyalty? Are these foreign terms to you?"

I said, "It's not that simple. Wellspring says—"

"Wellspring!" he shouted. "He's no Terran, you fool, he's only a renegade, a traitor scarcely a hundred years old, who sold himself utterly to the aliens. They fear us, you see. They fear our energy. Our potential to invade their markets, once the star drive is in our hands. It should be obvious, Landau! They want to divert human energies into this enormous Martian boondoggle. We could be competing with them, spreading to the stars in one fantastic wave!" He held his arms out rigid before him, his wrists bent upward, and stared at the tips of his outstretched fingers.

His arms began to tremble. Then he broke, and cradled his head in his corded hands. "C-K could have been great. A core of unity, an island of safety in the chaos. The Investors mean to destroy it. When the Market crashes, when the Queen defects, it means the end."

"Will she really leave?"

"Who knows what she means to do." The Coordinator looked exhausted. "I've suffered seventy years from her little whims and humiliations. I don't know what it is to care anymore. Why should I break my heart trying to glue things together with your stupid knickknacks? After all, there's still the discreet!"

He looked up ferociously. "That's where your meddling sent the Councilman. Once we've lost everything, they'll be thick enough with blood to swim in!"

He leapt from his desk top, bounced across the carpet, and dragged me bodily from the chair. I grabbed feebly at his wrists. My arms and legs flopped as he shook me. The tiger scuttled closer, clicking. "I hate you," he roared. "I hate everything you stand for! I'm sick of your Clique and their philosophies and their pudding smiles. You've killed a good friend with your meddling.

"Get out! Get out of C-K. You have forty-eight hours. After that I'll have you arrested and sold to the highest bidder." He threw me contemptuously backward. I collapsed at once in the heavy gravity, my head thudding against the carpet.

The tiger pulled me to my feet as the Coordinator clambered back into his oversized chair. He looked into his Market screen as I climbed trembling onto the tiger's back.

"Oh, no," he said softly. "Treason." The tiger took me away.

I found Wellspring, at last, in Dogtown. Dogtown was a chaotic subcluster, pinwheeling slowly to itself above the rotational axis of C-K. It was a port and customhouse, a tangle of shipyards, storage drogues, quarantines, and social houses, catering to the vices of the footloose, the isolated, and the estranged.

Dogtown was the place to come when no one else would have you. It swarmed with transients: prospectors, privateers, criminals, derelicts from sects whose innovations had collapsed, bankrupts, defectors, purveyors of hazardous pleasures. Accordingly the entire area swarmed with dogs, and with subtler monitors. Dogtown was a genuinely dangerous place, thrumming with a deranged and predatory vitality. Constant surveillance had destroyed all sense of shame.

I found Wellspring in the swollen bubble of a tubeway bar, discussing a convoluted business deal with a man he introduced as "the Modem." The Modem was a member of a small but vigorous Mechanist sect known in C-K slang as Lobsters. These Lobsters lived exclusively within skin-tight life-support systems, flanged here and there with engines and input-output jacks. The suits were faceless and dull black. The Lobsters looked like chunks of shadow.

I shook the Modem's rough room-temperature gauntlet and strapped myself to the table.

I peeled a squeezebulb from the table's adhesive surface and had a drink. "I'm in trouble," I said. "Can we speak before this man?"

Wellspring laughed. "Are you joking? This is Dogtown! Everything we say goes onto more tapes than you have teeth, young Landau. Besides, the Modem is an old friend. His skewed vision should be of some use."

"Very well." I began explaining. Wellspring pressed for details. I omitted nothing.

"Oh, dear," Wellspring said when I had finished. "Well, hold on to your monitors, Modem, for you are about to see rumor break the speed of light. Odd that this obscure little bistro should launch the news that is certain to destroy C-K." He said this quite loudly, and I looked quickly around the bar. The jaws of the clientele hung open with shock. Little blobs of saliva oscillated in their mouths.

"The Queen is gone, then," Wellspring said. "She's probably been gone for weeks. Well, I suppose it couldn't be helped. Even an Investor's greed has limits. The Advisers couldn't lead her by the nose forever. Perhaps she'll show up somewhere else, some habitat more suited to her emotional needs. I suppose I had best get to my monitors and cut my losses while the Market still has some meaning."

Wellspring parted the ribbons of his slashed sleeve and looked casually at his forearm computer. The bar emptied itself, suddenly and catastrophically, the customers trailed by their personal dogs. Near the exit, a vicious hand-to-hand fight broke out between two Shaper renegades. They spun with piercing cries through the crunching grip-and-tumble of free-fall jujitsu. Their dogs watched impassively.

Soon the three of us were alone with the bar servos and half a dozen fascinated dogs. "I could tell from my last audience that the Queen would leave," Wellspring said calmly. "C-K had outlived its usefulness, anyway. It was important only as the motivational catalyst for the elevation of Mars to the Third Prigoginic Level of Complexity. It was fossilizing under the weight of the

Advisers' programs. Typical Mech shortsightedness. Pseudopragmatic material-ism. They had it coming."

Wellspring showed an inch of embroidered undercuff as he signaled a servo for another round. "The Councilman you mentioned has retired to a discreet. He won't be the last one they haul out by the heels."

"What will I do?" I said. "I'm losing everything. What will become of the Clique?"

Wellspring frowned. "Come on, Landau! Show some Posthuman fluidity. The first thing to do, of course, is to get you into exile before you're arrested and sold. I imagine our friend the Modem here can help with that."

"To be sure," the Modem enunciated. He had a vocoder unit strapped to his throat, and it projected an inhumanly beautiful synthesized voice. "Our ship, the *Crowned Pawn,* is hauling a cargo of iceteroid mass drivers to the Ring Council. It's for the Terraforming Project. Any friend of Wellspring's is welcome to join us."

I laughed incredulously. "For me, that's suicide. Go back to the Council? I might as well open my throat."

"Be at ease," the Modem soothed. "I'll have the medi-mechs work you over and graft on one of our shells. One Lobster is very much like another. You'll be perfectly safe, under the skin."

I was shocked. "Become a Mech?"

"You don't have to *stay* one," Wellspring said. "It's a simple procedure. A few nerve grafts, some anal surgery, a tracheotomy . . . You lose on taste and touch, but the other senses are vastly expanded."

"Yes," said the Modem. "And you can step alone into naked space, and laugh."

"Right!" said Wellspring. "More Shapers should wear Mech technics. It's like your lichens, Hans. Become a symbiosis for a while. It'll broaden your horizons."

I said, "You don't do . . . anything *cranial,* do you?"

"No," said the Modem offhandedly. "Or, at least, we don't have to. Your brain's your own."

I thought. "Can you do it in"—I looked at Wellspring's forearm—"thirty-eight hours?"

"If we hurry," the Modem said. He detached himself from the table.

I followed him.


The *Crowned Pawn* was under way. My skin clung magnetically to a ship's girder as we accelerated. I had my vision set for normal wavelengths as I watched Czarina-Kluster receding.

Tears stung the fresh tracks of hair-thin wires along my deadened eyeballs. C-K wheeled slowly, like a galaxy in a jeweled web. Here and there along the network, flares pulsed as suburbs began the tedious and tragic work of cutting themselves loose. C-K was in the grip of terror.

I longed for the warm vitality of my Clique. I was no Lobster. They were

alien. They were solipsistic pinpoints in the galactic night, their humanity a forgotten pulp behind black armor.

The *Crowned Pawn* was like a ship turned inside out. It centered around a
core of massive magnetic engines, fed by drones from a chunk of reaction mass.
Outside these engines was a skeletal metal framework where Lobsters clung like
cysts or skimmed along on induced magnetic fields. There were cupolas here
and there on the skeleton where the Lobsters hooked into fluidic computers or
sheltered themselves from solar storms and ring-system electrofluxes.

They never ate. They never drank. Sex involved a clever cyber-stimulation
through cranial plugs. Every five years or so they "molted" and had their skins
scraped clean of the stinking accumulation of mutated bacteria that scummed
them over in the stagnant warmth.

They knew no fear. Agoraphobia was a condition easily crushed with drugs.
They were self-contained and anarchical. Their greatest pleasure was to sit along
a girder and open their amplified senses to the depths of space, watching stars
past the limits of ultraviolet and infrared, or staring into the flocculate crawling
plaque of the surface of the sun, or just sitting and soaking in watts of solar energy through their skins while they listened with wired ears to the warbling of
Van Allen belts and the musical tick of pulsars.

There was nothing evil about them, but they were not human. As distant
and icy as comets, they were creatures of the vacuum, bored with the outmoded
paradigms of blood and bone. I saw within them the first stirrings of the Fifth
Prigoginic Leap—that postulated Fifth Level of Complexity as far beyond intelligence as intelligence is from amoebic life, or life from inert matter.

They frightened me. Their bland indifference to human limitations gave
them the sinister charisma of saints.

The Modem came skimming along a girder and latched himself soundlessly
beside me. I turned my ears on and heard his voice above the radio hiss of the
engines. "You have a call, Landau. From C-K. Follow me."

I flexed my feet and skimmed along the rail behind him. We entered the radiation lock of an iron cupola, leaving it open, since the Lobsters disliked closed
spaces.

Before me, on a screen, was the tear-streaked face of Valery Korstad.
"Valery!" I said.

"Is that you, Hans?"

"Yes. Yes, darling. It's good to see you."

"Can't you take that mask off, Hans? I want to see your face."

"It's not a mask, darling. And my face is, well, not a pretty sight. All those
wires . . ."

"You sound different, Hans. Your voice sounds different."

"That's because this voice is a radio analogue. It's synthesized."

"How do I know it's really you, then? God, Hans . . . I'm so afraid. Everything . . . it's just evaporating. The Froth is . . . there's a biohazard scare, something smashed the gel frames in your domicile, I guess it was the dogs, and now
the lichen, the damned lichen is sprouting everywhere. It grows so fast!"

"I designed it to grow fast, Valery, that was the whole point. Tell them to use a metal aerosol or sulfide particulates; either one will kill it in a few hours. There's no need for panic."

"No need! Hans, the discreets are suicide factories. C-K is through! We've lost the Queen!"

"There's still the Project," I said. "The Queen was just an excuse, a catalyst. The Project can draw as much respect as the damned Queen. The groundwork's been laid for years. This is the moment. Tell the Clique to liquidate all they have. The Froth must move to Martian orbit."

Valery began to drift sideways. "That's all you cared about all along, wasn't it? The Project! I degraded myself, and you, with your cold, that Shaper distance, you left me in despair!"

"Valery!" I shouted, stricken. "I called you a dozen times, it was you who closed yourself off, it was me who needed warmth after those years under the dogs—"

"You could have done it!" she screamed, her face white with passion. "If you cared you would have broken in to prove it! You expected me to come crawling in humiliation? Black armor or dog's eyeglass, Hans, what's the difference? You're still not with me!"

I felt the heat of raw fury touching my numbed skin. "Blame me, then! How was I to know your rituals, your sick little secrets? I thought you'd thrown me over while you sneered and whored with Wellspring! Did you think I'd compete with the man who showed me my salvation? I would have slashed my wrists to see you smile, and you gave me nothing, nothing but disaster!"

A look of cold shock spread across her painted face. Her mouth opened, but no words came forth. Finally, with a small smile of total despair, she broke the connection. The screen went black.

I turned to the Modem. "I want to go back," I said.

"Sorry," he said. "First, you'd be killed. And second, we don't have the wattage to turn back. We're carrying a massive cargo." He shrugged. "Besides, C-K is in dissolution. We've known it was coming for a long time. In fact, some colleagues of ours are arriving there within the week with a second cargo of mass drivers. They'll fetch top prices as the Kluster dissolves."

"You knew?"

"We have our sources."

"Wellspring?"

"Who, him? He's leaving, too. He wants to be in Martian orbit when *that* hits." The Modem glided outside the cuploa and pointed along the plane of the ecliptic. I followed his gaze, shifting clumsily along the visual wavelengths.

I saw the etched and ghostly flare of the Martian asteroid's mighty engines. "The iceteroid," I said.

"Yes, of course. The comet of your disaster, so to speak. A useful symbol for C-K's decay."

"Yes," I said. I thought I recognized the hand of Wellspring in this. As the ice payload skimmed past C-K the panicked eyes of its inhabitants would follow it. Suddenly I felt a soaring sense of hope.

"How about *that?*" I said. "Could you land me there?"

"On the asteroid?"

"Yes! They're going to detach the engines, aren't they? In orbit! I can join my fellows there, and I won't miss the Prigoginic catalyst!"

"I'll check." The Modem fed a series of parameters into one of the fluidics. "Yes . . . I could sell you a parasite engine that you could strap on. With enough wattage and a cybersystem to guide you, you could match trajectory within, say, seventy-two hours."

"Good! Good! Let's do that then."

"Very well," he said. "There remains only the question of price."


I had time to think about the price as I burned along through the piercing emptiness. I thought I had done well. With C-K's Market in collapse I would need new commercial agents for the Eisho jewels. Despite their eeriness, I felt I could trust the Lobsters.

The cybersystem led me to a gentle groundfall on the sunside of the asteroid. It was ablating slowly in the heat of the distant sun, and infrared wisps of volatiles puffed here and there from cracks in the bluish ice.

The iceteroid was a broken spar calved from the breakup of one of Saturn's ancient glacial moons. It was a mountainous splintered crag with the fossilized scars of primordial violence showing themselves in wrenched and jagged cliffs and buttresses. It was roughly egg-shaped, five kilometers by three. Its surface had the bluish pitted look of ice exposed for thousands of years to powerful electric fields.

I roughened the gripping surfaces of my gauntlets and pulled myself and the parasite engine hand over hand into shadow. The engine's wattage was exhausted, but I didn't want it drifting off in the ablation.

I unfolded the radio dish the Modem had sold me and anchored it to a crag, aligning it with C-K. Then I plugged in.

The scope of the disaster was total. C-K had always prided itself on its open broadcasts, part of the whole atmosphere of freedom that had vitalized it. Now open panic was dwindling into veiled threats, and then, worst of all, into treacherous bursts of code. From all over the system, pressures long held back poured in.

The offers and threats mounted steadily, until the wretched cliques of C-K were pressed to the brink of civil war. Hijacked dogs prowled the tubes and corridors, tools of power elites made cruel by fear. Vicious kangaroo courts stripped dissidents of their status and property. Many chose the discreets.

Crèche cooperatives broke up. Stone-faced children wandered aimlessly through suburban halls, dazed on mood suppressants. Precious few dared to care any longer. Sweating Marketeers collapsed across their keyboards, sinuses bleeding from inhalants. Women stepped naked out of commandeered airlocks and died in sparkling gushes of frozen air. Cicadas struggled to weep through altered eyes, or floated in darkened bistros, numbed with disaster and drugs.

Centuries of commercial struggle had only sharpened the teeth of the cartels. They slammed in with the cybernetic precision of the Mechanists, with the slick unsettling brilliance of the Reshaped. With the collapse of the Market, C-K's industries were up for grabs. Commercial agents and arrogant diplomats annexed whole complexes. Groups of their new employees stumbled through the Queen's deserted Palace, vandalizing anything they couldn't steal outright.

The frightened subfactions of C-K were caught in the classic double bind that had alternately shaped and splintered the destinies of humanity in Space. On the one hand their technically altered modes of life and states of mind drove them irresistibly to distrust and fragmentation; on the other, isolation made them the prey of united cartels. They might even be savaged by the pirates and privateers that the cartels openly condemned and covertly supported.

And instead of helping my Clique, I was a black dot clinging like a spore to the icy flank of a frozen mountain.

It was during those sad days that I began to appreciate my skin. If Wellspring's plans had worked, then there would come a flowering. I would survive this ice in my sporangial casing, as a windblown speck of lichen will last out decades to spread at last into devouring life. Wellspring had been wise to put me here. I trusted him. I would not fail him.

As boredom gnawed at me I sank gently into a contemplative stupor. I opened my eyes and ears past the point of overload. Consciousness swallowed itself and vanished into the roaring half existence of an event horizon. Spacetime, the Second Level of Complexity, proclaimed its noumenon in the whine of stars, the rumble of planets, the transcendent crackle and gush of the uncoiling sun.

There came a time when I was roused at last by the sad and empty symphonies of Mars.

I shut down the suit's amplifiers. I no longer needed them. The catalyst, after all, is always buried by the process.

I moved south along the asteroid's axis, where I was sure to be discovered by the team sent to recover the mass driver. The driver's cybersystem had reoriented the asteroid for partial deceleration, and the south end had the best view of the planet.

Only moments after the final burn, the ice mass was matched by a pirate. It was a slim and beautiful Shaper craft, with long ribbed sun wings of iridescent fabric as thin as oil on water. Its shining organo-metallic hull hid eighth-generation magnetic engines with marvelous speed and power. The blunt nodes of weapons systems knobbed its sleekness.

I went into hiding, burrowing deep into a crevasse to avoid radar. I waited until curiosity and fear got the better of me. Then I crawled out and crept to a lookout point along a fractured ice ridge.

The ship had docked and sat poised on its cocked manipulator arms, their mantislike tips anchored into the ice. A crew of Mechanist mining drones had decamped and were boring into the ice of a clean-sheared plateau.

No Shaper pirate would have mining drones on board. The ship itself had undergone systems deactivation and sat inert and beautiful as an insect in amber, its vast sun wings folded. There was no sign of any crew.

I was not afraid of drones. I pulled myself boldly along the ice to observe their operations. No one challenged me.

I watched as the ungainly drones rasped and chipped the ice. Ten meters down they uncovered the glint of metal.

It was an airlock.

There they waited. Time passed. They received no further orders. They shut themselves down and crouched inert on the ice, as dead as the boulders around us.

For safety's sake I decided to enter the ship first.

As its airlock opened, the ship began switching itself back on. I entered the cabin. The pilot's couch was empty.

There was no one on board.

It took me almost two hours to work my way into the ship's cybersystem. Then I learned for certain what I had already suspected. It was Wellspring's ship.

I left the ship and crawled across the ice to the airlock. It opened easily. Wellspring had never been one to complicate things unnecessarily.

Beyond the airlock's second door a chamber blazed with blue-white light. I adjusted my eye systems and crawled inside.

At the far end, in the iceteroid's faint gravity, there was a bed of jewels. It was not a conventional bed. It was simply a huge, loose-packed heap of precious gems.

The Queen was asleep on top of it.

I used my eyes again. There was no infrared heat radiating from her. She lay quite still, her ancient arms clutching something to her chest, her three-toed legs drawn up along her body, her massive tail curled up beneath her rump and between her legs. Her huge head, the size of a man's torso, was encased in a gigantic crowned helmet encrusted with blazing diamonds. She was not breathing. Her eyes were closed. Her thick, scaled lips were drawn back slightly, showing two blunt rows of peg-shaped yellowing teeth.

She was ice-cold, sunk in some kind of alien cryosleep. Wellspring's coup was revealed. The Queen had joined willingly in her own abduction. Wellspring had stolen her in an act of heroic daring, robbing his rivals in C-K to begin again in Martian orbit. It was an astounding fait accompli that would have put him and his disciples into unquestioned power.

I was overcome with admiration for his plan. I wondered, though, why he had not accompanied his ship. Doubtless there were medicines aboard to wake the Queen and spirit her off to the nascent Kluster.

I moved nearer. I had never seen an Investor face to face. Still, I could tell after a moment that there was something wrong with her skin. I'd thought it was a trick of the light at first. But then I saw what she had in her hands.

It was the lichen jewel. The rapacity of her clawed grip had split it along one of the fracture planes, already weakened by the lichens' acids. Released from its crystalline prison, and spurred to frenzy by the powerful light, the lichens had crept onto her scaly fingers, and then up her wrist, and then, in an explosive paroxysm of life, over her entire body. She glittered green and gold with devouring fur. Even her eyes, her gums.

I went back to the ship. It was always said of us Shapers that we were brilliant under pressure. I reactivated the drones and had them refill their borehole. They tamped ice chips into it and melted them solid with the parasite rocket.

I worked on intuition, but all my training told me to trust it. That was why I had stripped the dead Queen and loaded every jewel aboard the ship. I felt a certainty beyond any chain of logic. The future lay before me like a drowsing woman awaiting the grip of her lover.

Wellspring's tapes were mine. The ship was his final sanctum, programmed in advance. I understood then the suffering and the ambition that had driven him, and that now were mine.

His dead hand had drawn representatives of every faction to witness the Prigoginic implant. The protoKluster already in orbit was made up exclusively of drones and monitors. It was natural that the observers would turn to me. My ship controlled the drones.

The first panic-stricken refugees told me of Wellspring's fate. He had been dragged heels first from a discreet, followed closely by the bloodless corpse of sad Valery Korstad. Never again would she create delight. Never again would his charisma enthrall the Clique. It might have been a double suicide. Or, perhaps more likely, she murdered him and then herself. Wellspring could never believe that there was anything beyond his abilities to cure. A madwoman and a barren world were part and parcel of the same challenge. Eventually he met his limit, and it killed him. The details scarcely matter. A discreet had swallowed them in any case.

When I heard the news, the ice around my heart sealed shut, seamless and pure.

I had Wellspring's will broadcast as the iceteroid began its final plunge into the atmosphere. Tapes sucked the broadcast in as volatiles peeled smoking into the thin, starved air of Mars.

I lied about the will. I invented it. I had Wellspring's taped memories to hand; it was a simple thing to change my artificial voice to counterfeit his, to set the stage for my own crucial ascendancy. It was necessary for the future of T-K, Terraform-Kluster, that I proclaim myself Wellspring's heir.

Power accreted around me like rumors. It was said that beneath my armor I *was* Wellspring, that the real Landau had been the one to die with Valery in C-K. I encouraged the rumors. Misconceptions would unite the Kluster. I knew T-K would be a city without rival. Here, abstractions would take on flesh, phantoms would feed us. Once our ideals had slammed it into being, T-K would gather strength, unstoppably. My jewels alone gave it a power base that few cartels could match.

With understanding came forgiveness. I forgave Wellspring. His lies, his deceptions, had moved me better than the chimeric "truth." What did it matter? If we needed solid bedrock, we would have it orbit us.

And the fearsome beauty of that impact! The searing linearity of its descent! It was only one of many, but the one most dear to me. When I saw the milk-drop splatter of its collision into Mars, the concussive orgasmic gush of steam from the Queen's covert and frozen tomb, I knew at once what my mentor had known. A man driven by something greater than himself dares everything and fears nothing. Nothing at all.

From behind my black armor, I rule the Polycarbon Clique. Their elite are my Advisers. I remember the cold, but I no longer fear it. I have buried it forever, as the cold of Mars is buried beneath its seething carpet of greenery. The two of us, now one, have stolen a whole planet from the realm of Death. And I do not fear the cold. No, not at all.

# Sunken Gardens

**M**irasol's crawler loped across the badlands of the Mare Hadriacum, under a tormented Martian sky. At the limits of the troposphere, jet streams twisted, dirty streaks across pale lilac. Mirasol watched the winds through the fretted glass of the control bay. Her altered brain suggested one pattern after another: nests of snakes, nets of dark eels, maps of black arteries.

Since morning the crawler had been descending steadily into the Hellas Basin, and the air pressure was rising. Mars lay like a feverish patient under this thick blanket of air, sweating buried ice.

On the horizon thunderheads rose with explosive speed below the constant scrawl of the jet streams.

The basin was strange to Mirasol. Her faction, the Patternists, had been assigned to a redemption camp in northern Syrtis Major. There, two-hundred-mile-an-hour surface winds were common, and their pressurized camp had been buried three times by advancing dunes.

It had taken her eight days of constant travel to reach the equator.

From high overhead, the Regal faction had helped her navigate. Their orbiting city-state, Terraform-Kluster, was a nexus of monitor satellites. The Regals showed by their helpfulness that they had her under closer surveillance.

The crawler lurched as its six picklike feet scrabbled down the slopes of a deflation pit. Mirasol suddenly saw her own face reflected in the glass, pale and taut, her dark eyes dreamily self-absorbed. It was a bare face, with the anonymous beauty of the genetically Reshaped. She rubbed her eyes with nail-bitten fingers.

To the west, far overhead, a gout of airborne topsoil surged aside and revealed the Ladder, the mighty anchor cable of the Terraform-Kluster.

Above the winds the cable faded from sight, vanishing below the metallic glitter of the Kluster, swinging aloofly in orbit.

Mirasol stared at the orbiting city with an uneasy mix of envy, fear and reverence. She had never been so close to the Kluster before, or to the all-important Ladder that linked it to the Martian surface. Like most of her faction's younger generation, she had never been into space. The Regals had carefully kept her faction quarantined in the Syrtis redemption camp.

Life had not come easily to Mars. For one hundred years the Regals of Terraform-Kluster had bombarded the Martian surface with giant chunks of ice. This act of planetary engineering was the most ambitious, arrogant, and successful of all the works of man in space.

The shattering impacts had torn huge craters in the Martian crust, blasting tons of dust and steam into Mars's threadbare sheet of air. As the temperature rose, buried oceans of Martian permafrost roared forth, leaving networks of twisted badlands and vast expanses of damp mud, smooth and sterile as a television. On these great playas and on the frost-caked walls of channels, cliffs, and calderas, transplanted lichen had clung and leapt into devouring life. In the plains of Eridania, in the twisted megacanyons of the Coprates Basin, in the damp and icy regions of the dwindling poles, vast clawing thickets of its sinister growth lay upon the land—massive disaster areas for the inorganic.

As the terraforming project had grown, so had the power of Terraform-Kluster.

As a neutral point in humanity's factional wars, T-K was crucial to financiers and bankers of every sect. Even the alien Investors, those star-traveling reptiles of enormous wealth, found T-K useful, and favored it with their patronage.

And as T-K's citizens, the Regals, increased their power, smaller factions faltered and fell under their sway. Mars was dotted with bankrupt factions, financially captured and transported to the Martian surface by the T-K plutocrats.

Having failed in space, the refugees took Regal charity as ecologists of the sunken gardens. Dozens of factions were quarantined in cheerless redemption camps, isolated from one another, their lives pared to a grim frugality.

And the visionary Regals made good use of their power. The factions found themselves trapped in the arcane bioaesthetics of Posthumanist philosophy, subverted constantly by Regal broadcasts, Regal teaching, Regal culture. With time even the stubbornest faction would be broken down and digested into the cultural blood-stream of T-K. Faction members would be allowed to leave their redemption camp and travel up the Ladder.

But first they would have to prove themselves. The Patternists had awaited their chance for years. It had come at last in the Ibis Crater competition, an ecological struggle of the factions that would prove the victors' right to Regal status. Six factions had sent their champions to the ancient Ibis Crater, each one armed with its group's strongest biotechnologies. It would be a war of the sunken gardens, with the Ladder as the prize.

Mirasol's crawler followed a gully through a chaotic terrain of rocky permafrost that had collapsed in karsts and sinkholes. After two hours, the gully ended abruptly. Before Mirasol rose a mountain range of massive slabs and boulders, some with the glassy sheen of impact melt, others scabbed over with lichen.

As the crawler started up the slope, the sun came out, and Mirasol saw the crater's outer rim jigsawed in the green of lichen and the glaring white of snow.

The oxygen readings were rising steadily. Warm, moist air was drooling from within the crater's lip, leaving a spittle of ice. A half-million-ton asteroid from the Rings of Saturn had fallen here at fifteen kilometers a second. But for two centuries rain, creeping glaciers, and lichen had gnawed at the crater's rim, and the wound's raw edges had slumped and scarred.

The crawler worked its way up the striated channel of an empty glacier bed. A cold alpine wind keened down the channel, where flourishing patches of lichen clung to exposed veins of ice.

Some rocks were striped with sediment from the ancient Martian seas, and the impact had peeled them up and thrown them on their backs.

It was winter, the season for pruning the sunken gardens. The treacherous rubble of the crater's rim was cemented with frozen mud. The crawler found the glacier's root and clawed its way up the ice face. The raw slope was striped with winter snow and storm-blown summer dust, stacked in hundreds of red-and-white layers. With the years the stripes had warped and rippled in the glacier's flow.

Mirasol reached the crest. The crawler ran spiderlike along the crater's snowy rim. Below, in a bowl-shaped crater eight kilometers deep, lay a seething ocean of air.

Mirasol stared. Within this gigantic airsump, twenty kilometers across, a broken ring of majestic rain clouds trailed their dark skirts, like duchesses in quadrille, about the ballroom floor of a lens-shaped sea.

Thick forests of green-and-yellow mangroves rimmed the shallow water and had overrun the shattered islands at its center. Pinpoints of brilliant scarlet ibis spattered the trees. A flock of them suddenly spread kitelike wings and took to the air, spreading across the crater in uncounted millions. Mirasol was appalled by the crudity and daring of this ecological concept, its crass and primal vitality.

This was what she had come to destroy. The thought filled her with sadness.

Then she remembered the years she had spent flattering her Regal teachers, collaborating with them in the destruction of her own culture. When the chance at the Ladder came, she had been chosen. She put her sadness away, remembering her ambitions and her rivals.

The history of mankind in space had been a long epic of ambitions and rivalries. From the very first, space colonies had struggled for self-sufficiency and had soon broken their ties with the exhausted Earth. The independent life-support systems had given them the mentality of city-states. Strange ideologies had bloomed in the hot-house atmosphere of the o'neills, and breakaway groups were common.

Space was too vast to police. Pioneer elites burst forth, defying anyone to stop their pursuit of aberrant technologies. Quite suddenly the march of science had become an insane, headlong scramble. New sciences and technologies had shattered whole societies in waves of future shock.

The shattered cultures coalesced into factions, so thoroughly alienated from one another that they were called humanity only for lack of a better term. The Shapers, for instance, had seized control of their own genetics, abandoning mankind in a burst of artificial evolution. Their rivals, the Mechanists, had replaced flesh with advanced prosthetics.

Mirasol's own group, the Patternists, was a breakaway Shaper faction.

The Patternists specialized in cerebral asymmetry. With grossly expanded right-brain hemispheres, they were highly intuitive, given to metaphors, parallels, and sudden cognitive leaps. Their inventive minds and quick, unpredictable genius had given them a competitive edge at first. But with these advantages had come grave weaknesses: autism, fugue states, and paranoia. Patternists grew out of control and became grotesque webs of fantasy.

With these handicaps their colony had faltered. Patternist industries went into decline, outpaced by industrial rivals. Competition had grown much fiercer. The Shaper and Mechanist cartels had turned commercial action into a kind of endemic warfare. The Patternist gamble had failed, and the day came when their entire habitat was bought out from around them by Regal plutocrats. In a way it was a kindness. The Regals were suave and proud of their ability to assimilate refugees and failures.

The Regals themselves had started as dissidents and defectors. Their Posthumanist philosophy had given them the moral power and the bland assurance to dominate and absorb factions from the fringes of humanity. And they had the support of the Investors, who had vast wealth and the secret techniques of star travel.

The crawler's radar alerted Mirasol to the presence of a landcraft from a rival faction. Leaning forward in her pilot's couch, she put the craft's image on screen. It was a lumpy sphere, balanced uneasily on four long, spindly legs. Silhouetted against the horizon, it moved with a strange wobbling speed along the opposite lip of the crater, then disappeared down the outward slope.

Mirasol wondered if it had been cheating. She was tempted to try some cheating herself—to dump a few frozen packets of aerobic bacteria or a few dozen capsules of insect eggs down the slope—but she feared the orbiting monitors of the T-K supervisors. Too much was at stake—not only her own career but that of her entire faction, huddled bankrupt and despairing in their cold redemption camp. It was said that T-K's ruler, the Posthuman being they called the Lobster King, would himself watch the contest. To fail before his black abstracted gaze would be a horror.

On the crater's outside slope, below her, a second rival craft appeared, lurching and slithering with insane, aggressive grace. The craft's long supple body moved with a sidewinder's looping and coiling, holding aloft a massive shining head, like a faceted mirror ball.

Both rivals were converging on the rendezvous camp, where the six contestants would receive their final briefing from the Regal Adviser. Mirasol hurried forward.

When the camp first flashed into sight on her screen, Mirasol was shocked. The place was huge and absurdly elaborate: a drug dream of paneled geodesics and colored minarets, sprawling in the lichenous desert like an abandoned chandelier. This was a camp for Regals.

Here the arbiters and sophists of the BioArts would stay and judge the crater as the newly planted ecosystems struggled among themselves for supremacy.

The camp's airlocks were surrounded with shining green thickets of lichen, where the growth feasted on escaped humidity. Mirasol drove her crawler through the yawning airlock and into a garage. Inside the garage, robot mechanics were scrubbing and polishing the coiled hundred-meter length of the snake craft and the gleaming black abdomen of an eight-legged crawler. The black crawler was crouched with its periscoped head sunk downward, as if ready to pounce. Its swollen belly was marked with a red hourglass and the corporate logos of its faction.

The garage smelled of dust and grease overlaid with floral perfumes. Mirasol left the mechanics to their work and walked stiffly down a long corridor, stretching the kinks out of her back and shoulders. A latticework door sprang apart into filaments and resealed itself behind her.

She was in a dining room that clinked and rattled with the high-pitched repetitive sound of Regal music. Its walls were paneled with tall display screens showing startlingly beautiful garden panoramas. A pulpy-looking servo, whose organo-metallic casing and squat, smiling head had a swollen and almost diseased appearance, showed her to a chair.

Mirasol sat, denting the heavy white tablecloth with her knees. There were seven places at the table. The Regal Adviser's tall chair was at the table's head. Mirasol's assigned position gave her a sharp idea of her own status. She sat at the far end of the table, on the Adviser's left.

Two of her rivals had already taken their places. One was a tall, red-haired Shaper with long, thin arms, whose sharp face and bright, worried eyes gave him a querulous birdlike look. The other was a sullen, feral Mechanist with prosthetic hands and a paramilitary tunic marked at the shoulders with a red hourglass.

Mirasol studied her two rivals with silent, sidelong glances. Like her, they were both young. The Regals favored the young, and they encouraged captive factions to expand their populations widely.

This strategy cleverly subverted the old guard of each faction in a tidal wave of their own children, indoctrinated from birth by Regals.

The birdlike man, obviously uncomfortable with his place directly at the Adviser's right, looked as if he wanted to speak but dared not. The piratical Mech sat staring at his artificial hands, his ears stoppered with headphones.

Each place setting had a squeezebulb of liqueur. Regals, who were used to weightlessness in orbit, used these bulbs by habit, and their presence here was both a privilege and a humiliation.

The door fluttered open again, and two more rivals burst in, almost as if they had raced. The first was a flabby Mech, still not used to gravity, whose sagging limbs were supported by an extraskeletal framework. The second was a severely mutated Shaper whose elbowed legs terminated in grasping hands. The pedal hands were gemmed with heavy rings that clicked against each other as she waddled across the parquet floor.

The woman with the strange legs took her place across from the birdlike man. They began to converse haltingly in a language that none of the others could follow. The man in the framework, gasping audibly, lay in obvious pain in the chair across from Mirasol. His plastic eyeballs looked as blank as chips of glass. His sufferings in the pull of gravity showed that he was new to Mars, and his place in the competition meant that his faction was powerful. Mirasol despised him.

Mirasol felt a nightmarish sense of entrapment. Everything about her competitors seemed to proclaim their sickly unfitness for survival. They had a haunted, hungry look, like starving men in a lifeboat who wait with secret eagerness for the first to die.

She caught a glimpse of herself reflected in the bowl of a spoon and saw with a flash of insight how she must appear to the others. Her intuitive right brain was swollen beyond human bounds, distorting her skull. Her face had the blank prettiness of her genetic heritage, but she could feel the bleak strain of her expression. Her body looked shapeless under her quilted pilot's vest and dundrab, general-issue blouse and trousers. Her fingertips were raw from biting. She saw in herself the fey, defeated aura of her faction's older generation, those who had tried and failed in the great world of space, and she hated herself for it.

They were still waiting for the sixth competitor when the plonking music reached a sudden crescendo and the Regal Adviser arrived. Her name was Arkadya Sorienti, Incorporated. She was a member of T-K's ruling oligarchy, and she swayed through the bursting door with the careful steps of a woman not used to gravity.

She wore the Investor-style clothing of a high-ranking diplomat. The Regals were proud of their diplomatic ties with the alien Investors, since Investor patronage proved their own vast wealth. The Sorienti's knee-high boots had false birdlike toes, scaled like Investor hide. She wore a heavy skirt of gold cords braided with jewels, and a stiff wrist-length formal jacket with embroidered cuffs. A heavy collar formed an arching multicolored frill behind her head. Her blonde hair was set in an interlaced style as complex as computer wiring. The skin of her bare legs had a shiny, glossy look, as if freshly enameled. Her eyelids gleamed with soft reptilian pastels.

One of her corporate ladyship's two body-servos helped her to her seat. The Sorienti leaned forward brightly, interlacing small, pretty hands so crusted with rings and bracelets that they resembled gleaming gauntlets.

"I hope the five of you have enjoyed this chance for an informal talk," she said sweetly, just as if such a thing were possible. "I'm sorry I was delayed. Our sixth participant will not be joining us."

There was no explanation. The Regals never publicized any action of theirs that might be construed as a punishment. The looks of the competitors, alternately stricken and calculating, showed that they were imagining the worst.

The two squat servos circulated around the table, dishing out courses of food from trays balanced on their flabby heads. The competitors picked uneasily at their plates.

The display screen behind the Adviser flicked into a schematic diagram of the Ibis Crater. "Please notice the revised boundary lines," the Sorienti said. "I hope that each of you will avoid trespassing—not merely physically but biologically as well." She looked at them seriously. "Some of you may plan to use herbicides. This is permissible, but the spreading of spray beyond your sector's boundaries is considered crass. Bacteriological establishment is a subtle art. The spreading of tailored disease organisms is an aesthetic distortion. Please remember that your activities here are a disruption of what should ideally be natural process. Therefore the period of biotic seeding will last only twelve hours. Thereafter, the new complexity level will be allowed to stabilize itself without any other interference at all. Avoid self-aggrandizement, and confine yourselves to a primal role, as catalysts."

The Sorienti's speech was formal and ceremonial. Mirasol studied the display screen, noting with much satisfaction that her territory had been expanded.

Seen from overhead, the crater's roundness was deeply marred.

Mirasol's sector, the southern one, showed the long flattened scar of a major landslide, where the crater wall had slumped and flowed into the pit. The simple ecosystem had recovered quickly, and mangroves festooned the rubble's lowest slopes. Its upper slopes were gnawed by lichen and glaciers.

The sixth sector had been erased, and Mirasol's share was almost twenty square kilometers of new land.

It would give her faction's ecosystem more room to take root before the deadly struggle began in earnest.

This was not the first such competition. The Regals had held them for decades as an objective test of the skills of rival factions. It helped the Regals' divide-and conquer policy, to set the factions against one another.

And in the centuries to come, as Mars grew more hospitable to life, the gardens would surge from their craters and spread across the surface. Mars would become a warring jungle of separate creations. For the Regals the competitions were closely studied simulations of the future.

And the competitions gave the factions motives for their work. With the garden wars to spur them, the ecological sciences had advanced enormously. Already, with the progress of science and taste, many of the oldest craters had become ecoaesthetic embarrassments.

The Ibis Crater had been an early, crude experiment. The faction that had created it was long gone, and its primitive creation was now considered tasteless.

Each gardening faction camped beside its own crater, struggling to bring it to life. But the competitions were a shortcut up the Ladder. The competitors' philosophies and talents, made into flesh, would carry out a proxy struggle for supremacy. The sine-wave curves of growth, the rallies and declines of expansion and extinction, would scroll across the monitors of the Regal judges like stock-market reports. This complex struggle would be weighed in each of its aspects: technological, philosophical, biological, and aesthetic. The winners would abandon their camps to take on Regal wealth and power. They would roam T-K's jeweled corridors and revel in its perquisites: extended life spans, corporate titles, cosmopolitan tolerance, and the interstellar patronage of the Investors.

When red dawn broke over the landscape, the five were poised around the Ibis Crater, awaiting the signal. The day was calm, with only a distant nexus of jet streams marring the sky. Mirasol watched pink-stained sunlight creep down the inside slope of the crater's western wall. In the mangrove thickets birds were beginning to stir.

Mirasol waited tensely. She had taken a position on the upper slopes of the landslide's raw debris. Radar showed her rivals spaced along the interior slopes: to her left, the hourglass crawler and the jewel-headed snake; to her right, a mantislike crawler and the globe on stilts.

The signal came, sudden as lightning: a meteor of ice shot from orbit and left a shock-wave cloud plume of ablated steam. Mirasol charged forward.

The Patternists' strategy was to concentrate on the upper slopes and the landslide's rubble, a marginal niche where they hoped to excel. Their cold crater in Syrtis Major had given them some expertise in alpine species, and they hoped to exploit this strength. The landslide's long slope, far above sea level, was to be their power base. The crawler lurched downslope, blasting out a fine spray of lichenophagous bacteria.

Suddenly the air was full of birds. Across the crater, the globe on stilts had rushed down to the waterline and was laying waste the mangroves. Fine wisps of smoke showed the slicing beam of a heavy laser.

Burst after burst of birds took wing, peeling from their nests to wheel and dip in terror. At first, their frenzied cries came as a high-pitched whisper. Then, as the fear spread, the screeching echoed and reechoed, building to a mindless surf of pain. In the crater's dawn-warmed air, the scarlet motes hung in their millions, swirling and coalescing like drops of blood in free-fall.

Mirasol scattered the seeds of alpine rock crops. The crawler picked its way down the talus, spraying fertilizer into cracks and crevices. She pried up boulders and released a scattering of invertebrates: nematodes, mites, sowbugs, altered millipedes. She splattered the rocks with gelatin to feed them until the mosses and ferns took hold.

The cries of the birds were appalling. Downslope the other factions were thrashing in the muck at sea level, wreaking havoc, destroying the mangroves so that their own creations could take hold. The great snake looped and ducked through the canopy, knotting itself, ripping up swathes of mangroves by the roots. As Mirasol watched, the top of its faceted head burst open and released a cloud of bats.

The mantis crawler was methodically marching along the borders of its sector, its saw-edged arms reducing everything before it into kindling. The hourglass crawler had slashed through its territory, leaving a muddy network of fire zones. Behind it rose a wall of smoke.

It was a daring ploy. Sterilizing the sector by fire might give the new biome a slight advantage. Even a small boost could be crucial as exponential rates of growth took hold. But the Ibis Crater was a closed system. The use of fire required great care. There was only so much air within the bowl.

Mirasol worked grimly. Insects were next. They were often neglected in favor of massive sea beasts or flashy predators, but in terms of biomass, gram by gram, insects could overwhelm. She blasted a carton downslope to the shore, where it melted, releasing aquatic termites. She shoved aside flat shelves of rock, planting egg cases below their sun-warmed surfaces. She released a cloud of leaf-eating midges, their tiny bodies packed with bacteria. Within the crawler's belly, rack after automatic rack was thawed and fired through nozzles, dropped through spiracles or planted in the holes jabbed by picklike feet.

Each faction was releasing a potential world. Near the water's edge, the mantis had released a pair of things like giant black sail planes. They were swooping through the clouds of ibis, opening great sieved mouths. On the islands in the center of the crater's lake, scaled walruses clambered on the rocks, blowing steam. The stilt ball was laying out an orchard in the mangroves' wreckage. The snake had taken to the water, its faceted head leaving a wake of V-waves.

In the hourglass sector, smoke continued to rise. The fires were spreading, and the spider ran frantically along its network of zones. Mirasol watched the movement of the smoke as she released a horde of marmots and rock squirrels.

A mistake had been made. As the smoky air gushed upward in the feeble Martian gravity, a fierce valley wind of cold air from the heights flowed downward to fill the vacuum. The mangroves burned fiercely. Shattered networks of flaming branches were flying into the air.

The spider charged into the flames, smashing and trampling. Mirasol laughed, imagining demerits piling up in the judges' data banks. Her talus slopes were safe from fire. There was nothing to burn.

The ibis flock had formed a great wheeling ring above the shore. Within their scattered ranks flitted the dark shapes of airborne predators. The long plume of steam from the meteor had begun to twist and break. A sullen wind was building up.

Fire had broken out in the snake's sector. The snake was swimming in the sea's muddy waters, surrounded by bales of bright-green kelp. Before its pilot noticed, fire was already roaring through a great piled heap of the wreckage it had left on shore. There were no windbreaks left. Air poured down the denuded slope. The smoke column guttered and twisted, its black clouds alive with sparks.

A flock of ibis plunged into the cloud. Only a handful emerged; some of them were flaming visibly. Mirasol began to know fear. As smoke rose to the crater's rim, it cooled and started to fall outward and downward. A vertical whirlwind was forming, a torus of hot smoke and cold wind.

The crawler scattered seed-packed hay for pygmy mountain goats. Just before her an ibis fell from the sky with a dark squirming shape, all claws and teeth, clinging to its neck. She rushed forward and crushed the predator, then stopped and stared distractedly across the crater.

Fires were spreading with unnatural speed. Small puffs of smoke rose from a dozen places, striking large heaps of wood with uncanny precision. Her altered brain searched for a pattern. The fires springing up in the mantis sector were well beyond the reach of any falling debris.

In the spider's zone, flames had leapt the firebreaks without leaving a mark. The pattern felt wrong to her, eerily wrong, as if the destruction had a force all its own, a raging synergy that fed upon itself.

The pattern spread into a devouring crescent. Mirasol felt the dread of lost control—the sweating fear an orbiter feels at the hiss of escaping air or the way a suicide feels at the first bright gush of blood.

Within an hour the garden sprawled beneath a hurricane of hot decay. The dense columns of smoke had flattened like thunderheads at the limits of the garden's sunken troposphere. Slowly a spark-shot gray haze, dripping ash like rain, began to ring the crater. Screaming birds circled beneath the foul torus, falling by tens and scores and hundreds. Their bodies littered the garden's sea, their bright plumage blurred with ash in a steel-gray sump.

The landcraft of the others continued to fight the flames, smashing unharmed through the fire's charred borderlands. Their efforts were useless, a pathetic ritual before the disaster.

Even the fire's malicious purity had grown tired and tainted. The oxygen was falling. The flames were dimmer and spread more slowly, releasing a dark nastiness of half-combusted smoke.

Where it spread, nothing that breathed could live. Even the flames were killed as the smoke billowed along the crater's crushed and smoldering slopes.

Mirasol watched a group of striped gazelles struggle up the barren slopes of the talus in search of air. Their dark eyes, fresh from the laboratory, rolled in timeless animal fear. Their coats were scorched, their flanks heaved, their mouths dripped foam. One by one they collapsed in convulsions, kicking at the lifeless Martian rock as they slid and fell. It was a vile sight, the image of a blighted spring.

An oblique flash of red downslope to her left attracted her attention. A large red animal was skulking among the rocks. She turned the crawler and picked her way toward it, wincing as a dark surf of poisoned smoke broke across the fretted glass.

She spotted the animal as it broke from cover. It was a scorched and gasping creature like a great red ape. She dashed forward and seized it in the crawler's arms. Held aloft, it clawed and kicked, hammering the crawler's arms with a smoldering branch. In revulsion and pity, she crushed it. Its bodice of tight-sewn ibis feathers tore, revealing blood-slicked human flesh.

Using the crawler's grips, she tugged at a heavy tuft of feathers on its head. The tight-fitting mask ripped free, and the dead man's head slumped forward. She rolled it back, revealing a face tattooed with stars.

The ornithopter sculled above the burned-out garden, its long red wings beating with dreamlike fluidity. Mirasol watched the Sorienti's painted face as her corporate ladyship stared into the shining viewscreen.

The ornithopter's powerful cameras cast image after image onto the table-top screen, lighting the Regal's face. The tabletop was littered with the Sorienti's elegant knickknacks: an inhaler case, a half-empty jeweled squeezebulb, lorgnette binoculars, a stack of tape cassettes.

"An unprecedented case," her ladyship murmured. "It was not a total dieback after all but merely the extinction of everything with lungs. There must be strong survivorship among the lower orders: fish, insects, annelids. Now that the rain's settled the ash, you can see the vegetation making a strong comeback. Your own section seems almost undamaged."

"Yes," Mirasol said. "The natives were unable to reach it with torches before the fire storm had smothered itself."

The Sorienti leaned back into the tasseled arms of her couch. "I wish you wouldn't mention them so loudly, even between ourselves."

"No one would believe me."

"The others never saw them," the Regal said. "They were too busy fighting the flames." She hesitated briefly. "You were wise to confide in me first."

Mirasol locked eyes with her new patroness, then looked away. "There was no one else to tell. They'd have said I built a pattern out of nothing but my own fears."

"You have your faction to think of," the Sorienti said with an air of sympathy. "With such a bright future ahead of them, they don't need a renewed reputation for paranoid fantasies."

She studied the screen. "The Patternists are winners by default. It certainly makes an interesting case study. If the new garden grows tiresome we can have the whole crater sterilized from orbit. Some other faction can start again with a clean slate."

"Don't let them build too close to the edge," Mirasol said.

Her corporate ladyship watched her attentively, tilting her head.

"I have no proof," Mirasol said, "but I can see the pattern behind it all. The natives had to come from somewhere. The colony that stocked the crater must have been destroyed in that huge landslide. Was that your work? Did your people kill them?"

The Sorienti smiled. "You're very bright, my dear. You will do well, up the Ladder. And you can keep secrets. Your office as my secretary suits you very well."

"They were destroyed from orbit," Mirasol said. "Why else would they hide from us? You tried to annihilate them."

"It was a long time ago," the Regal said. "In the early days, when things were shakier. They were researching the secret of starflight, techniques only the Investors know. Rumor says they reached success at last, in their redemption camp. After that, there was no choice."

"Then they were killed for the Investors' profit," Mirasol said. She stood up quickly and walked around the cabin, her new jeweled skirt clattering around the knees. "So that the aliens could go on toying with us, hiding their secret, selling us trinkets."

The Regal folded her hands with a clicking of rings and bracelets. "Our Lobster King is wise," she said. "If humanity's efforts turned to the stars, what would become of terraforming? Why should we trade the power of creation itself to become like the Investors?"

"But think of the people," Mirasol said. "Think of them losing their technologies, degenerating into human beings. A handful of savages, eating bird meat. Think of the fear they felt for generations, the way they burned their own home and killed themselves when they saw us come to smash and destroy their world. Aren't you filled with horror?"

"For humans?" the Sorienti said. "No!"

"But can't you see? You've given this planet life as as art form, as an enormous game. You force us to play in it, and those people were killed for it! Can't you see how that blights everything?"

"Our game is reality," the Regal said. She gestured at the viewscreen. "You can't deny the savage beauty of destruction."

"You defend this catastrophe?"

The Regal shrugged. "If life worked perfectly, how could things evolve? Aren't we Posthuman? Things grow; things die. In time the cosmos kills us all. The cosmos has no meaning, and its emptiness is absolute. That's pure terror, but it's also pure freedom. Only our ambitions and our creations can fill it."

"And that justifies your actions?"

"We act for life," the Regal said. "Our ambitions have become this world's natural laws. We blunder because life blunders. We go on because life must go on. When you've taken the long view, from orbit—when the power we wield is in your own hands—then you can judge us." She smiled. "You will be judging yourself. You'll be Regal."

"But what about your captive factions? Your agents, who do your will? Once we had our own ambitions. We failed, and now you isolate us, indoctrinate us, make us into rumors. We must have something of our own. Now we have nothing."

"That's not so. You have what we've given you. You have the Ladder."

The vision stung Mirasol: power, light, the hint of justice, this world with its sins and sadness shrunk to a bright arena far below. "Yes," she said at last. "Yes, we do."

# Twenty Evocations

**1. EXPERT SYSTEMS.**   When Nikolai Leng was a child, his teacher was a cybernetic system with a holographic interface. The holo took the form of a young Shaper woman. Its "personality" was an interactive composite expert system manufactured by Shaper psychotechs. Nikolai loved it.

**2. NEVER BORN.**   "You mean we all came from Earth?" said Nikolai, unbelieving.

"Yes," the holo said kindly. "The first true settlers in space were born on Earth—produced by sexual means. Of course, hundred of years have passed since then. You are a Shaper. Shapers are never born."

"Who lives on Earth now?"

"Human beings."

"Ohhhh," said Nikolai, his falling tones betraying a rapid loss of interest.

**3. A MALFUNCTIONING LEG.**   There came a day when Nikolai saw his first Mechanist. The man was a diplomat and commercial agent, stationed by his faction in Nikolai's habitat. Nikolai and some children from his crèche were playing in the corridor when the diplomat stalked by. One of the Mechanist's legs was malfunctioning, and it went click-whirr, click-whirr. Nikolai's friend Alex mimicked the man's limp. Suddenly the man turned on them, his plastic eyes dilating. "Gene-lines," the Mechanist snarled. "I can buy you, grow you, sell you, cut you into bits. Your screams: my music."

**4. FUZZ PATINA.**   Sweat was running into the braided collar of Nikolai's military tunic. The air in the abandoned station was still breathable, but insufferably hot. Nikolai helped his sergeant strip the valuables off a dead miner. The murdered Shaper's antiseptic body was desiccated, but perfect. They walked into another section. The body of a Mechanist pirate sprawled in the feeble gravity. Killed during the attack, his body had rotted for weeks inside his suit. An inch-thick patina of grayish fuzz had devoured his face.

## 5. NOT MERITORIOUS.
Nikolai was on leave in the Ring Council with two men from his unit. They were drinking in a free-fall bar called the ECLECTIC EPILEPTIC. The first man was Simon Afriel, a charming, ambitious young Shaper of the old school. The other man had a Mechanist eye implant. His loyalty was suspect. The three of them were discussing semantics. "The map is not the territory," Afriel said. Suddenly the second man picked an almost invisible listening device from the edge of the table. "And the tap is not meritorious," he quipped. They never saw him again.

. . . A Mechanist pirate, malfunctioning, betraying gene-lines. Invisible listening devices buy, grow, and sell you. The abandoned station's ambitious young Shaper, killed during the attack. Falling psychotechs produced by sexual means the desiccated body of a commercial agent. The holographic interface's loyalty was suspect. The cybernetic system helped him strip the valuables off his plastic eyes. . . .

## 6. SPECULATIVE PITY.
The Mechanist woman looked him over with an air of speculative pity. "I have an established commercial position here," she told Nikolai, "but my cash flow is temporarily constricted. You, on the other hand, have just defected from the Council with a small fortune. I need money; you need stability. I propose marriage."

Nikolai considered this. He was new to Mech society. "Does this imply a sexual relationship?" he said. The woman looked at him blankly. "You mean between the two of us?"

## 7. FLOW PATTERNS.
"You're worried about something," his wife told him. Nikolai shook his head. "Yes, you are," she persisted. "You're upset because of that deal I made in pirate contraband. You're unhappy because our corporation is profiting from attacks made on your own people."

Nikolai smiled ruefully. "I suppose you're right. I never knew anyone who understood my innermost feeling the way you do." He looked at her affectionately. "How do you do it?"

"I have infrared scanners," she said. "I read the patterns of blood flow in your face."

## 8. OPTIC TELEVISION.
It was astonishing how much room there was in an eye socket, when you stopped to think about it. The actual visual mechanisms had been thoroughly miniaturized by Mechanist prostheticians. Nikolai had some other devices installed: a clock, a biofeedback monitor, a television screen, all wired directly to his optic nerve. They were convenient, but difficult to control at first. His wife had to help him out of the hospital and back to his apartment, because the subtle visual triggers kept flashing broadcast market reports. Nikolai smiled at his wife from behind his plastic eyes. "Spend the night with me

tonight," he said. His wife shrugged. "All right," she said. She put her hand to the door of Nikolai's apartment and died almost instantly. An assassin had smeared the door handle with contact venom.

**9. SHAPER TARGETS.** "Look," the assassin said, his slack face etched with weariness, "don't bother me with any ideologies. . . . Just transfer the funds and tell me who it is you want dead."

"It's a job in the Ring Council," Nikolai said. He was strung out on a regimen of emotional drugs he had been taking to combat grief, and he had to fight down recurrent waves of weirdly tainted cheerfulness. "Captain-Doctor Martin Leng of Ring Council Security. He's one of my own gene-line. My defection made his own loyalty look bad. He killed my wife."

"Shapers make good targets," the assassin said. His legless, armless body floated in a transparent nutrient tank, where tinted plasmas soothed the purplish ends of socketed nerve clumps. A body-servo waded into the tank and began to attach the assassin's arms.

**10. CHILD INVESTMENT.** "We recognize your investment in this child, shareholder Leng," the psychotech said. "You may have created her—or hired the technicians who had her created—but she is not your property. By our regulations she must be treated like any other child. She is the property of our people's corporate republic."

Nikolai looked at the woman, exasperated. "I didn't create her. She's my dead wife's posthumous clone. And she's the property of my wife's corporations, or, rather, her trust fund, which I manage as executor. . . . No, what I mean to say is that she owns, or at least has a lienhold on, my dead wife's semiautonomous corporate property, which becomes hers at the age of majority. . . . Do you follow me?"

"No. I'm an educator, not a financier. What exactly is the point of this, shareholder? Are you trying to re-create your dead wife?"

Nikolai looked at her, his face carefully neutral. "I did it for the tax break."

. . . Leave the posthumous clone profiting from attacks. Semiautonomous property has an established commercial position. Recurrent waves of pirate contraband. His slack face bothers you with ideologies. Innermost feelings died almost instantly. Smear the door with contact venom. . . .

**11. ALLEGIANCES RESENTED.** "I like it out here on the fringes," Nikolai told the assassin. "Have you ever considered a breakaway?"

The assassin laughed. "I used to be a pirate. It took me forty years to attach myself to this cartel. When you're alone, you're meat, Leng. You ought to know that."

"But you must resent those allegiances. They're inconvenient. Wouldn't you rather have your own Kluster and make your own rules?"

"You're talking like an ideologue," the assassin said. Biofeedback displays blinked softly on his prosthetic forearms. "My allegiance is to Kyotid Zaibatsu. They own this whole suburb. They even own my arms and legs."

"I own Kyotid Zaibatsu," Nikolai said.

"Oh," the assassin said. "Well, that puts a different face on matters."

## 12. MASS DEFECTION.  "We want to join your Kluster," the Superbright said. "We must join your Kluster. No one else will have us."

Nikolai doodled absently with his light pen on a convenient videoscreen. "How many of you are there?"

"There were fifty in our gene-line. We were working on quantum physics before our mass defection. We made a few minor breakthroughs. I think they might be of some commercial use."

"Splendid," said Nikolai. He assumed an air of speculative pity. "I take it the Ring Council persecuted you in the usual manner—claimed you were mentally unstable, ideologically unsound, and the like."

"Yes. Their agents have killed thirty-eight of us." The Superbright dabbed uneasily at the sweat beading on his swollen forehead. "We are not mentally unsound, Kluster-Chairman. We will not cause you any trouble. We only want a quiet place to finish working while God eats our brains."

## 13. DATA HOSTAGE.  A high-level call came in from the Ring Council. Nikolai, surprised and intrigued, took the call himself. A young man's face appeared on the screen. "I have your teacher hostage," he said.

Nikolai frowned. "What?"

"The person who taught you when you were a child in the crèche. You love her. You told her so. I have it on tape."

"You must be joking," Nikolai said. "My teacher was just a cybernetic interface. You can't hold a data system hostage."

"Yes, I can," the young man said truculently. "The old expert system's been scrapped in favor of a new one with a sounder ideology. Look." A second face appeared on the screen; it was the superhumanly smooth and faintly glowing image of his cybernetic teacher. "Please save me, Nikolai," the image said woodenly. "He's ruthless."

The young man's face reappeared. Nikolai laughed incredulously. "So you've saved the old tapes?" Nikolai said. "I don't know what your game is, but I suppose the data has a certain value. I'm prepared to be generous." He named a price. The young man shook his head. Nikolai grew impatient. "Look," he said. "What makes you think a mere expert system has any objective worth?"

"I know it does," the young man said. "I'm one myself."

## 14. CENTRAL QUESTION.  Nikolai was aboard the alien ship. He felt uncomfortable in his brocaded ambassador's coat. He adjusted the heavy sunglasses over

his plastic eyes. "We appreciate your visit to our Kluster," he told the reptilian ensign. "It's a very great honor."

The Investor ensign lifted the multicolored frill behind his massive head. "We are prepared to do business," he said.

"I'm interested in alien philosophies," Nikolai said. "The answers of other species to the great questions of existence."

"But there is only one central question," the alien said. "We have pursued its answer from star to star. We were hoping that you would help us answer it."

Nikolai was cautious. "What is the question?"

" 'What is it you have that we want?' "

**15. INHERITED GIFTS.**   Nikolai looked at the girl with the old-fashioned eyes. "My chief of security had provided me with a record of your criminal actions," he said. "Copyright infringement, organized extortion, conspiracy in restraint of trade. How old are you?"

"Forty-four," the girl said. "How old are you?"

"A hundred and ten or so. I'd have to check my files." Something about the girl's appearance bothered him. "Where did you get those antique eyes?"

"They were my mother's. I inherited them. But you're a Shaper, of course. You wouldn't know what a mother was."

"On the contrary," Nikolai said. "I believe I knew yours. We were married. After her death, I had you cloned. I suppose that makes me your—I forget the term."

"Father."

"That sounds about right. Clearly you've inherited her gifts for finance." He reexamined her personnel file. "Would you be interested in adding bigamy to your list of crimes?"

. . . The mentally unstable have a certain value. Restraint of trade puts a different face on the convenient videoscreen. A few minor breakthroughs in the questions of existence. Your personnel file persecuted him. His swollen forehead can't hold a data system. . . .

**16. PLEASURE ROAR.**   "You need to avoid getting set in your ways," his wife said. "It's the only way to stay young." She pulled a gilded inhaler from her garter holster. "Try some of this."

"I don't need drugs," Nikolai said, smiling. "I have my power fantasies." He began pulling off his clothes.

His wife watched him impatiently. "Don't be stodgy, Nikolai." She touched the inhaler to her nostril and sniffed. Sweat began to break out on her face, and a slow sexual flush spread over her ears and neck.

Nikolai watched, then shrugged and sniffed lightly at the gilded tube. Immediately a rocketing sense of ecstasy paralyzed his nervous system. His body arched backward, throbbing uncontrollably.

Clumsily, his wife began to caress him. The roar of chemical pleasure made sex irrelevant. "Why . . . why bother?" he gasped.

His wife looked surprised. "It's traditional."

**17. FLICKERING WALL.**   Nikolai addressed the flickering wall of monitor screens. "I'm getting old," he said. "My health is good—I was very lucky in my choice of longevity programs—but I just don't have the daring I once did. I've lost my flexibility, my edge. And the Kluster has outgrown my ability to handle it. I have no choice. I must retire."

Carefully, he watched the faces on the screens for every flicker of reaction. Two hundred years had taught him the art of reading faces. His skills were still with him—it was only the will behind them that had decayed. The faces of the Governing Board, their reserve broken by shock, seemed to blaze with ambition and greed.

**18. LEGAL TARGETS.**   The Mechanists had unleashed their drones in the suburb. Armed with subpoenas, the faceless drones blurred through the hallway crowds, looking for legal targets.

Suddenly Nikolai's former Chief of Security broke from the crowd and began a run for cover. In free-fall, he brachiated from handhold to handhold like an armored gibbon. Suddenly one of his prosthetics gave way and the drones pounced on him, almost at Nikolai's door. Plastic snapped as electromagnetic pincers paralyzed his limbs.

"Kangaroo courts," he gasped. The deeply creased lines in his ancient face shone with rivulets of sweat. "They'll strip me! Help me, Leng!"

Sadly, Nikolai shook his head. The old man shrieked: "You got me into this! You were the ideologue! I'm only a poor assassin!"

Nikolai said nothing. The machines seized and repossessed the old man's arms and legs.

**19. ANTIQUE SPLITS.**   "You've really got it through you, right? All that old gigo stuff!" The young people spoke a slang-crammed jargon that Nikolai could barely comprehend. When they watched him their faces showed a mixture of aggression, pity, and awe. To Nikolai, they always seemed to be shouting. "I feel outnumbered," he murmured.

"You *are* outnumbered, old Nikolai! This bar is your museum, right? Your mausoleum! Give our ears your old frontiers, we're listening! Those idiot video ideologies, those antique spirit splits. Mechs and Shapers, right? The wars of the coin's two halves!"

"I feel tired," Nikolai said. "I've drunk too much. Take me home, one of you."

They exchanged worried glances. "This *is* your home! Isn't it?"

**20. EYES CLOSED.**   "You've been very kind," Nikolai told the two youngsters. They were Kosmosity archaeologists, dressed in their academic finery, their gowns studded with awards and medals from the Terraform-Klusters. Nikolai realized suddenly that he could not remember their names.

"That's all right, sir," they told him soothingly. "It's now our duty to remember you, not vice versa." Nikolai felt embarrassed. He hadn't realized that he had spoken aloud.

"I've taken poison," he explained apologetically.

"We know," they nodded. "You're not in any pain, we hope?"

"No, not at all. I've done the right thing, I know. I'm very old. Older than I can bear." Suddenly he felt an alarming collapse within himself. Pieces of his consciousness began to break off as he slid toward the void. Suddenly he realized that he had forgotten his last words. With an enormous effort, he remembered them and shouted them aloud.

"Futility is freedom!" Filled with triumph, he died, and they closed his eyes.

# A SHAPER/MECHANIST CHRONOLOGY

2045 — Spider Rose born

2053 — Interdict with Earth

2050—2150 — Concatenate Period

2186 — Abelard Lindsay born

2195 — Kitsune cloned

2203 — Lindsay scholarshipped to Shaper Ring Council

2205 — Constantine scholarshipped

2209 — Nikolai Leng "born"

2210 — Simon Afriel "born"

2213 — Lindsay returns to Mare Serenitatis Circumlunar Corporate Republic

2215 — Lindsay exiled to Mare Tranquillitatis People's Circumlunar Zaibatsu

2216 — Coup in Republic; Lindsay joins the Red Consensus

2217 — Investors arrive

2217 — Lindsay and Nora Mavrides join Goldreich-Tremaine

2253 — Lindsay leaves Goldreich-Tremaine for Dembowska Cartel

2267 — Vera Constantine cloned

2283 — Nora Mavrides dies; events of "Spider Rose"

2284 — Czarina-Kluster founded

2286 — Lindsay duels with Constantine

2291 — Lindsay recovers from duel, moves to Czarina-Kluster

2328 — Hans Landau "born"

2354 — Events of the "Cicada Queen"; fall of Czarina-Kluster; Lindsay visits Earth

2386 — SCHISMATRIX ends

2554 — Events of "Sunken Gardens"